NAKED FLESH

His lean, powerful body was quite bare now, except for the line of curling dark hair that bisected his broad chest. And, to her surprise, he wasn't horrid or beastly at all. He was beautiful. Like a statue of a Greek athlete, powerfully muscled and deeply tanned everywhere, his skin burnished by a sun far hotter than that which shone on England's damp, chilly shores.

"So. Do you like this better, my dear? The two of us, naked as Nature intended? Unfortunately, we would be at a decided disadvantage should this flea-bitten hostel catch fire!" Laughter rumbling in his voice, he gathered her into his arms and drew her close.

He smelled of sandalwood soap, tobacco and brandy, and felt so deliciously warm. *Hot,* really. His naked flesh burned like a furnace against her own, warming her. Oh, God, yes, warming her in ways she'd never dreamed of. . . .

Other *Leisure* books by Penelope Neri:
STOLEN

SCANDALS

PENELOPE NERI

LEISURE BOOKS NEW YORK CITY

For Barbara Snyder, with love.

Leisure Entertainment Service Co., Inc. (LESCO Distribution Group)

A LESCO Edition

Published by special arrangement with Dorchester Publishing Co., Inc.

Printed in the United States of America.

"Love and Scandals are the best sweeteners for tea."
—Henry Fielding, *Love in Several Masques*

Chapter One

Hawthorne Hall, Whitby, Yorkshire, 1855

"I'm off for a gallop before luncheon, Joseph. Go on home to your Sunday dinner. I'll rub him down."

"That's very good of you, m'lord," Victoria heard Lovett, the head groom, murmur as he stepped away from her father's hunter. "I'll just take another look at that mare before I leave."

"Good man. Give my regards to Mrs. Lovett."

With her father erect in the saddle, the snorting gray lunged forward, eager for a gallop. A moment later, she heard the clatter of Samson's hooves on the cobbled stableyard as Father rode away.

"Old Thorny's, gone, he has," Ned declared in a low, pleased voice as he ducked back inside the stables. "Good riddance, I say! Now, come along wi' me, my lass. I've got summat for you."

"You have?" Victoria asked, giggly with a mixture of excitement and nerves as Ned took her by the hand. *Old Thorny!* So that was what the servants and workers called her father behind his back? Given his irascible temper, it was an appropriate nickname.

"Aye, lass," Ned murmured, leading her to a horse stall at the rear of the stables. The shadows were deepest there, the gloom filled with the pungent scents of horse, liniment and fresh straw.

"You're quite mad, you know, coming here in broad daylight. What if Father had seen you? What then?" The risk of their being discovered alone together made her breathless.

"But he didn't see me, did he?" Ned retorted cockily, catching her about the waist. He grinned and winked down at her as he clasped his hands behind her back. "I were careful, weren't I? I came over the fields, instead of up the lane to the Hall. Besides, you're worth the risk, my lass." He flashed her another smile. "Now, forget about him. Think about me, and what I've got for ye, instead."

"What is it? Must I guess?"

"Nay. Just close thy bonny eyes, and don't look till I tell thee to."

"Oh, Ned. It's lovely!" Victoria exclaimed, opening her hyacinth-blue eyes moments later. "Thank you!"

Her smile was dazzling as she looked down at the pretty little jet rose Ned was clumsily pinning

10

to her bodice. Jet jewelry was all the rage in society, and this piece was exceptionally beautiful. Each dainty petal had been faithfully rendered by a talented carver's hand, then polished to a high black gloss.

"Truly, I've never seen such a pretty piece of jet."

"The real name for it is lignite. Any road, that's what the Professor said," Ned explained in his broad-voweled Yorkshire dialect. "It forms when a bit o' driftwood gets packed down in the mud of the ocean floor. It takes thousands of years to make a great dull lump in the shale. But after it's carved and polished, it shines like thy hair."

Darling Ned. He was exactly like the jet, Victoria thought fondly, her heart swelling with love as she threw herself into his arms. A true diamond in the rough. But instead of being embedded in ocean mud, Ned was buried here, in the northeast of England. Forced—by virtue of his poor birth—to labor on her father's home farm, and as a miner in the rabbit warren of the Hawthorne jet mines, his dear, fine qualities hidden beneath layers of shale.

Surely her love, like the carver's tools, could cut away the dross. Free the precious, hidden gem that was Ned? After all, it was the honest sweat of him and others like him in the Hawthorne jet mines, cotton mills and coal mines that had made her father the very wealthy man he was.

Ned, bless him, provided the vital elements that were missing in her luxurious yet empty life.

11

The ones that no amount of money could ever buy. Warmth. Affection. *Love* . . .

Ah, yes. She loved him so much. And he loved her, too . . .

With a low sound, Ned tugged the pins and combs from her upswept hair. Freed from confinement, the long, glossy black curls unraveled to her waist. Her inky lashes trembled on flushed cheeks as he ducked his unruly golden head to hers. His gray eyes burned as he grasped a fistful of that shining mass and hungrily bent to kiss her.

Tossing propriety to the winds, Victoria tilted her glowing face to his and let him.

"By gum, I want thee, lass," Ned rasped, drawing her down onto the straw beside him. Taking her slender hand in his large, rough one, he drew it to his lips. "I want thee summat fierce."

With crystal clarity she saw his brown flat cap lying on the brick floor of the box. Felt the coarse cloth of the threadbare brown jacket he'd worn to chapel, spread over the fresh straw beneath her. Then the press of his hot lips burned against her palm, her throat, like the fiery wings of a moth, and thought was impossible . . .

"Victoria. I can't hardly bear it," he whispered thickly.

A thrill ran through her as she knelt there, her heart hammering in her breast like a steam engine. All fear of discovery paled beside her love for Ned. Oh, Lord. She would die if she ever lost him! Just die!

Ned made her feel beautiful. Special. *Wanted*.

And he was so handsome, too, in a rugged, working-man's sort of way, with that wiry build, that shaggy golden hair, those pewter gray eyes.

He was very different from the smooth, cultured young men Father had begun to dangle before her two years ago, when she became sixteen and he realized she was a woman. Men with titles, who belonged to her own class. Men who were all flattery and flowery phrases and insincere, painted-on smiles. They were nothing but fortune hunters, drawn to her by her father's wealth, like moths to a flame.

Ned was nothing like them. All he wanted was her.

"I love you, too, Ned. And I shall miss you terribly while I'm in London."

London! Just thinking about the weeks—no, months—without him made her miserable. As if she needed launching into Society like a—a sailing ship on its maiden voyage! And as for finding a husband during her first season, as Father and Aunt Catherine hoped—*never!*

The only man she wanted to marry was lying right here, beside her. *Edward John Thomas. Farm laborer. Jet miner.* The man she loved, and who loved her in return.

It should all have been so simple, but it wasn't. Lord, no. She sighed. She and Ned were worlds apart, in every way but the one that counted. Their love for each other.

Somehow, she vowed silently, *we shall be husband and wife, Father will have to give his per-*

*mission, once he realizes that I love Ned, and will
marry no one else.*

"I'll miss thee, too," Ned said in response to her
comment. When he smiled, as he was doing now,
she felt the warmth of it right down to her toes.
"Don't thee up and wed some rich toff while
you're in the City, my lass," he reminded her,
trailing a coarse knuckle down her cheek.

"Silly. Of course I will not."

"Promise? Cross thy heart and hope t' die?"

"I promise."

"Good lass. Now come thee here, my beauty."
He pulled her down to the straw beside him and
kissed her.

She moaned softly as his lips moved against
hers, stiffening as his large hand curled, ever so
lightly, over the curve of her breast—and remained there.

The bold caress made her gasp in shock and
disbelief. But his second kiss—harder than the
first, and given with open mouth and thrusting
tongue—devoured the protest she would have uttered. Swallowed it whole!

Pinned beneath Ned's chest, his knee pushing
against the place where her thighs were pressed
together, she felt smothered, trapped.

What on earth was Ned doing? What had come
over him? She could not speak—could hardly
breathe!—as his hand slipped beneath her
hooped petticoat. Seconds later, she felt his callused fingers squeezing her knee. "Don't!" she
whispered as his hand inched its way up her leg,

scraping the scalloped hems of her drawers, snagging on her silk hose.

"Stop it," she repeated sternly. Her hand covered his, halting his explorations.

Looking up into his blazing gray eyes, she was frightened by what she saw in their depths.

"Stop? But why, lovie? If you really loved me, ye wouldna ask me to stop, my lass," Ned said thickly. His gray eyes narrowed. "Or were ye but making sport of me when ye said ye cared?"

"No, no, of course not. I'd never make fun of you, Ned," she assured him earnestly. "Believe me, dearest, I love you."

"Aye? Then prove it, lass. Prove I'm good enough for the likes of her ladyship." He sounded taunting rather than gently teasing now. "Prove I'm suited for better than licking your father's boots, aye?"

"I love you, truly I do, Ned. But . . . but I can't do what you ask of me . . . not until—not unless—we are marr—"

She froze as a great black shadow fell across them.

"Father! Nooo!" she screamed as Ned was lifted off her by the scruff of his neck.

Her father towered over them, his broad frame black against the April sunshine that streamed through the high windows. He looked very tall and terrible, etched against that brightness. A dark god of retribution, sent from the Underworld to punish her.

Ned, red-faced and choking, dangled like a dead rat from Lord Hawthorne's clenched fist, while beyond the box the great hunter Samson snorted and stamped his hooves, his reins dangling.

"You bloody *bastard!*" her father roared, slamming Ned up against the wooden box with such force that his teeth rattled. His normally ruddy face was livid with outrage.

The horses in the other stalls whinnied nervously and kicked at the wooden partitions.

"Lay your filthy hands on my daughter, would you, you son-of-a-bitch? I'll give you a thrashing you'll never forget!"

Chapter Two

Grabbing a riding crop from the tack wall, Lord Hawthorne brought the whip down across Ned's head and shoulders, striking him again and again.

He did not stop even when crimson welts crisscrossed Ned's face, nor when the swelling made his handsome features grotesque and unrecognizable.

Victoria's heart ached for his hurt, yet his courage filled her with pride. Not a sound had escaped her brave darling, not even when blood flowed from the splits in his lips. Rather, Ned endured the whipping in stony silence, his gray eyes murderous and without remorse as he glowered up into her father's face.

"Enough, Father! Stop, before you kill him! Please don't hurt him any more! It was all my fault!" she sobbed, trying to tug the riding crop from her father's hand.

He thrust her away.

"Let go, you wretched girl. Get away from here," her father growled. "I'll deal with you when I'm finished with this—whelp who came sniffing at your skirts. *Lovett!*"

"Here, m'lord!" Joe Lovett called, hurrying into the stables at a run.

The head groom's eyes widened as he took in the scene.

His gaze flickered from Ned to her, his expression concerned.

Judging by Uncle Lovey's shocked expression, she must look a fright, with her hair spilling loose about her shoulders. God knows, she felt close to swooning.

"I can trust you to be discreet, aye, Lovett?" her father growled, breathing heavily yet maintaining his choking grip on Ned's collar.

"Always, m'lord," Uncle Lovey said firmly, glaring at poor Ned. "Let me take 'im for thee, sir."

"No. I'll see that young Master Thomas leaves the grounds personally. And while he's at it, the county, too! Escort her ladyship back to the house, if you will. Then come back here. Victoria, to your room, immediately. Remain there until I send for you."

"But, Father—"

"Do it!"

"Yes, Father," she whispered, casting a look of longing at Ned as Uncle Lovey took her by the elbow and drew her away. "Oh, Father! Please, don't hurt him any more! I beg you, please let him go—"

"*Lovett*," Hawthorne warned, cutting off her entreaty. "Get her out of here."

"Right away, sir."

"I won't just abandon Ned, Uncle Lovey. I can't! Father will k-kill him," she sobbed. Her eyes swam with tears. "And I—I love him."

"If ye're askin' me, lass, the lout's got less than he deserves. He'll survive, never fear. His sort always does. I just hope the same can be said o' you," he added fervently.

By now they had reached the kitchens at the rear of Hawthorne Hall.

"Cook? Ring for my Lily will ye, love?" Lovett instructed the fat, red-faced woman who was braiding strips of dough at the kitchen table. "Lady Victoria's taken a wee spill. Happen ye've something hot and sweet to calm her nerves, aye?"

"A spill is it? Poor lamb. Right away, Mister Lovett." Cook, beaming at being called 'love' like a slip of a girl, wiped her floury hands on her bibbed apron and yanked one of several bells set in the wall alongside the Welsh dresser.

There was an answering jangle in some distant corner of the Hall.

Victoria was trembling as Joe Lovett pressed her down onto a straight-backed chair beside the wide fireplace.

She leaned back and closed her eyes, unable to erase the memory of poor Ned, beaten and bleeding as he dangled from her father's fist. Her

19

hands were still trembling as she silently urged Lily, her maid, to hurry, *please* hurry.

She did not care if Cook and the rest of the kitchen staff were watching her with open curiosity. Nor did she dread the coming summons to her father's study. Nor did she consider for a moment what would happen if word of her indiscretions became grist for the gossip mills of London on the eve of her first Season.

Dear Lord, no!

All she could think about was Ned. All she wanted was to fly into Ned's strong arms. To kiss away Ned's hurts and become Ned's bride. *Ned. Ned. Ned.* Her every thought, her every wish was for Ned. He was the spring in her step, the song in her heart, the light in her eyes!

When Lily arrived, she would send her to the Thomas farm post-haste, carrying a note that urged Ned to be strong and patient. A note promising that she loved him—would *always* love him.

And then, when he'd recovered from her father's thrashing, they would run away together and be married, exactly as she'd dreamed. Despite her father's disapproval and her Aunt Catherine's plans to the contrary, she would be Ned's bride someday.

Come hell or high water . . .

Victoria paused before the door to her father's study, her courage deserting her momentarily.

She had not seen Father since the incident in the stables two days ago. Nor had Ned sent any replies to the urgent notes she had sent him via

Lily, her maid. Consequently, she felt cut off, abandoned, angry and frightened, by turns.

Surely Ned must be at death's door, if he was unable to answer her letters. Or—had her father killed him?

Surely not.

Her fears and doubts heated her anxiety to a fine boil. She was so on edge now, she thought she might shatter into a thousand fragments at the drop of a hat.

With nervous hands, she smoothed down the folds of her blue plaid morning gown with its fitted cap sleeves, patted the clusters of jet-black ringlets that bobbed over each ear to frame her face. Then, drawing a deep, calming breath, she tilted her chin and swept into the lion's den.

Her father, Lord Roger Hawthorne, stood before ceiling-to-floor windows draped in wine-red velvet.

Beyond lay a charming view of the gardens her mother had planted twenty years before, when she first became mistress of Hawthorne Hall. Sheaves of her roses had covered her coffin when they laid her to rest in the Whitby churchyard, Victoria remembered, for Mama had fallen from her horse and been killed when Victoria was just seven years old.

Hands clasped behind his back, her father did not turn to face her as she came to a halt before his desk. His stern, hawklike features seemed carved in granite as he gazed out at the tulips, snowdrops and daffodils nodding their pastel heads in the spring breeze.

He looks as always, she saw with a sinking heart. *Remote. Cold. Uncaring*. Her faint if irrational hope that his anger had evaporated since Sunday was instantly dashed.

There would be no softening, not from this angry man. But then, there had never been any softness, not from him, and certainly not for her . . .

"You wanted to speak with me, Father?" she began in a clear, bell-like voice. Her tone, her expression and her body language belied her longing for even the tiniest crumb of his affection.

"I did indeed. Your Aunt Catherine is on her way here from Lincoln, even as we speak," he announced, still facing away. "Her arrival is expected within the hour. See to it that your trunks are packed and that you are ready to travel by the time she arrives. After a change of horses, and some refreshments, you will travel on to London by train, as originally planned."

"Am I still to be presented at court, then?" Victoria asked, astonished. "Shall we be in London for the entire Season?"

"But of course. You sound surprised, Victoria. Was that not your aunt's original intention?" her papa barked, turning to face her. "How else are you to make a proper entry into Society?"

Taken aback, Victoria saw no anger in her father's face, as she might have expected. On the contrary, there was a deep and abiding sadness there, as if he'd aged ten years in the past two days.

Had she put that sadness there? she wondered with the tiniest twinge of guilt. Did he even care enough to be sad about anything she did?

"But I had thought, after last Sunday . . ." Her voice trailed away. She could not meet his piercing deep-blue eyes.

"Oh, I can imagine what you thought, lass. Aye, and hoped, no doubt. But with any luck, word of thy disgraceful behavior has yet to reach the hallowed drawing rooms of London," her father said with heavy sarcasm. "There's still a chance a suitable match may yet be made for you, if we act quickly."

Victoria uttered an impatient, unladylike snort and stamped her slippered foot. It was a childish gesture, but it was preferable to throwing something, as she itched to do.

"Why will you never listen to what *I* want, Father? I do not *seek* a brilliant match," she protested, the set of her jaw not unlike his own in its obstinacy. "I simply want to marry the man I love!" she implored with such fervor her voice cracked. "The man who . . . who loves me."

"*Love!*" he snorted. "What you have mistaken for love is common lust, my girl! Trust me in this. That coarse, illiterate clod would have ruined you had I not arrived in the nick of time. Over my dead body you'll marry the bastard. I promised your mama you'd have a husband worthy of you, and by God, you will, my lass," he thundered. "Or I'll know the reason why."

"If I can't marry Ned, I shall never marry," she vowed.

"Ha! The devil you'll remain a spinster in my house," he insisted. "You will make your entry

23

into Society exactly as your Aunt Catherine has so generously planned for you. You will be presented to Her Majesty, and make the rounds of balls and suppers and what-have-yous. And then, Victoria, you will wed the first suitable man who offers for thy hand, be damned if you won't!"

"Then damned I shall be, sir, for I assure you, I will do nothing of the sort," Victoria declared hotly, even paler now with anger.

Her father was clearly very determined, but so was she. Unfortunately, there was precious little time in which to send another message to Ned, if her aunt was arriving within the hour. All she could do was dig in her heels, defy her father, and hope for the best.

"Rest assured, you will wed, my girl—and I don't give a tinker's damn if your future husband is a snot-nosed twit of twenty or an old lecher of ninety-two! Whether he's hale and hearty or a toothless old reprobate with only one eye. If he's your social equal, and able to support you, I'll welcome him as a son-in-law with open arms. And once you're safely wed, I've a mind to re-marry myself, be damned if I don't! I've mourned your mother long enough, Victoria."

"*Mourned* her?" Victoria cried, stunned and heartbroken. "Mourning is for those we love, Father. You never loved my mother, any more than you l-love m-me—"

With that, she turned and fled the study in a flurry of plaid skirts and under-petticoats, loudly slamming the door in her wake.

"Wrong, my proud, foolish lass," Lord Haw-

24

thorne murmured into the echoing silence after she was gone. "I loved my beautiful Isabelle more than you'll ever know. And you! You are her image, child. Why else would it pain me to look at you . . . ?"

Chapter Three

Hawthorne House, Belgravia Square, London
Three weeks later

Victoria stirred as Lily marched into her room, her starched gray skirts rustling. She was followed by the chambermaid, Dora, who carried a brass scuttle of coal for the fire.

Although it was the end of April, afternoons and early evenings at the Belgravia townhouse were often chilly. A result, Papa had once complained, of their proximity to the River Thames, across which chilly damp winds blew unchecked.

Rolling onto her back and opening one eye, Victoria saw that the fire had died down while she napped, leaving only white ashes and orange embers behind the polished black grate.

While Dora knelt on the hearth rug, noisily feeding lumps of Hawthorne coal to the glowing embers, Lily bustled back and forth, setting a porcelain jug of hot water and two fluffy Turkish towels beside the washbasin on the dresser, then arranging face-flannels beside it.

When the preparations for her mistress's bath were completed, Lily drew the rose-brocade draperies and lit the lamps.

Light spilled from the pretty globes of painted milk-glass, forcing a groan from Victoria. She dived under a feather pillow to shut out the light.

"Are you awake, milady?" Lily sang out cheerfully.

Drat that Lily! She was always cheerful, whatever the hour, no matter how dire the circumstances, Victoria reflected, yawning and squinting gritty eyes. Such perpetual optimism was a most annoying trait.

"No," she denied, wriggling back under the covers. "Good Lord, Lily, I doubt even God is awake at this unearthly hour. Everyone civilized is still napping."

"Eeh, I know what ye mean, love. Danced the night away last night, didn't you, then came crawling home at four in the morning as tipsy as a lord. But it's past five o'clock in the afternoon now, so get up, do, before ye miss your tea. It's treacle tart tonight—your favorite, aye? Lady Catherine's already dressed, she is. Her Martha's doing her hair even as we speak."

Victoria grimaced and sat up. "Oh, all right then. But don't expect me to be enthralled about

28

the prospect of yet another ball this evening. This is my third in ten days, not counting the round of soirees, drums and crushes I've been dragged to by Aunt Catherine! My cheeks positively *ache* from smiling so much, and I'm sick of having to always be so very *nice* to everyone—especially when I hear those witches gossiping about me each time I turn my back."

Lily snorted. "You've no one to blame for that but yourself, my lady," she said with the frankness of an old and trusted friend, rather than a servant. "I warned thee no good would come of batting your eyelashes at that Ned Thomas, didn't I? But would you listen?" She shook her head. "The dirty dog! What your Master Thomas was after, he didn't need no proper young lady for, that he didn't. There's more than one factory lass has already lifted her skirts for Ne—"

"Stop it right now, Lily!" Victoria said sharply, heat flooding her cheeks. She was wide awake now. Oh, yes, indeed. "It was not like that at all. Ned . . . Ned loves me, and I love him."

"Aye. So ye say," Lily agreed with another sniff, clearly unimpressed. "But handsome is as handsome does, I always say. And that Ned Thomas—!"

"You *did* deliver my notes to him?" Victoria demanded, suddenly suspicious. She turned to look at Lily with narrowed eyes.

Lily had never approved of her meeting with Ned in secret. Nor had Uncle Lovey, Lily's father, or Lily's mother, Rose Lovett. In their own sweet way, they were all old-fashioned snobs, bless them. Dearly loved family retainers who—quite mistakenly—thought they knew what was best for the daughter of the household. They considered Ned Thomas far beneath her in every way, shape and form, and believed she should marry one of her own class. Didn't they understand that when love struck, it struck blindly, regardless of one's standing in society?

"Li-ly?" she warned. "Answer me this minute! *Did* you deliver my notes?"

"Never mind Ned Thomas for tonight, milady," Lily countered, airily sidestepping her mistress's question and refusing to meet Victoria's accusing hyacinth-blue eyes. "I told thee, he survived your father's whipping right well. Harry and my da' saw him down at The Collier's Arms soon after. Ned's face were swollen and he was drunk as a lord, bragging that he'd pay his lordship back for his beating."

Lily was frowning, Victoria saw. Her nose was wrinkled up. Harry Coombs, the Hall's coachman, who was walking out with her, had been heard to describe his intended as "a pretty brown rabbit of a lass." Now Victoria understood why.

She hid a smile.

"You'd best get yourself off that bed so I can get thee dressed, or Her Grace will be coming upstairs to see what's keeping you from tea, my girl."

The warning succeeded in stirring Victoria to action. Aunt Catherine, Her Grace, the Duchess of Lincoln, was a dear old thing, but she was also a martinet.

Besides, she'd suddenly realized that she was starving for treacle tart.

Later that evening, a freshly bathed and powdered Victoria sat once again before her dressing table. This time, however, instead of a simple tea-gown, she wore a royal-blue satin fan-fronted ballgown that bared her slender shoulders and the tops of her breasts.

Nine other equally gorgeous creations of various styles and colors hung in the large dressing room that adjoined this one. Whatever other faults her father might have, he was no pinch-penny. He had given Aunt Catherine carte-blanche when it came to Victoria's wardrobe for the Season. And martinet or no, her aunt had splendid taste when it came to dressing her brother Roger's "poor little gel," as she called Victoria.

The gown's enormous puffed sleeves concealed her upper arms, while the skirts that billowed over her hooped petticoat and lace-trimmed under-petticoat made her tightly cinched waist appear as slender as a wasp's. Long white gloves elegantly encased her hands and lower arms.

"Ooof! You laced me so tightly I can hardly breathe," she accused Lily, rapidly fanning herself with an osprey feather fan. The feathers had been dyed royal blue to match her gown and the small plumes in her hair.

Lily giggled. "Never mind breathing, milady.

31

Just so long as thee can still make eyes at the gentlemen over that fan."

Giving a final pat to her mistress's hair, she beamed at Victoria's reflection in the mirror.

"There. All done. Scandal or no scandal, there'll be precious few of the Upper Ten Thousand can hold a candle t'your looks, milady," Lily said smugly. "Ye look a proper treat in that royal blue. It makes your eyes look almost lavender, it does. Will you wear your mam's sapphires, or the diamonds?" she asked, selecting three velvet jewelry cases from the dressing table.

"The sapphires," Victoria decided. She eyed her reflection in the mirror with little enthusiasm, then sighed. "Two more months until this wretched Season ends! Two months until I can see him again. How on earth shall I endure it, Lily?"

"I know what I'd do. I'd find meself a replacement," Lily suggested with a wicked little grin as she handed Victoria an earbob. A teardrop sapphire dangled from the cup of a tiny golden tulip. "Get him to make an offer for your hand, then ask for a lengthy engagement. That way, your da' will be satisfied, and you can be back at Hawthorne Hall by month's end. Who knows what might happen in the weeks before you have t'wed the man? There's 'many a slip betwixt cup and lip,' aye?"

"Indeed there is," Victoria exclaimed thoughtfully. "How clever of you, Lily!"

"You heard what, Mariah? With a common laborer? Do tell! Yet the chit looks as if warm butter wouldn't melt in her mouth . . ."

". . . tonight. Rumor has it he's looking for another wife . . . no daughter of mine . . . surely not in decent company, the rogue! . . . murdered his first . . ."

". . . they say he murdered the first one . . . resigned his commission . . . but then, Lord Hereford . . . old friend of the family . . ."

". . . I seriously doubt the truth will ever be known . . ."

". . . hanging's too good for him, I say . . ."

". . . and her papa caught them together in his stables . . ."

"In the haystack, what? By Jove, old chap, why the deuce did the naughty gel choose a hayfield, do you suppose? . . . dashed prickly place . . ."

Her face flaming, Victoria walked quickly past the knots of gossiping ladies and gentlemen, keenly aware of the curious eyes, the salacious whispers, that followed her passage around the ballroom.

In the gallery above the gathering, the string orchestra began playing yet another of the popular Viennese waltzes. As its lilting strains drifted over the ballroom, ladies perused their dance cards to ascertain their next partner's identity. The gentlemen in question moved around the room, seeking out the fair creatures who had promised them this waltz.

Her own dance card spectacularly blank, her ears still ringing with the latest account of her scandalous escapades, Victoria sought escape on the veranda.

With a little groan of relief, she plunged through some french doors, drew them shut behind her, and leaned gratefully upon them.

Beyond the veranda, formal gardens with box hedges, flowerbeds and pathways were drenched in bright moonlight that bleached everything to the color of ashes. The cool evening air smelled deliciously of dew and spring flowers—and the fragrant aroma of Havana cigars.

Alone, with only the full moon to witness her disintegration, Victoria abandoned her haughty pose and let tears spill down her hot cheeks.

Despite her brave claims to the contrary, the spiteful gossip that had attended every social engagement for the past month hurt more than she'd ever imagined.

The gossips' barbs were so vicious and spiteful, so unfair—and so very *exaggerated*.

She and Ned had shared a kiss, no more, thanks to her father's timely intervention. *A single kiss!* Yet to hear those wagging tongues, she was like that American author's heroine—the one who shared her last name? Hawthorne. *Nathaniel* Hawthorne's lady of the scarlet letter! A wanton. A scandalous hussy who had lightly bestowed her favors on any number of her father's laborers, if their tales were to be believed.

What she and Ned felt for each other was beautiful, pure, true. But the gossip twisted and cheapened it. Reduced their relationship to something to be snickered at, or hidden. Locked away in the attic like a crazy aunt, forbidden the light of day . . .

Oh, she could not wait to be far, far from London! Out from under the hateful scrutiny of high Society, with its taste for . . .

A muffled sob from a shadowed corner of the veranda diverted her attention.

Blotting her teary eyes on white-gloved fingertips, she went to investigate.

Steede Warring was about to extinguish his cigar and go back inside when a breathtaking young woman swept out onto the veranda. He watched as she closed the double doors behind her and leaned upon them.

Most of her inky hair was swept up into a knot on the very crown of her head, while short ringlets framed her heart-shaped face, in which a pair of magnificent iris-blue eyes blazed like a brace of stars. Her mouth was ripe and full-lipped, with deep dimples at the corners. It was, he decided, wondering how such a mouth would taste beneath his own, the mouth of a born courtesan. Too lush and tempting by far to be the mouth of an innocent.

He frowned. *An innocent?* Perhaps. Perhaps not. Belatedly, he'd recognized the lovely creature as Roger Hawthorne's only daughter. The chit the gossips were tearing limb from pretty limb. What had they called her? *Lady Victoria.*

His jaw hardened. His sable eyes flashed in the starlight. No stranger to scandal himself, he would reserve judgment on the matter of her guilt or innocence. He had yet to forget the out-right lies and half-truths that had circulated about himself not so very long ago. No doubt they continued to do so . . .

As the young woman leaned back against the french doors, he saw how the starlight glistened on her damp cheeks. Good Lord. She was crying, he realized with an unexpected stab of pity.

So. Despite that defiant expression, that proud carriage, la belle Victoria was far from hardened to the cruelly wagging tongues. Unlike himself, who'd consigned the lot of them to the bloody devil.

Still, an unblemished reputation was far more important to a woman—especially an unmarried woman, newly launched into Society. This unfortunate beauty would be lucky if she found a suitor willing to brave her tarnished reputation for a single dance, let alone to ask for her hand. He did not doubt that she'd receive proposals, however—none of them decent.

Either way, he doubted she would welcome a witness to her tears.

Dropping his cigar to the dewy grass, he stepped on it before ducking back into the deep shadows beneath the trees, becoming a shadow himself.

As he did so, he was startled to hear a child's sleepy whimper from the wrought-iron chaise tucked in a corner of the long veranda.

A small boy, looking like a miniature ghost in his long white nightshirt, clambered down from the bench and toddled toward the Hawthorne woman.

"Nanny? Is that you, Nanny?"

"Well, hello, there. Why, it's Wee Willie Winkie, isn't it?" he heard the woman ask, warmth and laughter in her voice now.

She crouched down to speak to the child, face to face, her royal-blue skirts billowing about her like the petals of an exotic blue orchid.

But it was not only the vision of loveliness she presented in the starlight that had Steede straining forward, reluctant to miss a single word. It was the gentle warmth, the genuine concern for the child he could hear in her voice.

It was unusual, in this day and age, when women of her class routinely banished their children to a nursery, or gave them over into the care of a nanny or a nursemaid, as Aimee had done. Lady Victoria's natural way with the child was as surprising as it was refreshing.

"What are you doing out here all alone, darling?" she asked. "It's past your bedtime, I do believe."

"I can't find my Nanny Barlow," the little imp piped, his lower lip quivering. "I looked and looked, but I simply cannot find her. Cissy's gone, too." His lisping voice was muffled with tears as he twisted a finger in his tousled curls.

"Oh, you poor little man. It's very frightening when we can't find somebody, isn't it?" Victoria commiserated with the child.

"I'm not frightened!" he retorted, bristling like

37

a bantam cock. "Papa says Comptons aren't afraid of anything, ever."

"I'm sure they're not. In fact, you strike me as a very brave soldier indeed. Won't you tell me your name?"

The blond head dipped in a solemn nod. "It's Christopher. Christopher Charles Compton."

"I'm honored to make your acquaintance, Christopher Charles. I'm Victoria. Victoria Colette Hawthorne," he heard her say, equally solemnly.

Steede grunted in surprise. Unless he was mistaken, the little chap was the Eighth Earl of Hereford, and his host and friend's son and heir.

"Now. Tell me. How did you manage to get outside, Master Christopher?" the young woman quizzed.

The little lordling scrunched up his features. "I don't 'member. I just woked up"—he shrugged expressively—"and I was already here. But . . . I don't know where *here* is." His lower lip quivered despite his brave claims.

The child had probably been sleepwalking, Steede reflected. Mary often did, when she was having a nightmare.

"Then come along with me, darling. I shall take you back up to the nursery. I'm almost certain we'll find your Nanny Barlow there."

"And Cissy, too?" The reedy voice was hopeful. "Cissy's my nursemaid."

The young woman smiled. "Of course. And Cissy, too."

"You pwomise?"

"I promise. Cross my heart. Now up we go, darling."

To Steede's surprise, she bent and picked up the little boy, whose thumb was tucked in his mouth now. She appeared quite unconcerned about the prospect of wrinkling her expensive gown or of destroying her hair.

It was a cool evening. The child's hands and bare feet must have been icy as he wrapped them around her neck and waist, then rested his nodding head on her bare shoulder.

But, with the drowsy child clinging to her like a little monkey, she went back inside the house.

She left Steede staring after her, like a man who's discovered a diamond in a heap of shattered glass.

"Ah, there you are, Lady Victoria. I've been looking everywhere for you. I believe this waltz is mine, is it not?"

Victoria did not bother to consult her dance card. She knew without a shadow of a doubt that every line in it was blank. Just as she knew—also without a shadow of a doubt—that she had never seen, let alone been introduced to, the impeccably attired, strikingly handsome man before her.

"I beg your pardon, sir?" she murmured, blinking and looking about. Perhaps the dark stranger who carried himself with an erect military bearing was addressing someone behind her?

"What a delightful sense of humor your niece has, Your Grace," he murmured, giving her aunt a gallant half-bow. "You know very well you promised me this dance." He offered her his arm. When she made no move to take it, he took her gloved hand and tucked it through his own. "Shall we?"

Victoria was considered tall for a woman, but he was taller still. Tall, darkly tanned and very handsome, with black eyes and saturnine features that made her think of Miss Brontë's brooding Heathcliff in *Wuthering Heights*.

The instant the thought entered her mind, she looked quickly away. For despite her loyalty to Ned, her pulse had unaccountably quickened.

But before she could make some excuse, Aunt Catherine jabbed her in the small of the back with her folded fan. "Well? Don't just stand there, gel. Run along. The waltz is starting."

Propelled abruptly forward, Victoria had little choice but to rest her hand on her striking escort's, and follow his lead onto the dance floor.

There, he made a gallant half-bow, stepped forward and took her in his arms.

As if caught up in a dream, she let him.

Seconds later, they were circling the floor with the other couples.

The gentlemen were immaculate penguins in high-collared white shirts and dark frock coats, while the ladies were like perfumed blossoms, their tissue petals caught up by a lazy wind as they swirled to the strains of a Viennese waltz.

Overhead, the crystal chandeliers were ablaze with light that winked and sparkled off the rainbows of jewels emblazoning the women's hair, ears, throats, wrists or breasts.

Around and around they waltzed, yet her partner said not a word until the strains of the waltz had quite faded away.

The orchestra struck up the Quadrille. Then the Lancer's. Another waltz followed—a German one this time, rather than the more popular Austrian ones.

Still, her partner said nothing, accompanying her with a lithe masculine grace that succeeded in making the other men look stiff and awkward.

"Sir, my aunt will be wondering what has become of me," Victoria pleaded after he had partnered her in a fourth dance.

"On the contrary," he countered with an amused gleam in those snapping dark eyes. "Her Grace, the Duchess of Lincoln, has been watching us as avidly as a hawk watching a particularly plump fieldmouse ever since I took your elbow. Rest assured, Lady Victoria, Her Grace knows very well what has become of her charming protégée."

Victoria's cheeks grew warm under his knowing smile.

"But . . . what of my reputation, sir? To dance so many dances with the same partner is to . . ."

". . . invite speculation about us?" The thick, jet-black eyebrows rose.

"Well, yes," she admitted grudgingly.

"Let them speculate." He smiled, but there was precious little mirth to it. "Besides, I doubt a little more gossip need concern either of us, Victoria.

41

You and I are birds of a feather, after all."

"You know my name. But how can that be, when we have never met before?"

He shrugged as he turned her. "There is no mystery to it. *I asked.*"

"Still . . . we have not been properly introduced."

In mid-dance, he stopped dead and made her a very proper half-bow. "May I present myself, ma'am? Captain Steede Warring, formerly of Her Majesty's Sixth India Regiment, now retired, and the Eighth Earl of Blackstone. Your obedient servant, Lady Victoria," he finished, making a deeper bow.

"Captain Warring," she murmured, flustered, as she inclined her head. There was suspicion in her eyes now. He must have heard the gossip circulating about her. Was he making fun of her—or testing the truth of the rumors by being far too forward in his manner?

"Splendid! And now that we've been properly introduced, may we continue our dance?"

"Oh! Well, yes, of—of course."

Like Cinderfellow, rather than Cinderella, her partner refused to relinquish her until the strains of the very last waltz died away at the stroke of midnight.

With the last chime, he escorted her back to her aunt's side.

Bowing gallantly over the duchess's hand, then Victoria's, Captain Warring bade both ladies a very cordial good night, then was gone as abruptly as he'd appeared.

She could feel the tingling sensation where his gloved fingers had rested on her waist long after he vanished into the crush.

"Shall we stay and have a bite to eat, Victoria?" Aunt Catherine asked. She looked a little flushed and tipsy, and the gray plumes in her hair were askew.

The rest of the gathering was streaming from the ballroom to the buffet tables in the adjoining room, where oyster patties, shrimp vol-au-vents, cakes, jellies and champagne were being served.

"Madeline always serves a deliciously *lavish* midnight supper," the older woman added wistfully.

"Hmm? I'm sorry, Aunt Catherine. What did you say?"

The Duchess of Lincoln frowned. "I said, shall we stay for Madeline's midnight supper, child, or order the carriage and go on home?"

"Let's stay," Victoria declared impulsively, recognizing the expression in her aunt's face. Despite her tall, spare figure, the duchess was very fond of her food. "I'm starving."

"I don't wonder at it. All that dancing with Henrietta's youngest boy has given you an appetite, has it not, my gel?" Catherine declared, her gray eyes narrowed.

The duchess looked down her long nose at her niece, whom she considered too slender, too tall, too dark-haired and far too exotic to be fashionably beautiful, but whom she loved dearly, despite her faults, and sniffed.

"By rights, I probably should have told the

young scoundrel to find himself another partner, after that second dance. After all, the very last thing we need is to have 'the Brute's' dreadful reputation linked with your own . . . transgressions. However—"

"The Brute?" Victoria echoed. A shudder danced down her spine, as if someone had walked over her grave.

Catherine nodded. "Yes. I've heard that name applied to him in some circles. It has to do with his first wife, I believe, and her tragic demise. But pay no attention to rumors, dear gel. As we both know, there's rarely so much as a kernel of truth to such gossip, is there?" she added, gently but pointedly.

"Besides, under the circumstances"—she cast Victoria a fond if disapproving look and shrugged—"refusing the fellow hardly seemed justified. It's not as if you have a column of prospective suitors beating a path to your side, now, is it, my dear?"

"No, Aunt Catherine. It isn't," Victoria agreed demurely, helping herself to a cream-filled meringue and a glass of champagne.

She tried to adopt a suitably downcast, chagrined expression, but could not hide her smile of glee. Another night had come and gone, and she was no closer to finding a husband than she had been at the beginning of April. It was perfect!

To you, my darling Ned, she toasted silently, taking a small sip of the fizzy wine. Bubbles tickled her nose. *And to our future together*.

The gossip, however hurtful or exaggerated,

had actually helped her cause, for it had effectively discouraged any would-be suitors. She would not have to make promises she had no intention of keeping.

If she could endure just another few weeks of being "cut," talked about, shunned and ignored by polite society, she could go home to Yorkshire disgraced, yet still blessedly unattached.

Exactly as she wanted.

Chapter Four

"I expect you're wondering why I sent for you, are you not, Victoria?" Lord Hawthorne began the following morning. He looked unusually good-humored. A man with a secret, bursting to be told.

Victoria, ousted from bed by Lily, nodded yawning agreement, then winced. The sudden movement of her head worsened the throbbing headache bequeathed by last night's champagne. One glass that had quickly become three.

"Of course, Father. Why—er—why *did* you summon me?"

Her father exchanged a smug grin with her aunt, and the tiny knot of foreboding in Victoria's middle tightened.

"Last night, as I was playing billiards at White's, a gentleman approached me. With little ado, he declared his intention to speak with me in the morning at my townhouse, on a matter of some importance." Father paused. "He presented himself here very promptly at ten, and is even now in the library, awaiting my answer."

"Your answer? Your answer to what, Father?" *Oh, how her poor heart fluttered . . .*

"I won't beat about the bush, Victoria. Splendid news! A gentleman of some consequence has asked for your hand in marriage."

He paused, awaiting her delighted response, but she was so stunned she could make none. She could only stare at him.

"Well, child? What have you to say?" Aunt Catherine urged. Her long, elegant hands folded beneath her bosom, she beamed down her slim beak of a nose at Victoria like a benevolent heron.

"I—I am overwhelmed," Victoria said sincerely. It was no lie. Though she was outwardly calm, her emotions were in utter chaos. "What answer did you give this gentleman, Father?"

There was the faintest tremor to her voice. *An offer of marriage!* That explained the simmering excitement she'd sensed in Lily this morning. Servants always knew everything. Lily must have known all about the gentleman caller in her father's study, as well as his purpose there, but the wretched girl had said nothing, drat her.

"I am delighted to say that I have accepted his suit, my dear, providing you are also amenable. I know I swore to marry you off against your will, but . . . I find I am not the tyrant I would like to be. So. What is your answer to be, Victoria? Shall I tell the gentleman you accept or decline his proposal?" His tone was hopeful, his own wishes on the matter very much apparent.

Victoria's thoughts raced. If she told her father she would not marry this man, whoever he was, she ran the risk of rekindling his anger. On the other hand, if she meekly accepted the offer, but asked for a lengthy engagement, she could still avoid an actual wedding for several months. Plenty of time in which to find a way to run off with Ned, as Lily had so cleverly suggested.

"I have had time and opportunity to consider my actions over the past few weeks, Father," she murmured, crossing to the window and staring pensively out at the rainy square. "I have since resigned myself to marrying someone of whom you approve."

She demurely crossed her fingers within the folds of her skirts, so that her lies would not be counted a sin.

"I'm sure if my suitor meets your approval, he will be quite acceptable to me, too," she continued. "However, I do have one small condition to my acceptance of his suit."

Her father, clearly beside himself with relief and pleasure, almost beamed. "Name it, my girl. By jove, name it and it's yours."

"I need a short while to adjust to the reality of this marriage, and accept it. As you are well aware, Father—and you, too, Aunt Catherine—until very recently, my affections, however mis-

49

guided, were directed . . . elsewhere." She lowered her lashes.

"Hrrmph. Of course, child. You shall have the time you need, provided your betrothed is agreeable. Now. Don't you want to know the lucky fellow's name?"

"Why, of course," she said quickly, beside herself with glee. *She had done it! She had convinced him! Soon, Ned . . . oh, soon!* "Who is the gentleman, Father?"

"He is Steede Warring, Lord Blackstone. The master of a fine estate in Devon. According to your aunt, Blackstone captained a regiment out in India until he was widowed last year. There's a small child from the first marriage. A daughter, did you say, Catherine?"

"I did. The little Lady Mary. She's seven, I believe. His Lordship was widowed when their plantation bungalow—"

"Blackstone!" Victoria whirled to face her aunt. She frowned, her hyacinth-blue eyes darkening to gentian. "Isn't that the man who—"

"—danced with you so many times at Hereford House? Yes, that is he—and he's such a handsome young man, too. Isn't it wonderful? You must have made quite an impression with your dancing, my gel."

"But . . . they call him the Brute! You told me so yourself, Aunt," she accused. "How could you consider such a man for my husband, Father?" she cried.

But was it really such a surprise that he had done so? she reminded herself bitterly. Had her father not threatened to marry her off to the first man who asked for her, regardless of age or constitution? Besides, whom had she expected to offer her marriage, given her own somewhat tarnished reputation? Prince Charming? Hardly!

"Come, come, child," said Catherine. "Don't be frightened by Blackstone's reputation. I've known his mother for ages. Henrietta and I were presented at court at the same time. And believe me, no son of Henrietta's could possibly have done all the things young Blackstone's rumored to have done. Trust me in this, darling. Neither your papa nor I would dream of forcing you to marry the man, if we thought for one moment the rumors were true . . ."

The devil you wouldn't, Victoria thought, itching to ask exactly what dastardly deeds the dark-eyed stranger was accused of. Instead, she held her tongue. She had no intention of actually marrying the man, so what did it matter if he was a regular Bluebeard? A bloodthirsty monster who ate wives for breakfast, the way other men ate quail eggs?

Long before her supposed wedding day, she and Ned would be fleeing north, to Gretna Green, and his lordship, the Brute, would be left standing at the altar in Whitby.

The jilted bridegroom.

"Six months? Quite out of the question, sir. Six weeks, and not a day longer, or my offer's withdrawn," Blackstone said curtly. He raked his

51

hands through his ink-black hair and scowled at Victoria from across the study.

His moody, brooding expression was hardly the look of a fond bridegroom, she thought, startled by the fierceness of it. What sort of fellow was this black-haired Brute, really?

For an instant, she felt a twinge—a frantic flutter—of apprehension in her belly. Heard a tiny voice in her head that warned, *Be careful! This one will prove dangerous if crossed!* But then her father spoke, and her uneasy thoughts vanished like smoke on the wind.

"Victoria?" Lord Hawthorne was saying. "What have you to say?"

Victoria had a great deal she dearly wanted to say but couldn't. Six weeks was not nearly long enough to put into action the kind of plan she needed to make, but . . . it would have to do. Beggars could not be choosers, after all.

"Lord Blackstone, I am deeply honored by your proposal," she said at length. "And I am delighted to say that I accept your offer of marriage. A six-week engagement will be perfectly acceptable."

"Splendid! Then the wedding can take place the third week of June," Aunt Catherine said. "It will be a rush to get the banns read, but even so, I am persuaded a wedding gown can be sewn and a small but charming breakfast arranged in so short a time. That Mrs. Johns who sewed your ballgowns. The widow with the daughters? She would be perfect, don't you agree, Victoria?"

Aunt Catherine suggested, all atwitter with wedding plans.

"I shall have my secretary place the announcement of your engagement in the *Times* first thing Monday morning," Hawthorne declared. "Congratulations, Blackstone. Welcome to the family, Steede, my boy."

He shook Blackstone's hand, clapped him on the back, then drew him over to Victoria. Taking her chill hand, he placed it in Steede's. "I believe you and Blackstone will do very well by each other, Victoria. And by the way," he hinted gruffly, "I'm eager to become a grandfather." He winked. "Don't keep me waiting, you two, eh?"

"Roger," Aunt Catherine scolded. "How could you!"

"Father!" Victoria squeaked, pink-cheeked and stunned. She had never, ever seen her father wink before. Had not believed him even *capable* of so human a gesture, let alone such a shockingly risqué comment.

"And so you shall be, sir," Blackstone promised in answer to Lord Hawthorne's far from subtle hint. His Lordship's firm grip on her chill hand tightened, and the unfathomable look he shot her made the hairs stand up on the back of her neck, and sent a shiver skittering down her spine.

"Well, then. If that's everything, I must be off! I have some business to attend to in the City and closer to home that will take several weeks to conclude. With your permission, I shall present myself at Hawthorne Hall on the third Saturday of June, in good time for the wedding. Victoria, my dear, you may expect a betrothal ring from me later today. I shall send it around by special messenger."

She inclined her head. "I shall look forward to it, Lord Blackstone."

"My name is Steede, Victoria. Now, will you accompany me out to my carriage, my dear?"

"I really don't think I—"

"Nonsense, Victoria. The two of you are betrothed. Run along with your fiancé, gel," Aunt Catherine urged in a far too hearty voice.

For one wild, insane moment, Victoria hesitated, tempted to end this farce. To blurt out the truth. To scream that it was Ned she was going to marry, not this Steede brute. That their plans for June weddings and her aunt's fretting over wedding gowns and wedding breakfasts were all a silly waste of time, because she was going to be long gone by the third week in June.

But instead, she allowed Blackstone to take her arm and lead her out to his carriage. She even forced herself to smile up at him as he kissed her cheek, and to wave as the fine black carriage with the Blackstone crest and the matched black horses pulled away.

From this moment on, she decided, she would behave as if she truly intended to go through with the wedding. She need not show too much enthusiasm. That would only draw suspicion. But she *would* have to demonstrate resignation, courage, a false dedication to doing her daughterly duty.

No one—not Aunt Catherine, nor Father, nor

Uncle Lovey and *especially* not that turncoat, Lily—must suspect the truth, until it was too late to stop her.

She had been raised without love. Enough was enough.

She would not marry without it.

Chapter Five

Never had four weeks passed so swiftly.

In her mind's eye, Victoria envisioned an enormous hourglass through which the grains of sand slipped at breakneck speed. Two-thirds were already gone. The time remaining would fly by even faster.

Aunt Catherine had taken up residence at Hawthorne Hall upon their return from London. The Duchess of Lincoln was happily widowed and fabulously wealthy. Victoria's three female cousins were advantageously wed, and busily presenting their mama with grandchildren to the left and right, in various far-flung corners of England. The appearance of the newest arrival was not anticipated until the autumn.

And so, since Victoria had no loving mama of her own to supervise the wedding arrangements,

Aunt Catherine took it upon herself to do so. She would stay at the Hall while Victoria's wedding gown and trousseau were being sewn by the talented Mrs. Johns, a widowed modiste, and her two seamstress daughters from London. The woman had been paid a small fortune to close up shop and follow the duchess and her niece up to Yorkshire for six weeks.

It was the modiste who proved the inspiration for Victoria's plans to elope with Ned.

Quite recently widowed, but forced by necessity to work before her year of deep mourning was officially ended, Mrs. Johns dressed in black from head to toe. When busy at her sewing, the woman reminded Victoria of a little black spider, spinning her web of threads.

On those rare occasions when the Widow Johns left the Hall to shop in Whitby, or to attend chapel, she wore a pert black hat with a heavy veil that hid her face, and a concealing black cloak. They were, Victoria decided, the perfect disguise for her own elopement!

To that end, she had persuaded the shrewd Widow Johns to part with those items of clothing for a price that bordered on usury. All that remained now was to advise Ned of the plans she had made.

"Polly," she told the chambermaid, after she had sent Lily on a false errand that would take her to the farthest reaches of the Hall. "Please, come here. I would like to speak with you a moment."

Polly rose from kneeling on the hearth and

shuffled over to her side, hanging her head and looking as glum as a wet weekend. A sooty smudge on one freckled cheek confirmed that she'd been making up the fires all morning. "I didn't do it, mum. Whatever it were," she whined, "it weren't me."

The maid was considered simple by the rest of the servants. After just a few random words, Victoria could understand why. But since she no longer trusted Lily to deliver her notes, she desperately needed another messenger who would not go running to her father.

She'd thought and thought, and decided Polly would have to do. There was simply no one else she could trust.

"When is your next afternoon off, Polly?"

"Mine? Why, it's tomorrer, in't it, mum?"

Victoria nodded. "Perfect. And will you be going home to visit your mother then?"

"Aye, mum. That I will. Proper poorly, me mam is," the girl explained eagerly. She looked relieved that she wasn't going to be scolded. "Cook says I can take her a fresh egg or two, and a bit o' butter and bread and summat else, since Old Thorny's as rich as old King Midas, he is, an' he won't never miss 'em—"

Belatedly clapping her hands over her mouth, Polly's eyes grew round as saucers. "Oh, I never meant it, mum. Honest, I didn't. Don't give me the sack. Please don't!"

"No one's going to give you the sack, Polly. Calm down, do. I just want you to deliver a note for me. That's all. To Mr. Thomas at the Thomas farm."

Polly frowned. "The young mister Thomas, or the old one?"

"To the young one. Ned. *To Edward*. Do you know him?"

A foolishly broad grin wreathed Polly's freckled face. "Oooh, aye. He's a handsome one, he is." She giggled. "Cook says he were the one what Her Ladyship was—oh!" She broke off, looking fearfully up at Victoria. "Eeh, by gum, I've done it again, aye? What was I thinkin' of, mum? Now, you never mind me, Your Ladyship. You hear me? Everyone knows Polly's daft in the head."

Two furious spots of red color blazed in Victoria's cheeks, but she could not afford to dismiss either Cook or the impertinent girl at this late date, gossip or no gossip. Daft or no, she needed Polly's help, and badly.

"Can you deliver the note for me or not?"

"Aye, I can."

"And it may only be given to Ned. No one else, understand?"

"Aye, mum. Only t' Master Ned."

"And once you've given it to him, you're to wait for his answer. Do you understand?"

"Yes, miss. I can do it. Ye'll see."

"Very well, Polly. I am placing my trust in you. And in return, I shall have Cook make you up a proper basket of food for your mother. A great big one with a roasted chicken, perhaps, and a bit of mutton. A little fresh milk and cheese. And a pot of beef-marrow and barley broth, too. The broth will do wonders for Mrs. Paxton's strength," Victoria murmured, withdrawing a small envelope from the pocket of her rustling skirts. A delicate floral fragrance rose from it.

Polly's face glowed as she took the letter from her. She sniffed it, grinned, then tucked it under the bib of her sooty white apron. "Oh, God bless ye, mum! God bless ye. Think no more of it. Ye can count on Polly Paxton, ye can."

Exactly one week later, some two hours after dusk had fallen, a heavily cloaked and veiled female figure scurried down the circular driveway through the drizzling summer rain.

She hastened to a point just beyond the ornate wrought-iron gates of Hawthorne Hall, where the Hawthorne carriage waited beneath a spreading chestnut tree.

The coachman, dressed in top hat and cloak, was already seated on the box. Lanterns burned on either side of the vehicle, spilling golden light on the oily black puddles.

"Don't bother to climb down, driver," she called in a muffled voice that she prayed Harry would not recognize. "It's just Mrs. Johns. I'm late as it is, and anxious to be off. Lay on until we come to the crossroads, then stop. Did Her Ladyship tell you we're to take on another passenger there?"

Harry politely inclined his head and tipped his hat. "Very good, ma'am."

Drawing a deep breath, Victoria opened the door, tossed her carpetbag inside, then clambered aboard the conveyance unaided.

Fighting her voluminous skirts, she finally seated herself, then closed the door behind her. Spreading out the damp folds of her cloak to dry, she rapped her knuckles smartly on the front wall.

A moment later, the coach rumbled forward.

Victoria drew the short velvet curtain aside and peered back at Hawthorne Hall.

The home she had grown up in was a sprawling dark silhouette in the center of its perfectly manicured park. Greek statuary gleamed like white phantoms in the gloom.

She could see the glow of the lamp that burned in Papa's study, and another in Aunt Catherine's boudoir. She could also see a glow in the attic rooms tucked under the eaves, where the servants slept and where the real Mrs. Johns and her two daughters, eyes streaming, were feverishly sewing her wedding trousseau. One that would never be needed.

For even as they hemmed the brocade train, or attached seed pearls to the exquisite, fitted bodice, the bride was being whisked away. Carried off, into the arms of another man.

Soon, Ned! Very soon . . .

Within the hour, the rain had turned from a sulky drizzle to a heavy, stinging downpour, whipped to a frenzy by the howling wind.

The coach hurtled through pitch-black, unfamiliar countryside while the storm crashed and clattered all around it.

The vehicle's violent rocking slammed Victoria about like a rag doll, shaken in the jaws of a rabid mastiff. Bruised and disoriented, she clung desperately to the velvet squabs, both gown and cloak soaked through by the swirling rain that gusted inside.

What on earth was wrong with Harry? Had her father's head coachman lost control of the team?

Struggling to her knees on the floor between the two seats, she craned her head out of the carriage window to see what was going on.

Oh, no! Thanks to the storm, the blinding rain, they had passed the crossroads north of Whitby, where they were to have picked up Ned. And there was no indication that the coachman intended to either stop, or turn back!

Why, they must be almost to the Scottish border by now. What could Harry be thinking of?

Swirling rain stung her cheeks and stole her breath away. She flicked her head, just as the lightning flashed. In its eerie blue-white flare, she caught a glimpse of her coachman's face.

A profile etched in granite.

A hard, determined jaw.

Blazing dark eyes, fixed resolutely on the rutted track ahead.

Dear God in Heaven! It wasn't Harry at all!

It was her intended.

Heathcliff.

Or more properly, Steede Warring, Lord Blackstone. The man that Society had christened the Brute, for reasons as yet unclear to her.

Recognition—panic—fear—lanced through her

in the same awful instant that another jagged arrow sizzled down from the sky.

The stench of ozone filled her nostrils. Seconds later, a lightning bolt struck a tree alongside the road, which exploded in a flash of light and a deafening crack that lit the hedgerows and trees for several yards in every direction. The oak instantly became a roaring pillar of fire that was biblical in its intensity.

The terrified team screamed and bolted, their necks stretched out like steeplechasers'. Mouths gaping, nostrils flared, terrified eyes rolled back, the horses galloped blindly, trying to escape the traces and outrun the monstrous black coach that nipped at their heels.

The coach's yellow wheels spun furiously, lurching over bumps and rocks, jolting in and out of potholes and muddy ruts in the rough road. The carriage was rocked from side to side so violently the front axle suddenly snapped with a loud crack, like that of a gunshot.

Seconds later, Blackstone's dark head appeared in the coach window.

She gasped, a tiny squeak of shock escaping her.

Rain streamed down his striking face in silvery torrents. Wet, dark locks snaked over his collar, black as sin. More sodden elf-locks clung to his temples and brow. His eyes were dark as the stormy night, blazing like banked coals, as he roared at her:

"Victoria! Open the door and give me your hand! We must jump for our lives!"

Jump? From a runaway coach?

The man was insane.

No. Not insane, she amended, but *murderous*. He meant to kill her, just as he had his first wife!

This was what the rumors hinted at! Only God knew how his first bride had met her end, but Victoria knew exactly how she was to meet *hers*. By breaking her silly neck as she was thrown from a racing coach.

And she'd gleefully thought to *jilt* this monster? That was rich! She wouldn't live long enough to jilt anyone!

Her nerves were shredded, her courage lost, her body bruised and trembling. Even if, by some miracle, she survived this terrible night, she would never see Ted again. She shook her head. Gnawed her lower lip. What was wrong with her? *Ned*. She would never see *Ned* again.

Ted, indeed.

Opening her mouth as wide as she could, Victoria screamed—

—and sank her teeth deep into Blackstone's outstretched hand.

Chapter Six

At any other time, Blackstone's bellow of pain would have been gratifying. A testament to the strength of her jaws, the sharpness of her teeth—indeed, her very will to survive.

Under present circumstances, however, it served only to deepen the terror in her heart, for the roar ended with the Brute reaching through the carriage window.

Twisting his fist in her cloak, he used its folds to haul her bodily from the coach. Out of the runaway vehicle, and into his viselike embrace!

Locked in the arms of a madman, Victoria screamed as she plunged, headfirst, into the wet, dark night.

She landed across something solid and hard. Something that drove the breath from her lungs and proved, unfortunately, to be Blackstone himself.

The Brute had gone to great lengths to ensure she did not escape him, going so far as to take the brunt of their fall singlehandedly. Or rather, single-*bodiedly*.

Bracing her palms against his chest, she pushed herself off him, and scrambled up.

Her first thought was to escape him. To take flight. To run, screaming, into the night. But instead, she was paralyzed by the sight of the horseless coach as it reached the very edge of the world, a dark headland silhouetted against the livid sky like the rearing prow of a ship.

Above it, serpentine tongues of lightning flickered and did a jagged, jerky dance, illuminating the rainswept countryside like brilliant magnesium flares. By its light, she saw the racing vehicle teeter on the edge of a cliff. Then it tipped over the craggy edge—and vanished!

Between ominous clatters of thunder, Victoria thought she heard the coach shatter on the rocks below, followed by the angry crash of the sea as the shattered pieces became flotsam and jetsam.

Badly shaken, Victoria began to tremble uncontrollably. Dear God, she had come within moments of losing her life! In his efforts to do away with her, Blackstone had unwittingly been her salvation . . .

. . . for now!

She jumped in fright as her savior's hand cupped her elbow.

"The Scottish border is just up ahead," he

roared over the noisy cacophony of the storm. "Come on!"

Seen through a veil of swirling rain, with his thick black locks and the coachman's black cape whipping about him, he was Lord Lucifer himself. Satan incarnate. Old Nick, the devil, come to carry her off to Purgatory!

"We'll pass the night at an inn before going on," he continued.

"Going on where?" she demanded. "What do you intend to do with me in the morning, m'lord?"

He chuckled wickedly. "Why, the very worst thing you could ever imagine, my darling Victoria."

Her heart leaped with terror as he thrust his striking, terrifying face into hers. This close, she could feel his hot breath on her cheeks, the heat of his lean, powerful body pressed against hers.

Something flared and glittered in his night-black eyes as he rasped, *"I intend to marry you!"*

"M—marry me! Preposterous!" she insisted, shrugging his hand from her elbow. "I tried to run off with another man! I *jilted* you! Why on earth would you still want to marry me?"

Her lower lip wobbled. Tears brimmed in her eyes, mingling with the rain that streamed down her cheeks as she insisted, "Besides, if I can't marry Ned Thomas, I shall marry no one. I know Ned loves me—and I love him, too. Nothing can change that."

"You little fool! Your precious Ned has abandoned you. Aye, and a string of gullible girls just like you!"

"No," she murmured in disbelief, shaking her head from side to side. "My Ned would never do that. It's not true."

"Oh, it's true all right. And two of the poor drabs are carrying his babes, without benefit of wedlock."

"Liar!" she hissed, rounding on him in fury. Her hand rose to slap his hateful face. To wipe the vicious lies from his lips. "Liar! Liar!"

The powerful hand that caught and trapped her wrist was like a manacle of hot steel. One that threatened to snap her dainty bones in two, like twigs.

"On the contrary, my dear," he rasped softly. "It is no lie."

"It was Lily, wasn't it?" she demanded bitterly, switching tactics. Her voice broke. "She told my father. Then he sent for you, did he not? That wretched girl must have found the note I gave Polly to give Ned. How else would you have known where Harry was to wait with the coach? It was that wretched Lily Lovett who betrayed our plans, wasn't it?"

"They were *your* plans, Victoria," Blackstone corrected in a tone that was brutal by virtue of its very gentleness. But he neither confirmed nor denied her suspicions about Lily.

"Mine and Ned's!" she insisted.

"No, Victoria. Yours and yours alone. Ned had no plans, beyond ruining his employer's daughter. I made it my business to inquire—discreetly, of course—"

"Oh, of course!"

"—and he left Whitby soon after your father's thrashing, spurred on by several other town fathers whose daughters he had ruined. I have it on excellent authority that he hasn't returned since."

"Do you really? And on whose authority would that be?" she scoffed, shooting him a withering look.

"His mother's. I'm very much afraid you mistook Ned's lack of response for silent agreement to your elopement, my dear."

Her face burned. There was such pity in his voice. Oh, God! Blackstone *pitied* her!

Slender fingers curled into small, tight fists. Her head came up at a haughty, defiant angle. She made her spine so rigid it hurt.

Foul weather be damned! She would not just stand there and let someone like him feel sorry for her. Her Hawthorne pride would not permit it. She could bear anything—*anything*—but pity!

Indeed, it was easier to be angry with him—with Lily—with Father—the wretched world at large!—than to believe Ned was not the plain but decent, working-class man she'd believed him to be.

"Horsefeathers, m'lord!" she declared with a haughty snort.

Turning, she squirmed away from him, stalking down the rutted, muddy tracks with her chin held high.

The Widow Johns's black pillbox-hat was sadly askew. It flapped against the side of her head, clinging by a solitary hatpin. The attached widow's veil whipped about in the wind. The violent tugging threatened to scalp her.

Wrenching the offending chapeau from her head, she hurled it into the night and stalked on, headed—despite her protests—in the direction Blackstone had pointed. Toward the nearest village just over the Scottish border.

Alone.

In the morning, she would hire a public conveyance to take her back to Whitby. And once there, she would go directly to the Thomas farm, and find out for herself if what Blackstone claimed was true. . . .

In the deepest ruts of the track, the mud was so deep she had to lift her knees very high in order to extricate her feet from its sucking hold. To prance, almost, like a circus pony. A very *slow* circus pony.

The wretched stuff was over her ankles. Indeed, her sturdiest boots were quite ruined by it. Great muddy splotches stained the hems of her borrowed black cloak, as well as several inches of the gown beneath it. But her sorry appearance paled beside the enormous significance of what Blackstone had said.

"*. . . a string of gullible girls, just like you.*"

"*And two of the poor drabs are carrying his babes, without benefit of wedlock . . .*"

She swallowed. If—and it was a very large if—His Lordship was telling the truth, Ned—*her*

Ned—had fathered children on two other Whitby women. He couldn't have behaved so badly, could he? Not the Ned she knew and loved?

No, she told herself firmly. A man of Blackstone's sinister reputation was not to be believed. Rumor hinted that he had murdered his first wife, after all. Now he seemed determined to do away with her!

"Well, we'll see about that," she muttered, fighting the quagmire that sucked at her stout walking boots.

She dragged her sodden carpetbag behind her as she struggled along, for it contained her most treasured personal possessions, including a framed sepia daguerreotype of her mama—the only picture of her that Father had not locked away. If only her poor little mare, Calypso, had not been left behind, she thought with a pang, but it couldn't be helped. Planning the elopement had been difficult enough, without adding a horse to her plans.

As she struggled along, she told herself she did not believe Steede's claims. No, not for a moment.

Ned had sworn he loved her, and she believed *him* utterly. He could never have feigned the tender way he'd held her. No man could. Nor could he have fabricated that—that light in his eyes when he kissed her. If it had not been the light of love, then what had it been, pray?

What, indeed? the tiny voice of her conscience asked, but she turned deaf ears to it.

". . . Not his name, nor his wedding ring, nor even his protection. Just a tawdry brooch . . ." Blackstone was saying from somewhere above her. *Like God*.

Looking over her shoulder, she saw that, while she struggled through the mud, His Lordship had caught and mounted one of the carriage horses. He must have cut the team free of the traces before instructing her to leap from the coach. He was now riding the lead horse alongside her.

There was no sign of the other three animals.

". . . and even that, not simple, honest silver, but a garish rose of polished jet. The sort of bauble you'd win at a country fair."

His scornful words filtered through the layer of cotton wool that cocooned her mind.

Her hand flew to the brooch beneath her cloak. To the carved jet rose, worn pinned at the throat of her high-necked shirtwaist, amidst rows of tucks.

"Aye, and that's all the sly bastard gave them for their favors," Blackstone continued in the same mocking tone, making no apology for his strong language. "He ruined those poor lasses' lives, and for what? A paltry trifle!"

She heard no more. She was too busy swallowing the wail that rose into her throat. The anguished sob of the betrayed. Of the heartbroken. Of the disillusioned.

She had shown the brooch to no one, not even to Lily. How could Lord Blackstone have known about it, unless . . . unless . . . ?

Her heart hammered in her ears . . .

. . . *unless he was telling the truth!*

But if he was, it meant that Ned had never loved her. That he had set out to seduce her from the very first.

That she was to have been but one of many conquests.

For an instant, she remembered looking up into Ned's eyes in the gloomy stables, and being frightened by the spark of anger she'd glimpsed when she stalled his advances.

"If you really loved me, ye wouldna ask me to stop. Or were ye but making sport of me when ye said ye cared?" he'd challenged her.

Had his challenge been a working-class man's need for assurance from a sweetheart he considered above him, as she had told herself? Or a sly attempt to bring about her surrender?

". . . prove it, lass," he'd urged her. *"Prove I'm suited for better than licking your father's boots . . ."*

Something shattered within her then. Like priceless crystal dashed against a stone wall, something splintered into a million icy slivers.

". . . the gifts, followed by his victims' seduction," she heard Blackstone say, as if from very far away.

In that moment, she hated him. Hated him with every fiber of her being! For there was—lost in the shattered fragments that were her heart— a burgeoning suspicion that he was right.

"If your father had not whisked you off to London, you might well have shared their fate, my dear," Blackstone continued.

And the jet brooch seemed to burn through the stuff of her blouse. To scorch her throat with a brand of shame.

No letter 'A' would label Victoria Hawthorne an adulteress. No, indeed. She would wear the letter 'F' instead. For gullible, naive, trusting, stupid *Fool!*

The high collar of her blouse was suddenly so tight it choked her. The curtain of rain, the dark night pressed all around her, were claustrophobic in their closeness. She felt hot and cold by turns, and shivered uncontrollably.

Oh, Ned, how could you hurt me so? her soul cried out within her. *I loved you! I would have endured anything!—gone anywhere!—relinquished all!—had you but said the word.*

"Take me up," she demanded brokenly.

"What's that?"

Blackstone's voice was deep, startled.

"I said, take me up behind you. *Please*. And for pity's sake, do it *now*, m'lord!"

She deplored having to ask him for anything, but she had no choice, murderer or nay. Her legs refused to hold her. Whether it was the shock of Ned's betrayal or something else entirely, she did not know, but she could not walk another step. Could not utter another word over the painful knot of unshed tears in her throat.

Blackstone's dark eyes flickered over her. Without another word, he reached down and lifted her up before him, onto the carriage horse's bare back. His hands, some still-aware part of her mind registered, were surprisingly gentle as he did so.

Drawing her back against his chest, he grasped a handful of the horse's coarse mane in one fist, and a length of its broken harness in the other. "Get up there, sir!"

At a sedate walk, the horse carried them through the drizzling rain toward the lights of Gretna village that twinkled just over the border.

Victoria stared at her hand in the flickering light of the fire.

A slim gold band etched with flowers encircled her wedding finger like a noose.

Above it, the magnificent betrothal ring he'd sent her by special messenger the day he'd asked for her hand—an oval Indian sapphire, surrounded by alternating sapphires and diamonds—flashed their brilliant blue and icy fires in the meager light.

As pretty a pair of shackles as any girl could hope for, she thought with a sigh, reaching for the poker to stoke the fire. Aye, and those shackles had been set on her for life over a blacksmith's anvil, of all things, in a ceremony that had lasted less than ten minutes!

Even so, those ten short minutes had altered the course of her life irrevocably, for they had bound her to a man she hated. A man who, in all probability, wanted only to murder her.

Oh, dear God, what had she done?

Burned her bridges behind her, that was what!

Agreeing to marry Blackstone while her mind still reeled from Ned's betrayal had been rash beyond belief. She should have waited. She should have thought things through, coolly, logically. She should have tried to find out if Blackstone was telling the truth.

But, she had done none of these things, and there was no going back now.

She waited until the logs on the hearth were a glowing fiery orange, then unpinned the jet rose and hurled it into the fire.

The bauble caught and burned like a lump of coal.

Within the half hour, only smoke and ashes remained, like her dreams of a life with Ned. A rich, warm life, filled with all the love and affection, the caring and warmth her childhood had lacked.

Still feeling numb, she turned down the bed to allow the linens to air, hoping the warmth given off by the fire would rid them of dampness. Or at the very least, dispel the musty odor that clung to them.

Perched on a grubby needlepoint stool by the chimney nook, she hugged her knees and gazed into the fire, letting her thoughts wander aimlessly.

The bedchamber was a disgrace.

Cobwebs festooned its highest corners. Sluts' wool drifted across the dull floorboards with every draft. The narrow bed would better have accommodated a single occupant—or a corpse—

than a bride and her husband on the night of their wedding.

Still, there had been no choice, really. The other three inns the small village boasted had been full. This flea-bitten lodging on the outskirts of Gretna had been all that Blackstone could find them.

Or so he claimed.

Secretly, she suspected that an inn with such a—a sinister aspect had proven more to the Brute's liking than a more reputable establishment with lavender-scented linens, bountiful hot water and a lavish board to offer its patrons.

Still, he had duly registered them below, at the small scarred desk in the lobby, incensed by the landlord's inquiry as to whether His Lordship wanted the room for an entire night or just an hour or two.

She could not fathom any reason for his anger, for the man's query had seemed perfectly reasonable to her.

Tipping the scruffy porter a halfpenny to bring up Lady Blackstone's small bag, His Lordship had escorted her up a narrow flight of stairs to this large, drafty chamber on the second floor.

After instructing the slatternly chambermaid to bring Her Ladyship a tray of hot food, fresh towels and jugs of hot water, he had promptly disappeared. In parting, he'd murmured only that he would join her later.

But His Lordship's sable eyes had said volumes.

She shivered, despite the heat thrown off by the fire.

Now here she sat, fed, watered and bathed, awaiting the dragon's return like some virginal sacrifice.

Her freshly washed black hair gleamed in the firelight as she nervously pleated and unpleated the folds of the flannel nightgown she'd salvaged from her carpetbag, wondering when . . . or even if . . . Blackstone would return to claim his husband's rights.

If? That was rich! A man like Blackstone was unlikely to forgo any rights he was due—a husband's or otherwise.

She bit her lip. He could surely have taken his pick of second wives, scandalous past notwithstanding. Great wealth like the Blackstone fortune had a way of making fathers with marriageable daughters strangely forgetful, after all. Why, then, had he chosen *her*, when there must have been droves of eager innocents who would have begged him to kiss them? Touch them . . . intimately.

She swallowed, her palms suddenly moist.

The very thought of the dangerous, yet strikingly handsome, Blackstone touching *her* intimately made queer little currents eddy up and down her spine. Aye, and in certain other places where she knew none should have eddied.

For some reason, she remembered how safe she had felt earlier when Blackstone held her before him on the horse. The firm way his strong arms had encircled her, and how his broad chest had supported her weary head.

A peculiar lethargy came over her

Perhaps it would not be so awful, after all, to endure His Lordship's most intimate attentions. Perhaps he would even be kind, and not the unfeeling beast that Aunt Catherine had implied bridegrooms so often were on their wedding nights.

Immediately, she rejected the thought. Kindness? Gentleness? From a man who, by all accounts, had *murdered* his first wife? Was she mad? That was probably his dastardly scheme. His entire modus operandi, so to speak.

First he lulled his unsuspecting bride into a false sense of security. And then, after the marriage had been consummated, he killed her just like the black widow spiders she'd read about, who killed their mates once they had mated. Though in this instance, of course, it would be a black widower and—

"Oh!" A log on the fire suddenly collapsed in ashes, scattering sparks over the hearth. Her nerves were wound so tightly, she sprang up like a child's jack-in-the-box.

Leaping across the chamber, she flattened herself against a grimy, whitewashed wall, brandishing a weighty brass candlestick before her.

But the chamber door remained closed.

It was, she judged by the muffled chimes of the village clock, very late when she finally heard footsteps on the landing.

Exhausted and half-asleep, the damp, musty covers tucked firmly beneath her chin, she stiffened, holding her breath. Her heart skipped a beat as someone stopped outside her door! Seconds later, the brass doorknob turned, first this way, then that.

Stiff as a board, her fingers locked in a death grip over the fraying hem of the sheet, she stared at the door, waiting for Lord Lucifer to step through it. *Willing* him not to.

"Victoria?" Blackstone's deep, resonant voice murmured against the jamb. It sounded slurred, as if he'd been drinking. "Lady Blackstone? Are you still awake?"

Slowly, the door swung inward.

Chapter Seven

Eyes squeezed shut, Victoria pretended to be fast asleep as Blackstone moved about the room.

She heard the swish of fabric against fabric, felt the lumpy mattress sag as he perched on the far side of the bed, followed by the dull thud of his boots striking the floorboards, one by one, and the mutter of a low oath when a fastening eluded him.

Her bridegroom was undressing, she realized with a frisson of horror. And after he had undressed, what then?

Oh, Lord! What then, indeed . . .

"Victoria?" he murmured. His deep voice was so close to her ear she could not hide the violent twitch her body gave in response to it.

"Damn it, sit up, Victoria. I know you're not asleep. Here. I've brought something to warm you. This blasted room is as cold as a meat pantry."

Was the "something" poisoned? she wondered. Mulled cider, laced with arsenic? Probably. Obviously, she would have to engineer a little spill . . .

Pushing herself up to a sitting position, she arranged the bolster at her back and fluffed the goosedown pillows, playing for time.

To her surprise, the quaint pewter tankard Blackstone thrust into her chilly hands was steaming. She sniffed the contents suspiciously. To her dismay, they smelled divine, a mixture of creamy milk and rich, dark chocolate. Flavors that would mask even a hefty dose of rat poison or hemlock, surely.

"Why don't we share it?" she offered in a very small voice. "I—I couldn't possibly drink it all on my own, and as you said, it is very cold in here."

"It is only hot cocoa, Victoria," he assured her sternly, the half-smile vanishing. In its place was a dark scowl that, on one with such saturnine features as his, created a devilish aspect indeed. "Not a whiff of hemlock nor a grain of deadly nightshade anywhere!"

"Deadly nightshade?" she echoed. "Don't be ridiculous, sir!"

But by the guilty pink color that filled her cheeks, Steede knew his suspicions had been correct.

His bride had been as pale as whey until that guilty flush restored the color to her cheeks. Anger filled him. Devil take the gossips of London!

Thanks to their wagging tongues, his own wife believed he intended to murder her! Dear God, had the rumors that surrounded Aimee's death been so badly distorted?

Obviously they had.

"I certainly wasn't implying that you . . . that you . . ." Her voice trailed lamely away, denying her protests.

"The devil you weren't!" he scoffed. "Here. Hand me the bloody tankard!"

"No, really, I—"

"Give it here, I said!" he thundered.

Snatching the tankard from her hand, he took a deep swallow of its contents. "Hmm. Bloody marvelous. Cocoa and hot milk, madam—and that's all it is. Here. Try some."

She looked as if she'd rather drink hemlock from a skull—preferably his—than sip from any vessel his lips had touched. Nevertheless, she did so. Gingerly.

"Warmer?" he inquired when she had drained the mug.

"Much, thank you," she agreed primly, shrinking back against the pillows.

God, she looked primed to bolt if he so much as touched her—yet he doubted he could help himself in that regard. That aura of innocence, of unawakened beauty, made him want her more than he'd ever wanted a woman, including his first wife. And he was, after all, her bridegroom. For such beauty, he could almost forgive her the deep bite wounds on his hand, which still

85

throbbed painfully, despite the stiff brandy with which he'd doctored himself.

Taking the tankard from her, he took her slender hand in his and drew it to his mouth. His lips brushed the tips of her long, tapering fingers, before he turned her hand over and kissed the well of her palm.

She flinched violently.

"Please, don't!" she whispered, trying to free her hand.

"Shhh," he murmured, placing the hand he had kissed on his cheek. "We are married, are we not, my dear? And this is what married couples do on their wedding night." He smiled. "And any other night it may please them."

Pressing her back against the soft feather pillows, he followed her down.

Her coal-black hair was strewn across the pillows in inky coils. Her pale, heart-shaped face bloomed like an exotic orchid amidst its ebony petals. And at its heart, that lush carnal mouth, and lips the deep, velvety red of roses . . .

The ache in his loins mounted, along with his growing desire, despite his vow to proceed slowly and gently. God knows, it was becoming more difficult by the minute, for he had wanted her from the first instant he saw her, that night at the Herefords' ball.

Her blue satin skirts had billowed about her like the petals of a rare hothouse flower as she knelt to speak with little Lord Christopher. Her dark hair had gleamed in the moonlight. Glittering sapphire tears had swung from the tips of pink earlobes as delicate as seashells, while still more sapphires had encircled a swanlike throat he yearned to kiss.

One look, and he'd been lost . . .

The image of graceful white shoulders, of creamy breasts rising from blue satin, had imprinted itself on his memory. As had the scandalous lady herself . . .

Yet once she had left the toddler and returned to the ballroom that night, she had become another woman entirely. An ice-maiden in blue—cool, regal, untouchable—who had deigned to come down from her crystal tower to rub shoulders with the common folk. A woman who was, at least on the surface, impervious to the racy scandal surrounding her.

And, despite his determination to dismiss that gossip as false, his wicked imagination could readily conjure up the image of quite another Victoria. A temptress who sprawled elegantly across the straw in some idyllic stable. A wanton beauty who rode astride his hips without a stitch of clothing to her name!

In his dreams, her cool reserve became wild abandon. Her head was thrown back, and her gypsy curls flowed in inky ripples over her ivory breasts. Her eyes smoldered with invitation, and that carnal mouth was parted in a gasp of pleasure as he drove into her, time and time again. . . .

This—this, by God!—was the tantalizing image that had driven him from the study of his townhouse to White's, and Roger Hawthorne, in the wee hours following the Herefords' ball. The same tantalizing image that had haunted his dreams, and prompted his offer for the lady's hand the following morning, too. *Lust. Desire.* Not the image of a nursemaid for his daughter! Hell, no! Finding a new mama for little Mary had quickly become a secondary reason for his pursuit. A welcome bonus? Truth was, he wanted Victoria. Lusted after her, craved her, had to have her. . . .

Nor had his rampant desire diminished in the following hours. Rather, memories of her provocative scent, the way she'd felt and moved in his arms, had served to fuel his desire.

He might try to convince himself that his motives were pure. Paternal, even. But he'd be a liar. It was *lust* that had prompted his offer for Victoria's hand. No more, no less. And if he had to marry the woman in order to bed her, then so be it, he'd decided.

Three years ago, when Aimee proved unfaithful, he'd decided that marriages of convenience were best for both parties. Nothing had happened since then to alter that belief. He'd accepted long ago that a loving marriage such as his parents had enjoyed was not in the cards for him.

Still, his five weeks' engagement to Victoria had proven the longest five weeks of his life. If he were honest with himself, he had welcomed the arrival of Hawthorne's frantic note, informing him of his betrothed's plans to elope with the Thomas lout, for her actions had precipitated a speedy end to his torture. He would take the coachman's place, he'd promised himself, then persuade the faithless Victoria to elope with him, instead.

No more nights filled with dreams of her dancing naked in his arms, warm and pliant with surrender, he'd thought as he donned Harry's cape and top hat and took his place upon the box of the coach.

No more days fractured by glimpses of raven-haired women he'd mistaken for her, then followed up hill and down dale like a hound after a bitch in heat!

Here, in this godforsaken corner of the world known as Gretna Green, he would make Victoria his own.

Firelight danced over her pale, lovely face as he ducked his head to hers. His broad chest crushed the rounded breasts hidden by her voluminous nightgown as he leaned over her.

He teased her soft lips apart with the tip of his tongue, tasting, sampling. A lovely woman was like a fine vintage wine. Lust or no, one did not swig great gulps from her lips, like champagne swigged from the bottle. One sipped, savored her bouquet lingeringly, as if drinking her essence from the finest crystal.

When she drew away in confusion, he firmly took her chin between his thumb and finger and held it steady while he deepened the kiss.

To his surprise, she yielded her mouth with only a soft, breathy murmur. Her arm curled around his neck. Her fingertips idly ruffled the waves at his nape.

Promising. Very promising.

Even that careless little caress sent an electric jolt through his loins.

Spun silk, he thought as he plunged his hands into her midnight hair. Its soft coils felt like warm silk as they slipped through his fingers, as alive and vital as the lovely woman whose lips he kissed.

He felt her shiver as his hand splayed around her throat. Fingers curled around its elegant column as he deepened the kiss, tracing the pink whorls of her ears down to her nape.

A half-smile played about his lips as Victoria sighed and relaxed beneath him, murmuring like a cream-fed kitten.

He continued to kiss and caress her, deftly unfastening the narrow blue ribbon bows that closed the front of her nightgown as he did so. When the last tie was undone, he drew the fronts of her bodice apart to bare her breasts for his pleasure. And pleasure it was, indeed, to look upon them.

She sucked in a shocked gasp and shivered as cool air kissed her skin, then gasped again as his warm breath fanned her snow-white bosom, steepled with small raspberry-pink buds.

"How lovely you are," he breathed, his dark gaze shifting from her face to her perfect breasts. *"Everywhere."*

He gazed deep into her eyes, tracing each delicate mauve areola with his fingertip as he did so.

The soft, velvety nipples stiffened in response, until a flushed pink bud rode taut upon the swell of each ivory mound.

With a groan so deep it was more a growl, he dipped his dark head and covered one breast with his mouth.

Blackstone's mouth engulfed her breast, then drew hard upon the tiny peak as if it were a succulent berry. She could not hold back a cry of surprise, for his mouth was unbelievably hot, the feel of his wicked tongue unbearable!—*unbearably sweet!*—as his hungry mouth danced over her flesh.

Delicious sensations filled her. Ones that traveled—in some mysterious fashion—from her breasts to the secret place between her thighs.

For one delicious, wicked moment, she could not help wondering how it would feel if Blackstone were to touch or even kiss her there, like the Eastern couples she had seen once in a book of erotic drawings found in her Father's library.

Oh, wicked girl! Oh, wicked wicked thoughts!

What was wrong with her, she wondered, shame flaming her cheeks? Blackstone would do what had to be done to consummate their marriage, and then he would tell her what a brave girl she'd been and leave her bed, God willing, just as her stammering aunt had so nervously described.

She had only to submit to her husband's will for a few moments. To lie there, grit her teeth and do her duty, however distasteful, bolstered by the knowledge that it would soon be over.

She was not supposed to feel pleasure—no decent woman did, Aunt Catherine had assured her. Only *males* took pleasure in carnal matters, be they human or animal.

Consequently, confused by the considerable pleasure she was feeling, Victoria stiffened as Blackstone pushed her nightgown up her legs to her hips, kissing the petal-soft ivory legs he bared as he did so.

"Don't!" she murmured, knotting her fingers in his hair to halt his explorations.

"Let go, darling. You're my bride. I want to look at you. *All* of you. Come. Let's get this wretched tent out of the way, shall we?" He sounded amused, his voice even deeper and huskier than usual.

Mortified, she crossed her arms over her bare breasts as he tugged the nightgown down, over her hips, down her legs and feet, and finally stripped it off her.

She cringed as he flung the garment aside, for he made no effort to hide his laughter

"Good Lord! Drawers, *too*? On your wedding night? I shouldn't be surprised if you're wearing a chastity belt beneath them!" the hateful man roared. "One that is stoutly padlocked, of course."

His sable eyes dancing with wicked merriment, he planted a kiss on the tip of her nose, then deftly slipped his hand between her ruffled drawers.

She shot up off the bed as if he had stuck a pin in her, although he had done no more than gently stroke the undefended flesh he found there.

"Then again," he murmured, his eyes even darker now, his voice unaccountably thicker as he caressed that part left bare by the divided garment, "perhaps not, hmm?"

Her drawers quickly went the way of her nightgown, soaring across the bedchamber in an unseemly flash of white that made her cheeks burn.

"Now, then. Turn and turn about, hmm, sweetheart? It's only fair," he murmured. Sitting up, he unfastened his breeches and shoved them down and off his body. His drawers followed.

Oh, God. His lean, powerful body was quite bare now, except for the line of curling dark hair that bisected his broad chest. And, to her surprise, he wasn't horrid or beastly at all. He was beautiful. Like a statue of a Greek athlete, powerfully muscled and deeply tanned everywhere, she saw, his skin burnished by a sun far hotter than that which shone on England's damp, chilly shores.

"So. Do you like this better, my dear? The two of us, naked as Nature intended? Unfortunately, we would be at a decided disadvantage should this flea-bitten hostel catch fire!" Laughter rumbling in his voice, he gathered her into his arms and drew her close.

He smelled of sandalwood soap, of tobacco and brandy, and felt so deliciously warm. *Hot*, really. His naked flesh burned like a furnace against her own, warming her. Oh, *God*, yes, warming her in ways she'd never dreamed of.

Stiff as a porcelain doll, she allowed Blackstone to caress and kiss her breasts, her shoulders, her back. To trace the path of her spine down to the flare of her hips and buttocks. To follow the lush curves of her bottom, until he found the swollen folds of her womanhood.

Pressing her down to the sheets, he dipped his head to kiss her navel, then teasingly stirred the patch of dark curls below it with several low, puffing breaths, chuckling softly as she gasped in shock. Tousling the same curls with his hand, he delved lower, inserting a probing finger between the pouty folds.

"My poor love," he murmured thickly. "So sweet and wet and wanting. Come, now. Open for me, my lovely. Wider. Aye, there's a love. There's a good lass . . ."

He crooned endearments and nonsense words in her ear, and all the while his finger pressed deeper, deeper, until her world revolved around it. Around the hot, hard length of it, which although a little painful was at the same time strangely pleasant.

While his mouth was busy at her breasts, he smoothly worked that finger in and out of her, going deeper with each inward thrust until she thought she would faint from sheer delight.

As if her own body were allied with his against her, a silky dew poured from her body to aid his intrusion.

And—despite what she had told herself, and the fact that she hardly knew the man, for all that they were husband and wife—she thrilled to his touch. Could not get enough of what he was doing, nor the way he made her feel. She wanted more. *More!*

Little cries broke from her lips as her body suddenly pulsed with an excess of pleasure.

"Oh! Oh, Blackstone!" she cried.

In the wake of those exquisite flutters came delicious contentment—followed by a deep sense of shame. What had happened to her? And what must Blackstone think of his innocent bride, who found pleasure in The Act like a common trull?

But to her dismay, she had no time to consider the question further, because her husband chose that moment to lift himself over her, and kneel between her legs.

"Blackstone, don't!" she cried, suddenly panicky. She shoved at his chest with her palms.

"I must, my sweet. But I shall not hurt you, after the first time. Once your maidenhead has been fully broached, there will be only pleasure, for both of us."

Gently pinning both hands to the bed above her, he stopped her protests with a long, deep kiss and spread her wide with his knees.

"Blackstone—Steede—wait! Let me—*ohhh!*"

She gasped as the hard, blunt head of his shaft pressed against her opening. And then, his face a dark, intent mask, Blackstone thrust forward, driving deep inside her.

In that single thrust, the worst of it was over. Done with. A moment's searing pain, the splash of something hot against her thigh, and he was lodged deep within her body.

For better or worse, their marriage had been consummated. She belonged to him. Now. For better, or for worse.

She offered no comment when, some while later, he withdrew and rolled off her. Rather, she lay stiffly beside him, breathing shallowly as she stared up at the patches of mildew on the ceiling.

His own heart still racing, he took her rigid hand in his and kissed her knuckles.

"Give me a few moments to recover, then I shall attend to your pleasure again, my dear," he promised, smiling down at her, still ridiculously pleased that she had come to him untouched.

To his disappointment, she did not eagerly return his smile but quickly looked away, refusing to meet his eyes.

A knot of ice formed in his belly. "My eagerness for you undid me. The next time will be better for both of us. You will see. I shall show you pleasures you have only dreamed of, my sweet," he promised, for he had felt her passion ignite with his touch, and her soaring response to his caresses. "Games of love that I learned in the East, where a beautiful woman like you is a jewel beyond price."

"I will submit to you, as is my wifely duty, m'lord," she whispered, her voice breaking. "But I shall never find pleasure in it, nor come to your bed willingly."

His dark eyes heavy-lidded now, gleaming with

amusement, he leaned on one elbow and looked down at her. She had the flushed, sleepy look of a woman who has been well loved by a man. The liquid darkness of spent passion was in her eyes. "What's that? Do you challenge me, Victoria?"

"No, m'lord. I simply stated a fact."

He grinned and chucked her under the chin. "Bloody little hypocrite! You enjoyed what I did as I enjoyed doing it. In your innocence, do you think a man cannot tell whether a woman feels pleasure? Especially a man like myself? The fluttery little pulses here," he murmured, cupping her mound, "the nectared welcome here," he added, touching her between the thighs again. "The rosy flush that suffused your body!" He chuckled. "Your lovely body betrayed you, my darling Victoria—even as your lovely eyes betray you now. They are windows to your thoughts— and to your most intimate feelings. Do you hate me so much, then?"

Angry that he had read her so accurately, she turned her head away and stared steadfastly at the smoke-blackened beams and grimy ceiling above the bed instead.

That he had given her pleasure—and worse, that he *knew* he had done so—infuriated her. She was furious for enjoying his lovemaking like a common trollop, and for forgetting Ned and all he had meant to her so easily.

"And to think you would have given your maidenhead, your fresh loveliness, your heart, for a tawdry brooch and a collier's grimy cottage, had I not intervened!" Steede murmured, sweeping his hand down the length of her body. "And that, my sweet, would have been a terrible mistake. You see, you were born to be a rich man's bride."

She flushed, dangerously close to slapping his hateful face. "I'll have you know I loved Ned, although he was only a 'grimy collier' to you. And I'm not someone who easily forgets those I love."

"Believe me, I have more admiration for the hard-working poor of this country than do most men, Victoria. But that—that lout was unworthy of you in every way."

"Let me be the judge of that!" she insisted.

"If you had such great faith in your Ned, why did you marry me?" he demanded.

"You confused me. I—the storm, your talk of brooches—I didn't know what to think."

"Don't give me that. In your heart of hearts, you knew what Ned was. Aye, and what he wanted. When I told you about those other women, it struck home, did it not? You recognized something of Ned in what I told you, didn't you? That—that is why you married me."

"It was nothing of the sort!"

Infuriated by her obstinacy, he got up and began dressing, moving about the room with clipped, brisk movements that—had she known him better—would have eloquently betrayed his anger without need for words.

Blasted woman! While she lay there, his wedding ring on her finger, his seed in her belly, still clinging to her memories of that bastard Thomas, his own treacherous body was stirring once again. Her nearness and the delicate feminine scent of her, which still clung to his body like a musky perfume, enflamed him.

He wanted her again, damn her. And if he didn't make himself scarce, he'd be hard put to leave her alone. His bride or no, he had no intention of ravishing the blasted woman on their wedding night. Perhaps she'd come around once she'd had time to recover and think things through . . .

As he strode across the room to retrieve his cravat, she shrank back against the pillows, as if fearful he might hurt her in some way.

"For pity's sake, Victoria, I won't strike you! Surely you don't believe those damned rumors?" he accused.

"What else am I to believe? I hardly know you—"

"Nor I you, madam! But I, at least, gave you the benefit of the doubt," he flung back at her.

"Why did you do it? Why did you have to offer for my hand and ruin *everything?*" she demanded.

She saw him square his jaw at the word "ruin."

"Because my little daughter needs a mother," he snapped through clenched jaws. "And because, quite by accident, I saw you with Lord Hereford's small son the night of the Herefords' ball. I was impressed by your way with children, and thought you'd do admirably as Mary's stepmama."

She swallowed. "You wanted a mother for your little girl? That was the only reason you offered for my hand?"

It wasn't, of course, but he was too angry to admit it. "Yes," he snapped, the single word like a gunshot.

Dear God, it was even worse than she'd feared. He had not wanted her for herself at all, although he had done his duty and bedded her. He'd wanted a mother for his little girl. And that was all he wanted.

A lump of misery swelled in her throat. What kind of woman was she, that she'd enjoyed his dutiful bedding?

"Well, Victoria? What have you to say? You *are* fond of children, are you not?" he repeated impatiently when she said nothing.

She swallowed over the knot in her throat and nodded.

"Yes. Very fond, m'lord," she whispered.

The tawny flicker of firelight bronzed his broad shoulders, chest and powerful arms as he shrugged angrily into his shirt. The ruddy glow behind him made a red-gold nimbus about his dark head as, arms akimbo, legs braced apart, he scowled down at her.

"The name is Steede, Victoria," he snapped. "Now that we are husband and wife, in every sense of the word, I shall expect you to use it."

"Very well, *Steede*," she echoed, hyacinth-blue eyes mutinous as she glared up at him.

He nodded, moving about the chamber as he dressed, tying his cravat, dropping a gold cufflink in the gloom, swearing softly as he retrieved it.

"I have never bedded any woman against her will. But we *are* married now, Victoria. And, since I have already dismissed my mistress of the past two years in deference to your position as my wife, I shall expect you to see to my . . . needs." A faint smile played about his sensual lips. His black eyes were filled with a lambent fire. "As I, my lovely wife, shall most certainly attend to yours."

His husky declaration was very nearly a threat, she thought. Or was it not a threat at all, but a wickedly sensual promise?

Either way, it made her shiver. Stirred a quiver of response in the very place that still throbbed from her bridegroom's ardent attentions.

His sable gaze impaled her as he added softly, "You do understand?"

"Perfectly, m'lor—Steede," she agreed, her cheeks burning.

He nodded and slung his coat over his shoulder. "Excellent. Then I urge you to rest for the remainder of the night. We leave Gretna for Blackstone on the milk train."

And then, to her utter amazement and confusion, he leaned down and pressed his lips to the dimple at the corner of her mouth in a chaste kiss. "Sweet dreams, Lady Blackstone," he murmured softly.

With that surprisingly tender farewell, he left her staring into the shadows, filled with regret— though whether it was regret over losing Ned, or that she had not met Blackstone first, she could not have said.

Chapter Eight

Blackstone Manor, Devonshire, Southwest England

"Mother," Blackstone murmured, crossing the drawing room to kiss his mother's brow. "Allow me to present my bride, Victoria. Victoria, my mother, Lady Henrietta Warring."

"Victoria, dear girl! Welcome to Blackstone Manor!"

Steede's mother rose gracefully from her chair by the drawing room fire to greet them as, exhausted by the endless train journey down from Yorkshire to the farthest reaches of England, Victoria tottered into the room after Steede.

Her first view of imposing Blackstone Manor with its twelve chimneys scraping the sunset and its sprawling wings bathed in the sun's dying rays had drained her of her last drop of energy.

"Lady Henrietta," she murmured, politely inclining her weary head and extending her hand. "I'm delighted to meet you, madam."

"And I you, my dear girl," Henrietta responded, squeezing Victoria's hand. "Steede, she's lovely, simply lovely!" the older woman exclaimed, turning to her son. "My felicitations to both of you on the occasion of your marriage. I pray it will be as long and happy as mine was to Steede's father."

Aware of Victoria's startled expression, Steede explained, "I couldn't keep my eagerness to wed you a secret, *darling*. Before I left Devon, I confided our intentions to elope with my mother."

"Indeed?" Victoria murmured, hyacinth eyes flashing angrily. "Then it appears your bride was the last to know."

Henrietta laughed as Steede crossed the room. In a low voice she said, "Oh, dear girl, don't be cross with him, I beg you. He was so impatient to make you his bride! And—now that I've seen you—I quite understand why. I hope you'll be very happy here as the mistress of Blackstone Manor. My maid and I have spent the past few days moving my things into the Lodge. You must come to take tea with me there from time to time, and to visit, as I intend to take dinner here with the two of you on occasion. If," she added pointedly, "I'm invited."

"Oh, madam, of course you will be! And there was no earthly reason to remove yourself from your home on my account," Victoria exclaimed, aghast. "Please, do come back. You must remain here. It is where you belong."

Henrietta patted Victoria's hand. "I appreciate your generosity of spirit, my dear, but you are the mistress of Blackstone Manor now. And besides, it is my belief that newlyweds need time alone to acquaint themselves more fully with each other, without interfering in-laws to take sides in their little love spats. As it is, you are taking on a small child. One who—I have little doubt!—will resent your marriage to her father, at first. Being a new stepmother is enough for any young bride to contend with," she added with a chuckle, "without the addition of an opinionated old woman like myself. Our Mary is a darling girl, but somewhat . . . well, perhaps I should let you form your own opinions of my granddaughter, without mine to color them."

Henrietta Warring rose, a tall, slender woman elegantly gowned in pale amethyst. Hair pins tipped with the deep purple gemstones sparkled in her silver chignon, while a very fine oval amethyst pendant hung on a gold chain about her neck.

It was immediately obvious to Victoria from which parent Steede had inherited his dark, striking good looks. In her heyday, Lady Henrietta had clearly been a beauty. A brunette original, rather than the blue-eyed blonde Society fawned over.

"I was hoping that perhaps I could call upon you for advice in that regard, madam," Victoria murmured, and was surprised when Henrietta patted her cheek and smiled.

"Of course you may, of course! I will help in any way I can, dear girl, as long as my help falls short of interference. Come and see me often, won't you? It is my fond hope that we shall become friends, as I have always been close friends with your dear aunt. How is my Birdie?"

Victoria refrained from laughing at Her Ladyship's pet name for her beaky-nosed Aunt Catherine.

"I'm happy to say Her Grace, the Duchess of Lincoln, is very well, ma'am, and enjoying her many grandchildren. She speaks most highly of you, and of your long friendship and remembers her first Season in London with great fondness, because of meeting you there."

Henrietta laughed in open delight. "As well she might, oh, yes! As well she might! That naughty Birdie! What a wicked brace of gels we were back then, and no mistake. Our poor mamas quite despaired of us making suitable matches."

"Really?"

"Indeed they did. And then we stunned the lot of them by attracting the notice of not one, but *two* of the season's most eligible bachelors. Wealthy, titled gentlemen they were, too—and handsome? Oh, my dear, so handsome! Within the year, Catherine had married her duke, and was expecting her first daughter—that would be your cousin Imogene—while I married my beloved John, the Earl of Blackstone."

A shadow crossed Henrietta Warring's face.

"Our first son, John Minor, was born a little over a year later. We lost him at the very beginning of the Crimean, you know. To think he's dead, and yet the wretched war goes on. . . ."

"I'm so sorry."

"Bless you," Henrietta murmured. "My poor husband was never the same afterwards. He followed our John to the grave less than two years later, leaving Steede to inherit the earldom and the estates in his brother and father's stead. Thank God I have him left to me," she added in a lower voice. "Such a dear boy."

Victoria made appropriate murmurs, but it was difficult to think of the man who had taken Ned's place, married her, then made love to her so ardently the night before as his mother's "dear boy."

Ever since last night, she'd been having flashbacks of their intimate encounter. Ones that became especially vivid whenever Steede chanced to glance across the room at her, as he was doing now, his sleepy dark eyes filled with wicked promises.

Dear Lord. When he looked at her like that, her body grew hot and cold by turns, as if feverish. She could feel his lambent dark eyes upon her breasts like a scorching caress that seared through her clothing.

Just thinking about his lovemaking made her knees weaken and her breasts tingle. It also stirred a tickly pulse between her thighs.

Flustered, she quickly looked away, refusing to meet Blackstone's eyes. Clearing her throat, she told Henrietta, "Before our—elopement—my aunt expressed her intention to call at a later date, ma'am."

Her new mother-in-law nodded. "I shall look forward to it. Better yet, I shall write dear Birdie first thing in the morning, and extend my invitation to stay. Well, now. I've kept you standing about long enough. You must both be exhausted after that wretched train journey down from London! I shall go home to my dear little house and let Cook serve you your supper. My maid will be waiting up for me, fussing as always. A very good night to you, my dear boy," she murmured, pausing en route to the door to offer her cheek for Blackstone's lips.

To Victoria's surprise, Lady Henrietta also leaned forward and kissed her brow. "And to you, daughter. Welcome to your new home, and may God richly bless your marriage."

Touched and warmed by the woman's affectionate greeting, Victoria smiled. "Thank you, ma'am."

"*Mother*, dear. Please, call me Mother. Or Henrietta, if you prefer the modern way. Ma'am makes me feel positively ancient."

And with that, she was gone, still laughing gaily as she left the two of them alone.

"What a charming lady," Victoria observed in the yawning silence that followed Lady Henrietta's departure.

"What did you think? That I'd crawled out from under a rotted log?" His dark brows rose questioningly. "Cook suggested we dine by the fire. I accepted for both of us. I trust you'll find that acceptable?"

"Of course. Thank you," Victoria said stiffly, jumpy now that she was alone with her husband.

What was wrong with her?

Each time she looked at the wretch, she remembered him as he'd looked in their room at the inn, a naked savage, an untamed brute with powerful muscles that rippled under sun-browned skin burnished by firelight. Or looming over her, his handsome face, broad shoulders and darkly furred chest filling her vision.

Her erotic memories intensified the delicious ache between her thighs and stirred flutters in her belly.

His every gesture brought back images of tanned hands caressing the slope of her hip, or the gentle graze of his knuckles as they followed the curve of her cheek down over the hollows of her throat, to a velvety nipple.

Her response to his touch had been shameless, wanton—but, oh, what pleasure he'd given her, she thought with a shiver. She would have liked to deny it, but doubted she had the strength, let alone the will. And as for refusing him, as she'd so rashly sworn—she could not, even had she wanted to!

And there was, too, that strangely tender kiss of farewell. Hardly what she'd expected from a man with his dangerous reputation.

Obviously there was more to Blackstone than met the eye . . .

"Excellent!" Steede declared. Striding across

the room, he yanked the tasseled bellcord to summon a servant.

Exhausted, Victoria sank down into an over-stuffed horsehair chair by the fire without waiting for an invitation.

Peeling off her mud-stained kid gloves, which had shrunk as they dried and become so tight overnight that they pinched her fingers, she held her hands out to the fire's warmth.

She was surprised—and pleased—by the drawing room's charming appearance. With the addition of a few polished copper or brass bowls of brilliantly colored flowers, and perhaps a glowing landscape or two, the room would have the warm, inviting feeling she preferred. . . .

She caught herself in mid-thought and scowled.

Good Lord! Here not five minutes, and already she was making changes, thinking as the mistress of Blackstone, she realized, annoyed with herself for so readily slipping into the role of Blackstone's wife. The least she could do was feel a *twinge* of discomfort. A soupçon of remorse.

"May I pour you a sherry or a glass of port, Victoria?"

"No, thank you," she refused, discreetly smothering a yawn. "The tiniest sip would send me to sleep."

"Ah. My apologies, Lady Blackstone," her husband murmured, his roguish grin showing no remorse whatsoever. "I'd forgotten how little sleep you had last night—"

"Heavens! I have nothing to wear tomorrow,

except for these mud-stained rags!" she declared suddenly, abruptly changing the subject as she sprang to her feet. Her cheeks had turned beet red.

"If you recall, my dear, I offered to purchase you a new wardrobe in London when we changed trains," he reminded her with gentle reproof in his tone. "But you would not hear of it."

To his credit, he *had* offered, she remembered as she sat back down. But she had not felt comfortable allowing a gentleman to purchase clothing for her, any more than she was prepared to answer to a gentleman for everything she did. She doubted she would ever be *that* married to anyone, least of all a rogue like Blackstone. She valued her independence much too highly.

"Be that as it may, I should still like these sponged, brushed and ready to wear in the morning," she insisted with a sniff, gesturing at her clothes. Several inches of her skirt were dark with dried mud, as was her under-petticoat beneath it. More splatters stained the tucked bodice of her high-necked blouse.

"Of course. I shall have my housekeeper attend to it immediately after dinner, and assign you one of the housemaids to help you dress until we can engage a ladies' maid for you. If it's any consolation, you shouldn't have to make do for very long. Before I left Yorkshire, I took the liberty of asking your father to have your things sent down here."

"You did what?" she exploded, springing to her feet.

"Really, darling, you don't have to thank me," he bantered, enjoying the way her rising temper intensified her coloring. "I'm sure everything will be here within a day or two. Until then, perhaps you could borrow a few things from my mother?"

An angry scowl distorted his bride's lovely face.

"You were supremely confident of the success of your plan to take Ned's place, were you not, m'lord?" she snapped, her pallor revived by a surge of color that pinkened her cheeks in a most delightful fashion.

His black eyes sparkled. "Supremely," he agreed. "But then, a man's confidence ensures his success in most undertakings, be it marriage— or *murder*," he added ominously, taking wicked delight in the sudden darkening of her eyes.

"Undoubtedly," she ground out, not entirely convinced he was teasing. "So, my father and your mother knew," she continued, counting on her fingers and pretending she had not heard his last comment, although she had. Oh, yes—and it had chilled the blood in her veins, and struck terror in her heart. "Then there's Harry and Lily, too, obviously. Who else did you tell? What about your butler? Did he know? And the gardener? What about him? And was the Archbishop of Canterbury privy to your plans? And how about Her Majesty, the queen? Was there *anyone* you neglected to inform about our elopement, prior to commandeering my coach and telling *me*?" she demanded, sticking out her chin.

"Nooo, not that I can think of," he admitted airily, flashing her an evil grin. "Ah ha! Arthur.

Saved by the timely arrival of our supper, I do believe. Come in," he barked as someone knocked discreetly at the door. "Ah, it is you, Arthur. You're a godsend, man!"

"Sir?"

"Never mind. Set the card table up over there in front of the fire, would you?"

"Very good, m'lord." With a nod, the startled young footman pushed a wheeled serving cart into the room, laden with domed silver dishes. Delicious aromas escaped them.

Arthur unfolded a cherrywood card table before the fire, then drew two straight-backed chairs up to either side of it.

Whisking a snowy linen cloth over the green baize surface, he set two places with fine napery, gold-plated cutlery, and white china elegantly banded in gold.

"Please," Steede murmured, gesturing his toe-tapping, fuming wife into the chair the footman held for her. "Be seated."

"Your Ladyship," Arthur murmured politely as she took her seat.

"Thank you . . . Arthur, is it?" she ground out, dropping into her seat with more flounce than grace.

"Yes, milady."

When they were both comfortably seated, Arthur draped serviettes over their laps and began ladling creamy asparagus soup into their soup bowls from a silver tureen.

The soup course was followed by thin slices of tender pink lamb, dressed with a delicate pearl-onion gravy and accompanied by tangy mint sauce.

Early garden peas, tiny roasted potatoes cooked to a mouthwatering golden brown, and a delicious green salad of torn lettuce, spring onions and watercress made flavorful light accents to the lamb for Victoria. Anything heavier after their long, cramped journey would have been *de trop*.

Both anger and hunger were mollified by the delicious repast. As she ate, Victoria felt the irritation draining from her, along with the very last dregs of energy.

"I shall assemble the staff for your inspection first thing in the morning," Blackstone promised after Arthur had left them to enjoy their meal alone.

"Thank you. I shall look forward to it. If the caliber of tonight's meal is anything to go by, you have an excellent staff," she complimented him grudgingly. "But when shall I meet little Mary? I am most anxious to do so."

"And you shall, first thing tomorrow. I'll have Kalinda bring her down from the nursery as soon as she finishes her breakfast."

"Kalinda?"

"Her nursemaid."

"Ah. M'lord—Steede, does Mary take all of her meals upstairs with this woman?"

"She does, yes." He frowned. "Why? Is there something wrong with that?"

"I believe there is, yes. Very wrong," she told him frankly, determined to start off as she intended to go on. He'd offered for her hand solely because of her way with children, and she intended to give him what he wanted. Her way.

Setting down both knife and fork, she dabbed her mouth on the corner of a snowy serviette.

"How is Mary to learn proper etiquette or the social graces she will need as an adult if she is shut away from everyone? Expected to eat all of her meals off a tray in the nursery or schoolroom? From now on—with your permission, of course—I would suggest we dine together. *En famille*, as the French call it. *As a family*. Unless, of course, we are having guests for dinner."

"Oh, of course," he quickly agreed.

She cast him a suspicious look. Was he laughing at her? But no, he appeared quite solemn and attentive, except for that little twitch about his lips. A nervous tic, perhaps?

"I deplore the practice of banishing one's offspring to the nursery the minute they are born, and parading them out only on festive occasions. I shall keep my children with me as often as possible. You see, er, Steede, I intend to devote a great deal of love and time to their care. Not to relinquish them to nursemaids and nannies and governesses for months on end!"

Her lovely face glowed. That, and her passionate, almost accusatory tone, made it obvious his wife's feelings on the subject were strong and very personal.

Was that how she had been raised, after her mother's death? Steede wondered with an unexpected pang of sympathy for the little girl she'd been. By a succession of nursemaids and nannies? Had his bride been denied a proper family life when her father—a taciturn, stern fellow at the best of times, from what little he had seen of Lord Hawthorne thus far—retreated into himself, mourning the beloved wife he had lost forever?

He believed so.

A thrill of excitement ran through him. If anyone could give him back the old Mary, his little daughter the way she had once been, Victoria could. He was sure of it. And her affectionate, nurturing presence at Blackstone Manor would, God willing, prevent his own little daughter from sharing her stepmother's fate.

"In this household, you may raise your family—*our* family—in any way you deem fit, my dear," he said softly, casting her a heated look. Reaching across the table, he placed a heavy hand over hers and fondly squeezed the slim fingers. "Ah, Victoria, Victoria! Call me optimistic, if you will, but I have a strong intuition our family will be a large one." He shot her a sly, wicked wink. "*Very* large indeed."

Judging by her sudden, delightful blush and the nervous way she fussed with her hair, his comment had reminded her of the way those babies would be conceived.

Just as he'd intended.

Tonight, he would permit his beautiful bride a brief respite in which to recover from their wedding night and the wearying train journey, and to reflect—with pleasure, he hoped—upon her wifely duties in his bed.

But tomorrow, he promised himself, splashing brandy into a balloon glass, he would join her there.

She might never come to love him, or he her. But he would awaken her passions so fully she would never sleep alone again, willingly . . .

Cupping the snifter in both hands to warm the tawny golden liquid inside it, he lifted the glass in silent salute to his belle Victoria.

"So be it!" he murmured, and drank long and deep.

Chapter Nine

The following morning, Victoria awoke from restless, erotic dreams to find her mud-stained clothing had been miraculously restored to serviceable condition and set out, ready for her to wear.

With the help of Belinda, the nervous little housemaid who had been chosen by the housekeeper, Mrs. Hastings, to assist her with her morning toilette, she sailed down the gracefully curved front staircase in search of the dining room and breakfast.

At the foot of the staircase, she found the manor's staff assembled according to rank and household position.

The footmen were neatly attired in bottle-green livery, while the maids wore dark gray dresses and snowy bibbed aprons and caps.

She greeted each one with a smile and a gracious word or two, from Titchy, the youngest tweenie, to the butler, Mister Jessup, a tall, thin, formal fellow who performed the introductions in a plummy voice accompanied by hand motions.

"Have you seen Lady Mary this morning, Jessup?" Victoria asked the thin majordomo, once the staff members had been dismissed to their various duties.

"I have indeed, ma'am. You will find Her Ladyship awaiting you in the dining room." He indicated with a flourish in which direction she would find the room. "His Lordship instructed her nursemaid to bring her down to meet you, before he left for the station."

"Very good, Jessup. That will be all for now."

She found her stepdaughter in the dining room, as the butler had promised. Mary was standing by the window, looking out, her hands primly clasped before her.

What an exquisite child, Victoria thought.

Mary's long, curling hair was the tawny gold of clover honey. Caught back from her profile by a pair of tortoiseshell combs, it streamed down her back in shining ringlets. Her eyes were lovely, too. A deep smoky gray, they tilted up like a kitten's at the outer corners.

To Victoria, those eyes seemed peculiarly solemn and adult as Mary looked up at her from beneath long, coal-black lashes clearly inherited from her darkly handsome papa, and in sharp contrast to her peachy complexion and red-gold hair.

She would be a beautiful young woman someday, Victoria thought as she crouched down, eager to greet her little stepdaughter eye to eye.

"You must be Mary," she began gently. "How wonderful to meet you at last. I'm Victoria. Did your papa tell you that he and I are married? I shall be living here at Blackstone Manor from now on. I do hope we can be friends?"

She waited, expecting some response from the child. Not necessarily a warm one—what intelligent child *would* welcome the woman who had replaced her beloved mother?—but *something* other than this silent, unwinking stare. Even a surly welcome would be preferable to that.

Hiding her dismay, Victoria decided to behave as if nothing out of the ordinary had occurred. The little girl would surely speak to her in her own good time. Perhaps she first needed to decide for herself whether Victoria was going to be a friend or an enemy.

Once her initial surprise had worn off, Victoria's tender heart went out to Steede's daughter. So this was what Henrietta had hinted at. That her granddaughter was an unhappy, perhaps difficult, child.

Well, Victoria knew all about unhappiness from her own lonely childhood. Following her mama's accidental death, her childhood had been overseen by a steady procession of nursemaids, nannies and later, governesses and companions—even an occasional housekeeper.

The women had come and gone through the doors of Hawthorne Hall in their turn, and each one had been shrewdly assessed by the hostile little imp she had been, before battle plans could be drawn up.

There had been Nan the Ninny, who could be intimidated by loud screams, cross looks and threats to "tell Papa." Mademoiselle Priscilla Poireau, who wanted to become Victoria's stepmama and the new mistress of Hawthorne Hall. Sylvia the Sneak, who had carried tales of Victoria's smallest misdeeds to Father, embellishing them until they achieved truly demonic proportions. Theodora the Tippler, who had sneaked sips of Papa's liquor, and Spiteful Sybil, who had delighted in pinching so hard she had left bruises on Victoria's cheeks, upper arms and thighs.

Ah, yes. She had met them all, and liked none of them, for they had kept her apart from the only person she wanted to be with: her Papa.

But Papa had changed after Mama went to heaven, and he had wanted no part of her, Victoria remembered, a painful lump forming in her throat just thinking about it. And, in the years that followed her father's rejection, the gulf between them had widened irrevocably.

She was already sixteen when he realized she was no longer a child, and prevailed upon Aunt Catherine to help him get her married off. But the affection and attention she had received from her aunt—delighted to have a fourth daughter to pamper and cosset, now that her own brood had flown the nest—had been a case of far too little, too late.

By then, Victoria had become an intelligent, well-educated hoyden, with few social graces other than that of being an expert horsewoman— a talent that was quite useless in a drawing room. What manners she could lay claim to had been largely a result of Lily Lovett's bullying.

Consequently, it had taken poor Aunt Catherine almost two full years and a procession of dancing masters, music teachers, seamstresses, milliners and a considerable portion of her father's fortune to make her presentable for her debut into polite Society. And then, just when her first Season was approaching, she had met Ned, and her aunt's plans for a brilliant match for her had been toppled.

Poor, dear Aunt Catherine! Her aunt had had her work cut out for her, in order to make a silk purse out of the proverbial sow's ear she had been. For, although Victoria had come to womanhood lacking no luxury, she had been sorely lacking any male influence in her life, let alone a civilizing *female* one.

Was that why she had been drawn so readily to Ned? she wondered suddenly. Had she found in Ned's quick grin, his apparent adoration of her, the attention and affection she craved from her father? And, believing she had found it at last, had she mistaken it for love, because she had wanted so desperately to be loved?

She would never know.

"Come, darling. Sit beside me," she urged the

little girl, patting the straight-backed chair beside her own at one end of the long walnut dining table.

Mary continued to regard her solemnly.

"I thought it would be nice if we breakfasted together this morning, just the two of us," Victoria continued. "Perhaps your papa will join us later, wouldn't that be fun? And afterwards, I thought we could pick some roses from the gardens. I'm sure your grandmama wouldn't mind. We'll cut some for the house, and some to take to her at the Lodge. They smelled heavenly when I opened my window this morning! I expect you can smell them from the nursery, too, can you not?"

Stony silence.

"The Lady Mary takes her breakfast in the nursery each morning, Memsahib Warring. It is her custom to be served there, yes? The servants, they already know this. They will have carried her tray upstairs, to her room."

Victoria gasped, her hand flying to her breast.

In her fascination with her stepdaughter, she had not noticed the slender woman who stood by the window, cast in shadow. The low, singsong voice coming out of nowhere startled her.

A gauzy wine-colored veil draped the woman from head to toe. She wore a short-sleeved pink tunic under a cranberry silk sari, the folds of which were ingeniously wound about her slender body. Several inches of rose silk trousers and burgundy velvet slippers appeared below the hem of the sari.

The colors of the woman's garments blended so perfectly with the cranberry velvet of the draperies, she almost disappeared among their folds. An accident, or a clever design, Victoria wondered suddenly, then dismissed the idea as foolish.

A crimson dot the size of a farthing was centered directly between the woman's brows. A Hindu caste mark, Victoria thought it was, though she couldn't be certain, having only read about India and her many peoples.

The woman's lustrous black hair was caught back in a heavy coil, fastened by silver combs at the nape. The slanted sloe-black eyes were very bright in the slim-nosed, exotic café-au-lait face. They were as inquisitive as a bird's above prominent cheekbones.

"And who, pray, might you be, madam?" Victoria inquired, her jet eyebrows arched.

The woman bowed gracefully, her palms pressed together. "I am Kalinda, memsahib. The Lady Mary's humble ayah. That is to say, her nursemaid, yes? I have taken care of the little missy since she was a small baby. Sahib Warring brought me to England from Calcutta, memsahib."

Although her words were very proper and correct, there was no mistaking the woman's proprietary tone, which bordered, Victoria thought, on insolence. Little Mary was her charge, and she would welcome no interference on Victoria's part, her tone implied.

We shall see about that, Victoria thought, wondering if Kalinda's possessiveness was the reason Steede had suddenly decided to find Mary a stepmother. She would ask him later.

"And I am sure you have done so admirably," she complimented the woman. "However, in the future, I want Mary to join me for breakfast each morning. A brief period spent apart each day can only be good for you both. Mary and I must get to know each other. Mustn't we, Mary?"

She smiled at Kalinda, then at the little girl, who still stood demurely before her. Demurely *and* silently.

Mary's small hands were clasped together over the folds of a snowy, ruffled pinafore, worn over a severe navy-blue frock. The small fingers were entwined so tightly the knuckles were white. The skirts that reached to her mid-calf were finished in yet another deep ruffle.

Scrawny, knobbly-kneed sparrow legs stuck out beneath the frock, like pipe cleaners encased in ugly black wool stockings, then planted in black button boots.

There was something very endearing about those skinny little legs and awful boots. Victoria ached to replace them with the slippers of dainty white kid that she had dreamed of as a little girl.

There was nothing endearing or touching about the child's expression, however. Mary's gray eyes smoldered. Her lower lip jutted. Her narrow shoulders were rigid with anger.

The Lady Mary was obviously livid about her new stepmama's interference in her daily routine.

Not twenty-four hours at Blackstone Manor, and already the child declares war on me, Victoria thought. *Nor will her ayah improve the situation, if I leave them to each other's company. Ah, well. There's no help for it.*

"That will be all for now, Kalinda. You may go," she ordered crisply.

Kalinda's dark eyes widened. Her brows rose. "Go, memsahib?" she echoed. "But to where must I go?"

"Why, to your room." Did the woman not understand English? "Or perhaps you'd prefer to take a walk down to the village. The time is yours, to do with as you wish. Surely you have some personal errands to occupy you?"

"Errands, memsahib? But I have none. My only joy is to serve the Lady Mary! That is the purpose for which Sahib Warring brought me here, from my own country." Panic flared in the sloe-black eyes.

"I'm sure it was, Kalinda. But all of us—even nursemaids as devoted as you undoubtedly are—need time to ourselves. Now that I'm the mistress of Blackstone Manor, some things will be changing—for the better, I hope. With His Lordship's approval, I have decided that Mary and I are going to spend the mornings together, getting to know each other. Are we not, Mary?"

When Mary ignored her, she continued briskly, "I'm quite certain Lord Blackstone did not want you to devote every waking moment to your charge when he engaged you. Run along now, and enjoy an hour or two alone. Mary and

I are going outside to pick some roses for the house. They smell heavenly! You may join Lady Mary later."

Kalinda's face darkened. Mary's lips likewise tightened in displeasure, thinning to a bad-tempered line that quite spoiled her pretty little face.

Ah ha. A reaction—albeit an angry one. It was a start, of sorts.

Kalinda bowed again. She looked no happier than her little mistress, but—eyes carefully blank—she inclined her veiled head nonetheless. The movement made her silver bangles and anklets chime merrily, like tiny temple bells. "Very well, memsahib. It shall be as you wish."

"Excellent!" Victoria declared with an enthusiasm she was far from feeling. "You may go now, nurse."

Kalinda had no choice but to leave the room, gracefully bowing and backing away in the Eastern fashion.

Victoria was hard put not to smile at the befuddled expression on the Indian woman's face. Clearly, the mother hen had never been parted from her chick before. Poor Kalinda. Victoria had no wish to be cruel to anyone, but in this instance, a brief daily separation was not only necessary, but vital, she believed. If not for Mary, then for her own relationship with her step-daughter.

How were they ever to become close when Kalinda stood between them, jealously guarding her charge? And surely such an attachment on the part of a nursemaid could not be healthy for the child.

"Well, now. Where were we?" Victoria asked when the ayah was gone. "Ah, yes. Breakfast. Thank you, Arthur."

She took the chair that the footman held out for her.

With a wink and a grin, lanky Arthur pulled out the chair on Victoria's right for Lady Mary. The little girl made no effort to climb up onto it, or to return Arthur's engaging smile.

Instead, her arms crossed over her chest, she continued to pout and scowl at Victoria. And, though not a word passed her lips, her mutinous expression spoke volumes.

Just like her father, Victoria thought to herself. *If looks could kill, I would be hanged, drawn and quartered even as I stand here!*

"I expect the Lady Mary needs assistance, Arthur," Victoria murmured calmly. She carefully avoided any eye contact with the child. "Please. Help Her Ladyship into her seat."

"Certainly, madam."

But as Arthur bent to lift the child up, Mary quickly stuck out her elbows and shrugged off his assistance.

Glaring at the poor footman, she scrambled up into her chair unaided, proving Victoria's fears that Mary might be deaf quite unfounded.

She turned away, hiding a smile.

"Splendid! Arthur, you may inform Mrs. Hastings that Lady Mary and I are ready to be served now. There is no point in delaying any further.

His Lordship will not be joining us until later, if at all."

"Very good, madam," Arthur agreed with a grin and a bow, then left them alone.

Mary, Victoria soon discovered by the simple process of observation, enjoyed Mrs. Hastings's buttery scrambled eggs very much. She was inordinately fond of plump browned sausages and crispy rashers of grilled bacon, too. She preferred her morning porridge sweetened with honey and cream, rather than salted, and liked her toast dark and spread thickly with butter and marmalade.

She had no fondness whatsoever for fried liver, and the mere sight of deviled kidneys made her gag. She was also adept at drinking large glassfuls of milk without leaving the suspicion of a milk moustache on her upper lip.

In short, except for her extraordinary ability to remain silent, she was a perfectly normal seven-year-old.

Earlier that morning, as Victoria had sat before the dressing table in her airy, sunlit room, making her toilette with Belinda's eager if clumsy assistance, and sorely missing the capable services of Lily Lovett, Steede had entered her room through the connecting door to his own.

After bidding her a very good morning, kissing her cheek and asking if she had slept well, as if they were a perfectly ordinary, happily married couple, he had announced his intention to ride down to the railway station before breakfast.

"You're going away?" she had inquired uncertainly, unable to decide whether she wanted him gone or not.

"And abandon my lovely bride so soon after our wedding day? Not a chance, my dear!" he had vowed with a roguish grin that she felt deep in her belly. "No, the stationmaster sent a lad up to say several trunks had arrived from Whitby on this morning's milk train. Apparently your belongings are already here, and must be signed for."

She confided to Mary as they breakfasted that she thought her papa had a secret up his sleeve, too.

"He sounded very mysterious and was smiling when he went out. I expect we'll find out what he's up to soon enough, don't you?" Victoria observed, spreading marmalade on her buttered toast and talking animatedly, as if she expected Mary to contribute or answer her.

The child made no attempt to respond, however.

The meal finished, Victoria rang for a housemaid to fetch them straw sun hats, gardening gloves, a flat basket and pruning shears.

"There!" she declared when they were both suitably outfitted. "Don't we look grand! Come along, darling. Off we go!"

Taking Mary's small hand—which was swimming in a too-large canvas glove—she led the way outside, to the rose gardens at the rear of the manor.

The heady perfume was intoxicating on the warm air.

Keeping up a stream of lively chatter intended to put the child at ease, Victoria went from bush to bush, like one of the busy bumblebees that buzzed from flower to flower, gathering roses instead of nectar.

She snipped a woody stem here, another there, carefully removing the thorns and placing each exquisite bloom in the flat wicker basket she'd given Mary to carry.

"My mama was very fond of roses, I recall. She had her own rose garden at Hawthorne Hall— that's in Yorkshire, where I grew up. We used to pick them together, just like this. Everyone calls it Isabelle's rose garden now, because Mama loved it so. I was just your age when she went to heaven, but I still miss her very, very much."

No comment. No change in expression.

Victoria shrugged, then added, "I expect I always shall, don't you?"

When they had first gone outside, she had expected Mary to balk and run off, rather than carry the basket, as she'd asked.

But to her surprise, the child had dutifully trotted after her, following her down the crazy-paving pathways that wound between the rosebeds, where every variety and color of rose was in glorious bloom.

A thrush threw out its plump speckled breast and serenaded them from a trellised archway in the tall box hedges that surrounded the rose garden. Through it, Victoria could see a driveway of golden shingles that swept around a grassy paddock to the rear of the manor house, where the carriage houses, stables and storerooms were located.

In the distance, above the treetops, rose the crenellated Norman tower of the village church of St. John.

Once or twice as she picked, Victoria thought she saw a glimmer of interest in the child's cool gray eyes as she named each variety, comparing the Blackstone roses to those grown at Hawthorne Hall.

As a little test, she intentionally selected an overblown rose with falling petals, and saw the little girl's eyes narrow with dismay. When Victoria gripped the rose's woody red stem with her shears, Mary seemed on the verge of protesting.

Victoria paused, then selected another, less overblown rose, and the girl's shoulders sagged in relief.

"There. Finished. Your turn to pick now, Mary," she sang out. "Let me carry the basket, while you do the clipping," she suggested casually.

Mary's head jerked around as if pulled by a string. Eyes widening, she pointed to herself.

"Of course I mean you, silly-billy!" Victoria laughed, responding to the child's brief pantomime. "Here." She carefully handed the child the clippers, positioning Mary's small fingers correctly on the handles. "Perfect. Go ahead. Try one."

With a startled yet eager glance, Mary chose a

beautiful blushing pink rosebud. At a point about ten inches from the bud, she deftly snipped the woody stem. Knocking off the sharp thorns with the side of the pruning shears, as she had seen Victoria do, she placed the rosebud in the basket with the others.

She could not resist flashing Victoria a look of triumph when she was done, coupled with an expression that was very nearly a smile.

"Clever girl. I just knew you could do it!" Victoria praised her. "You and I make an excellent team, do we not? Would you cut some of those cream roses, too? I love the ones with just a blush of yellow, don't you?"

Chapter Ten

It was in his grandmother's rose garden that Steede found them on his way back from Blackstone Station, one a beautiful rose herself, the other a lovely bud that had yet to bloom. But the sight of them together—one fair-headed, the other dark, was bittersweet. Neither his radiantly beautiful bride nor his lovely little daughter had any love in their hearts for him, he reflected as he rode his gray stallion toward the trellis set in the hedge, leading a second horse by its halter.

A fat pony and cart, loaded with three enormous trunks, followed him down the shingled driveway, its yellow wheels spinning. Driving the vehicle was young Sam Woods, one of his undergrooms, who had accompanied him to the railway station.

Tucked between Sam and the trunks was the

Penelope Neri

new head groom he had hired just a few days ago, and a slender young serving woman who was holding her hat down on her head and squealing with fright as the cart sped merrily up the driveway.

"Good morning, Victoria. Mary, my poppet! I see you two have met. How are my girls getting along?" he greeted them.

"We were just cutting some roses for the house. Weren't we, Mary?" Victoria said, shading her eyes with her hand to look up at him. "Oh, what a fine animal!" she exclaimed, her eyes shining as she admired his silver-gray stallion.

"Isn't he?" Steede agreed, patting Mercury's neck. "What's your opinion of the new mare?" he asked, deliberately casual.

She glanced past him, and her eyes widened in delight. *"Calypso!"*

The black Arabian tossed her dainty head and whinnied in greeting to her mistress.

"My sweet baby!" Victoria exclaimed, running under the trellis into the shingled drive. "How I've missed you!" She flung her arms around the mare's neck and hugged her.

Steede laughed. "Before I left here, Mama warned me that you would be happier in familiar company. So, when your father told me about your fondness for this pretty lady, I asked him to send her down to us by train, along with your trunks and other belongings. A—er—certain lady's maid and her young man insisted upon accompanying the mare, too."

"Lily? It *is* she! Oh, and there's Harry, too!" Victoria exclaimed as the cart drew level with them, then briefly slowed.

" 'Morning, Your Ladyship!" Harry Coombs sang out, grinning as he doffed his cap.

"Harry, hello!"

"Good morning, my lady."

"And to you, too, Lily," Victoria muttered less eagerly.

She was obviously in two minds about whether to be happy to see her maid or not, for she frowned and pursed her lips, Steede saw.

But, before she'd made up her mind whether to be gracious or cool, Sam had whisked the cart around to the carriage house and kitchens at the rear of the manor, sweeping Lily and her young man away with it.

Lily's face was a pale anxious oval as she looked back over her shoulder at her mistress, Steede observed. He felt moved to say something on the girl's behalf, since she had abandoned family and home to be with his bride.

"Before you condemn your poor Miss Lovett out of hand, my dear, perhaps I should explain," he began. "It was not Lily who 'betrayed' your plans to elope that night, but the Widow Johns."

"The Widow Johns!"

"She told your father you planned to elope with a most unsuitable young man, and that you'd borrowed her widow's veil and black cloak for that purpose."

Victoria's lips tightened in displeasure.

"When he questioned the maids, Polly caved

in. She handed over a note you'd written to your Mr. Thomas, still undelivered."

"I should have known. That wretched girl!"

"Lord Hawthorne immediately telegraphed me, and the rest you know. Fortunately—or so some might think—I reached Hawthorne Hall in the nick of time to save you from yourself."

He grinned, but he had forgotten that their marriage was nothing to smile about, at least as far as his bride was concerned. She glared back at him, her deep hyacinth-blue eyes electric in her anger.

"Some might think it was fortunate. Others would disagree." She sniffed in displeasure. "I wonder. Why on earth would the Johns woman go tattling to my father in the first place? What possible reason did she have to betray me?"

He shrugged. "She told your father she was afraid she would not be compensated for the trousseau she and her daughters had sewn, once the bride had flown. But who really knows? By the way, I've hired Harry away from your father permanently. He agreed to let him go, since he still has Mr. Lovett. Said he wouldn't get a bit of work out of him, with his betrothed so far away. You know, to give her her due, Lily insisted on coming here to attend you."

"I'm sure she did," Victoria said, feeling a little guilty now for ever doubting Lily's loyalty.

"So. How are you, poppet?" he asked, turning to Mary. He had done all he could for Lily. The rest was up to the two of them.

While he and Victoria talked, Mary had sidled

over to Victoria's mare. After casting her a beseeching look, she had received her stepmama's nod of approval to pet Calypso's velvety black nose. Steede felt a sharp, irrational stab of jealousy at the look of understanding that flashed between them.

Like her papa and her new stepmama, his daughter adored horses and riding. So much so, he planned to give her a pony of her own for her eighth birthday next month, if Victoria agreed it would be good for her.

"Would you like to sit up here on Mercury and ride back to the house?"

The child froze, her hand in midair, staring up at him from wide, frightened gray eyes. In that instant, she reminded Steede of a startled doe caught in the glow of a poacher's lantern.

He held his breath, hoping against hope that this time it would be different. That Mary would once again be the affectionate, loving child she had been before the fire that claimed her mama's life. The little girl who had adored her papa and followed him everywhere, toddling at his heels like a chubby little shadow.

But it was not to be. At least not this time.

Mary dropped the shears, turned and ran back to the house, losing her straw hat as she bolted.

"Well! What brought that on, I wonder?" Victoria exclaimed. "Jealousy, do you think? I suppose it's only natural, now that you have remarried. Please overlook Mary's rudeness this time, Steede. My arrival has obviously upset the poor child. She hasn't said a word all morning."

A harsh bark of laughter escaped him.

"I would have been surprised if she had, Victoria. My daughter is mute, you see. She hasn't spoken since her mother died, almost two years ago."

He knew he sounded bitter, but Aimee had a great deal to answer for. Although dead and buried, she still managed to reach out from the grave to disrupt his life—as she had while she lived.

"Not spoken?" Turning from the beautiful little mare she'd been petting, Victoria shaded her eyes to look up at her husband, who was still mounted. "Has she been examined by a physician?"

He nodded. "The finest doctors in Europe. Specialists from Edinburgh, Vienna and Paris, as well as London. They all made the same diagnosis. There is nothing wrong with her."

"But, if that's true, why can she not talk?"

"It's not that she can't talk, but that she won't, for whatever reason. The doctors believe the loss of her mother is responsible for her silence. The shock of her death, perhaps? Grief? The ability could return as readily as it was lost."

"I see," Victoria murmured, frowning. Things were more complicated than she had thought. She picked up the basket of roses and slipped it over her arm. "Well. Thank you for having Calypso sent to me here, my lord. And for letting Lily come to me, too. It—it was most kind of you."

He liked her this way, he thought. Off-balance, the grateful supplicant. Her glossy black hair was pulled away from her face and spilled loosely down her back, like his daughter's. She looked young, desirable, and so bloody lovely, lust slammed through him like a fist to the belly.

"Do you really mean that?" he asked huskily, reaching out to rub a silky black ringlet between two of his fingers. He wanted to feel that hair spilling through his fingers, slippery as watered silk. To wind its glossy length about his throat as he made love to her. "That I'm kind, I mean?"

A familiar throb had asserted itself in his loins now. Astounded, he found he was hard with desire for the lovely witch he had married.

Uncomfortable in his aroused state, he shifted position on the English saddle, hoping to God she wouldn't notice. Or if she did, that she was as yet too naive to know what was happening to him.

"Of course," she answered. "Very kind."

For a man who murdered his first wife, he could almost hear her silently adding.

"Kindness has nothing to do with it," he said curtly. "I want you to be happy here, damn it."

She nodded politely, but offered no comment.

"Especially since it seems I am so soon placed in your debt," he added reluctantly.

"Debt?" Her lovely head came up. "How so?"

"It seems you have already made your influence felt upon my daughter. For that, you have my deepest gratitude. Kalinda stays as close to Mary as her own shadow, despite my best efforts to separate them. This is the first time I have seen Mary without her nurse."

"You mean, since her mama died?"

"No, Victoria. *Ever*. It was Kalinda who raised her, you see. Aimee was—well, my first wife was more concerned with her social engagements than she was with her children. And for some time, she was . . . unwell. Having an ayah meant she didn't have to worry about them."

"Them? Then Mary has brothers and sisters?"

"*Had*. An infant brother named Johnny. He was six weeks old when he and his mama were killed."

"Oh. I'm so very sorry," she murmured softly. But she did not ask him what had happened.

Why? he wondered heavily. Because she thought she already knew the answer? Because she had heard—and believed—the rumors that his first wife had died by his hand?

She looked uncomfortable, he saw, and knew he had guessed correctly.

"It must have been terrible for you," she whispered, refusing to meet his eyes. She did not sound as if she believed it for a minute.

"Very," he agreed, gathering the reins into his hands with brusque, clipped movements. "But it is past, and we must all go on with our lives. Enough of dark memories on such a glorious day! What do you say to a ride? By the looks of her, your mare is eager for an outing. A gallop would do her good, after being cooped up in that cattle-car all night. And this brave fellow is always up for a gallop, aren't you, boy?"

He patted his gray's arched neck. The stallion

tossed his proud head and snorted, as if agreeing with his master.

Calypso whinnied and tossed her head.

"I would like that very much, yes," Victoria accepted, laughing despite herself at the antics of their horses, who had seemed to understand their words. His offer provided a welcome change of subject.

The smile that lit up her face touched something inside Steede that had nothing to do with lust or even desire. A vulnerable, lonely spot that he'd believed had been boarded up long ago, hardened and protected from all tender emotions.

What would it take, he wondered, to make her smile like that for him . . . ?

"I'll put these roses in water, and change. I'm sure Lily will know where she packed my habit."

"Run along then," he urged, pleased that she had accepted his invitation. "I'll meet you in the stableyard."

Chapter Eleven

True to his word, Steede was waiting in the stableyard with her mare saddled, bridled and raring to run when she came down.

In just the few minutes it had taken Victoria to make amends with Lily and change her clothes, he had acquired a picnic basket from the kitchens. A fringed woolen carriage rug of red-and-black plaid was also draped over his arm.

"I thought I'd show you over the estates, then introduce you to our legendary Dartmoor. There's a pretty tor with a marvelous view where we can have our picnic," he suggested, cocking a hopeful brow.

"Tor?"

"That's what we call our rocky hills here in Devonshire."

"I'd like that very much," she said simply. "Will

145

you give me a leg up?" There was no mounting block.

"My pleasure." Setting the picnic basket on the cobbles, he helped her to mount by cupping his hands together as a stirrup for her dainty boot, then boosted her up into the sidesaddle.

Her rounded derriere, draped in blue velvet, swayed temptingly before him until she had settled herself securely in the awkward sidesaddle; then she caught her leg over the peg and gathered up the reins. "Thank you."

Her easy grace confirmed her father's claims that she was an expert horsewoman.

"My pleasure. You make a fetching sight, Lady Blackstone. I'd say you've ridden a time or two before, by the looks of you," he observed as he mounted his own, much larger stallion.

She blushed prettily. "Father insists I could ride before I could walk. I don't know about that, but I do love horses, despite what happened to my mama." Her hyacinth-blue eyes were suddenly very bright. Too bright.

"Is that how she died? In a riding accident?"

She nodded, sorrow darkening her expression. "Oh! Just look how pretty everything is! I hardly noticed last night, I was so tired . . ."

The catch in her voice and the damp sheen in her eyes warned him that she was perilously close to tears.

He frowned as they walked their horses down the gravel driveway, toward the tree-lined lane that led into the village a half-mile away.

As a former military man, he had seen first-hand the devastating effects of silence following the horrors of battle. Bad memories, like poisoned wounds, needed to be lanced. He knew that better than anyone, though to date, he'd been unable to take his own advice. Perhaps when Victoria learned to trust him, she would choose him to talk to.

Silently, he vowed that if she would only meet him halfway, he would try to make her forget her lonely childhood. He would lavish on her all the love and affection she had been denied, and give her babies on whom to shower her own love and affection. Their days would be filled with warmth, sunshine and laughter, and their nights . . . their nights with passion and, perhaps, even love.

But he made no reference to his plans, nor to her mercurial change of subject as they trotted their mounts up the cobbled high-street of Blackstone, lined with cottages, to the village green.

Rather, he kept up his end of the conversation by telling her the history of Blackstone, and about the good people who lived there, many of whose families had been in domestic service at Blackstone Manor, or laborers on the Blackstone Home Farm or estates for centuries.

Lined with an assortment of thatched cottages, shops and public houses built of green Hurwick stone, with quaint swinging signs and narrow granite pavements like the nearest town of Tavistock, the village green was a bustling place, with carts and drays coming and going. Friday was pannier-market day, as it had been since medieval times.

Numerous stalls with striped awnings had been set up on the grassy green. Stallholders were busily selling the fresh vegetables, eggs and other produce in their baskets to those who had come on foot or by cart to Blackstone from the surrounding hilly countryside for which Devon was justly famous.

"So many public houses for such a small village!" Victoria exclaimed. "Surely they cannot all turn a profit?"

"You'd be surprised," Steede told her, pleased by her shrewd—if blunt—comment, so typical of Yorkshire folk, whatever their origins. "Although we require just the one church for the saving of our souls, all *three* of our drinking establishments are very well supported by our local shepherds, who graze their masters' flocks upon Dartmoor."

She laughed and reined her horse's head to the left. "Obviously a very thirsty occupation. Shepherding, I mean."

"Obviously. No, this way," he urged her when they reached the fork in the road just outside the village. "The left fork takes you across the stone bridge over the Tamar, while the other leads to a bridle path through the woods, then up, onto the high moors. That's where we're going."

Turning her mare's head, Victoria rode after him between an avenue of cyprus and yew trees, guiding her horse in and out of sun-dappled shadow where leaves rustled and birds twittered in the green-gold hush.

"Tired?"

"Not in the least."

"Hungry?"

"Starving!"

"All right. We'll have our picnic up on the tor," Steede suggested after he had shown her around his estate. "There's a view from the top unlike any in Devon, except the view from High Willhayes." Seeing her questioning expression, he added, "Dartmoor's highest point."

"Ah."

When they reached the hill's peak, he sprang down from his horse, came over to her mare and held out his arms.

Unhooking her leg, she slipped easily into his arms, her slender body flowing through his hands like water.

He steadied her, hands clasping her waist, her soft curves pressed against his lean, hard body. The warmth of her body rose through the midnight-blue velvet of her riding habit to heat his hands.

In that moment, their mouths were so very close he could feel her unsteady breath as it fanned his throat and cheek. The urge to kiss her, to crush those berry-red lips beneath his own, was strong indeed, but he mastered it—not from any noble motive, but in the hope that, by moving slowly, one step at a time, he would gain her confidence and trust—and the invitation he had sworn she must offer before he took her again.

"Thank you," she murmured breathlessly, looking up into his eyes, then quickly away.

"My pleasure," he said thickly, breathing in her scent.

Her breasts, confined by the velvet of her jacket, their lush curves hidden beneath the frothy lace of her jabot, were crushed against his chest as she arched against his flanks. He stood with one leg thrust forward, his knee lost within the folds of her skirts, where it pressed against her upper thighs.

Sweet Blessed Lord! It was all he could do to keep from sweeping her beneath him, or lifting her astride his aching shaft.

"You can let go of me now," she murmured, sounding breathless and no less husky than he did.

"Hmm? Of course," he recovered, itching to bite the petal-pink earlobe that, like a creamy pearl, peeped out from beneath a glossy black curl.

For several seconds, they remained very close together, their hearts beating in harmony, their eyes locked, mouths very close, bodies touching, until the plaintive cry of a curlew, circling high above the windswept tor, shattered the sexual spell between them.

Abruptly, she stepped back.

Reluctantly, he turned away, spreading the plaid carriage rug across the springy turf, grabbing the wicker picnic basket.

From a dish covered with a knotted napkin,

he withdrew golden Cornish pasties. The half-moons of crumbly pastry were filled with minced roast beef, peas, carrots and potatoes, the crimped edges running with thick brown gravy.

Slices of last night's cold lamb followed, along with a small pot of Mrs. Hastings's Indian chutney, thick slices of buttered farm bread, wedges of damson pie and a small crock of Devonshire clotted cream.

"Cook is to be complimented," he exclaimed, pleased. "What a grand feast the old girl provided for our impromptu picnic. I must thank her."

Waving Victoria to a seat on one edge of the plaid, he slipped the horses' bits from their mouths so that they could graze, and threw himself down on the rug beside her.

From their vantage point atop Tamar's tor, they could see clear across the rolling moors to the looming gray walls of Dartmoor Gaol at Prince Town, to the far west.

The prison was one from which few convicts escaped, he told her as they ate, washing down the repast with bottled apple cider.

Those desperate few that managed to evade the guards fell prey to the treacherous moors themselves, for by day, patches of brilliant green against dark turf betrayed the presence of bottomless mires. But at night, when a thick mist fell over the moors, the telltale emerald went unseen. Then the greedy bogs swallowed up the unwary like quicksand, leaving no trace of their passing.

To the southwest of the tor lay the sea, a

choppy blue-gray crested with whitecaps as bright as shattered glass this morning. Seagulls wheeled and cried over the cliffs, swarming like gnats over something coming into the distant harbor.

"The fishing fleet's coming in," Steede observed, nodding in the direction of the cloud of gulls as he took a hefty bite of a savory meat pasty. "The gulls will be fighting for the innards."

"About my mother," Victoria began, quite unexpectedly.

"She must have been wonderful. I'd like to hear about her."

"I—I was with her the day of the accident."

"Really?"

She nodded. "We used to ride together every afternoon, you see. Horses were in Mama's blood—as, I suspect, they are in mine."

"My mama remembers your mother's debut into society," he said. "She said she was the loveliest woman she had ever seen."

"She was beautiful, yes. I don't remember her features much at all, but I remember the—the presence of her as clearly now as I did then. She made me feel so very safe."

"Did your father have no portraits painted of her?"

"Oh, several. But after she died, he ordered them taken down. He said he couldn't bear to look at them. I have a daguerreotype of her, though. Did you know her family came from France originally? For generations, the de Blanchards raised beautiful horses in the French countryside, crossbreeding European horses to the beautiful, swift Arabians they brought to France from the deserts of the East.

"Then the Revolution came, and with it, Madame Guillotine. My mama's family were aristocrats, which made them enemies of the people!" She shrugged expressively. "They were forced to flee France for the safety of England—though not before my great-great-grandparents had lost their heads in the Place de la Concorde."

"You have my sympathies. But what became of the horse breeding?" Steede asked, genuinely curious.

"They were able to send a few of their blooded brood mares and stallions across the English Channel to our British cousins before they made good their own escape. It was not easy, but eventually they returned to breeding their beloved horses here in England. My mother and father met when my father went to an auction. He came to see a stallion my grandfather was offering for sale, and instead, saw Mama. Isabelle Colette de Blanchard. He returned the next week, and offered her father for her hand. *One look*. Mama said that was all it took for them to fall in love," she added with a dreamy expression.

"Sometimes it happens that way," Blackstone murmured, remembering his first glimpse of Victoria in the moonlight.

She nodded. "As it did with Ned and me. We met at his mother's sick bed, you know, and from that moment on, we—oh! Forgive me!" she begged, clapping her hand over her mouth, clearly devastated by her slip of the tongue. "Please. Forget I ever spoke of that meeting."

"Believe me, I intend to," he promised, tight-lipped. "But please, go on with your story."

"That afternoon, Mama was teaching me to jump," Victoria continued, a faraway, remembering look in her eyes. "Papa had given me a little pony for my seventh birthday. Goblin, his name was. There was a fallen log in the field. A very little one. Mama went over it several times without incident, to show me how easy it was. The last time, a rabbit bolted from its burrow, right beneath her horse's nose. It reared up, and she tumbled from its back."

"Good God!"

"I didn't realize it at the time, of course, but the fall broke her neck instantly. She was dead before I reached her. Both our mounts bolted and raced home to their stables. Later, I overheard Papa talking to my aunt. He told her he would never forget the sight of those riderless horses, clattering into the stableyard, nor the dread he'd felt on seeing them.

"He never spoke of Mama, or of that dreadful day, ever again. He blamed me for her death, you see? And over the years, I believe he grew to hate Mama, too, for leaving him so soon."

He glanced down and saw that she had twisted her serviette into knots, her hands restlessly wringing the square of fabric, over and over again. The edges were badly frayed now.

Blackstone frowned. "Hate you? But you were only a child! What sort of father hates his own child? Besides, how could you possibly have been at fault for anything, little as you were? Did he ever tell you he blamed you?"

"Not in so many words, no. But then, he didn't have to. I've always known it," she insisted huskily, swallowing several times and blinking back tears.

"Don't cry, damn it," he growled. Women's tears always unmanned him. Taking her hand, he drew her across the plaid rug, onto his lap. "Darling Victoria, don't cry."

Murmuring her name, he kissed her, tasting the salt of her tears on her lips. Crooning little nonsense phrases, he nibbled her neck, breathing in the sweet, soapy scent of her skin, her hair, cupping and gently stroking her breasts until he could feel the hardened nipple under his thumb through the velvet jacket.

"I want you, my lovely Victoria," he whispered raggedly, slowly lowering her to the plaid rug. When she lay beneath him, her hair fanned across the plaid like a skein of black embroidery silk, he kissed her, parting her lips with his tongue to stroke her own, then nipping at her pouty lower lip.

The intimacy of his kisses made Victoria moan softly with pleasure, for she knew they were a prelude to a more intimate joining.

"Say it. Tell me you want me," he commanded, kissing the hollows of her throat.

"I want you," she echoed, arching her throat for his kisses like a cat arching its back against its master's hand. She hated the little purring, throaty sounds she was making, but couldn't seem to help herself.

Wanting him no less than he wanted her, she made no protest when he unbuttoned her riding jacket and drew the fronts apart.

Unlacing the busk and chemise beneath it, he freed her breasts, taking a long hungry look at them before setting his mouth to each mauve-tipped swell.

A shudder moved through him at his first taste of her. Her skin was smooth as cream, sweet as honey on his tongue. The small nipples were like sugared raspberries, crowning a sumptuous sweet he could never get enough of!

Lifting her skirts, he uncovered her lower limbs, inch by sensual inch.

"You, Lady Blackstone, are a sight to drive men mad," he breathed in her ear. "A study in delicious contrasts. Refined lady—unbridled wanton."

Her feet were shod in dainty high-heeled riding boots that hugged her leg to mid-calf. Beneath them, she wore stockings of sheer black silk, gartered just above the dainty knees she pressed so modestly together. Snowy silk drawers, edged with scalloped white eyelets, met lacy blue garters.

While a bachelor soldier, he had seen many examples of Eastern erotica. "Pillow books" the men enjoyed when parted from their wives and sweethearts, filled with drawings of couples engaged in various methods of intercourse. He had also seen dozens of racy sepia daguerreotypes of naked women in alluring poses and exotic costumes. Yet not one had ever made him as hard as he was now, looking down at his own bride.

Pillowed by the turf, her skirts and petticoats gathered up about her waist, her lower limbs displayed in all their lacy finery, she was a sight that had him close to exploding, and yet, only her pretty breasts were bared. It was that wild combination of lady and sensual wanton, that carnal mouth and those wide, angelic blue eyes that aroused him, he thought, wanting her more than ever.

And so, kneeling between her thighs, he ducked his head and took her with tongue and lips and hands on that wild, windswept tor, his passion running free and savage as any stallion's as he plundered those soft feminine folds. They were swollen with desire—and wet. Dear Lord, so wet! So ready for him, he discovered, pushing his fingers deep into her satiny heat, and gently strumming the tiny moist bud of her desire with his thumb.

Softly whimpering his name, she arched up against his hand, trying to increase the pressure, the heat, the friction of his skin as it moved in and over hers.

"Steede . . . oh, Steede!"

"Yes, my beauty. Yes, Victoria, yes! Don't fight it!" he commanded her.

Still plying her with thumb and finger, he captured her mouth beneath his own and kissed her deeply, feeling the contractions of her body begin as he eased himself onto her.

157

Unbuttoning his breeches, he freed his rigid shaft, groaning as it sprang forth, hard, hot and demanding. A fiery brand that throbbed against her cool, silk-clad thigh.

Sliding his palms beneath her derriere, he raised her up, and drawing back, prepared to thrust deep into her heat and seek his ease.

But, while he was still poised on the threshold of paradise, the silly baaing of a flock of sheep and the tuneless whistling of their shepherd intruded. The sounds were growing closer by the second.

Looking down the hill, he cursed, silently and vehemently, as he saw the ancient fellow wending his way up the rocky tor toward their lofty picnic spot. The shepherd was someone Steede knew well.

"I regret we must postpone our pleasure, my sweet," he murmured, smartly whisking down her skirts. "Hide that pretty pair for now and sit up, there's a good girl. We're about to be visited by Old Tom Foulger—and I'm not about to share so much as a glimpse of your charms with the old reprobate."

Leaning forward, he planted a farewell kiss on each breast, then drew her bodice fronts together and deftly adjusted his breeches.

"Hallooo, there, Tom. A good day to you. How is the flock?" he inquired loudly.

Winking at Victoria, he stood and started down the hill to cut off the shepherd who, corduroy cap in hand, was grinning broadly and tugging at a gray forelock as he clambered up the slopes to meet his master.

A gnawing, nagging ache, a sense of incompletion lingered on the ride home—and an uncomfortable ride home for Steede it was, too, Victoria believed, if the black scowls he cast her were anything to go by.

"Tonight, madam," he rasped through clenched jaws, his breath so hot in her ear that gooseflesh prickled down her arms, "I shall come to your bed and finish what was started on the tor. And I give you fair warning, Victoria. Lock your door to me tonight, and I shall tear it off its hinges, so help me God!"

"Very well, Steede," she promised shakily. Her limbs were weak as a kitten's as he lifted her down from her mount.

He leered at her, a mere baring of teeth, his eyes hot, his body tense. "No protests? No arguments?"

She shook her head, too shaken by her churning emotions to speak. And then, unable to look him in the eye a moment longer, for fear he would read the longing there, she scuttled back to the house like a frightened rabbit.

Once inside, she hurried upstairs to wash herself and change her clothing, relieved that Lily was nowhere in evidence to ask the inevitable questions.

Composed once more, she came back down to the scullery almost an hour later, intending to

arrange the roses she and Mary had picked before it was time for afternoon tea.

She had stood the flowers in a large tin tub
filled with water before she went to change for
her ride. But to her surprise, she discovered both
tub and roses were gone.

"Where's Mrs. Hastings?" she asked Cook as
she went into the kitchens. The large ruddy-
cheeked Devonshire woman was perspiring
heavily as she oversaw the preparations for the
evening's dinner.

In the kitchens, three serving women were
busily peeling vegetables, or kneading bread
dough on a floured table set beneath the window.
Another was covering a platter of tiny crustless
cucumber-and-cream cheese and salmon sandwiches with a dampened tea-towel, to keep the
bread from drying out.

"Out, mum. Happen I might be able t' help
you?"

"Has someone moved the roses that I picked
earlier?"

"Not that I know of, mum. They was there in
the scullery earlier, stood up in that old tub,
aye?"

"That's right, but they're gone now."

"Oh, ah? I'll ask Arthur if he's moved them,
shall I, mum?" Cook suggested, mopping a ruddy
face on the hem of her apron.

"No, no, don't trouble yourself. You have more
than enough to do here without bothering about
this. I'll just look around. I'm sure they're here

somewhere. Perhaps Arthur put them outside . . ."

"The little miss and that Egyptian woman was rummaging about in the scullery a while ago. Happen they'll know what's become of your roses, mum?"

"You're absolutely right. Lady Mary has probably arranged them already. Thank you, Cook— oh, and by the way, the picnic was delicious. Thank you so much."

Cook beamed. "My pleasure, mum. I'm right happy you enjoyed it."

But Victoria's search turned up no sign of either the missing roses or her stepdaughter and the nursemaid.

When she questioned other members of the household staff as to their whereabouts, she was told they had been seen walking down to the village earlier that afternoon, while Her Ladyship was out riding.

"Isn't it strange?" she observed to Lily later that evening as she prepared for bed, still none the wiser. "I must have picked three dozen roses this morning, and not a single one of them can I find, anywhere!"

"That's rum doings. Perhaps that little Lady Mary knows where they are," Lily suggested, removing the hairpins from Victoria's chignon and stowing them in a small porcelain box.

Unwinding the long black ringlets, Lily briskly applied a silver-backed brush to their length, brushing her mistress's hair until it fell to her waist in a shining waterfall of black silk.

"There you are, my lady. One hundred strokes," Lily said after brushing it for several minutes. "I'll just turn down the bed for you, then I'll be off myself, aye?"

"Please, do," Victoria murmured, only half listening. Far from paying attention to Lily, she was staring off into space, remembering Steede's wicked instruction to leave her door unlocked. . . .

"Tonight, madam. I shall come to your bed and finish what was started on the tor. And I give you fair warning, Victoria. Lock your door to me tonight, and I shall tear it off its hinges, so help me God!"

Oh, Lord. Just the thought of him making love to her again made her shiver. Anticipation and excitement filled her.

How could she be so weak, so wanton, so easily won over by another man? One who was, moreover, practically a stranger, and whose past—in all honesty—she knew very little about, although she had married him.

Why, just a few days ago, she had sworn she loved Ned—had been prepared to abandon wealth and title—everything!—in order to elope with him. And yet now, less than a week later, she could hardly remember the last time she'd thought of the man.

Slipping a silk nightgown over her head—a scandalously sheer, scanty one that Lily had chosen from the trousseau the Widow Johns had sewn for her—she critically appraised her reflection in the mirror.

162

Rather than voluminous folds of gathered flannel concealing her figure, this skimpy silken wisp accented everything, baring half her bosom, then skimming her slender waist to cling alluringly about the hips.

Would Steede step through the adjoining door tonight, as he had threatened? she wondered. And if he did, would he like the frivolous scrap she was wearing . . . ?

She shivered. She had the feeling she would not be wearing it long enough to find out whether he did or nay.

"Eeh, by gum! Will ye look at that!" Lily suddenly exclaimed.

Victoria spun around, gasping as she looked over at the bed.

She had expected a spider, or even a mouse. But it was neither. In the soft lamplight, she could see what had made Lily scream so.

She had folded back the top sheet, to discover that blood soaked the bottom one. Great crimson, scarlet and deep-red gouts of it were splashed all over the lavender-scented linens.

"Dear Lord!" Victoria exclaimed, her hand flying to her heart. "Where in the world did that come from?"

"I don't know, my lady—but I know where it's bound, and that's a fact!"

Grim-faced and thin-lipped with anger, Lily leaned over the bed to remove the stained linens. But at the last moment, she stiffened, her hand frozen over the sheet's lace edging.

"Well, I'll be blowed! It ain't blood at all, my

lass. Look. It's *rose petals*. Red ones. There must be hundreds of 'em!" She chuckled. "I've see nowt like this before, not in all my days!"

"Rose petals?" Victoria exclaimed. "Are you sure?"

On closer inspection, she could see that Lily was right. Red rose petals had been strewn across the snowy bottom sheet, then the bed neatly remade over them.

Victoria shivered. Innocent rose petals they might be, but in the low lamplight they were indistinguishable from blood.

And now that the bed had been turned down, the smell of their perfume filled the room, sickly sweet, overpowering.

"Take them away, Lily. I can't bear the sight of them!" she whispered with a shudder.

"Now then, love, don't take on," Lily advised, giving her a comforting hug. "Whoever did this, it were someone what wished ye well, aye? Life like a bed o' roses, so to speak. How were they t' know we'd think it were blood, aye, chick?"

"I suppose you're right," Victoria agreed, forcing a smile she didn't feel. She rubbed her bare arms, where goosebumps had sprouted. "It's just that . . . well, I think these petals are from the roses Mary and I were picking when you and Harry arrived this morning."

"And what if they are?"

"After I came back from riding, I wanted to arrange them in vases for the house and Lodge. But I couldn't find them anywhere. If these are the same roses, why not use all of them? The pink, or the yellow, say? You don't think whoever put these here wanted to frighten me? You know, to make me think it was blood?"

Lily shrugged. "I doubt it, love. Besides, why would anyone want t' frighten ye? You've been here but the one day, after all. Hardly time t' have made any enemies. No, my lass, I'd wager it were the little girl's doings. Bonny little thing, she is, to be sure, but an odd little soul, from what I heard below stairs. Who knows. Perhaps she only likes the red ones?"

"You're probably right." On reflection, perhaps she'd overreacted. Sprinkling rose petals in her bed could have been Mary's silent welcome to Blackstone Manor. Or maybe one of the chambermaids was following some bizarre Devonshire tradition to welcome her to Blackstone Manor. After all, there was nothing malevolent about rose petals. She would think of them as her "bed of roses," just as Lily had said, she told herself.

But even so, the uneasy feeling lingered.

"Well, then, if you're all set, I'll be off to my own bed. Worn out, I am, what with that wretched train journey. Thought it would never end, I did. 'Devon!' I told Harry. 'More like the end o' the world, you ask me!' "

Victoria smiled and kissed her maid's cheek. "I'm really glad you came. And Harry, too. Good night, Lily, darling."

"Me, too." Lily smiled and squeezed her hand. "Sleep well, love. I'll see thee in the morning, aye?"

With that, Lily blew out the chimney lamp and left her alone.

Slipping between the cool sheets, Victoria lay back upon the pillows, bathed in moonlight, to wait for her dark, handsome lover.

He joined her only moments after Lily's departure—so soon that she knew he'd been listening for her maid's footsteps outside his door.

Like a lean, dark shadow, he stepped through the connecting door with the stealth of a thief. Dropping the Turkish towel he had fastened about his flanks, he slid into bed beside her.

"God, look at you. Like a shaft of moonlight," he murmured thickly as he took her in his arms, running his hand the length of her slender, silk-clad body. "My lovely huntress, Diana. Goddess of the moon. Skin as luminous as moonflowers, and hair as dark and glossy as a starlit sky. That's what you are, ma belle Victoria . . ."

Drawing down the shoulder straps, he kissed her bared shoulders, his hot tongue laving silky flesh that smelled of hyacinths.

". . . my moon goddess," he whispered.

He kissed her everywhere, drawing the gown down her body inch by inch, as if peeling the skin from a ripe peach. The comparison, though indecent, was an apt one, Victoria thought with a frisson of pleasure.

When the gown's silky folds were pooled about her waist, he dipped his dark head to her bosom and cupped both snow-white mounds in his hands. As his tongue flicked over the flushed, swollen nipples, low gasps and moans escaped her. Both areolas rucked, like rumpled mauve velvet.

When each adorable mound had been well loved, he removed her nightgown completely, tossing it aside with an impatient growl as he had on their wedding night. Then, rearing back, he looked down at her, his night-black eyes dancing with wicked pleasure.

Taking her hand, he placed it over his manhood, which jutted, hard and hot, from the dark forest at his groin.

"Take him in your hand," he urged her, gazing deep into her eyes. "Feel what you do to me!"

He gritted his teeth as her hand closed over him, her fingers lightly stroking, then shuddered as she pushed back the sensitive skin, exposing the swollen ruby beneath.

Despite his sternest efforts, his manhood bucked with a will of its own.

"Damn and bless you, Victoria," he breathed, his kisses belying his curse. "Shall I ever get enough of you? Have you bewitched me? Is that why I feel like this? Come, now. Open for me, darling. Let me make you ready . . ."

She took his hand as he had done hers, her courage fed by the desire that sizzled through her veins. Placing it over her mound, she whispered, "I *am* ready." A shiver moved through her. "Oh, *God*, so ready . . . Now. Steede. Take me. Oh, take me now!"

He squeezed her swollen mound very gently, then slid his fingers deep inside her.

167

"Don't," she hissed, plucking at his wrist. Yet her hand fell away and she moaned helplessly as he worked his maddening fingers in and out of her, moving them deeper each time. The pleasure built, until she arched up, off the bed, imploring him to end her torment with little broken bird cries that spurred his own arousal.

"Now," she begged in a hoarse, strangled voice. "*Inside me*. Oh, God! Please, now!"

"Soon, my sweet," he promised her huskily, his dark eyes heavy-lidded with desire. "I want to taste you . . ."

He trailed his tongue down her silky abdomen, lingering to lap at the dimple of her navel.

". . . like a hummingbird, sipping nectar from a lovely orchid . . ."

She whimpered as he planted a trail of tiny wet kisses down her belly, gasping as he nuzzled the dark curls below.

". . . like this one," he murmured, ducking his ebony head.

He kissed her there, tasted the very essence of her, his tongue dancing over her exquisitely sensitive pearl until she was sobbing with delight against the fist pressed to her mouth.

And then, guiding his manhood home, he slid inside her so deeply, fully, she cried out in pleasure.

Pulse after golden pulse shimmered and danced through her belly, like flames flickering behind her closed eyelids. Each pulse, each flutter, drew him deeper into her body.

"Again," he commanded savagely, lifting her

hips higher. His muscular buttocks flexed as he thrust again and again into her searing heat.

His eyes were closed as he ground his flanks against her. The erotic slap of bare flesh against bare flesh was loud in the shadowed hush.

"Climb with me, Victoria!"

She shook her head from side to side on the pillow. Her hyacinth eyes were dreamy with spent pleasure. Her limbs felt loose, heavy with satisfaction.

"Hmm, too soon. Not yet," she protested drowsily.

"Now," he commanded, black eyes heavy-lidded as he thrust back and forth against her. "Let go. Let go, and you will *soar!*"

"I can't . . . I just ca . . . Oh! Oh! *Oooh!*"

Wrapping her legs around his waist, she began to move with him, her body rising and falling to meet his driving loins.

Taking him in her arms, she felt the powerful cords that shimmied across his shoulders and down his back when he flexed his muscles. Raw, virile strength sheathed by smooth, hot flesh. Power and beauty that hummed beneath her fingers, her hungry lips.

Like magic, the fire rekindled, bursting through her with the explosive heat and flash of a Roman candle.

"Steede!"

Suddenly the night shattered, splintered into a million blinding shards of light. The world spun crazily on its axis, reeling out of control.

And as he had promised, they soared to the stars. *Together.*

Chapter Twelve

Mary awoke with a start. For the first time in ages, she had dreamed she was back in India, and that it was the night of the fire. The same night she had fallen asleep in the peacock chair on the verandah outside Mama and Papa's room, and woken to hear Mama screaming. . . .

Pushing the covers aside, she padded barefoot across the room and stared at the fireplace, still sleepy and confused.

Pretty orange and yellow temple dancers swayed before her eyes—no, not dancers, *flames!*

Flames that writhed in the draft . . .

Flames that roared and gobbled up everything in their path with angry crackling, snapping sounds, like a gold and red crocodile . . .

Flames that lit up the sky outside her window, so that the night was as bright as day.

It was happening again!

She had to wake everybody. Kalinda first. Then Kalinda would help her wake Papa and the others . . .

But tonight, like that other, dreadful night, Kalinda was not asleep in her bed in the adjoining room.

Whimpering and still only half awake, Mary stumbled through Kalinda's darkened room with its lovely smells of India, to the other door, which led out into the hallway.

Barefoot, she pattered along the Turkey runner to her parents' room at the far end of the upper gallery, still dreaming she was in the bungalow and sobbing softly for her papa as she went.

Victoria woke to hear muffled weeping outside her door.

Opening it, she found Mary huddled on the threshold, sobbing her heart out.

"Mary! What on earth—? Oh, you poor little thing!"

The summer storm that had broken soon after midnight must have woken the child and sent her looking for comfort. The booms of the thunder overhead now were as loud and frightening as cannonfire.

"What is it, darling? Oh, sweetheart, don't cry so. Come to Victoria," she murmured. "There's nothing to be afraid of."

Picking up the little girl, she carried her back

to her bed, lay down beside her and pulled the covers up over them both.

But Mary continued her whimpering, muttering about "Mama" and "fire." She was still more than half asleep, Victoria realized, and a thrill ran down her spine. Half asleep, and talking— proof that, physically at least, she was capable of speech. In the six weeks since she had been at Blackstone, they were the only words she had ever heard Mary utter. She could hardly wait to tell Steede when he returned from his business in London.

Wanting to reassure herself that there was no fire, and that the little girl was only dreaming, Victoria left her briefly and hurried down the drafty gallery to the nursery.

The fire had died down to a heap of glowing embers. Embers that—to Victoria's relief—were still safely contained behind a sturdy fireguard.

The connecting door to Kalinda's room stood slightly ajar. Curious, Victoria peeked inside.

As another flash of lightning lit up the room, she could see embroidered silk shawls draped over lamps, the dull wink of brass figurines—and the mounded shape of the ayah's body beneath a fringed counterpane.

So. The nursemaid had not heard her little charge leave her bed, nor her frightened sobs. Nor, it seemed, had Mary tried to wake her. Why not, she wondered?

Returning to her own bed, she slid between the sheets and cuddled Mary closer.

". . . sorry, 'Toria," the child murmured drows-

173

ily, turning to her and burrowing her head in the curve of Victoria's neck.

Tears filled Victoria's eyes. The way Mary cuddled up to her and mumbled her name meant she was making progress, surely.

"Yes, darling. I'm right here. And it's all right. There's no fire. Go on back to sleep, darling. Only sweet dreams this time . . ."

She stroked her hair, loving the baby fragrance of Knight's castille soap, the warmth and weight of the little body curled so trustingly against hers. What was it Mary was so sorry about? she wondered. For the rose petals in her bed? For her scowls and dark looks? Could a child's sense of guilt, highly magnified, have caused her nightmares, rather than the storm?

"Hush, darling, hush. Go back to sleep. I know how sorry you are. I know, too, that you don't want to love me—but I do want to love you. And when we love someone, we sometimes have to fight very hard to make them love us, too," Victoria whispered.

"But when that someone is worth loving, then they are worth fighting for." Victoria hugged her closer. "Just as I shall fight to make you love me, even if it takes years and years. Remember that there is nothing—nothing!—you could ever do or say that would make me stop loving you, my darling girl."

How could anyone ever harm a child, she wondered, stroking Mary's flushed cheek, and still live with themselves afterwards? But people did, every day, in countless cruel and uncaring ways, and often in the name of Christian charity, as in the work- and poorhouses.

She fell asleep cradling Mary in her arms, waking some time later to hear the storm still raging, its violence unabated.

Mary was wide awake and staring up at her.

In the flashes of lightning that lit the room, Victoria could see the confusion and fear in the child's eyes. Not fear of her, Victoria was almost certain, but of the storm.

"I expect you're wondering how you came to be here, aren't you? Well, you had a bad dream and walked in your sleep," Victoria explained, smiling as she brushed locks of tawny hair back from Mary's flushed cheeks. "I found you outside my door, curled up like a kitten. Your feet were two little blocks of ice, so I picked you up and popped you into my bed to get warm. If you want to go back to the nursery, I'll carry you," she offered.

After a moment's hesitation, the tousled head shook vehemently from side to side. *No!*

Thunder crackled loudly again, rattling the windows in their frames. Rain pattered against the panes, as if someone outside were hurling handfuls of shingle at the windows.

"Do you want to stay here, then?" she asked.

In answer, Mary burrowed her face against Victoria's body, her little fingers digging into her arms.

"All right. I know. Why don't I tell you a story until you fall asleep? One about a little girl, just like you. Her name was . . . Colette. She was

175

seven years old, and she lived in a beautiful brick house by the sea, just like this one.

"Little Colette's papa was very, very rich. He gave her everything a little girl could ever ask for. Pretty dresses, jam tarts, strawberries and cream, a whipping top, French dolls—even a pony of her own. In fact, Colette always had everything she wanted—except what she wanted most. For her papa to love her.

"You see, her mama had gone away to heaven, and Colette missed her very, very much. It wouldn't have been quite so awful if only her papa had not been so very sad, but he was. Colette thought he didn't care about her anymore, but it wasn't true. Then one day, Colette's papa came to her and said . . ."

"You're worried about Mary, aren't you?" Victoria asked her mother-in-law as they lingered over afternoon tea in the burgundy-and-cream drawing room the following afternoon.

"Yes," Lady Henrietta admitted. For the first time since Victoria had met her, Steede's mother looked troubled. The slim hand that held the dainty bone-china cup with such aplomb trembled.

"I hardly knew the child's mother, I must admit, what with my son being stationed in India. Steede brought his bride home to Blackstone only once, when they were on their honeymoon tour, you understand? But that one time, I received the impression that Aimee was a self-centered, flighty gel who gave little thought to anyone but herself. My husband, John, God rest his soul, agreed. Aimee reminded him of a female cat he'd had as a boy, or so he said. Every spring, the cat would drop her litter wherever the fancy took her, then run off and leave her poor, helpless little kittens to fend for themselves."

"So Aimee and Mary were not close?"

"Heavens, no! Far from it. And from the few rare comments Steede has made, I concluded that his marriage had proven disappointing, although he never discussed it with me. I believe Aimee was something of a social butterfly when they met in India. She continued her social whirl even after she became a wife and a mother." Henrietta sniffed in disapproval. "True, she was very young, and quite lovely, but such singleminded pursuit of her own diversions left her poor child very much in her nursemaid's care. A most unsuitable set of circumstances, to my mind."

"If Kalinda was her *only* influence, I would agree wholeheartedly," Victoria allowed. She firmly believed that Kalinda's influence over her charge should have been limited by both her mama and her papa.

"Before he met you, my dear, Steede was at his wits' end. He was seriously considering sending Mary off to a good boarding school somewhere, you know. He thought, in the long view, that it would prove the best path for my granddaughter. May I ask your opinion on the subject?"

"I would have to disagree, ma'am."

Henrietta leaned across and patted Victoria's

knee. "It's Mother, my dear. Remember? Or if you prefer, Henrietta."

"Thank you, Henrietta." She smiled. "I believe Mary feels abandoned. As if her mama and baby brother have deserted her. And with her papa so wrapped up in his own grief, Steede was, perhaps, unable to give Mary the reassurance she needs."

"Reassurance?"

She nodded. "That she is safe and loved. Sending her off to boarding school now, when I have been here only a short time, would be devastating for her, don't you think? Mary could not help but think of me as the reason for her—her banishment."

"I expect you're right," the older woman admitted. She took a sip of tea, gazing thoughtfully into the fire that had replaced the tapestry fire screen last week. "But what of her education? The child has a keen intelligence, and I am of the modern school of thought. I believe women's minds should be challenged and nurtured. Not allowed to become porridge! I want Mary to have all the opportunities that I was denied as a young gel, regardless of whether she can speak. If you do not think boarding school appropriate, my dear, would you instead find a suitable governess for my granddaughter?"

"With your permission—and Steede's, of course—I have a better idea. Thanks to the excellent staff that you engaged, Henrietta, the Manor virtually runs itself, while I have far too much time on my hands. Rather than spend my days in idleness, why shouldn't I teach Mary the fundamentals myself? A little French, botany, mathematics, geography and such, to start with. And then later, perhaps we could go on to some Latin and Greek."

Henrietta's face lit up. "Would you really? Oh, dear girl! That would be *splendid*."

As the two women continued their tea and conversation, a slender shadow separated itself from the draperies. The eavesdropper slipped out into the hallway, then hurried up the back stairs to the second floor.

"They take tiffin and make their plans to send you away, my jewel!" Kalinda wailed. "Trust me. I heard them with my own ears."

No. You are wrong, Mary wrote on the slate. *Not Victoria.*

"Are you sure of that?" Kalinda asked slyly.

Loves me, Mary wrote again.

"Loves you! Who? Your grandmother?" A vigorous nod from Mary. "And the Lady Victoria, too?" Another nod. "You are mistaken, my dove!"

Not, Mary wrote.

"No? Then let us test her, precious blossom. If the memsahib truly loves you, as she claims, your beloved Victoria will forgive you any naughtiness, no matter what it may be. Is that not what she told you, little one?" Kalinda murmured.

Her voice was silky-soft now. She was purring like old Sal, Cook's kitchen cat, Mary thought.

"Test her, my baby," Kalinda urged. "Let us discover, once and for all, if your Victoria means what she says—or if her mouth is full of lies."

How? Mary wrote.

"I have the perfect way. You must go into her room when she is riding with your papa, and destroy the picture she showed you. The one of her mother that she treasures so. Break the glass! Stamp upon the frame! Tear the photograph into the smallest pieces. See if she still loves you, after that, my little one."

No, Mary scrawled on the slate, shaking her head from side to side. She wrote again, *No*.

"Ah. So you are afraid to discover the truth, my bright jewel," Kalinda purred again, stroking her head.

For once, Mary twisted out of her reach. *No!*

"But you have nothing to fear if your step-mother truly loves you, as she says. You will only be testing the truth of her promises. And if she has lied! Well, what does it matter to you? If she and the old one have their way, you will soon be sent far, far from Blackstone."

Where? the little hand scrawled frantically, panic and terror in the wide gray eyes.

"Why, to a boarding school, my dove. To a cruel, lonely place far from Kalinda, who is the only one who truly loves you."

No. No more, Mary wrote, although the words "sent away" and "boarding school" had made her tummy ache. She pressed so hard with the nub of chalk, she almost carved the words into her slate. Her fingers were sore as she glared at Kalinda, her lower lip jutting obstinately.

In the end, her ayah had to look away—though

not before Mary saw Kalinda's brown eyes grow hard as a cobra's.

The cold place in Mary's tummy grew colder still. What was wrong with Kalinda? Why had she been so horrid since Victoria came to Blackstone? Had Kalinda stopped loving her, like Papa? Was that it?

"It is time for your afternoon nap, Memsahib Mary," Kalinda said, still in the cross voice that was quite unlike her gentle sing-song tone. "Into bed with you!"

Milk? Mary wrote. *Gingersnaps?*

"Gingersnaps! There will be no gingersnaps for you today, my naughty one. Gingersnaps are only for little girls who obey their ayahs. Take your nap—but before you sleep, consider your disobedience, yes?"

After Kalinda had gone into the small room adjoining the nursery to take her own nap, Mary climbed up onto the velvet window seat. She pulled a crocheted shawl up to her chin, trying to get warm.

The nursery fire had burned down and the coal scuttle was empty because Kalinda had not rung for Em to bring more coal, as she usually did. She must be very cross indeed, to forget such a thing. Ever since they came to England, Kalinda had complained of the cold.

Feeling abandoned by everyone, and miserable, Mary rested her chin on her knees and gazed through the lead-paned windows at the deserted park below, where an early mist was rising off the lawns.

Most of the time, she liked living here. England was always green and pretty, always cool and damp, so that she was never exhausted by the heat. And, although it rained a little almost every day, there was no monsoon season here, with endless roaring rains, and afterwards, the discovery of horrid snakes that had crawled inside the bungalow to stay dry.

But when she was miserable, as she was now, she missed India and her little monkey, Kiki, who had been left behind with the gardener. She missed India's vivid skies and bright flowers, too, and the hot, heavy breezes that smelled of spices, dung and ghee, and carried the smells and clamor of the marketplace on their warm currents.

If she squeezed her eyes shut and tried very hard, she could still go back there in her thoughts and dreams, though her memories were not as clear as they had once been, and her dreams far less frequent.

At the end of every spring, His Royal Highness, the Rajah, had left his white palace and moved his wives and royal court to the highest slopes of the mountains, where it was cool during even the hottest months of the year.

In her mind's eye, Mary could see the gaily draped royal elephants swaying through the streets, swinging their trunks from side to side. Inside the canopied howdahs on their backs rode the turbaned Rajah and his many wives, their fingers, earlobes and wrists glittering with jewels.

Papa had told her that just one of those jewels

could buy enough food for an Indian village for several lifetimes.

She remembered the men of her papa's cavalry regiment lined up in their pretty scarlet uniforms on the parade ground. Their gold buttons, fringed gold epaulets and steel saber blades had flashed in the sunlight as they stood stiffly at attention beside their mounts, like rows of lead toy soldiers.

As the elephants lumbered past the bungalow and the parade ground where the regiment was assembled, the soldiers smartly saluted the royal procession as it left the city, headed toward the dusty foothills.

Papa used to look so handsome in his uniform, Mary remembered. She had loved it so when he came striding into the bungalow each evening, calling her name and holding out his arms for her to run into them.

"Mary! Where are you, poppet? Where's my Mary, quite contrary?" he would call, his deep voice ringing through the airy rooms as he tossed his pith helmet to his batman.

Squealing in delight, she always dropped the toy she was playing with and ran to him. "Papa!"

Papa would laugh and lift her up, to ride on his shoulders.

"Look at me! Look at me, Kalinda! I'm tall as an elephant!" she had screamed in delight from her lofty perch.

"That you are, minx! And naughty as a little monkey!" Papa had said, his eyes twinkling. "Where's your mama?"

She had wrinkled her nose, but before she could answer Papa's question, Kalinda had bowed and answered it for her.

"Memsahib Aimee has gone out, Sahib Warring. She went to take tiffin with Memsahib Miriam, sir."

Papa's smile had vanished.

"Tea with Miriam again, eh?" he had snapped. "Blast it!" His eyes had been angry, too. "Who was her escort? No, don't tell me. The colonel's bloody adjutant, Sahib Blake, am I right?"

Kalinda had bowed. "It is so, sahib. But never fear, the memsahib is in very good hands, sahib. Very safe. Very proper. Never fear."

But despite Kalinda's smiling assurances, Papa had not smiled again that afternoon. He had said bad words, lots of them. And when Mama came home, they had gone into their apartments and quarreled. She knew, because she had crept outside, onto the verandah in front of their French doors, and she had heard them before she fell asleep.

And then, later that same night, later . . .

Remembering, Mary bit her lip, blinking back tears as she tried to swallow over the lump in her throat.

After the fire that took Mama and Baby Johnny away to heaven, Papa had tried to hug her and kiss her and get her to talk to him.

"What is it, poppet?" he asked, over and over again. "Tell Papa? Has the cat got your tongue?"

But she just couldn't talk to him, not anymore. She was too afraid that once she started talking, she might never be able to stop. And then she might blurt out her dreadful secret and tell Papa the truth. That it was *her* fault that Baby Johnny was d-dead—*everything!*

He wouldn't love her if he knew.

Fresh doubt began to worm its way into Mary's heart, which was thumping loudly now.

Kalinda had been her nurse for as long as she could remember. She loved her ayah, and she was almost certain Kalinda loved her in return. On the other hand, she had known her stepmama for such a little while.

Perhaps Kalinda was right about Papa's new wife? Perhaps Victoria was not what she seemed? Perhaps—she swallowed over a knot of tears—perhaps Victoria's mouth really was full of lies? Should she tell Kalinda that she was sorry for being such a naughty demon-child?

Yes, she decided. As Kalinda kept reminding her, she was the only one Mary had left. The only one who still cared about her, despite knowing the terrible secret Mary carried.

Mary's lips wobbled. Tears stung in her eyes. If Papa ever found out—or Grandmama, or Victoria—they wouldn't love her anymore. But Kalinda would love her always, come what may. Hadn't she proved it?

Mary scrambled off the window seat. Smoothing down her ruffled white pinafore, she trotted over to the door that led to Kalinda's room.

She knocked and, receiving no answer, opened the door a few inches, expecting to see her nurse fast asleep on her bed.

But to her surprise, the room was empty. Only the faint scents of curry, tea and patchouli lingered there.

Mary frowned. Kalinda had said she was going to rest, but she must have gone out through the other door, instead. The one that opened onto the upper gallery. Where could she have gone?

A peculiar cold heaviness settled in the very bottom of her tummy that made her want to be sick.

She had a horrid feeling she knew where Kalinda had gone—and what she had gone to do. . . .

Chapter Thirteen

The mare's hooves drummed the hard-packed turf as Victoria galloped Calypso across the edge of the moors, turning her mount's dainty Arabian head toward the gloriously colored woods that had yet to shed the last of their jewel-toned leaves.

The crisp wind and exertion had painted roses in her cheeks, Steede saw as she reined Calypso in just a few yards from his hiding place. Her glowing creamy skin was in sharp, lively contrast to her jet-black ringlets, her sparkling hyacinth-blue eyes, her sapphire velvet riding habit

"Steede! Where are you? Show yourself. I know you're here somewhere. Harry promised I'd catch up with you here!" she demanded, rising up from her sidesaddle to peer between the trees.

There was a husky catch to his wife's voice.

Laughter, underscored by something more; something earthy and female.

Its rich, seductive quality made him hard as the iron ground beneath his boots.

Stepping out from behind a massive, ancient oak just a few feet from her, he caught her elbow and tugged her, still laughing, from the mare's back and into his arms.

"Damned right I'm here," he said thickly, and crushed his mouth down over hers, slaking his hunger for the taste of her like a thirsty man drinking water from a spring.

Her lips were soft and yielding, yet as eager as his. He drank from them thirstily, pressing her back against the rough trunk of the oak to deepen his kiss.

A small cry broke from her when he paused to draw breath.

"*Now, my love.* Oh, God, Steede, hurry, hurry . . ."

He kissed her again, urgently now; her throat, her ears, her eyelids, cupping her face with one hand and plucking the pins from her hair with the other.

Still clinging fiercely to each other, they tumbled to the ground. Drifts of leaves, bright as the feathers of some exotic bird, stirred beneath them as, with shaking fingers, they tore off each other's clothes.

The sight of her naked, framed by colored leaves, made Steede groan with pleasure as he lowered himself over her. She was a wood-nymph, celebrating an ancient fertility rite, and he was her Pan . . .

"You've bewitched me," he growled as he guided his straining shaft to her silky folds. Pressing deep, whispering words in her raven hair, he began to move upon her, flexing buttocks and flanks that were hard with muscle to fill her. "And—God help me—I pray your spell is never broken . . ."

Victoria's face was flushed with the afterglow of their lovemaking as she ran upstairs to her room two hours later.

The cream-colored draperies had been drawn and several lamps lit in readiness for her return. They cast pools of gentle radiance over the room, catching the bright wink of several shiny objects scattered beside the bed.

What on earth could they be? she wondered, unpinning the top hat with the trailing veil as she crossed the room.

A small cry escaped Victoria as she knelt down. The shiny objects were pieces of broken glass, strewn over the Turkey carpet at her feet. To one side lay the twisted remains of an ornate picture frame. A raised pattern of flowering vines and leaves was stamped into the heavy silver.

The frame had once held her most prized possession: a sepia picture of her beautiful mama. Her *only* picture of her.

But the frame was badly bent now, and her mama's picture was nowhere to be seen.

"Please, God, don't let it have been Mary," she

told herself. She had shown the picture to the child just the week before, the morning after the storm. She'd told Mary that it was her only picture of her mama, and that she treasured it.

"There you are, love! I thought I heard you come up. I've brought your laundry and—oh, my. What a shame," Lily cried as she peered over Victoria's shoulder. She was carrying a wicker laundry basket piled high with Victoria's carefully pressed and starched undergarments.

"How in the world did that happen?" Lily asked as she began stowing frothy garments in dresser drawers. The faint fragrance of lavender, rose and hyacinth sachets rose from them as she did so.

"I have no idea. It was like this when I came in. A draft knocked it down, I expect," Victoria said with a shrug, carefully avoiding Lily's eyes as she sank wearily onto the bed.

"A draft?" Lily rolled her eyes and snorted. "Not likely, love. The windows are all closed, aye—and with good reason! It's right nippy out there this afternoon, it is," she said, plucking a stray bronze leaf from Victoria's hair with a knowing little grin. "No, I reckon it were that child. Your precious Lady Mary," Lily sniffed. "The little imp needs her bottom smacked, if you ask me."

"What the little imp needs is someone who loves her," Victoria scolded softly.

"She already has someone. That nurse of hers." Lily shuddered as she tucked neatly folded camisoles and ruffled pantalets into a drawer. "And

190

a proper odd kettle of fish, she is, too. Talk about unfriendly! Turned everyone below stairs against her, she has. Mrs. Hastings says she worships the devil—aye, and the small lass with her. The maids say her room smells peculiar. Of heathen incense, no doubt. And that Em—"

"It's probably curry, not incense," Victoria corrected, shaking her head.

"Curry? What's curry?"

"An Indian spice usually eaten as a sauce with lamb or mutton. It has a hot yellow spice called turmeric in it—one that our English cooks are unfamiliar with. Steede—His Lordship—claims he likes it, and he's certainly no heathen. And as for Kalinda worshiping the devil—! What utter nonsense! Tell the kitchen staff not to be so silly. The poor woman is different because of her Indian upbringing, but that is all. Customs vary across the British Empire, you know. And I'm sure my coming to Blackstone has frightened the woman even more than it did Mary."

Lily frowned. "I can understand the little lass being jealous of her da's attention, but her nursemaid—?"

"I don't mean she's jealous of me, exactly. Just fearful and afraid of what the future will bring. Kalinda is all alone in a foreign country, don't you see? I'm sure she wonders what will become of her if His Lordship relieves her of her duties as Lady Mary's nurse. The child is already quite old enough for a governess, after all, and perhaps Kalinda has no family or ties left in India."

"I expect you're right," Lily murmured, sounding as if she expected nothing of the sort. "Now, get your 'ands out of that there glass before ye cut yourself, my lady. I'll ring for one of the maids to shake out the rug and sweep up the little imp's mess."

"Lily," Victoria scolded. "I told you. I don't think Mary's responsible."

"No? Then who did it? Answer me that," her maid demanded, pulling the bellrope to summon Emmie. With her lips a thin, determined line, her indignant expression quite detracted from her fresh, pretty looks. "And where's Lady Isabelle's likeness, tell me that?"

"I really don't know," Victoria murmured, thinking she had a very good idea who might have done it, although it would be next to impossible to prove.

"Hmm. Well, what's done can't be undone, me mam always said. We just have to go on with our lives and do the best we can, aye? Now. Let's get thee out of that riding getup, shall we? Before ye know it, it'll be time for dinner. Don't want to keep His Lordship waiting, do we now?" Lily grinned, plucking another stray leaf from her mistress's velvet skirt. "Impatient lad, His Lordship, aye?"

"Very," Victoria murmured in agreement, silently deploring the guilty flush that rose to her cheeks in response to Lily's comment. Steede was her husband, for pity's sake. Why on earth was she blushing?

Lily actually laughed, drat her.

* * *

Refreshed by a sponge bath followed by a short nap, Victoria rose and, with Lily's assistance, dressed for dinner.

She came downstairs to dine that evening in a simple yet becoming gown of eau-de-nil satin. Silk flowers of the same shade decorated the simple knot into which Lily had twisted her black hair.

She found Mary standing in the marble-floored entrance hall to Blackstone Manor. The child was lost in thought, her face rapt with concentration as she gazed up at the lifesize painting of her beautiful mama, which hung on the wall opposite the main doors.

Soon after her arrival, Steede had asked Victoria if she would prefer that it be hung elsewhere, but she had told him to let it be, for Mary's sake more than anything.

"Good evening, Mary,"

"Ohh!" The child jumped in surprise. Obviously, she had not heard Victoria coming down the staircase. She bobbed a sketchy curtsy.

"Good evening, Mary," Victoria repeated gently. "I was wondering. Were you looking for me this afternoon? Did you perhaps go into my room to find me?"

Mary's gray eyes widened. She shook her head, sending red-gold ringlets flying about. *No.*

"Then you have no idea how this might have been broken?" Victoria held out the twisted picture frame. "It was in its usual place on my dressing table when I left to go riding. Remember, I showed it to you the morning after the storm?

But when I came back, it was lying on the floor. There was a pile of broken glass beside it, and the picture of my mama was missing."

Mary simply stared at her.

"Mary, if there was an accident, and it got knocked down and broken, I shan't be cross in the least. But I really would like my mama's picture returned to me."

Mary sucked in a shaky breath. She stared at the mangled frame in Victoria's hand as if it were a hooded cobra that might suddenly sink its deadly fangs into her cheek.

But after only a moment's hesitation, she looked away, shrugging narrow shoulders and shaking her tawny head in denial.

"Ah, well. Perhaps a draft knocked it down," Victoria conceded. She straightened up and held out her hand, smiling. "Shall we go in to dinner, darling? I don't know about you, but I'm starved."

Mary nodded, her head downcast.

With a sinking feeling in her stomach, Victoria realized that the tiny hand tucked inside her own was trembling.

"Everything all right, Victoria?" Steede asked as the three of them sat at dinner a short while later beneath a chandelier of shimmering Waterford crystals.

"Everything's wonderful!" she assured him.

Steede frowned at his bride over an exquisite centerpiece of gold, bronze and rusty-orange chrysanthemums arranged with sprays of vivid autumn leaves in a huge copper bowl. *Victoria's handiwork*, he thought admiringly, amazed by his bride all over again.

Since her arrival, the entire house glowed with a new warmth. Instead of echoing caverns that housed antiques and pieces of expensive furniture, the rooms of Blackstone Manor now reached out to embrace one. The library practically invited a visitor to curl up by the fire and lose himself in the classics or an exciting first edition, or the conservatory visitor to explore the exotic profusion of orange and lemon trees and lush tropical greenery, thanks to the small changes Victoria had implemented.

His mother could not say enough in praise of her new daughter-in-law. Praise that was, he'd noticed, growing more and more fond.

"Of course everything's all right. Why shouldn't it be?" Victoria said brightly, laughing as she dabbed her mouth on an Irish linen serviette.

Her husky laughter reminded him of their lovemaking that afternoon. Not four hours had passed, and he wanted her again—itched to kiss the corner of her mouth, or slip the pins from her hair and let it pool like ink over his bare chest . . .

He shrugged. "Just a feeling I had," he forced himself to say, losing himself in the depths of her eyes. "What about you, poppet? Are you well? Harry tells me you didn't visit the stables today," Steede said, forcing his attention back to his small daughter.

Mary refused to look at him. Small red-gold head bowed, she peered steadfastly into her soup bowl, as if expecting to find the secrets of the universe in its depths.

Her withdrawal was disappointing. She had seemed to be opening up, softening toward him of late, thanks to Victoria. But now, he was not so sure. Tonight, Mary was the same as she had been immediately after the fire. Silent. Hostile. Withdrawn.

He sighed. In his deepest heart, he knew why she had not spoken since that dreadful night, although he had tried to deny it. It was because of him. She blamed him for the deaths of her mama and her baby brother. Perhaps she always would. . . .

"I've never known you to forget old Jasper's carrot or Mercury's sugar lump," he continued, forcing himself to sound cheerful. "Feeling poorly, were you? Or was it something else? Did my girls have a falling out? Victoria?"

Dark brows lifting in inquiry, he looked down at Mary, then across at Victoria. Something had happened. He could feel it in the air, despite Victoria's apparent composure. His daughter, then. What had his tiny hellion been up to now, in her jealousy of her new stepmother?

But despite the questions that sprang to mind, demanding answers, he did not voice them. Victoria's handling of the situation was very likely the best one. Unlike himself, she seemed to know instinctively what needed doing.

"What's that doing there?" he asked casually,

nodding at the mangled silver frame alongside Victoria's place setting.

"That? Oh, the draft knocked it off my dressing table. I meant to ask you where I could get another."

"Let me take care of it for you," he offered. Reaching across the table, he brushed the tips of her fingers with his own. A tingle ran up his arm like an electrical shock.

At his touch, a delicate blush rose up from her cleavage to stain her throat and creamy cheeks a pale pink.

He had the sudden, insane urge to play robber-baron. To sweep her up into his arms, carry her off to his bedchamber, peel away the layers of eau-de-nil satin, lace and silk, and there discover just how far that pretty blush extended. . . .

But, since he could hardly yield to his baser instincts or indulge his lust for his wife with his little daughter present, he contented himself with casting Victoria a long, smoldering look that promised a reckoning—of sorts—to come.

It was enough to send her hand flying to her throat like a fluttering white dove, and to darken her hyacinth-blue eyes with confusion and desire.

It was going to be a very long evening, Steede decided with a heavy sigh, leaning back to let Arthur replace his soup bowl with a lamb chop.

Steede came to her that night as she had known he would, waiting only moments after Lily left to join her in bed.

As he slid beneath the cool linen sheets, she shivered and wrapped her arms around him, her head falling back as he kissed the hollows at the base of her throat.

"I'm falling in love with you," she whispered much later, stroking the heavy dark head pillowed on her bosom.

Steede slept on, oblivious to her words, his breathing even, deep and undisturbed.

"I never meant to—never intended to—but, God help me, I am."

For some reason, the realization terrified her.

Chapter Fourteen

"I hope you don't mind taking tea out here in the gazebo for once, my dear," Henrietta murmured, pouring steaming orange pekoe from an almost translucent bone china pot. "But I adore the view from my summer-house, and soon it will be too cold to take tea outside. We should make the most of the warm weather, don't you think?"

"Oh, yes. It's lovely here, and so very tranquil. Just listen to that birdsong!" Victoria sighed with pleasure as she looked around her.

In the three months she had been at Blackstone, her occasional afternoon teas with Steede's mother had become regular visits she looked forward to. She couldn't have asked for a more charming hostess nor for a lovelier setting, she had to admit.

Blackstone Lodge was like a doll house of soft

red brick. Crisp white shutters framed the windows, and a honeysuckle vine twined about the small portico, spilling intoxicating perfume everywhere, while English ivy clung to the walls.

Built on a small rise, the Lodge was hidden from the Manor by graceful silver birches, and reached by a stone path that meandered between charming gardens. The flower beds were so cleverly landscaped they seemed natural. Mother Nature at her loveliest.

The gazebo where they were taking afternoon tea was a small white gingerbread structure that overlooked the river. Several times, Victoria spotted the iridescent blue wings and orange breasts of kingfishers as they darted over the water in search of fish, despite Mary, who was perched on the river bank.

She was wearing a new dress with a ruffled bodice—one of several Victoria had commissioned Mrs. Stacey, the village seamstress, to sew for her from yard goods discovered at a Plymouth clothier's when she went there with Steede. The lively tartan of greens, blues, grays and whites was set off by narrow black lines. Matching emerald-green ribbons caught up Mary's red-gold hair in bouncy ponytails.

Wearing a dreamy expression, Mary sat on the daisy-strewn bank, dabbling bare pink feet in the slow-moving river and chewing the wispy end of her ponytail. Stockings, garters and dainty kid boots were scattered across the grass, discarded within minutes of her arrival.

The child was miles away, prodding a stick at

the newspaper sailing boat bobbing below her in the water.

Victoria smiled fondly. She enjoyed seeing her stepdaughter involved in a new pastime, rather than in dour Kalinda's company.

She had shown Mary how to make paper boats at breakfast that morning, using the current edition of the *Times* for building material. Mary had quickly caught on, and was soon folding her own sailboat, the tip of her tongue sticking out in concentration as she worked.

Unfortunately, the two of them had been so carried away with their model-making, they had pressed almost every page of the daily newspaper into service before Steede had read it!

When he found out, he shot them both black looks as he scanned the few pages he'd managed to rescue, before they were added to the "fleet."

To Victoria's surprise, Mary had begun to giggle at her papa's expression. Her infectious gurgles of laughter had made Victoria laugh, too, for some reason.

Soon, both of them had been laughing helplessly until their sides ached.

Steede, however, had cocked a disapproving eye at Victoria, who had tears running down her cheeks, and scowled.

"What the devil's wrong with you two this morning?" he had growled, before he stalked off to his study, taking the *Times*'s remnants with him.

It wasn't until he was gone that Victoria realized he probably thought they were laughing at *him*.

Poor Steede. He was always so stern and serious, except in their bed. Had losing his first wife made him that way? Did he look at her, remember Aimee, and find her wanting? Or dream of distant India and the life they'd had together, and wish he could go back there? Then again, perhaps it was his nature to be serious and stern.

Mary still missed her birthplace, Victoria believed. The child was probably dreaming her paper vessel could carry her back to India right this minute. Back to the time before her mama and baby brother were taken to heaven, Victoria reflected, setting down her empty cup and saucer with a heavy sigh.

Speaking of happier times, she had not yet recovered her mother's picture, she reminded herself. Nor had she found out who had destroyed the silver frame.

The maids flatly denied it, and both Kalinda and Mary had protested their innocence. Innocent or no, since that incident, there had been other minor occurrences.

One afternoon, she returned from riding with Steede to find that the contents of her drawers and armoire had been riffled, her belongings subtly disturbed. Lily claimed someone had gone through Victoria's Chinese jewelry chest, too. They'd checked the contents, and were almost certain nothing was missing, but the sense of violation and unease lingered.

Unfortunately, although Victoria had her suspicions about who was responsible for the malicious pranks and the snooping, she had no real proof and refused to make unfounded accusations against anyone.

"More tea, my dear?" Henrietta murmured, breaking into her thoughts.

"Hmm? Oh, yes, please," she accepted, smoothing down the rose-pink skirts of her afternoon gown as Henrietta poured. There was nothing she enjoyed more than a perfectly brewed dish of hot tea, and Henrietta's housekeeper, Dotty, brewed a superior one.

"You know, my dear, you're very good for my son," the older woman observed suddenly as she handed the cup and saucer to Victoria. "And for my granddaughter, too."

"Why do you say so, ma'am?" Victoria asked, surprised by her comment. She had been thinking exactly the opposite.

"Until you came here, Steede and Mary seemed to have forgotten how to laugh or cry, or feel any of the emotions that make up the fabric of our lives! They simply . . . existed, day in, day out, until you arrived. Now look at the dear child, barefoot as a tinker's brat, dabbling her toes in the river!"

"You approve?" Victoria asked, surprised.

Laughing, Henrietta nodded her silver head. "I certainly do! Another grandmama might not, but it does my heart good to see the darling girl so— so carefree, after all the sorrow in her young life. What did you do with that wretched nursemaid of hers? Lock her in the cellars?" Henrietta asked, lowering her voice to a conspiratorial whisper.

Victoria smiled. "Not at all. Kalinda and I have come to an understanding. She understands that I will not back down, and *I* understand that I will not back down!"

Henrietta laughed in delight.

"I told her Lady Mary would be taking tea with her grandmother and myself this afternoon, and that her services would not be required until five. Kalinda wisely remembered she had some unfinished darning to do in her room."

"Do you intend to dismiss the woman eventually?"

After a moment's thought, Victoria shook her head.

"No. Merely to wean Mary away from her by degrees, so that she is exposed to influences other than Kalinda's, and to places other than the nursery and schoolroom.

"I want Mary to see me as a trusted friend, not someone who is trying to take her mother's place in her heart. Someone who cares deeply about her. And because I care, I want her to become comfortable in those social situations in which she will find herself as an adult. Kalinda has been her nurse since she was an infant. Naturally, the child loves her like a mother. It can only hurt Mary if they are separated. I believe she has endured hurt enough."

"Mary would also bitterly resent you, were you to separate them entirely. I'm sure you've considered that? This way is far less upsetting, for everyone concerned. You're a clever girl, Victoria—wise beyond your years."

Victoria conceded her point and accepted the compliment with an incline of her head.

"Steede's changing, too. Likewise for the better. There's a—a sparkle in his eyes that wasn't there before." Henrietta's dark eyes twinkled as Victoria blushed.

"If there is a change, it is a very little one, I'm sure, ma'am."

"Do not be so modest, Victoria!" Henrietta scolded. "Take credit where credit is due, and thank me for my compliments, do."

Victoria laughed. "Then, thank you."

"Why *did* you marry my son, Victoria?" the older woman asked suddenly. "I'm afraid I don't believe that fairy tale he told me. The one about love at first sight? Lovely as you are, my son has never been impulsive."

"That question is one you must ask Steede, ma'am, for I shall never answer it."

Now it was Henrietta who laughed softly. "Ah. Then I was right. Well, whatever your reasons, I foresee a happy future for the two of you, nonetheless. You are becoming fond of him, despite your determination not to—no, my dear, don't even begin to deny it! And he—well, I see the same softening in him."

"With all due respect, ma'am, I believe you are mistaken," Victoria protested stiffly. "What my husband feels for me is—well, it is not love." She quickly looked away, her cheeks growing warm.

"What is it then? Desire?" She smiled at Victoria's shocked expression. "And why should he not desire you? You are an intelligent, beautiful, desirable young woman, and he is a normal, hot-blooded man. Of course he desires you, child! Ahh. You consider it improper for ladies to discuss such matters. Perhaps it is so, in polite company. But you and I are quite alone here, are we not? And becoming, I thought, close friends?"

"I hope so, yes."

"Then consequently, I say to you, Victoria, that there is nothing wrong with the two of you desiring each other." She leaned across and patted Victoria's knee. "And remember. Great and enduring love has been founded on far less than mutual passion."

"But Aunt Catherine says that—"

Henrietta threw up her hands. "Catherine! That explains it. I should have realized. Victoria, your Aunt Birdie—while a dear gel, and my oldest friend—is far too prim and proper for her own good. Her mother, Maude, was exactly the same way, God rest her soul. My John used to say it was a consequence of lacing their corsets too tightly!" Henrietta confided with a wicked chuckle.

"To Birdie, the part her poor husband played in the conception of their daughters was a necessary evil. Something to be endured but never, ever enjoyed." Henrietta's dark eyes sparkled naughtily. "I feel sorry for all that she missed, for I welcomed my darling John into my bed every single night of our marriage."

"Then it is proper for a young woman such as

myself to . . . to take pleasure in her marriage bed?"

"Why on earth not? You are husband and wife, after all. Besides, I suspect those who say that it is improper are those who have never sampled its true delights, darling girl. Be proper at the table, if you must. Be proper at church, too, of course. And most certainly be proper in polite society. But in your marriage bed, in your husband's arms—? *Never!* Be his mistress. His beautiful, mysterious lover. His delightfully *improper* wanton. Then you will be the wife he never tires of—or replaces with another woman."

"Another woman?" a deep voice exclaimed. "And what other woman would that be, *Mother*?" Steede demanded, climbing the gazebo steps and shooting Victoria such a wicked glance, she knew he'd overheard at least the end of their conversation.

She smothered a sigh of irritation, for his unexpected arrival had once again prevented her from asking her mother-in-law the question that, lately, was always on the tip of her tongue. The one about Aimee, her first daughter-in-law, and how she had died.

"Why, Steede. How wonderful of you to join us. Won't you have some tea? I'll have Dotty bring us another cup, shall I?" Henrietta offered, squeezing the hand Steede placed on her shoulder as she looked up at him.

He shuddered. "Lord, no. Never touch the wretched stuff. I prefer more civilized drinks," he declared, taking a seat and stretching out his long legs.

"Whisky or brandy, no doubt," his mother supplied dryly.

"To name but a few." His smile faded. "Look here, I didn't come to take tea, pleasant though the company may be. I came to escort my wife and daughter back to the house. Mother, tell Dotty to be sure to lock your doors tonight."

"Why? What's happened?" Henrietta demanded quickly.

"Some convicts escaped from Dartmoor Gaol last night—nothing to be alarmed about yet," he added quickly, noting the widening of Victoria's eyes. "But until they're apprehended, or we have proof that they've fallen victim to the moors, we should all be on our guard. They'll be hungry and desperate for money and a change of clothing in which to make good their escape. And desperate men commit desperate deeds."

A short while later, Victoria walked back to the Manor, her arm linked through her husband's as they strolled along.

Mary—now fully dressed in her white kid boots and white stockings—skipped along beside them both.

As they walked, Victoria considered the surprising advice Henrietta had given her before Steede's unexpected arrival. A smug little smile spread across her face.

Perhaps it was more by accident than by design, but she was doing the very things her mother-in-law had suggested to draw Steede closer to her. In their bed, she was his mistress, his mysterious lover, his very improper wanton. The question was, did she really *want* to draw him closer?

She caught his lambent dark eyes upon her as she looked up, and her heart raced in response.

More and more of late, it seemed, her answer was an unqualified "yes!"

Chapter Fifteen

The end of August was as glorious as its beginning, with long golden summer days that melted into sultry evenings filled with the scent of the night-blooming cereus, the bright wink of fireflies in the hedgerows—and her husband's ardent lovemaking.

Though she had yet to discover how his first wife had died, it didn't seem so important anymore. Steede was proving a most attentive husband, both in her bed and out of it. And, much to her surprise and delight, he was fast becoming her friend and companion, too, for they had discovered other mutual passions besides their love of horses. The works of Shakespeare, Dickens and the American writer Hawthorne.

All things considered, she was happier than she had ever been. Her life had settled into a rou-

tine that, while fulfilling and pleasurable, was
not at all boring.

Most mornings, she and Steede took breakfast
with Mary, then Steede went to his study to meet
with his secretary and attend to the estate's correspondence and accounts, or else he rode out to
the Home Farm or nearby towns such as Tavistock or Plymouth on the estate's business.

Immediately after breakfast, Victoria met with
Lily. Together, they went over her schedule for
the day, selected what garments she would need.
She left Lily to determine whether the chosen
items would have to be set out, brushed, laun-
dered or pressed.

The day's wardrobe taken care of, she then met
with the butler and the housekeeper in turn to
balance the household accounts and discuss the
menus, then tackled her own correspondence,
which included personal letters from Aunt Catherine and her three cousins, Imogene, Lettie and
Patience, and numerous formal invitations.

When Victoria asked Steede's advice about
whether to accept the invitations they were receiving, he in turn suggested she ask his mother.

"For my part, I'm not eager to regain entry into
Society. Devil take the lot of them, I say! After all,
the bloody gossips haven't been exactly kind to
either of us, have they, my dear?" he reminded
her with a thin-lipped smile. "You, they labeled
the scarlet lady, while I was Lord Scandal himself!"

Henrietta, however, became very excited and
dismissed Steede's reservations out of hand.

"What do men know of such matters, my dear? You should accept as many invitations as your calendar permits! They are the means by which you and Steede may properly take your places in Society. And—whether my son admits it or not—trust me, Victoria; it is in your best interests to be accepted by your peers. Since the ton will not be returning from the Highlands until after the end of September, these invitations will provide you with the means to make valuable allies before the others return from Scotland!"

Henrietta's eyes sparkled as she shuffled through the stack of stiff cream envelopes.

"Look at how many you have, my dear! Here's one to a Harvest Ball to be given by the Duchess of Devonshire, no less! Marguerite is a darling, you know. And this one here is to Lord Linden's country estate for a shooting weekend in September. You'll have such a grand time! Steede's an excellent shot, you know, and Lindy's not one to pinch pennies when it comes to entertaining. And this one here, to Viscount Sheffield's evening of caroling and entertainments in London at Christmastide—oh, the timing couldn't be more perfect."

It was the custom for Society couples to follow the royal family to Balmoral, Scotland. They would take up residence in the Highlands for endless rounds of houseparties and shoots during the grouse season, which began on August 12, and lasted through the end of September, before returning to London in October.

"Naturally, these invitations are largely the result of everyone's curiosity about your sudden marriage. There are many who will presume—because of your elopement—that Steede compromised you in some way. Your appearance together as a devoted couple will scotch the rumors. Truly, it is an auspicious beginning. A decided change in the way the wind has been blowing since that other sad business."

Since Henrietta—insofar as Victoria knew—was unaware of the gossip about herself and Ned, the "sad business" she was referring to could only be the death of Steede's first wife, and his subsequent resignation from the Army and return to England.

Here was the perfect opportunity for her to ask her mother-in-law the question she'd been burning to ask, ever since she came to Blackstone Manor. *Lady Henrietta, I've been wondering. How did Lady Aimee meet her tragic end?*

But as so often happens, the moment, once there, was quickly past and gone. Henrietta's voice trailed away, and the conversation moved on to the matter of which invitations to accept, and which to decline, and her question, once again, went unasked.

The next two hours of each morning she spent with Mary in the schoolroom, a time she was beginning to look forward to enormously, for Mary was far from being the unschooled child they had thought her. On the contrary. She would answer the questions Victoria put to her by scrawling her reply on a slate—replies that were, invariably, spelled correctly, too. For a child of her age and sex, the extent of her knowledge and vocabulary was quite remarkable.

When Victoria asked Mary who had taught her to read and spell, she wrote a single word by way of answer: *Papa*.

But when Victoria asked Steede about it, he was as astonished to hear of his daughter's talents as Victoria had been.

"I did try to teach her to read and write, after a fashion," he admitted. "It was after the doctors had examined her and found nothing wrong. I thought if I could teach her to write down what she wanted to say, it might help. So I spent an hour or two with her every day. But after a few months with no apparent progress, I gave up. On the surface, it appeared my efforts had failed. Apparently, I was wrong."

He was obviously delighted, if perplexed, by this revelation.

Twice a month, Victoria asked Harry to ready the little curricle with the yellow wheels and bring it around. With Mary perched on the seat beside her, she drove into the village of Blackstone to pay calls on the vicar, Reverend Mortimer, and his lady, Charlotte Mortimer, at St. John's Manse. Other afternoons, the two of them took baskets of fresh produce, jams and bread from the Manor's kitchens to the cottages of the parish's poor or infirm.

It was while on a similar charitable visit to Whitby's sick that Victoria had first met Betty Thomas's youngest son, Ned, she recalled, and lost her foolish heart. And perhaps—she now believed—her mind, too!

She shook her head. It was amazing how time could change one's entire outlook. Whereas once, Ned had been the center of her universe—her moon, sun and stars—this was the only time she'd thought of him in *weeks*. Her feelings for him had been fragile, false things, compared to those she had for her husband.

On a glorious afternoon in early September, Victoria hurried downstairs to meet Steede for their afternoon ride, buttoning her kid riding gloves as she went.

Mary and her ayah were in the marble entryway when she reached the foot of the stairs, either having just come in from some excursion or other, or preparing to leave.

Mary was wearing an adorable blue dress with a white sailor collar and a red bow this afternoon, yet another of the talented Mrs. Stacey's creations. A saucy straw boater with a trailing blue ribbon crowned her red-gold hair.

"Why, how very grown-up you look today, Lady Mary," Victoria greeted her gaily, making her a sweeping curtsey. "Kalinda, good afternoon." She nodded graciously to the nurse. "Where are you ladies off to?"

Mary eyed her guiltily, flushed, then quickly looked down at her boots. She seemed uneasy, Victoria thought. As if she wanted to say something—a decidedly unlikely event, given the child's continued silence.

The Indian woman inclined her dark head, her expression carefully blank, her silver bracelets chiming musically.

"If it please the memsahib, we are going to the village shop to buy silk. The Lady Mary, she is embroidering the sampler for Sahib Warring's Christmas stocking, yes?"

"A sampler? How ambitious of you, Mary. I had no idea. Do you enjoy embroidery, then?" Victoria asked, curious.

It was plain from the way Mary glared at her nurse that she did not.

Victoria laughed. "I don't blame you. I detested sewing when I was your age. Dancing was all right, but I much preferred riding Goblin, my pony, although I had a very handsome dancing master," she added, eyes twinkling.

Mary's scowl lifted. Her eyes shone at the mention of ponies.

According to Lily, who talked to Harry every chance she had, the little girl haunted the stables whenever she could escape her nurse, feeding the horses with carrots and sugar lumps, and petting them.

Their mutual love of horses was an interest worth pursuing, Victoria decided, if it would bring her closer to the child.

"I've been thinking. Perhaps we should ask your papa about getting you your own pony soon, hmmm?" Steede had mentioned that he intended to buy one for Mary's birthday, so she was not giving her stepdaughter false hopes. "And riding lessons, so that you may accompany us on our rides from time to time. What do you say to that?"

A radiant smile would have been reward enough for the suggestion. But, to Victoria's delight, Mary flung her arms around Victoria's legs and hugged her.

Bending down, Victoria gathered the little girl to her, stroking her bright hair.

"Oh, darling Mary," she whispered, wrapping her arms around the little girl. "I've been wanting to cuddle you again for such a long time."

But, obviously embarrassed by her show of emotion, Mary soon tugged herself free of Victoria's arms and bolted back upstairs.

After a few seconds, Kalinda bowed and hurried after her—though not before Victoria saw the smirk of triumph on her face.

"Go ahead. Smirk all you want, Kalinda," she told the gleaming suits of medieval armor and the busts of Shakespeare and Socrates in their niches. "Perhaps Mary did run away this time. The important thing is, she *hugged* me first. I'm gaining ground with her, Kalinda, whether you like it or not!"

Elated by Mary's show of affection, she hurried outside, eager to tell Steede of this new development.

To her surprise, when she went outside, Steede was leading Calypso and Mercury from their stalls. Both animals were saddled and bridled. None of the grooms, with the exception of the tackboy, Toby—who was simple, according to Lily—were anywhere in evidence.

"Where is everyone?"

"Gone. I sent Harry and the lads ahead. If all goes well, I'll need them to bring back the new horses."

"Horses?"

He nodded. "That's right. I was just about to come inside and offer my apologies. I can't accompany you this afternoon, Victoria. There's a horse fair in Tavistock," he explained. "And I need plough horses for the Home Farm. I should have told you before, but I didn't realize today is the last day."

"I see. So it has all come down to this. Married but four months, and I have been passed over in favor of a horse," she said, trying to sound sad but unable to keep from smiling, for he cut a dashing figure in his black riding jacket, breeches and boots.

"Ah, yes. And a plough horse, at that," he agreed, winking at her. "Two plough horses, in fact. I need them for the Home Farm, as our poor old fellows are ready to be put out to pasture. Then there's the matter of finding a likely pony for Mary. It's her eighth birthday next Wednesday, and she loves horses."

"I know. Oh, I'm so glad you're getting her one! I just this minute told her we thought she should have a pony. When I promised to remind you, she actually hugged me!"

"Did she really?" Steede shot her an envious look.

"She did. She loves horses so much. She must take after you."

He grinned down at her, his black eyes sparkling like jet in the sunlight, his crisp black hair tousled by the wind, as if she'd just rumpled it, she thought suddenly, her thoughts wandering.

"Or her stepmama," he added, tossing the horses' reins to Toby. Catching her about the waist, he drew her against him, ignoring the tackboy's slack-jawed grin.

"How long will you be gone?" she asked, smoothing down the lapels of his hacking jacket and trying to hide her disappointment that they wouldn't be able to ride together. All morning, she'd looked forward to having him to herself.

"I should be back by this evening, if I find what I want."

"Good. Then I'll ask Cook to delay dinner until you get home, and we'll dine together by the drawing-room fire, as we did my first evening at Blackstone."

"Splendid." He seemed surprised by her suggestion, yet pleased, too, if his broad grin was anything to go by. "And after supper, I think we should have an early night, don't you? Damned tiring things, these horse auctions . . ." His voice dropped, becoming a sensual growl as he nuzzled her hair, her ear, then gently blew into it.

"I'm sure they are," she agreed demurely, as goosebumps prickled down her arms.

"And? Will you miss me this afternoon?" he demanded.

"Of course. I always look forward to our rides."

"I see. And exactly how much will you miss me?"

"Oh, a little, I expect."

"A little? That's all?" His black brows rose.

"Oh, all right. A lot."

"You won't miss me horribly? Dreadfully? Hugely?"

She sighed, laughed and playfully punched his chest. "I shall miss you terribly, horribly—awfully—you wretched man! Now are you satisfied?"

"I am indeed. And I suppose I shall miss you, too. A little."

"You rogue!"

Instead of lifting her into the saddle, he continued looking down at her, his hands clasped about her waist.

"A penny for your thoughts, my lord Blackstone?" she teased huskily, wondering what was going on behind her husband's broad tanned brow and onyx eyes.

"Hmmm?"

"I said, a penny for your thoughts, milord," she repeated.

"Just a penny? What I was thinking about is worth far, far more than your penny, Lady Blackstone," he murmured, chucking her beneath the chin.

His smile had become sad somehow, his tone bittersweet, all teasing gone.

Was he thinking about his first wife, she wondered suddenly, jealous of a woman long gone.

". . . for it is unobtainable, and therefore priceless," Steede continued. "Now I must be off, or I

221

shall have to forgo inspecting the horses before I bid on them. Up you go, my dear!"

With that, he lifted her up onto the saddle.

As she settled, Calypso shied violently. If Steede had let go, Victoria would have fallen from her back to the cobbles.

Snorting, the edgy mare tossed her head.

"Whoa, there!" Steede commanded, grasping the shying horse by the cheek-strap to hold it steady, while Victoria recovered her seat.

Calypso snorted as Victoria hooked her right foot over the sidesaddle peg. Then she shortened the reins, and the mare circled, kicking up her back legs.

"Steady on, girl. What's wrong with you today, hmm?"

Victoria tried to sooth the snorting, pawing mare. "Steady, now, baby. Steady."

In answer, Calypso tossed her dainty head. Ears laid back, she rolled her eyes so that the whites showed, still sidestepping and circling nervously, her hooves clattering on the cobble-stones.

"She doesn't seem herself today," Steede said. "I'd feel better if Harry took a look at her before you took her out. Ride another horse, Victoria."

"But she's perfectly fine now. Look. She's just a little skittish, that's all. Aren't you, my sweet baby?" Victoria crooned, patting the mare's glossy neck.

Steede frowned, still doubtful, but as she said, the animal did appear to have settled.

"I don't like you riding alone when she's acting up."

"I promise you, I'll be perfectly all right. I always rode alone in Yorkshire."

She was reluctant to mention such a delicate matter, but it was possible the mare was coming into season, and was acting skittish because Steede's stallion was nearby.

"Go! Go and find Mary the perfect pony for her birthday," she urged. "A little coal-black one, just like Calypso here."

"You're sure?" Steede said, eyeing first Victoria, then the mare. "You'll be all right?"

"I'm positive," Victoria confirmed, warmed by his obvious concern for her safety. "See you this evening at dinner!" she called over her shoulder as she rode off.

"Miss me!" he ordered.

"I will! *Horribly!*" she responded with a silvery peal of laughter.

He watched as Calypso walked away from him, down the driveway.

All four of the Arabian's elegant legs looked sound enough, but the horse still seemed edgy, sidestepping and tossing her head.

"What d'you think, Toby?" he wondered aloud, aware that the tackboy was hovering at his elbow. "Should I go after her?"

"Music," Toby said excitedly, tugging at Steede's sleeve. "Pretty fairy music. Toby hear. Come. Toby show you."

"Not now, lad," Steede said kindly, patting

223

Toby's shoulder. "Go muck out those stalls for Harry."

"Mr. Harry gone," Toby said, nodding happily. "Harry my friend."

As Toby shuffled off, Steede continued to stare after his wife. Victoria was an excellent rider, an accomplished horsewoman who knew her mount well. If she felt the mare would settle, then it would, he told himself.

Shading his eyes against the dazzling sun, he watched the trim figure in royal-blue velvet ride gracefully away.

But as he stared after her, a cloud came from nowhere to cover the sun, and cast him in shadow.

And, although it was a warm August day, he shivered.

Chapter Sixteen

Victoria regretted refusing Steede's offer of another mount long before they'd clattered through the village's cobbled streets and plunged into the woods beyond.

Calypso was so difficult to control that riding her was no pleasure at all today. Indeed, it took every ounce of Victoria's strength, not to mention her skills as a horsewoman, just to keep her saddle. She rarely used her crop, but today she touched it sharply to the mare's flanks to urge her forward.

"Come on, baby. Don't you want to run? Let's go!" she coaxed.

With a shrill scream, Calypso reared up, almost unseating her. Her front hooves struck solid ground only briefly before she kicked up her hindquarters and bucked, trying to unseat

Victoria. The very second all four hooves landed again, she took the bit between her teeth and bolted.

The autumnal woods flashed by in a blurred band of red and gold as Calypso gained speed, Victoria clinging desperately to her reins.

As the mare plunged blindly through the heavy undergrowth, springy branches whipped back, slashing Victoria's cheeks, leaving behind red, angry weals and bloody scratches.

As the horse burst out of a thicket, it startled several ravens feasting on a dead rabbit in a tiny clearing. The huge birds rose into the air in an ominous black cloud, flapping their black wings directly beneath Calypso's hooves and cawing loudly.

The sounds and their sudden violent movement panicked the mare even more, forcing a fresh burst of speed from her.

Seconds later, they were up on the high moors, the mare's hooves drumming the turf as she thundered on, careening toward the hazy band of blue and gray of the distant sea, with Victoria clinging to her back like a limpet.

At any moment, Calypso could step in a rabbit hole and shatter her leg, Victoria thought, desperately hauling on the reins in a frantic effort to halt the mare. Then they would have no choice but to shoot her, she thought, a sob catching in her throat.

Afraid for her beloved mare, she spared no thought for what her own fate might be if she were thrown at such a speed.

The possibility did not even enter her head until she was airborne, sailing over Calypso's head, with the ground rushing up to meet her.

I'm going to die, she thought incredulously.

A brilliant flash of white filled her skull as she landed. Then there was only blackness, dark and infinite.

Steede found his stablehands at the horse auction being held on the commons outside the market town of Tavistock.

Nearby, a band of Gypsies had set up camp, their colorful wagons, or *vardos*, drawn up about a cooking fire from which a thin ribbon of smoke unraveled, rising between the treetops.

A number of sloe-eyed, handsome women dressed in long skirts and with bright kerchiefs fastened over their black hair were milling about the camp, as were several ragged children. But there was no sign of their Gypsy menfolk. They must have taken the band's horses to be sold at auction.

The camp dogs barked and snapped at Mercury's heels as Steede rode past, giving chase until an old crone smoking a clay pipe screeched at the beasts to quiet down.

A crowd of onlookers was bidding on several riding horses as he rode up. The auctioneer, Jeremiah Price, was a man Steede had done business with in the past, and respected.

Price was touting the mounts being walked by the grooms as "eminently suitable for genteel or elderly ladies desirous of a docile, steady mount."

Steede stopped to watch the animals being put through their paces, his attention caught by a spry little Welsh pony as black as polished jet.

A long, shaggy forelock spilled over its forehead, almost hiding its bright, liquid brown eyes. An equally luxuriant black mane and a long, full tail completed the little gelding's handsome looks. The small, sturdy beast also had a beautiful gait and a gentle if mischievous temperament.

"Ah, good. You've spotted him, too, my lord! I were looking at that little 'un afore they started the bidding," Harry observed as he appeared at his master's shoulder. He jerked his chin at the pony. "Handsome little beast, ain't he, sir? And just as gentle as ye please, for all that he's a bit of a rascal. Sound in wind and limb, too, from what I could tell, and will ye look at the shine to him! He's been well cared for, I wager. If ye like him, milord, I think he'd do right well for Lady Mary."

"I agree," Steede murmured, watching as the pony trotted nimbly after its handler, then nuzzled the lad's pockets for a carrot.

When he was satisfied that all appeared well, he started back toward his horse.

"Harry," he told the groom over his shoulder, "stay here and bid on that pony, then pick me out a pair of good plough horses for the Home Farm. Tell the auctioneer—his name's Mr. Price—tell him that you're my head groom, and to send all bills to the Manor for settlement."

"You're leaving, Your Lordship? But—beggin'

your pardon, sir—where will you be, sir?" Harry called after him as he headed back toward his horse.

Steede stopped and turned to Harry, his expression grave. "Have you ever had the sense that something was wrong?" he asked heavily, as if he were wondering out loud. "A feeling so strong in here"—he gestured to his gut—"that it consumes you?"

"Aye, sir. I have."

Steede nodded. "Well, I have that feeling now, about Her Ladyship. I've had it all the way over here. I still have it now, and I can't ignore it any bloody longer. Calypso was acting up when I left Blackstone. I should have stayed. Gone with her. Made sure Her Ladyship was all right. But I didn't, damn it. So, I'm going back there right now. I only hope to God I'm not too late."

"My old granny says we should heed such feelings, milord—and that little mare, she's usually as steady as they come. Always has been! With all due respect, milord, I'm coming back with you," Harry insisted gruffly, his jaw stubbornly set. "My Lily 'ud never let me hear the end of it if summat happened to Her Ladyship and I did nowt to stop it!"

"All right, man. The bloody horses can wait—except for that pony. Price!"

"Aye, Your Lordship?" the auctioneer responded, doffing his hat and peering at Steede over his gold-rimmed spectacles. The circle of bidders turned to stare at him, too.

"That black Welsh pony, Lot Fifteen, what was the last bid?"

Price named a figure.

"I'll top it by twenty guineas!"

"Very good, sir." The auctioneer looked about the circle of faces. "Do I hear fifty guineas?" Silence. "Fifty guineas am I bid?" Nothing. "Very well, then. Fifty going once, going twice—*sold!*" His hammer came down. "Lot Fifteen goes to Lord Blackstone of Blackstone Manor!" the auctioneer bellowed. He nodded in Steede's direction. "Thank you very much, milord. An excellent choice.

"Next on the docket, we have a steady mare, five years old, stands fifteen hands . . ."

Steede's blood ran cold as he rode into the Manor's stableyard a little over an hour later.

Calypso stood alone in the stableyard, neither rider nor saddle on her back. Her dainty head hung down dejectedly, and even from a distance, Steede could see the dried lather that crusted her black coat, the congealing blood that caked her side. Fresh blood trickled from a raw pink wound where the saddle pad should have rested.

As Steede reined Mercury in, frozen by dread, Harry hurried forward, whistling under his breath as he went to catch the horse's cheekstrap.

Calypso shied away from him at first, then snorted in greeting and stood quietly, twitching once or twice as Harry ran gentle hands over her, crooning the soothing words she'd learned as a filly in his care.

"Eeh, the poor little lass has a right nasty rip right here, sir. Apart from that, she seems unharmed. Just a bit upset, aren't ye, my lass? I'll put her in a stall; then we'll look for Her Ladyship."

Steede nodded, so filled with dread he was unable to speak. He stared at the trees lining the driveway, trying to see beyond them, to Victoria. Afraid he might actually be able to see her—and not like what he saw one bit.

All he could think of was the day of their first picnic. Of Victoria telling him that her mother had been thrown from her horse and broken her neck on a day very much like this one. Of her father's sense of foreboding when he saw her mother's horse clatter, riderless, into the stableyard at Hawthorne Hall. . . .

Had Victoria suffered the same fate as her mother? he wondered. Was she out there somewhere, sprawled on the muddy turf, her lovely neck broken, her iris-blue eyes staring blindly up at the sky above her . . . ?

So great was his fear that history had repeated itself, the blood seemed to chill in his veins.

"*No!*" The anguished word burst from his throat unbidden, like a curse. His fingers curled into huge fists at his sides. "No, d' you hear me?" he seethed under his breath. "Not again. Never again!"

Whom he was addressing was unclear, but Harry thought His Lordship was probably talking to God. He clamped a hand on His Lordship's shoulder and squeezed.

"Now then, milord. Don't ye be after thinking about that," Harry murmured in the firm voice he used to calm his horses. "I wager we'll find Her Ladyship walking home an' cursing like a bloomin' trooper because her girth broke!"

"I pray to God you're right, man," Steede said fervently, his jaw set and hard, his black eyes emptied of light. "Let's go!"

Touching his heels to old Jasper's flanks, Harry clattered after him.

Victoria opened her eyes to find something cold and wet plastered to her brow. Her right temple throbbed. Her head ached terribly.

An ancient face was looking down at her, like a gargoyle. It was a seamed, whiskery face, with numerous moles that sprouted white hairs. Straggly gray locks hung down to bony shoulders shrouded by a grubby smock. The lips were sunken in over the mouth, like a drawstring, as if the man—for a man it was, and an old one, at that—was missing most of his teeth.

The old fellow looked like something out of a nightmare, except for his eyes, which were watery blue and very gentle and kind.

"Now, now, don't ye fret, mum," he soothed as she struggled to sit up. " 'Tis only Old Tom Foulger, what tends His Lordship's sheep hereabouts. My little Blackie found ye, aye, Blackie?"

A cold, wet nose pushed its way into her hand.

She heard a dog whimper. Blackie, then, was his sheepdog.

"My—my horse," she whispered hoarsely. She struggled to sit up, but her head swam so much she was overwhelmed by nausea. Sinking back down, she closed her eyes and waited for the dizziness to pass.

The shepherd replaced the wet rag that had fallen off her temple. Its icy coolness soothed the bruise, and helped to silence the hammer that was pounding in her skull.

"Don't try t' stand yet, mum. 'Twere a powerful thumpin' ye took when yer horse threw ye."

"Her legs. Is she sound?" she asked, terrified of what his answer would be.

Old Foulger chuckled. "Oh, arr. She sartainly looked that way t' me, mum. Racing like a black wind, she were, when last I saw 'er. I were still looking for the poor beastie's hurt when her took fright an' run off."

Victoria tried to raise herself again. This time she succeeded, though not without her stomach heaving in protest.

Tom Foulger and his little collie dog, Blackie, watched as she struggled to stand up. Carefully wiping his hands on his smock, Foulger offered her a helping hand, which she gratefully accepted.

On a slab of black rock several feet away, she saw Calypso's saddle.

"What happened? Did the girth break?" she asked, swaying from side to side as she nodded at it.

The shepherd shook his head. "Nay, mum. It were me. I took t' saddle off of her."

"You did? But why?"

"Hold 'ee hard, mum, an' I'll show ye." Hefting the saddle up into his scrawny arms, he carried it back to her.

"Blood was a-coming from under here, mum," he murmured, indicating the saddle pad, "so I unbuckled this 'ere strap t' see where it might be a-coming from, aye? But the very moment I lifted it off 'er, the lass ran away, quick as winking, like she were right happy to be rid of it, aye? An' here's the reason for it, mum, make no mistake."

Old Tom turned the saddle over, and Victoria gasped.

Fully half of the saddle pad was soaked with blood—and like Tom, she could see the cause.

It was an intricately designed cravat pin, she saw, and quite exotic. The shaft tapered to an ornately detailed, engraved silver head that was shaped like an eagle's talons, gripping a perfect black pearl. Its steel shaft had been threaded through the cloth several times. The exposed inch of sharp steel caught the sunlight with a dull wink, while the point showed traces of dried blood. *Calypso's* blood.

Victoria bit her lip. Oh, the poor little baby! Every time she'd rested her weight on the saddle, this wickedly sharp pin had been driven into her mare's back, time and time again. No wonder the mare had thrown her! But how in the world had a cravat pin ended up in such an unlikely place?

Her hands started to shake as she considered

234

the possibilities. An accident? Hardly! A cravat pin did not find its way into a saddle pad by chance, nor thread itself in and out of the cloth, so that most of its wicked length lay hidden, like a snake in the grass!

No, someone had put the pin there intentionally, then made certain it would not easily come out. And that someone could have only one reason for doing such a thing.

They had wanted her horse to throw her. Had wanted her hurt—perhaps even killed!

But who in the world would do such a thing? Who hated her that much?

Harry, the head groom? Never. Harry would no sooner harm a hair on her head than would Lily. Somebody else, then. Someone who not only hated her, but stood to benefit from her death.

The name that sprang to mind immediately was Kalinda—or failing Kalinda, Mary herself. But she immediately dismissed both woman and child as unlikely suspects. Whoever had done this had also had access to her horse, and Kalinda did not. Which under-groom had saddled Calypso that afternoon? she wondered, trying to gather her thoughts despite the painful throb in her temple. . . .

The last of her strength ebbed when she remembered that it had been no groom. Steede had led the mare from the stable himself, along with his stallion. And both animals had already been bridled and saddled when he did so.

Her hands shook as she withdrew the sharp

pin from the saddle pad and slipped it into the deep pocket of her velvet skirt. What was it Steede had told her? That all the grooms, including Harry, had been sent ahead to the horse auction on Tavistock common.

Which meant he'd had ample opportunity to saddle their mounts. Had he also hidden the cravat pin beneath hers?

Dry-mouthed, she swallowed, overwhelmed by sadness and doubt, and by the crushing sense of betrayal that filled her. Had all the scandal, the rumors about Steede, been true, then? Had he really murdered his first wife? Was he now trying to murder his second?

No, screamed her heart. Steede was gentle, kind—and falling in love with her, just as she was with him! She knew it, *felt* it. The man who held her in his arms each night, and kissed her with such tenderness would never hurt her.

Would he?

Of a sudden, she remembered him as he'd been the night of the storm, with the rain and wind swirling his cloak and ebony hair about him. The threatening, powerful figure he'd cut, backlit by flashes of white lightning as the runaway coach careened toward the cliffs.

Rain had streamed down his furious, handsome face in silvery torrents. Wet black locks had snaked over his collar and clung to his temples and brow. Black eyes had blazed like banked coals as he roared at her to leap from the coach.

In that moment, he had looked like Lord Lucifer, in the flesh. A violent, deadly dangerous man, who was more than capable of murder. . . .

"Mum? Don't be getting up, now! White as a blessed ghost, ye are," Old Tom exclaimed.

But she ignored him and scrambled to her feet, her legs wobbling as she tried to stand, her poor head reeling.

Deaf to the shepherd's pleas for her to wait while he fetched help, she stumbled toward the woods and Blackstone Manor beyond them.

Which was the real Steede, she wondered dazedly as she went? The tender lover who made her heart and body sing with delight when she lay in his arms? Or the calculating Bluebeard who, for motives known only to himself, killed his brides, one by one?

She shuddered. Until she knew the truth, one way or the other—until she'd decided what to do, and where to go—he must never suspect that she'd found the pin. She would have to be very careful.

Her life depended on it.

Chapter Seventeen

Still dazed and disoriented, she managed to find her way down from the high moors, into the woods.

Moving at snail's pace in her bruised and confused state, she tottered to and fro like a drunkard, burrs clinging to her riding habit, stray twigs whipping at her face, leaves catching in her hair. From time to time, she was forced to halt and cling to rough tree trunks for support, fighting the nausea and dizziness that threatened to overwhelm her.

She heard the two horsemen riding at breakneck speed through the dense woods long before they reached her.

Frightened that whoever had engineered her fall had returned to finish the job, she quickly hid behind a broad oak tree, pressing herself up against its rough bark. Moss crumbled beneath her scratched and bloodied cheek, and a twig snapped loudly under her riding boot as she hid herself. But, breathing shallowly in case they heard her, she stood perfectly still as the pair halted their horses in the center of the little clearing.

The carcass of the dead rabbit, abandoned now by the greedy ravens, lay like a forgotten bundle of rags and fur to one side.

"Which way now, sir?" she heard Harry ask, adjusting his flat cap and flicking a brown cowlick from his eyes.

"To the left. Look at all the broken branches, those trampled grasses over there," Steede said, indicating the route by which Calypso, startled by the huge birds' flapping wings, had fled the open area. "Something big crashed through there, wouldn't you say?"

Harry gave a low whistle. "That I would, m'lord. The mare must ha' been travelin' summat fierce, to do that. I'm thinking she bolted."

"Or else threw her rider." Standing in the stirrups, Steede cast about him on all sides. His black eyes narrowed as he scanned nearby bushes, drifts of leaves and grassy tussocks, looking—she knew—for her crumpled body.

Her heart raced so violently she thought that at any moment it might leap from her breast. Calypso must have galloped straight back to the stables at Blackstone Manor. But what had Steede been doing there? And Harry, too? Steede had told her he and his grooms were riding over to the horse auction on Tavistock Common—close to an hour's distance on horseback. Had the horse auction been a ruse to persuade her to go riding alone? Perhaps his talk about needing plough horses and birthday ponies had been nothing more than a smokescreen.

To give the devil his due, if Steede was guilty, he was a consummate actor. He looked beside himself with anxiety as he sat his silvery-gray stallion in the glade. He'd certainly convinced Harry of his sincerity, she saw, for the head groom gave his master an anxious side glance, then clapped a reassuring hand across his back.

"Now, then, m'lord. Chin up, aye? We've found nowt yet. And chances are, there's nowt to find, eh?"

"I hope to God you're right, man," Steede agreed, looking no less anxious, despite his words.

Her husband's handsome, sun-browned face was gray and drawn beneath its tan, his brow furrowed with concern. Deep worry lines bracketed his sensual mouth and winged away from the outer corners of his eyes. Even his hair and clothing appeared disheveled, quite unlike his usually immaculate attire. But was his anxiety due to his concern for her safety—or to his burning desire to know if she had survived the fall from her horse?

She could hear her heart thundering in her ears in the few seconds it took for the men to ride on. When they were gone, she swayed, clutching the oak's trunk for support. Earth and sky swapped places momentarily, before she could recover her equilibrium.

God, she felt so queasy still, so terribly dizzy. And her head—! It was pounding so badly she was afraid she would be sick. She should have listened to Tom, the shepherd, and waited until he could bring someone to take her home, to Blackstone.

If only Harry had been alone. She would have called to him, begged him to take her up behind him on old Jasper. But until she had determined Steede's true motives, she dare not.

After the two men had ridden off, she stumbled on, weaving her way between the endless, silent oaks, the birches and chestnuts, until she had left the woods behind.

Tottering shakily across the ancient stone bridge that spanned the Tamar, she reached St. John's Manse on the outskirts of Blackstone.

As she stumbled down Church Lane, lined with Italian cypresses and somber yews, clutching the iron palings that enclosed the churchyard for support, she saw the vicar talking to the sexton. The gnarled little man was up to his armpits in the grave he was carving from the black Devonshire soil.

The macabre thought crossed her mind that perhaps her husband had ordered the grave dug in readiness for her . . .

The thought left her feeling faint and dizzy.

Sick to her stomach, she leaned against the lych-gate, badly in need of its support.

"Reverend Mortimer!" she called, but could manage only a reedy croak for help.

Reedy or not, it served its purpose.

The reverend turned. A broad smile of greeting broke over his cherubic pink face. The brown eyes twinkled behind the classical scholar's gold-wire spectacles.

"Lady Victoria! My, my, what a pleasure to see you again so soon," Reverend Mortimer exclaimed, striding toward her down the grassy path that wound between the mossy gravestones. "Charlotte will be delighted to—*Your Ladyship!*"

He caught her just as her knees buckled.

"Willie, here!" she heard a frantic voice calling the gravedigger.

And with a sigh, she fainted into Mortimer's arms.

"How is she, Alec?"

"Sleeping. I gave her a draft of laudanum. She seemed very agitated, I thought."

"Unusually so?"

"Yes. Any idea why she should be?"

"None whatsoever, no. But she will recover?"

"Good Lord, yes. I thought you knew that."

"Damn it, Alec, you're the physician, not me! What was I supposed to think? Her mare returns without her, or its saddle, and the next thing I hear, my wife has swooned in Dick Mortimer's arms and is at the vicarage, being tended by Charlotte Mortimer. What the deuce was I supposed to think?"

"Sorry, Steede. I wasn't thinking. Rest assured

that I have every expectation that your lady will make a complete recovery in just a day or two. And while I'm here, may I offer you my warmest congratulations on your marriage, old man, despite the fact that I was conspicuously absent from the wedding feast?"

"You and everyone else I know." Steede rolled his eyes heavenward. "I may as well tell you, before you hear it from someone else. Truth is, we eloped. Back in June."

"Did you, indeed? Well, I can certainly see why! You do manage to wed the most incredibly lovely women, you rogue! Personally, I can't imagine what they see in you."

Steede smiled grimly, the laughter never quite reaching his eyes. "Nor I, Alec. Nor I."

"Anyway, I've ordered complete bed rest for a week, to allow the swelling on Her Ladyship's temple to go down. A few days' rest won't hurt her. After that, she may resume all of her usual activities, if she feels up to it. But if she complains of nausea or problems with her vision, send for me immediately, all right?"

Steede nodded. "Will do. Now, how about a drink?"

"Don't mind if I do. Perhaps a toast to your wedding?"

Steede went to the liquor cabinet and opened the doors. "Whisky?"

"No, thanks. A glass of port, if you have it. I find strong spirits in the middle of the day tend to make me sleepy—and I still have a surgery full of patients to see, not to mention house calls this afternoon."

"Port it is then," Steede agreed, splashing the deep-red wine into a glass.

Victoria lay in her bed, unclothed, the sheet drawn up to her chin. Her eyes widened with terror as the connecting door that led to her husband's room—grown to several times its normal height, in some incredible fashion—slowly opened, its hinges screaming like souls in torment.

As if motion could be slowed, she watched Steede as he strode slowly toward the bed. He stood there, towering over her, looking impossibly tall and dark and devilishly handsome. His striking black eyes were bottomless pools that glittered with nameless desires.

"I love you, Victoria," Steede mouthed, but she could not hear what he was saying. She could only read his lips.

Casting aside the white Turkish towel he'd wrapped about his lean waist and muscular flanks, he joined her in the bed, caressing and kissing her with lips and hands of fire until, all pride vanquished, she broke and begged him for more. Implored him to take her, make love to her. To hurry, please hurry!

Immediately, he lifted himself over her. Kneeling between her thighs, he raised her hips and entered her in one powerful thrust that arched her up off the bed.

Head thrown back, eyes closed, she parted her

lips in a primitive scream of sheer pleasure as he began to thrust, caressing her breasts, kissing her throat, filling her and withdrawing again and again.

"Steeeeede! Oh, God!" she screamed as wave after wave of pleasure ricocheted through her. Colored lights exploded like fireworks against her closed eyelids. Exquisite pulses tugged at her womb, making her gasp in delight.

"Oh, love, my dearest love!" she sobbed breathlessly.

But when her eyes flew open, it was not her husband who towered over her. Not the Steede she knew and loved who rode her mercilessly.

The creature that mated with her was a demon, caped in swirling crimson satin that spread, like wings, over them both! The great, hairy devil-goat had curling horns and blazing black eyes that brimmed with crimson and gold. The demon was Lord Lucifer in the flesh! The devil incarnate! Satan, Prince of Darkness—

—and her lover. Her husband. The man that scandal had once christened "the Brute"!

"Noooooo!" she wailed, tossing her head wildly from side to side. "Let me gooooo!"

"Hush, darling. It's only a dream. Victoria! Wake up!"

She heard Steede's deep voice commanding her to wake up as if she were at the bottom of a well.

Opening her eyes—*really* opening her eyes this time—she saw him standing over her.

Rather than a flowing crimson cape, he wore

a simple white shirt of Egyptian cotton, minus the collar and studs, the sleeves rolled up to the elbows, and trousers with braces. Instead of curling horns upon his head, his black hair was only disheveled, his stern face unshaven and dark with stubble.

No demon lover at all, in fact, but a weary, concerned husband. One who gripped her wrists and shook her gently to rouse her from her frightening dreams. A man who, though he might not have donned the horns of Satan, was, nevertheless, a possible murderer behind that mask of handsome normalcy.

She cringed from him.

"Let me go," she croaked. "Take your hands off me! I'm awake, I tell you. Let go!"

He released her and stepped back.

"You were screaming and thrashing about," he explained. "I was just trying to keep you from hurting yourself. What was it? A nightmare?"

She nodded but would not meet his eyes. "Yes," she whispered.

"Would you like some hot milk or cocoa to calm you?"

His words recalled their wedding night, when he had given her hot cocoa to warm her, and she'd been afraid he had poisoned it.

She feared the same thing now. . . .

Looking up at him, she knew by his expression that he had guessed what she was thinking.

"Victoria, what is it—?" he began, reaching out to caress a stray curl that fell across her brow.

Immediately, she shrank back against the pillows, squirming out of his reach.

"You need not be afraid of me, damn it!" he snapped, his patience splintering. He ran an agitated hand through his hair. "Surely by now you know that I could never hurt you, Victoria. Victoria? Look at me! For God's sake, talk to me!"

"I'm—tired, that's all. And I need more sleep. These wretched nightmares give me no rest at all. I told Dr. Riggsby that laudanum always makes me worse. You must . . . you must forgive me."

Her apology seemed to mollify him, for he nodded. The broad shoulders sagged. "Victoria, whatever you may believe to the contrary, I had nothing to do with your accident," he told her quietly. "Any more than I had anything to do with my first wife's death."

She met his impassioned response with stony silence, one he realized now that he would never breach by words alone. Nor would she permit him to soften her resolve, her fear of him, with gentle kisses and caresses. For when he would have brushed his lips over her cheek, she stiffened. And when he tried to hold her hand, she quickly drew it aside.

After several moments of crackling silence, he murmured, "Well, if there's nothing you need, I shall bid you a good night. Sleep well, Victoria."

With that, he left her alone and went below in search of a badly needed whisky.

But it wasn't until he had been gone for several moments that Victoria released the breath she'd been holding.

*   *   *

She awoke again in the wee hours of the night, as had become her habit in the week since her fall from Calypso, to find that someone—probably Lily—had turned the lamp wicks very low. Only a gentle golden radiance flowed from the gas lamps' flower-painted globes. The banked coals behind the gleaming black grate glowed a pure orange-pink.

She sucked in a breath as she turned her head on the pillow, startled to discover that she was not alone.

A man was seated in an overstuffed wing chair before the hearth, his shoulders slumped, his dark head cradled in his hands.

Dr. Riggsby? she wondered. No. Not the doctor. It was Steede.

Giving no indication that she was awake, she watched as he suddenly got to his feet, muttered something unintelligible, then strode across the room. He went straight to the huge mahogany wardrobe that stood in the corner, where her clothes were hung.

He turned once to look over his shoulder—perhaps to make certain she was still asleep?—before opening the wardrobe door.

With bated breath, she watched through slitted eyes as he riffled through the garments that hung there, stirring the lacy sachets and pomanders as he slid aside several rustling gowns on padded satin hangers.

The faint fragrance of dried rose petals, lavender and honeysuckle wafted across the room. It tickled her nose and made her want to sneeze. But with an effort, she managed to smother the urge and lie absolutely still.

After several moments, Steede obviously found whatever he was looking for, because he stopped searching. She saw the lamplight wink off a small, shiny object in his hand, before he quickly tucked it into his trouser pocket and closed the wardrobe door.

The cravat pin? she wondered.

"Victoria?" he asked softly, coming to stand at the foot of her bed.

Through half-closed eyes, she could see he was holding a needlepoint pillow in both hands. *Oh, dear God! He intends to smother me with it!*

"Victoria?" he repeated. "Are you awake?"

She gave no answer, squeezing her eyes tightly shut. But, despite her apparently deep, heavy sleep, inside she was rigid, coiled like a spring, ready to roll aside and leap from the bed the instant he pressed the pillow over her face.

But a moment later, he swore under his breath, turned on his heel and left the room, closing the door carefully behind him with a barely audible "click."

When, after several minutes, she opened her eyes again, she saw the cushion was back on the wicker chaise longue next to the window, where he had found it.

Thank God, he had gone.

But she did not dare fall asleep again that night, in case he returned to finish the job.

And so she lay there, wide-eyed and wakeful,

staring up at the rose wallpaper until the first rays of sunlight fingered their way between the parting in the draperies, to crawl across her flower-strewn walls.

"Well, now. You're looking better this morning," Lily greeted her cheerfully as she bustled into the room what seemed like moments later.

Better, despite the fact she'd hardly slept a wink? Despite the fact that her eyes were red and gritty-feeling, and that she could not seem to stop yawning?

"Glory be! That great bruise has faded. Do ye feel like getting up today, my flower?"

"Do I! I've wasted an entire week lolling about in this wretched bed. An entire week, can you believe it? That horrid Dr. Riggsby simply won't listen to reason! Lay out my plaid morning gown, would you, Lily dear—the one with the red sash and piping? I think its bright color will lift my spirits." *And perhaps lend me some Dutch courage?* she added grimly.

For, until she could devise a way to leave his household, she was virtually a prisoner at Blackstone Manor, and at its master's mercy.

"Right you are, my lass. Brrr." Lily shivered, rubbing her hands together and hunching her shoulders. "It's nippy this morning. Thee'll be wearing a woolen shawl t'go down t'breakfast or I'll know the reason why, my lass," Lily said firmly, sounding even more like Rose Lovett, her mother, than usual.

"Bossy wretch! But if you insist," Victoria conceded readily as she tossed aside the covers.

Lily was right. There was a distinctly wintry chill in the air this morning. Fastening the sash of her dressing gown, she took her seat on an overstuffed stool before the dressing table.

While Lily unplaited her hair, she kept up a stream of cheerful chatter that washed over Victoria, only half-heard. Instead, she inspected her reflection in the looking glass, turning her head this way and that.

The face that stared back at her was very pale against the midnight hair that spilled in a wild black torrent down her back. Her face looked thinner, too. The high cheekbones were more pronounced than before, the iris-blue eyes larger and shadowed with pale lilac. The phrase "her haunted eyes" leaped to mind from the pages of some tawdry novel or other. On her reflection's temple was a faded green-and-yellow bruise the size of a fist. It served to remind her of her husband, and her need for caution.

"By the way, where is everyone?" she asked Lily casually.

Behind her own reflection, Lily paused to consider the question, a silver-backed hairbrush in hand.

"Well, let me see. Lady Henrietta popped in a while ago from the Lodge. She left a nice bunch of mums downstairs for ye, and says she'll be back t' take tea with ye this afternoon, if ye're feeling up to it."

"Lovely. I'm sure I shall be. And what about Mary? What's she been doing?"

"She's either in t' schoolroom or t' nursery,

where she's been every day since thee were laid up. Proper glum she's lookin', too, poor little mite. Not much of a birthday for her, is it, the lamb, not with you abed and all? Just eight, and her actin' like she's eighty!"

" 'Poor mite,' is it! I thought you didn't like my stepdaughter?" Victoria asked, amused. In the week she had been laid up, there had apparently been considerable changes made, in terms of attitude, at least.

"I didn't, but the little lass has grown on me, like, aye? The child can't be all bad, I told mesel', not if she loves my Lady Victoria so."

"Do you really think she does, Lily?" Victoria asked eagerly. "Love me, I mean?"

"Do I ever. Been like a pale little shadow, Lady Mary has, ever since ye took that spill. Once or twice I caught her hanging about by your bedroom door, like she wanted to come inside, aye? I told her ye weren't dead, if that were what she was worried about. That ye'd banged your head, but were on the mend, you know?"

"You should have let her in."

"I told her if she wanted t'see ye, she could. But she looked at me with those great gray eyes, then ran off like a frightened rabbit! Still, Cook's making a chocolate birthday cake with icing for this afternoon's tea, and there'll be trifle and custard and her favorite sandwiches, too. Cream cheese and cucumber. Not to mention sausages for breakfast, too!"

"Wonderful!" Bangers sounded delicious, after the bland invalid's fare she'd been served this week. "And what of—what of His Lordship? Where is he? Is he at home?" Dare she hope he'd gone to the Quarterly Assizes in Plymouth?

"Bless him, His Lordship's downstairs in his study. He says if ye're feeling up to it, he'd like ye to come down to the breakfast room, so ye can give the little lass her birthday gift together." Lily's almost dreamy smiled betrayed that her sentiments were well and truly in her master's camp.

"Ah, the long-awaited pony," Victoria declared, thrusting aside unsettling memories of Steede, his striking features gilded by ruddy firelight as he rummaged through her wardrobe, searching for the weapon with which he'd hoped to bring about her destruction. Or of Steede looming over her bed like a hovering hawk with glittering jet eyes, hugging a tapestry pillow to his chest. Or of Steede smiling as he offered her hot chocolate, laced liberally with hemlock . . .

"Oh, but I wouldn't miss it for the world!" she lied gaily, swallowing her misgivings. "Have you seen the pony yet?"

"Have I! By gum, he's a bobby dazzler, that 'un." Lily grinned. "Black as coal, he is, and just as fat as a barrel of lard! But he's not all looks— he's a canny little beast, too, and just as gentle as they come."

"He sounds wonderful. Hurry up and finish my hair, do!" Victoria urged. "I can't wait to see him."

"And His Lordship?" Lily asked hopefully.

Victoria wrinkled her nose, a grimace designed

to hide the uneasy flutters that filled her belly whenever she thought of Steede now. "I suppose I'll have to see him, too, if we're to give Mary her gift together, don't you think?" she said levelly, refusing to look at Lily.

"But you're not looking forward to it? Being wi' His Lordship, I mean. Not like ye were before?" Lily prodded, obviously disappointed by her mistress's lack of enthusiasm.

"I really don't know what you mean," Victoria hedged airily. "Lord, my stomach is queasy still. I think just some tea and toast for me this morning, don't you?"

"Stop it, do. Don't ye go changing the subject on me, my lass. You know very well what I mean. Ever since the accident, ye've shied away from that handsome husband of yours, whereas before, ye were fairly panting after him, like—well, I don't rightly know what like!"

"How can you say such a thing?" Victoria protested indignantly. "Panting, indeed. I certainly was not panting!"

"Ye were, too. But summat's happened, hasn't it? Ye can hide it from others, my girl, but not from me. I know ye too well. Do you blame him for it—is that it?" Lily asked earnestly, her brown eyes shiny with tears.

"For my accident, you mean?" Victoria asked warily. What did Lily mean by *blame*, exactly? Did she share her own suspicions about Steede?

"Aye. Because he didn't come with ye that day. And because he didn't save ye when Calypso threw you. God knows, the poor love blames himself for it. I've never seen a grown man so glum about owt as your husband about this. You wouldn't believe the questions he's been asking my Harry and the other grooms about that afternoon—!"

"I . . . I suppose I do blame him, in a way," Victoria lied. Better Lily should believe that than guess the truth: that Steede had probably tried to kill her! "Gracious! What on earth has become of the tea this morning? Did they go to Ceylon to pick the leaves? Be an angel and fetch me a cup, would you, Lily dear?" she coaxed. "I'm parched."

"Right away, love." Lily clicked her teeth in annoyance as she set down the brush and patted Victoria's neatly arranged hair.

The wild tangle of Gypsy curls had been tamed, fashionably parted in the middle, then swept up on either side of her head and braided. The end result, of intricate, glossy black braids looped against petal-pink skin, was very fetching.

"Wednesday must be Em's day to bring up the morning tea trays, I warrant. Always late, that one is. I told Mrs. Hastings she's just as simple as that Toby, what with his spoutin' on about hearing fairy bells an' such nonsense!"

While Lily, still clucking like an old hen, bustled downstairs to fetch her up a cup of tea, Victoria sped across the room to the wardrobe. Opening the door, she burrowed inside and quickly found what she was looking for—her blue velvet riding habit, beautifully steamed and brushed and mended, following the accident.

She reached deep into the skirt pockets, hoping against hope that she would find what she had hidden there.

Empty.

Crushed with disappointment, she quietly closed the wardrobe door and returned to her padded stool before the dressing table, sitting down again in a sort of daze.

Now she knew exactly what Steede had been searching for last night. *The eagle claw cravat-pin.*

Now it was gone. The last trace of evidence that would link Steede to her fall had been safely removed.

The scene was set for him to try again. . . .

Chapter Eighteen

"Are you ready for your present? Good. Then, close your eyes, birthday girl!" Steede instructed, nodding at Victoria to fasten the silk scarf around Mary's eyes. "And mind you keep them shut until I tell you to open them. Victoria, you take her right hand, I'll take the left."

Holding a giggling Mary between them, they led the blindfolded girl out of the breakfast room, across the marble entry hall and through the kitchens.

There, a beaming Cook and her three scullery maids bobbed their little mistress curtsies and chimed in unison, "Happy birthday, Lady Mary. Many happy returns of the day!"

From the kitchens, the trio skipped outside, urging Mary to be careful of the step leading down to the cobbled yard.

Victoria noticed that Mary's breathing had quickened as they left the house. A rosy flush was beginning to add a blush of color to her fair complexion. The little girl must have guessed what was coming next. She could hardly contain her excitement!

Sure enough, in the stableyard stood Harry, a red leather bridle in hand. He was wearing a broad grin as he tipped his cap to them. "Mornin', Your Lordship. Lady Victoria. Happy birthday to ye, Lady Mary."

"Morning, Harry. Are you ready, poppet?" Steede asked his daughter, also grinning.

For the moment, caught up in the fun, Victoria forgot her fear of him. "Nod if you're ready for your surprise, darling!"

After a moment's hesitation, Mary nodded vigorously. She gripped Victoria's fingers even tighter and bit her lower lip.

"All right. Victoria. Take off the blindfold," Steede urged her.

Her eyes met his. "No," she softly refused. "This is your gift to Mary. That honor is yours."

"Thank you," he said gratefully, clearly surprised by her generosity.

A deft flick of the wrist, and the blindfold slid away.

"You can open your eyes now, pet," Steede said softly.

Mary blinked. Her jaw dropped as Harry stepped aside, whisking away a horse blanket.

For the first time, Mary saw the adorable little

black pony that was hidden beneath it, tossing its flowing black mane.

"Happy birthday, poppet," Steede murmured. "His name is Sooty, and he's all yours!"

A look of joy, of disbelief and wonder, suffused the child's face as she looked wildly from the pony, then back to Victoria and Steede, as if she could not comprehend her good fortune.

"Go ahead. Harry will put you up on his back," her papa urged, laughing at her dumbfounded expression.

To his delight, his daughter threw her arms about him and hugged him, then did the same to Victoria, before Mary went flying across the stableyard. She came to an abrupt halt before the coal-black pony.

Little girl and horse stared at each other for an endless moment, the pony's liquid brown eyes meeting Mary's solemn gray ones.

It was clearly a case of love at first sight for both of them, for the Welsh pony snorted and nuzzled his new little mistress's hands, into which Harry had slipped a lump or two of sugar, and an apple.

While the pony nibbled his treat, Mary threw her arms around Sooty's neck and buried her face in his rough mane, her eyes shining beacons of happiness.

"Ye'll ride astride like a lad until your twelfth birthday, Lady Mary. Then I'll teach ye t' ride with the sidesaddle, like Her Ladyship," Harry promised with a grin. "Oopsadaisy, my lass!"

So saying, he lifted the girl astride the tiny

saddle of soft scarlet leather, then placed her little hands correctly on the matching reins. "Heels down," he instructed. "Toes up. Sit up straighter—aye, that's it, my lass. That's the way of it! Ye'll be riding like a champion, come next birthday! Come along wi' ye, Sooty, my lad," he crooned, leading the Welsh pony toward the paddock behind the stables.

Mary squealed in delight as the pony broke into a bouncy trot that tossed her up and down in the saddle, her joyful laughter ringing out on the damp October morning.

Steede and Victoria exchanged quick, pleased glances. The rare sound brought lumps to their throats and moisture to their eyes.

"You couldn't have done anything that would have made her happier, Steede," Victoria observed.

"This once, I would have to agree with you," he murmured, a ghost of a smile playing about his lips. "And, now that my daughter's happiness has been assured, I believe it is only fair that I secure my own. Wouldn't you agree?"

She would have turned and walked back inside, but he caught her elbow. "I said, wouldn't you agree, Victoria?" he repeated.

"I suppose it would be fitting, yes," she agreed uncomfortably, wanting only to run and hide from him.

"Ah. And how do you suppose I could secure my happiness?"

"I really couldn't say, sir—nor am I in any mood for parlor games," she said coolly. Color filled her cheeks that had nothing to do with the weather, but a great deal to do with the hungry way his black eyes devoured her—like a starving man devoured hot bread!

"Perhaps, for a start, I could convince Mary's stepmother that she truly has nothing to fear from me? That I want only her happiness, and nothing more? How about that, for a beginning?"

"Let go of me. You're hurting my arm." He wasn't, but she didn't want him to touch her. Couldn't trust herself if he did.

"No. You've avoided me long enough. You, Toby! Wait there!" he ordered, without letting her go. Rather, he strong-armed her toward the stables by her elbow, propelling her along so swiftly her feet hardly touched the ground. "Tell Her Ladyship what you heard that afternoon. The one when Harry left you in charge of the horses, remember?"

They stood where Toby loitered, half in and half out of the stables, blocking his exit. Perhaps sensing the underlying anger in Steede, the slow-witted tackboy looked shifty-eyed and sullen, ready to bolt past them to freedom.

It was apparent he had not come to expect much kindness in his fifteen or so years, for when Steede reached out to give him an encouraging pat on the back, he ducked his greasy dark head in reflex, as if expecting a hefty clout instead.

"Mr. Harry, he say Toby's in charge," he volunteered suddenly, puffing up with pride. "Toby grooms His Lor'ship's horses, like Sammy an' Mr. Harry."

263

"I'm sure you're an excellent groom," Steede agreed mildly. "Can you saddle a horse, too, Toby?"

"Aye!" Toby declared, grinning and showing a crooked fence of yellow teeth. " 'Tighten the girth like so, Toby, my lad! Don't let 'er blow out 'er belly,' " Toby said in a deep voice quite unlike his own. He was obviously repeating instructions Harry had given him.

Steede nodded. "Good man. And what about that afternoon? The one when Harry went to Tavistock to buy Sooty? What happened that afternoon? Did you saddle any horses for Harry that day?"

Toby nodded eagerly. "Cally and Merc'ry. Later, Uncle Willie come up from the vicar's. Uncle Willie say the pretty lady hurt! Pretty lady, there!" he repeated, pointing at Victoria. His expression was sad as he touched the side of his own head.

"And how was she hurt?" Steede persisted with far more patience than Victoria would have thought him capable of—and more gentleness than any other man she knew, she thought uncomfortably.

The gentle image of him did not sit well with her convictions that he was a homicidal lunatic, though if she were honest with herself, he had never been less than gentle with any man or beast, that she knew of.

"Do you know what happened to her?"

"Cally hurt. Cally throw the pretty lady off!"

"Cally? By that, you mean Calypso?"

"Caly'so," Toby agreed, vigorously nodding his head.

"I wonder. Why would she do that? Cally's a gentle little lady. Do you know why, Toby?"

To Victoria's amazement, Toby's eyes filled with tears that rolled down his cheeks and dripped off his chin. He nodded and looked down at his scruffy boots. "Aye."

"Tell me, Toby."

"No! Toby go now!" he insisted, wiping his runny nose on his jacket sleeve.

"Not yet. You can go as soon as you tell me. *Why* did Cally throw the pretty lady?"

"Cally hurted," Toby whimpered, rubbing his side. "Cally hurted here. Blood, blood all over! Poor Cally . . ."

"Is this what hurt her, Toby?" Steede demanded, taking the cravat-pin from his pocket. "This pin here?"

The lad gasped. His muddy brown eyes became saucers. He tried to lunge past Steede, bent on escaping, but Steede caught him by the shoulder and would not let him go. In his desperation, he shook the boy. "Toby, please. Answer me!"

"Wasn't Toby! Wasn't!" the lad sobbed. "Lemme go!"

"Who was it then? Just tell me who it was and you can go home. Don't you want to go home, Toby?"

Toby nodded, fresh floods of tears streaming down his grimy cheeks. "Toby go home. Toby's a good boy."

"The name, then. Just tell me the name. Who

asked you to saddle the horses that day? Who hid this pin under Cally's saddle?" His tone was urgent as his black eyes bored into the youth's. "Tell me, lad!"

Toby's lower lip wobbled tremulously. "It were t'fairy-music lady. She tell Toby, saddle Cally and Merc'ry, boy! The fairy lady!"

"Good lad. Run along home now," Steede urged, releasing the lad and patting his shoulder.

With a sudden relieved grin, Toby bolted, loping off down the driveway like a frightened hare.

"Well. You heard him. Now do you believe I had nothing to do with your accident?" he demanded, turning to Victoria.

"What is there to believe, my lord? The poor lad is a simpleton—hardly a reliable witness to anything! What's more, I don't have a clue who his 'fairy-music lady' might be. Don't tell me you do?"

Steede shot her a thin-lipped smile. "Yes. Don't you? Really?"

"I told you, no."

"Then you've never noticed the pretty sounds made when silver bracelets strike each other? There's a silvery chime—an almost fairy-like musical ringing. And there's only one person in this household who wears such bracelets."

"Kalinda," she whispered.

He nodded. "That's right. She's Toby's fairy-music lady. It can be no other."

Victoria said nothing. What he was suggesting confirmed the suspicions she had harbored about Kalinda from the very beginning, when she found the rose petals strewn in her bed. But she was equally convinced that Kalinda had not acted alone. No. Steede was also deeply involved. He must be. How else would he have known about the pin? Toby's story was merely the result of coaching on Steede's part. Nothing more. A desperate attempt to divert suspicion from himself, onto his cohort, and lull her into trusting him. After all, whose story would prove more convincing to the authorities? The testimony of a respected, wealthy peer of the realm—or that of an Indian serving woman?

"My God! You still think I'm involved, don't you?" he exclaimed, reading her expression. "No, no, don't bother to deny it, my dear! I can see it in your face. All right, then. You tell me. Who has a better reason to want you gone than Kalinda?

"Mary has reached the age when she needs a mother and a governess, rather than a nursemaid. And she has both in *you!* Like it or not, when you married me, you became a very real threat to Kalinda's future here, Victoria, don't you see?" he asked earnestly, his expression grave. "With you at Blackstone Manor, there is *no longer a reason for Kalinda to be here!* She knows it, and she is terrified she's going to be dismissed. That is why she has gone to such great lengths to make Mary completely dependent on her. I didn't realize it at first, but now that I've put two and two together, it's obvious. It's the same reason she must get rid of you. As long as Mary needs her, and rejects me, her place here is secure."

"It's a possible explanation, true," Victoria admitted. "And plausible, too, after its fashion. Unfortunately, she is not the one I hold ultimately responsible!"

Whirling around so that her skirts flew up and the fringes of her fluffy angora shawl whirled around her, she ran over to the paddock.

There Mary, her pretty face transported with delight under a small black hard-hat, was riding around and around, perched on Sooty's broad back, while Harry called encouragement from the fence.

Steede glared after Victoria, cursing under his breath as he followed her. He knew she neither liked nor trusted Kalinda. So why the devil didn't she believe him?

When it came, the answer, although obvious, was one he found distasteful in the extreme.

For all that she mistrusted Kalinda, she mistrusted him—*her own husband!*—even more!

Chapter Nineteen

"Victoria? You have to wake up!"

"Hmm?" she murmured drowsily. Opening heavy-lidded eyes, she saw Steede leaning over her. He was stern and unsmiling in the dim lamplight. A glance at the window showed the yellow and charcoal skies of dawn through a gap in the draperies.

"Where's Lily? And what on earth is the time?" she asked drowsily. "It isn't even light outside yet! What are you doing in my room?" She had locked both the connecting door between their rooms and the door that led out onto the gallery, before retiring. He must have a second key.

"It's just after five-thirty. Lily will be here soon to help you dress. Victoria, I have some bad news for you, I'm afraid."

"Bad news?" His announcement banished the

last residue of sleep. Suddenly filled with apprehension, she sat up. "What is it? Tell me."

"Lovett arrived on this morning's milk train from London. He brought a letter from your Aunt Catherine. It seems your father is missing."

"Missing!" Victoria echoed, swinging her legs over the side of the bed. "What do you mean by missing? Lost at sea?"

"No, nothing like that. Apparently your father went down to the jet mines to meet someone last Monday evening, and has not been seen since." Steede hesitated, wondering how best to continue. "They fear . . . they fear he may still be down there. In the mines, I mean."

"Those shafts are like a rabbit warren! They riddle the cliffs! People have wandered around down there for weeks, and never been found! How long has he been missing?" she demanded.

"As far as I can determine, he disappeared a week ago."

"That long! Why wasn't I informed sooner?" she demanded, furious that no one had bothered to let her know.

"According to your Uncle Lovey, Lord Hawthorne's people have been busy scouring the countryside for him ever since. It was not known that he was down in the mine until he'd been missing for three days. When your Aunt Catherine arrived from Lincoln, she elected to wait another day or two before informing you, hoping against hope that her brother would be found."

"But he wasn't," she declared indignantly, sounding very much like her father in that moment. Her blue eyes narrowed shrewdly. "What else is there? There's something you haven't told me, isn't there?"

He nodded, wishing he could spare her this. "Victoria, my dear," he said very gently, "I'm afraid it doesn't look good for your father."

"Tell me anyway," she insisted, although she had gone very pale. Steede sounded grim indeed.

"The police believe he arranged to meet someone down in the mine. He and this man then quarreled and came to blows. They believe . . . they believe he beat your father very badly."

Victoria's hand flew to her mouth, to stifle the sob that would have escaped it. "I must go home. I have to leave immediately!" she whispered.

"Of course. I'll join you as soon as I can," he promised firmly, as if he expected some argument. "By this weekend, if all goes well. Lily will go with you, of course. I asked Mrs. Hastings to wake her. She'll be readying your things even as we speak."

"Thank you," she murmured, wondering, not for the first time, how he could seem so genuinely concerned for her well-being if he truly wanted her dead.

"You will tell Mary why I've left so suddenly?"

"Of course."

"I—don't want her to think I've abandoned her."

"I'll take care of it."

Standing, she slipped her arms into the ruffled white dressing gown he held out for her, and with a shiver, wrapped its folds tightly around her.

"Cold?" Steede asked, noticing the shudder.

"And frightened," she whispered, stiffening as he drew her back against his chest. And, although she did not soften in his embrace, nor did she shrink from it.

She closed her eyes, yearning to melt into his arms, wanting him to hold her and soothe away her fears.

How many other mornings had he held her in almost the same way, cupping her breasts, stroking and caressing her, until her knees grew weak with longing? How many mornings had he drawn her back against his lean frame like this, so that she was pressed against the hard ridge of his loins, as she was now. And how many times had he whispered endearments in her ears, promising endless delights, until he led her back to bed?

Now, as then, he dipped his dark head, angling it to kiss her throat, her cheek, the skin still warm and flushed by sleep.

"Please, don't," she whispered.

"Tell me why you shivered just then? Is it me?"

She shook her head. "Noo," she told him truthfully. "For a second, I felt as if someone had walked over my grave. I'm all right now, really. You can let go."

"It's going to be all right, Victoria," he promised softly, sensing her unspoken needs. "They'll find your father, and they'll bring him safely home. You must believe that."

"I do. Truly, I do," she replied, yet her voice was breaking. Dear Lord, she was so frightened, so close to surrendering, she was almost willing to accept his claims of innocence, in her need for comfort.

She stepped forward, so that their bodies were no longer touching. His hands fell away from her. "Ring for Lily, would you?"

He nodded. "Of course." With an unfathomable expression in his black eyes, he stepped away. "I'll leave you to get dressed, while I arrange for Harry to bring the carriage around. If you hurry, you can make the six-fifteen to London. Oh, and wear something warm. It's cold outside."

"I will. Thank you," she murmured politely, turning her head away and refusing to look at him. Yet she could still feel where his hands had cupped her breasts, as if her flesh were branded by his touch.

"You are very welcome, my dear," he said softly. "As always."

The timbre of his voice somehow filled her with shame.

When she turned back again, he was gone.

By six, they were ready to board the coach that would whisk them away to the railway station. Fifteen minutes to spare. Lily—ever efficient— had outdone herself, Victoria though absently.

"Take care of yourself, Victoria," Steede urged, taking her hand and squeezing it as they stood by the waiting coach.

"I shall," Victoria promised stiffly, giving him a nod.

"Aye. And if she don't," Lily piped up from the depths of the coach, "we will, right, Da'?"

On the seat opposite the women, Uncle Lovey smiled and nodded. "That's right, love. Don't thee worry about nowt, m'lord. Her Ladyship will be right as rain."

"Since she will be in your capable care, Lily, Mr. Lovett, how could I ever doubt it?" Steede murmured, smiling.

Though she remained stiff and unyielding, Steede drew Victoria's kid-gloved hand to his lips, then cupped her pale face and kissed her full on the lips.

"I shall join you by week's end, my dear," he murmured, lifting her up, into the coach. "I'm sure your father will have been found by then."

"I pray to God you are right," Victoria whispered. Rather than the poised, remote woman of moments ago, she knew she sounded like a frightened little girl, fearful for her missing father, but she couldn't seem to help it.

"Sir! The six-fifteen! See the smoke above the trees? She's coming down the Blackstone line, sir!" Harry sang out urgently.

"I see her! Lay on, man. My guinea says you miss it!" Steede wagered his new head coachman, slapping the side of the coach and stepping back.

"Not a chance with these beauties, sir! Yeehaa! Gee' up there, lads!"

As the whip cracked in the air above their

glossy backs, the matched team of grays pulled swiftly away from the grand entrance of Blackstone Manor, headed for the Blackstone Station in the village at a fine clip.

From the lead-paned nursery window high above the portico, a small, distraught face watched the high-stepping grays enter the avenue of glowing beeches, afire with autumn foliage. Seconds later, both horses and coach vanished from view.

Chapter Twenty

"Tell me what happened, Carter. Everything!" Victoria instructed the Hall's butler, peeling off her gloves and unpinning her hat as soon as she entered Hawthorne Hall.

Without so much as a sidewards glance, she handed gloves and hat to Lily, who—like her mistress—had already removed her cloak and was bustling about, instructing a footman where to put their bags.

Carter's expression was grave as she led the way into her father's study.

"I expect Mr. Lovett has told you all there is to know, Your Ladyship. His Lordship received an anonymous note a week ago, instructing him to come alone to the jet mines at dusk, where he would meet the sender and learn 'something of the utmost importance.'

"I didn't like the sound of it one bit, madam, so I recommended that His Lordship ignore the missive. Unfortunately, being of an obstinate nature, the master regrettably refused my advice. He implied that he knew very well who had sent it, but that he intended to meet the bast—er, that is to say, madam, the—er—the blighter—anyway and have it out with him, once and for all. When I suggested that myself and some of the lads from the Hall accompany him, he refused, on the grounds that it smacked of cowardice."

"I see. And who did my father think the sender was?"

Carter's eyes slid uncomfortably away from hers. He cleared his throat. "I—er—I'd rather not say, madam."

"On the contrary, Carter," she repeated in a stern voice. "You will tell me, at once."

"You're your father's daughter or I'm a Dutchman, madam!" Carter muttered. "It was Ned Thomas, madam."

Victoria's shoulders sagged. "I see." The identity of the letter writer answered several questions she'd had. "And my father has not been seen since he left here to meet Mr. Thomas?" It was not so much a question as a statement.

"No, Your Ladyship. When he failed to return home by dawn, Lovett and I took a few of the lads and went to the mine. Just in case His Lordship had run afoul of Ned Thomas in a vengeful frame of mind, you understand?"

Victoria nodded. Carter had his origins in the cockney stews of London, her father had told her once. The strangely crooked nose, which had been broken several times in fistfights and left to heal by itself, revealed that—despite his polished veneer—the butler was no stranger to the rougher elements of society.

"Well, me an' the lads, we took a look 'round, but there was no sign of them, or the 'orse."

Samson. Her father's hunter.

"With His Lordship's nag gone, we reckoned His Lordship had left the mines and gone elsewhere."

"Don't blame yourself, Carter. I would have come to the same conclusion—although I gather yours was proved incorrect?"

"Regrettably, yes, madam. Me and the lads came back to Hawthorne Hall to await His Lordship's return. We were still waiting two evenings ago, when the copper—that is, the police constable—came to the Hall. He'd ridden over from Haverleigh village in the next county, he said. Ned Thomas had been drinking in a pub there the night before, shouting up pints and flashing pound notes like a nabob. Come into an inheritance, he had—or so he claimed," Carter added darkly.

"Apparently, someone in the pub had bought a fine gray hunter from the bloke for a fraction of its worth. Another bought a gold pocket watch off him. When the inscription on the watch and the name of the man in question didn't match, the authorities decided t' take the bloke in for questioning. But before they could nab him, he'd scarpered."

"Scarpered, Carter?" Victoria frowned.

"Right, madam. That is to say, *ran off. Escaped.*"

"I see."

"While Ned was in his cups, he boasted that he'd 'toed the scratch and gone a round or two' with Old Thorny, a mine owner from Whitby, then left him for dead in his own mine. He seemed to find the idea most amusing. Well, the Haverleigh police had heard that Lord Hawthorne was missing, so they dispatched a constable to Whitby to inquire after His Lordship's whereabouts."

"So what my husband told me is no exaggeration. My father could very well be dead," she whispered, abruptly sitting down behind the desk in her father's leather chair.

"I cannot lie to you, madam. I regret to say it is very possible, after all this time." His voice was thick with emotion.

"I see." Victoria fell silent, chilled by what Carter had told her. The situation was even worse than she had feared. "And I regret to say, I must agree. If my father was still alive, he would have found his way out by now, don't you think?" Victoria said softly, staring into the fire.

"It's very hard to say, Your Ladyship. But if you'll forgive me for saying so, His Lordship is a tough old bast—um, bird. If anyone can survive something like that, it's him." Carter grinned.

"Have they found Ned Thomas yet?"

"No, madam. But they're out looking."

She nodded curtly, reminded of the gaolers'

search for the three convicts who had escaped Dartmoor.

"Should my father be found in less than excellent health, I intend to have Master Thomas's head on a platter," she rasped softly. "Do I make myself clear, Carter?" Her jaws were clenched with anger.

"Perfectly, madam. And may I say that Your Ladyship's sentiments are my own, entirely?" the butler added.

Clasping his beefy hands together, he loudly cracked his knuckles, one by one.

Despite the late hour, the search party was still down at the mines when she arrived there. According to Uncle Lovey, they had been there each and every day since her father's disappearance.

"Mr. Huddersby, the mine manager, has taken charge of the search, Your Ladyship," he told her as he handed her down from the carriage.

"And what sort of man is Huddersby?"

"A most reliable one, my lady," Uncle Lovey reassured her, tucking her hand through his. "He's organized the lads into search teams, and drawn up a map of the mines, as best he can. Each team is given an area to search. If His Lordship is down there, they'll find him."

At the head of the jet mine's main shaft was a cluster of buildings used as offices, and also sheds where freight cars waited to be filled. Kerosene lanterns cast unwavering pools of amber light over the mine yard, where a group of men had congregated. Their coat and jacket collars were turned up against the damp, cold wind that blew inland off the sea, numbing fingers and reddening noses.

The searchers' grim gray faces—cast now in a ruddy glow, then in murky shadow by the lanterns' light—were a scene from a nightmare.

Many of the men she recognized from Sunday chapel, she realized, nodding and smiling to them when they tipped their hats to her.

"Good evening, Mr. Archer. Mr. Dougherty, how are your wife and little ones? Mr. Smith, thank you for coming."

These hardworking, decent men who labored long hours in her father's jet or coal mines had all turned out to help in the search when their shifts ended.

That they had done so astounded her! To be honest, she had never dreamed her irascible father was so popular, nor that so many would risk their own lives in the dangerous mine shafts to search for him.

The cliffs of Whitby were riddled with the shafts and tunnels left behind by centuries of jet-mining. In recent years, the increased popularity of jet had led to a marked increase in the number of tunnels, as more and more of the lignite was mined. Why, just a few years ago, a perfectly healthy man had been lost for *fourteen days* in that rabbit warren, unable to find his way to the surface! How much harder would it be for an injured man to find his way out—or for the searchers to find him?

"Anything, Mr. Huddersby?" she asked her father's mine manager as he led a party of men out of the main shaft.

"Nowt as yet, my lady," the manager responded in his broad Yorkshire accent, doffing his flat cap. "But we ain't giving up on His Lordship as yet. Nay, not by a long chalk! We're just calling off t' search till daylight. Then the lads will go back down, aye?"

"But . . . isn't it dark down there? What difference does it make, whether it is day or night, if they have miners' lanterns?" Victoria wondered aloud. Overwrought by fear, by the gloomy, depressing mood of the place, and by the fine damp rain that had been falling since her arrival, she sounded a little shrill.

"You're right aboot that, Your Ladyship. Black as pitch it is down there, right enough," Huddersby agreed. "But my lads are proper spent. Been at it all day long, they 'ave, aye? Let them have their bit o'rest, and they'll be all the fresher for it, mum."

"Forgive me, Mr. Huddersby. In my concern for my father, I completely forgot that they'd be tired. Of course they are. I'm so sorry," she murmured, embarrassed to have sounded so inconsiderate when the poor men had been searching for her father for days.

She turned to look about the circle of miners, at their grimy, coal-blackened, weary faces. The whites of their eyes, the rare patches of unblackened skin were startling—almost comic—in the shadows.

"I apologize to you, gentleman," she said sincerely. "I really wasn't thinking. All of you have my deepest gratitude for working so hard and so long to find my father."

"Well, we had to, didn't we, Your Ladyship?" one of the men piped up.

"Had to? You mean, someone forced you?" she asked, horrified.

"Nay, my lady. We had to look for 'is Lordship on account of we don't want to lose him, do we?" Cap in hand, the little sparrow of a man grinned. "There's few mine owners what would treat us lads as fair and square as your da'. Aye, and he's not so bloody tight with his silver as most, either—beggin' your pardon, Yer Ladyship."

"Aye, milady. He's a hard man, your da', but he's a right fair one, too," another miner added. "And that's more than can be said for most of 'em. Right, lads?"

"Right!" The loud masculine chorus echoed the spokesman's sentiments.

A lump of emotion clogged Victoria's throat.

"Then thank you, all of you. And rest assured that, whatever the outcome of your search, I shall not soon forget you, nor what you have done for me and my father in these trying times. I promise each and every one of you that, even if my father is—dead, nothing shall change for any of you, unless it changes for the better."

"Why, God bless ye, lass!" one man, overcome with emotion, said gruffly. "You're Old Thorny's daughter, an' no mistake. But we'll find him yet, God bless 'im. Aye, and alive and kicking, too! Just see if we don't!"

The miners were as good as their word, for find her father they did, at dusk the following day. And if not exactly kicking, he was—for the time being, at least—alive.

It was all Victoria could do to keep from crying out when the miners carried him into the Hall on a broad wooden plank.

A wave of love she never knew she felt for her father welled up and overflowed as she looked at him—and with it came anger.

Her father's iron-gray hair was matted with dried blood and dirt. His haggard face was gray, and had aged a full ten tears since she'd seen him last. Much of it was mottled with livid, yellowing bruises. His clothing was bloodstained in places and very damp.

Although he was unconscious and unresponsive, she could hear his crackling breathing from across the hall and knew he was not dead, although she believed he was close to it.

"Carry His Lordship up to his room, gentlemen; then Cook has some soup for all of you. Lily, fetch hot water and towels. Carter! Send a groom for Dr. Walters immediately!" she cried, lifting her skirts to hurry upstairs after the men and the makeshift stretcher.

Lily scurried off toward the kitchens, calling for Mrs. Oliver and her mother, Mrs. Lovett, as she went.

"Doctor's already on his way, my lady," Carter said, his normally florid complexion pale with concern. "I sent a lad to fetch him before they

285

brought His Lordship out of the mine. Is there anything else I can do while we wait?"

"Yes, Carter. There is. You can pray," Victoria whispered, and hurried upstairs.

Ian Walters was attending a difficult delivery when word reached him that his services were needed at the Hall.

By the time he arrived at Lord Hawthorne's bedside, the patient had been stripped of his damp garments, bathed and dressed warmly in a fresh nightshirt by his daughter, the housekeeper and his head groom's wife. Heated stone bottles were tucked all around him. Woolen blankets were heaped over him. But despite their best efforts, His Lordship shivered and shook, mumbling that he was cold, so very cold.

"Sorry business, this," Walters observed, peering at Victoria over the rim of his gold spectacles. "Lucky for His Lordship the beating didna finish him outright. Did they apprehend the Thomas lout yet?"

Victoria shook her head. "No. Not yet."

"Whist! Will ye look at this dark area! His attacker used a billyclub or a cosh on the old dev— on His Lordship, by the looks of it. Bruises like these aren't made by knuckles alone."

"Will he recover?" Victoria asked huskily, almost afraid to hope. She was almost dropping from exhaustion, first from two sleepless nights spent fretting that they would never find her father at all, and now that they had, from fear that he would not recover.

"I'm afraid it's too early to say. The bruising is the least of his problems. It's the pneumonia I'm worried about," Walters explained after he had listened to her father's breathing. He sounded his chest, pressing with two fingers, then tapping with his knuckles and listening intently. "His Lordship isn't a young man anymore, though his normally robust constitution should stand him in good stead. Here," he added, handing her a bottle from his black bag. "Give him this."

"What is it?"

"Paragoric linctus. Two teaspoons every three hours. A steam tent will help loosen the congestion in his lungs, too. You can rig one up by draping blankets around his bed, Your Ladyship. I'm sure Mrs. Lovett here can show you how it's done, can ye not, Mrs. Lovett?"

"Eeh, that I can, Dr. Ian," Aunt Lovey promised, favoring the young doctor with a doting smile.

"He'll need bed baths every few hours, too, to bring down the fever, as well as chest rubs with camphor and mentholatum."

"Whatever needs to be done, we'll do it," Victoria promised, tossing her head. She had long suspected that Ian Walters considered her a spoiled, frivolous dilettante, incapable of hard work. Well, she'd show him, by God!

Walters's blue eyes narrowed. He pushed back the lock of fine sandy hair that flopped over his brow. "And what of you, Your Ladyship?" he demanded.

"Me?" She snorted, tossing her black hair. Her

striking red-and-black plaid with fitted sleeves, a pert black collar and matching black cuffs, swished and crackled as she moved. "There's nothing wrong with me, Doctor. Nothing at all."

"Are you quite sure about that, madam? You're looking a wee bit pale and peaked, I'm thinking. No sickness early in the morning, aye? No wee fainting spells, or a sudden distaste for your favorite foods?"

His piercing blue eyes met her own as he lifted her wrist, inspected his watch and palpated her pulse.

"Whist, your pulse is racing. How so, Your Ladyship? Are your stays too tight?"

"That, sir, is none of your business!" she shot back, flushing. That wretched man! He had discerned her secret almost immediately. Still, if someone was going to notice the exhaustion, the pallor common to her condition, Walters would be the one to do so, she thought, hiding a weary smile.

Apart from the fact that he was a member of the medical profession, and an excellent physician, it was no secret to anyone in Whitby that the handsome young doctor had been sweet on Victoria since he was in short knickers. Their vastly different positions in society had prevented Walters from ever voicing his admiration, however.

Poor Ian! He must have wanted to kick himself when he'd heard about her wanting to elope with Ned—a miner and laborer—she thought ruefully. The knowledge filled her with shame, more than it did amusement. What had she been thinking of, that she hadn't recognized Ned Thomas for what he truly was, his origins be damned?

"I'm very tired, Doctor. That's all. Hardly surprising, since I haven't slept a wink in almost three nights. I hate to disappoint you, but I haven't had a 'peaked' day in my life!"

A faint smile played about Walters's lips. "If you say so, Lady Blackstone. But will ye allow me t'be the first to congratulate you and His Lordship, peaked or nay?" he asked in a lower voice, taking her hand in his and kissing it in the continental fashion.

Unfortunately, his voice had not been low enough, judging by the sudden gleeful, knowing looks the older women and Lily exchanged.

"You'll do no such thing," Victoria said crisply, jerking her hand away. "And if you are in such dire need of new patients, Doctor, I would recommend that you visit the parish poorhouse. Lord knows, there are numerous poor devils in need of your skills there."

"I will be sure to keep that in mind, Victoria," the saucy fellow assured her, although she had given him no permission to address her by her first name.

"Well, now. It's a chilly evening. Would you care for a drink before you leave, Doctor? Carter would be happy to pour one for you. Downstairs, of course."

"Och, of course, aye. But nooo, thank ye kindly," Walters refused, obviously wanting to laugh.

"Then, *good night, sir.*"

"A very good night indeed, ma'am," the doctor murmured, inclining his head as he went to the door. "Whist, don't bother t'ring for a servant. I know my way out."

"As you will, Doctor. When will you be back to see my father?"

"I'll drop round again tomorrow after the morning surgery. Meanwhile, if there's any change in his condition, call me immediately. My housekeeper knows where to reach me. Day or night."

"Wretched man," Victoria muttered under her breath when he was gone.

"Perhaps. But young Ian's a fine physician, like his da' before him," Mrs. Lovett observed softly, smiling as she stared at Victoria's middle.

Victoria could almost hear the knitting needles and the crochet hooks clacking!

"Have I spilled something on my skirts, Mrs. Lovett?" she snapped, annoyed that both Auntie Lovey and Mrs. Oliver's eyes had suddenly dropped to her belly, following Walters's unsubtle comment.

"Nay, my lass, not a blessed thing," Auntie Lovey assured her, fondly patting Victoria's elbow. Her smile now spread from ear to ear. "Come along, Mrs. Oliver. We've done all we can for His Lordship for the time being, bless him. The rest is up to him, and the good Lord. I was thinking I'd sort through my wool basket . . . I'd say we've earned a nice cup o' tea and a bit of a gossip, wouldn't you?"

"Me, too, Ma. Shall I bring you up a cuppa, love?" Lily offered, turning to Victoria.

On the verge of refusing, she nodded instead. "Hmm, please. I'd love one."

A telegram had been sent to Aunt Catherine, who had been forced to leave Whitby for the lying-in of one of her daughters, Lettie, following the birth of the duchess's seventh—or was it her eighth?—grandchild. Victoria and her father were quite alone, for the time being.

The draperies had been drawn against the draft. The fire roared behind the polished black grate. Its flames licked at a fragrant old apple bough on the hearth, dispelling the autumn chill, and gave a cheerful focus to the deeply shadowed room. The only sound other than her father's labored breathing was the loud, measured tick of the mantel clock, and the occasional crackle and hiss of the log on the fire.

Dragging a leather armchair over to the bedside for her vigil, Victoria sank down into it, drawing a fringed afghan around her shoulders to keep the chill at bay.

But soon, lulled by the room's cozy warmth and the clock's monotonous ticking, she fell fast asleep, fingers cradling her hardening belly as she dreamed of the child that would be born, come winter's end.

Chapter Twenty-one

"Victoria?"

The hoarse croak brought her head around.

"Father! You're awake!"

"Of course I'm awake. What the devil are you doing here?" her father growled, scowling up at her from faded blue eyes. "Don't tell me ye've left Blackstone?"

"Of course not! Well, not exactly. At least, not yet," she assured him, giddy with relief that he'd emerged from the fever. "I came because you needed someone. You know, to take care of you. You've been very ill, you know."

"I have?" He seemed surprised. "For how long?"

"It's been ten days since we found you. We were afraid we were going to lose you."

"That I'd die, you mean. Poppycock!" he

scoffed. "I've managed to take care of myself all these years. No bloody reason I can't continue to do so. And if I needed a nurse—which I don't— your Aunt Catherine can play Flo Nightingale. You, my girl, have a husband to tend to. Go home to him! You're not needed here."

"Not needed! Is this what you call taking care of yourself, you stubborn old man?" she demanded, too happy to be truly angry with him.

Her eyes twinkled as a shocked, indignant scowl deepened the furrows in her father's face. He had seen few glimpses of the temper she'd inherited from him before. Well, that was all about to change.

"Had I been here, I would have moved heaven and earth to keep you from going to that wretched mine—had Carter tie you down, if needed be! What in the world possessed you to meet Ned Thomas alone? You had the man horsewhipped, then dismissed from your employ! Meeting him alone was sheer stupidity. Asking for trouble!"

Her father had the grace to look a little ashamed of himself, for the few seconds it took to recover from her dressing down.

"Stupidity? Horsefeathers! My mistake was in expecting the lout to have an ounce of honor in him, my lass! The young pup jumped me from behind," Hawthorne grumbled, coughing thickly. "Blast this wretched cough! You call yourself a nurse? Fetch me a brandy, lass."

"I will not. I'll fetch you this instead, you disagreeable old goat. Aye, and you'll drink it too, every last drop. Like it or not," she warned, pouring a teaspoon of syrupy black cough linctus into a spoon. "Don't make me hold your nose, Father. Open wide."

"I will not. Be off with you! Devil take you, you wretched harpy. I'll not take another drop of your poison!" he declared, clamping his jaws together and waving his hands about.

"If you take it, I'll ask Walters about the brandy. Spit it out, and I'll recommend he prescribes you a purge. A very *strong* one," she added sweetly.

Still spluttering his indignation, Hawthorne opened his mouth and swallowed, grimacing as the linctus trickled down his throat.

"Blaaggh. Wretched stuff. You're a bloody tyrant, woman! A despot! A slave driver in petticoats," he muttered. "Aggh, by God, this muck tastes like horse liniment. What the devil is it?"

"Horse liniment!" she shot back, laughing. It was so wonderful to hear him bellowing, almost back to his usual cantankerous self.

"Horse liniment? What the devil are you trying to do?" Then, catching the twinkle in her eyes, he realized she was teasing and laughed, too.

The rare rumbling sound made Victoria think of a volcano about to erupt.

"You know, there's something different about you, my lass," her father observed at length, watching as she recorked the medicine bottle and set it on a tray with its fellows. "You look different. More womanly, and—eeh, I can't put my finger on it. A mite sad, too, aye? Are you not happy with Blackstone, love? Is that it?"

Good Lord. He had called her "love," she realized, stunned. And he actually sounded as if he cared whether she was happy or not.

"I—" She swallowed over the huge lump in her throat, wondering how best to begin. "I was very happy, until about a fortnight ago. Then it became apparent that Steede was trying to—to kill me."

"*Kill* you?" A roar of laughter burst from her father. Waving off her restraining hands, he struggled to sit up. His face was ruddy against the white of his nightshirt as he leaned heavily against the carved headboard behind him. "Where the devil did you get that idea? From the scandal mongers and their jabbering about his first wife's death?" He jabbed his thumb and fingers together, mimicking the gossips' clacking mouths. "Well? Did you?"

"In a way, I suppose I did, somewhat," she agreed reluctantly.

Her father shook his head. "By gum, I'm that disappointed in you, Victoria. The man was willing to ignore the scandal about you and that—laborer, was he not? He liked what he saw, and decided to find out for himself what sort of woman he was to wed, the gossip be damned! Could you not pay Blackstone the same courtesy, lass? Could you not have trusted *me*, if not *him*?" His tone was accusing now. And hurt.

"You? What had you to do with it?"

"What father would let his only daughter

marry a man known as 'the Brute' without first investigating his character? Not this father, by gum!

"I know you think poorly of me, Victoria, but I'm not so bad as all that. Within hours of Blackstone's offer for your hand, I knew everything there was to know about him, thanks to Carter and his backstreet connections. Good servants always know what's going on in a house. And I have it on good authority from Blackstone's servants—some that served him out in India, as well as here in England—that your husband was in no way responsible for his first wife's death. He was an excellent father and husband, and a bloody fine soldier and employer, to boot. True, he holds himself to account for the lady's death, but as for causing that death himself—*never*."

"But it isn't just the rumors!" Victoria protested, the wind taken out of her sails by her father's sterling defense of her husband. "There have been . . . incidents since I arrived at Blackstone Manor."

She described them all: the blood-red petals she'd found in her bed, the mangled picture frame and missing picture of her mother, Lily's belief that her belongings had been searched. She ended with her fall from Calypso and finding the cravat-pin fastened to the bloodied saddle pad. The incriminating pin that Steede had stealthily recovered from the pocket of her riding habit, believing she slept.

"If it wasn't Steede who engineered my accident, why would he sneak about at night trying to recover the pin?"

"I can't answer that. But . . . what does your gut tell you, Victoria? What do you feel for the man in here, and in here?" Hawthorne demanded, poking himself in the belly, then the chest. "If not for the gossip, would ye think him capable of murder?"

Never! screamed a small, persistent voice in her head. But she seriously considered her answer before reluctantly admitting aloud, "Well, no, I suppose not."

"And before the fall, how were things between you then?" He read her pinkening cheeks, her confused expression, and chuckled. "Ah. So that's how the wind blew! You were falling for the handsome scalawag, were you not, my lass?"

"I suppose I was, after a fashion. Oh, all right. Yes, yes I was!"

"Then think about it, my lass," he urged her in an unusually gentle voice. "Trust your instincts. Do you really think I'd give my only lass, my Isabelle's wee babby, to some coldblooded, murdering bastard who slaughtered his first wife?"

Tears welled up and spilled down her cheeks. He had never spoken so openly to her before, nor so fondly.

"I—really don't know what I thought. I was distraught, I suppose. Upset. And you—had threatened to marry me off to the first man who offered for my hand! I thought . . . I thought . . ."

"Well, you thought wrong, lass," her father said gruffly, taking her slender hand between his hard, large ones. He squeezed it so hard she winced. "I love you, my little Vicky. Always have, always will. Ever since the day you were conceived, I've wanted only the best for you. I know I haven't been a champion father, but was it so bloody easy to think the worst of me, lass? To believe I'd sell you to the highest bidder, never mind the man's reputation?"

"Yes! It was difficult to believe you cared for me at all," she told him frankly, her chin up, her voice husky with emotion.

"But you had everything a child could ask for! Toys. Pretty clothes. Tutors and instructors—the finest of everything money could buy. How else was I to show my love for you? What more could I have given you?"

"*Yourself*, Father," she told him earnestly. "That was all I ever wanted. Your love. Your affection. Your time. I didn't care about things or about money! Don't you see? It was so lonely for me here, after Mama died. You could have helped to fill that loneliness. We could have helped each other. But instead, you abandoned me, too. You shut me out of your life, so that I had no one."

"You're right, my lass. I didn't mean to do it, but I did," he admitted heavily, much to her surprise. There was a suspicious sheen in his own eyes now. "I had a bloody long time to think about my life while I was down those godforsaken mines, waiting for someone to find me. Time to think about the mistakes I'd made. I mourned your mother far longer and harder than was fitting or healthy for either of us, Victoria.

"The good Lord knows, there were times I ached to dandle you on my knee, or just hold you in my arms. But when I looked into your bonny wee face, it was always my Isabelle's face that looked back at me. . . .

"In the end, I had t' keep away. I couldn't bear to have ye near me. You reminded me of her too much, my darling girl. And it hurt. It hurt more than I could bear."

"And so you abandoned me, without ever leaving me alone," she whispered.

"It's too late now, I suppose?" he asked. "For you to forgive me, I mean?"

Teardrops trembled on the tips of her lashes. She wanted to weep, for all the years they had wasted. "We can't turn back time, nor undo the wrongs we've done." Her mouth quivered. "But we can go on from here, if you want to. I understand so much better now, Papa. All the time I was growing up, I truly believed you hated me. That you couldn't bear the sight of me."

"And now?"

"Now I know what it means to love somebody. And—oh, Papa!—I don't know if I could do any better than you, when—if!—it should happen to me!" What if the child was a boy, and the image of Steede? she wondered. How would she be able to bear it?

"It won't happen. I won't let it. Come here, my love," her father murmured brokenly, holding out his hands.

She took them in her own and kissed them. His

skin was cool, the fever gone. Yet his lips were warm as he pressed them to her brow. *Warm and infinitely loving.*

"I love you, Papa. I've always loved you. Please don't shut me out again?" she whispered brokenly.

"I won't. I swear it. I love you, too, darling girl," Hawthorne said through his tears as she leaned down to kiss his cheek. "This old place has felt so empty since you left us, chick."

Her head resting on his chest, she smiled as her father stroked her hair. A faraway look in his eyes, he began telling her about her mother, and how it had been before he lost her.

How fitting it is, she thought sadly as she listened to him, *that love gives us such insight into the hearts of others.*

She knew how it felt to love and lose someone now. For had she not lost Steede, lost her trust in him, which was even worse than losing him to death?

". . . and so, all going well, we're to be wed at Christmas. I'll understand if you can't give it, but we'd like your blessing, daughter. And we want you and Blackstone to come for the wedding, aye?"

Wedding? Whose wedding was he talking about? she wondered, only just realizing what he'd been saying.

"I'm sorry, Father. I didn't hear what you said."

He sighed. "I said, I've decided to wed again— start another family. A brace of strapping lads

301

would be grand, aye, lass? You know, to carry on the Hawthorne line?"

"I'm to have baby brothers? What a wonderful idea!" Victoria exclaimed, laughing. "But who's the lucky bride-to-be? Have you found her yet? Have you asked for her hand? Are you seeking my approval of your choice?"

"Aye, aye—and aye!" Hawthorne declared. "Her name's Delia Anne. She's the daughter of old Lord Chillingsworth in Haverleigh, and a bloody fine horsewoman, too. Her seat's almost as good as yours! We met at a hunt supper old Chillingsworth gave right after you ran off with Blackstone. She's a bit long in the tooth, my Del—saw her thirtieth birthday last year, aye? But still young enough to give me a babby or two, Lord willing. And—" He broke off.

"Go on," she urged, seeing his throat and cheeks suddenly redden. "And what?"

"Hmm?" he asked innocently.

"Oh, no, you don't! Tell me. Do you love her? Is that what you were going to say?"

A slow, sly grin spread across her father's gaunt face. And, for a moment, the years fell away. He was again the dashing young suitor that Isabelle Colette de Blanchard had fallen for at first sight, all those years ago.

"Aye, lass. I reckon I was," he admitted in a husky voice. "My Del's a good lass. We have fun together, and we like the same things. She'll make me a grand wife."

Still stunned—and delighted—by the thought of having a stepmother not much older than herself, who would be producing a son or a daughter for her papa soon after she produced his first grandchild, she could think of nothing to say, except to wish them every happiness. Which she did. Time enough later to broach the subject of leaving Steede. . . .

"Thank you, my lass. Now, where's that husband of yours, eh? Downstairs, drinking his way through my whisky cellar?"

She shook her head, a shadow crossing her face at his mention of Steede. Was her father right about him? she wondered. Was he truly innocent of his wife's death, as Papa so staunchly believed? Could the incidents she had taken for attempts on her life—or at very least, attempts to frighten her away—been nothing more than unhappy coincidences? A little girl's jealous attempts to rid herself of a rival for her father's attentions? Or—as Steede claimed to believe—Kalinda's desperate attempts to maintain her position as Mary's nurse?

"No, I'm afraid he's still at Blackstone. He was supposed to join me last weekend, but there were problems at the Home Farm and he couldn't get away," she lied. "He'll be happy to hear you're on the mend, however."

Hawthorne nodded, yet gave her a searching look. "I don't doubt it. And it's because I'm on the mend that I don't need you anymore. You can run right back where you belong. No, don't argue with me, my lass. Go! And when you get there, tell Blackstone I like the fire he's put in your eyes. Aye, by God! I like it right well, my lass!"

She tossed her head, her eyes flashing. "I'll go home when I'm good and ready—and it won't be until you're up and about again," she said firmly, although it was yet another lie. "By the way, shouldn't we let the Honorable Lady Delia know you're indisposed? I'm sure she'll want to hurry over and offer you some tea and sympathy."

"Tea! If I know Del, it'll be whisky and a cigar she'll be offering me, by gum!" her father chortled. His deep, rumbling laughter was music to her ears. "She's no milksop, my Del!"

Chapter Twenty-two

"Memsahib Victoria has been gone for two weeks, my darling girl. It is as I told you. She is not coming back. And now your father has left, too. Come away from the window and eat your breakfast."

She promised, Mary wrote on the slate. Her lower lip quivered as she clambered down from the cushioned window seat. She wrote again, *She will come back. I know it.*

Kalinda shook her head. "My sweet, trusting child. That is the way of the English memsahib. She is an evil woman who does not keep the promises she makes. First she casts a spell over your papa, to make him adore her and follow her to the ends of the earth. Then she lies to you, saying she loves you and will never leave you—"

Not a lie! Not! Mary wrote. Breaking down, she

305

sobbed, tears sliding down her pale cheeks like the rain that streamed down the nursery windowpanes.

"No? Then why did she leave Blackstone, hmmm, my pretty one? And why has she not come back in all these many days? The answer is that she is not coming back. *Ever!* And now Sahib Warring, he has gone, too."

Mary covered her face with her hands.

"Now, now, my baby. Don't cry," Kalinda crooned in her sing-song voice, stroking Mary's long, fair hair. "You still have me, yes? And your Kalinda would never lie to her beloved missie Mary. You can trust your ayah, my poor dear child, even when everyone else has failed you. Even if you were as wicked as the demons of Kali, Kalinda would still love you . . ."

But I am as wicked as the demons of Kali! Perhaps—perhaps even more wicked, Mary thought miserably. With a sob, she threw herself into Kalinda's arms and buried her face against the glittery folds of her sari.

For as long as she could remember, Kalinda's strong brown arms and soft bosom had comforted and protected her. She loved Kalinda more than she had ever loved her mama, she thought guiltily, for her ayah had always taken care of her every need, while Mama had complained that Mary's hugs wrinkled her pretty clothes, or that Mary's kisses made her pretty face sticky. Kalinda had never lied to Mary, either—until now.

Why didn't she believe Kalinda this time?

What was different about now? Why did she still believe that Victoria loved her, although she had gone away and not come back?

Was it because her heart said Victoria had meant what she said? That there really was nothing she could ever do that would make Victoria stop loving her. That when you really loved someone, it lasted forever and ever. . . .

Where? she wrote urgently on the slate.

"Where did your papa's woman go?"

Mary nodded.

Kalinda laughed. It was a harsh, ugly sound that hurt Mary's ears. Her nurse's face was twisted in a way Mary had never seen before, and her eyes were hard and spiteful, the way Mama's had sometimes been, after Baby Johnny was born.

Looking at her made Mary's tummy hurt.

"That one has gone home, little one."

More frantic scribbling. *Where home?*

"Aiieee, so many questions! You are as insatiable as the elephant's child," she declared, cupping Mary's face between her slim brown hands. "And as curious as a little monkey! I know only that the memsahib has gone away, my jewel. Gone to a far distant place."

Across moors? Mary wrote on the slate.

"Indeed, yes, my daughter. Across the moors and beyond them. Perhaps she has gone as far away as India, yes? And the memsahib will not be back. You saw her the morning she left. She looked happy to be leaving the wretched little monkey who destroyed her treasured picture."

Mary swallowed. It was very difficult, because there was a lump in her throat that hurt so much it made tears sting behind her eyes.

Perhaps she was dying? Perhaps the lump in her throat was her punishment for doing the naughty things Kalinda had told her to do? Perhaps . . . perhaps that lump would grow and grow, until it choked her to death?

Still . . . no matter what Kalinda had said about Victoria being glad to leave Blackstone, there was a small part of Mary that desperately insisted Kalinda was wrong.

"I love you, Mary, my pet. Never forget it!" Victoria had promised, holding her fiercely. *"And I shall fight to make you love me, even if it takes years and years. Remember that there is nothing— nothing!—you could ever do or say that would make me stop loving you, my darling girl."*

She loved Victoria, too. She truly, truly did. And she didn't want to be mean or cross to everyone again, the way she had been before Victoria married Papa and came to Blackstone.

She wanted to help Victoria arrange the roses for the house, or to take to Grandmama at the Lodge. She wanted to stand next to her in church on Sunday morning and sing so loudly that Mrs. Mortimer, the vicar's wife, stared at them both, and made them giggle. She wanted to wear the pretty dresses Victoria asked Mrs. Stacey to sew for her, and go riding across the moors with her each afternoon on Sooty's back. She wanted to cuddle up in bed beside Victoria while she told her wonderful stories that chased away her nightmares, as she'd done the night of the storm with her story of the little girl named Colette.

Colette was just like Victoria when she was a little girl. *And just like Mary, too,* a tiny voice whispered inside her head. Colette had believed her papa didn't love her anymore, too, but she'd found out she was very, very wrong. That all the while, he had loved her more than anything, but a cruel witch had cast a spell on him, so he couldn't tell Colette he loved her. . . .

Perhaps she should saddle Sooty and go after Victoria? Her darling little Sooty could take her anywhere, no matter how far away it might be! He was the fastest, strongest little pony in the whole wide world.

And when she found Victoria, she would promise to be good forever and ever if only she'd come back to Blackstone. Cross her heart and hope to die, she'd be so good.

Her mind was made up. She would go Sunday—most of the servants would be away from the house that day. She would go down to the stables and saddle Sooty when the clock's big hand was on the twelve and the little hand was pointing to the four. That was the best time, because the stables were empty while Harry came up to the kitchen for tea. It was also the time when she and Kalinda were supposed to take their naps, so no one would notice if she and Sooty were gone until supper time.

After she'd found Victoria, she would bring her back to Blackstone. Then Papa would come home, too, and he would smile and be happy again, the way he used to be when Victoria first came to live with them.

And if she could do that, perhaps Papa would someday forgive her for the other, terrible thing she had done? Something that was far, far worse than destroying Victoria's picture frame. . . .

Chapter Twenty-three

"Your father looks bloody lively for a man at death's door."

"Steede! You startled me! What on earth are you doing here?" Victoria demanded, her gloved hand flying to her breast.

Her heart skipped a beat as she swiveled to face him, for as always, he made the breath catch in her throat.

He leaned against the doorframe, looking immaculate yet somehow dangerous in black evening tails and high-collared snowy shirt and stock, the dazzling starched linen in striking contrast to his inky hair and unshaven jaw. His arms were crossed over his chest, and a cheroot dangled casually from between the fingers of his right hand; a narrow ribbon of blue smoke unraveled from the glowing tip.

Given his expression, she would not have been surprised had the smoke issued from his nostrils. He looked moody, angry, capable of anything.

The thought made her shiver.

Thrown off by his sudden arrival, and by her body's unexpected tug of response, she stared at him, the earbob she was clipping on forgotten. She'd been so lost in thought, so unhappy and confused, she hadn't heard the door open.

"I came to join you for dinner, darling. Why else would I be here, dressed like this?" His smile was a wolfish baring of teeth. "Well? Aren't you going to welcome me? Your father and his fiancée certainly did. Unless—don't tell me you haven't missed me?" he taunted, his tone mocking.

Victoria flushed but ignored the taunt. "Didn't you get my last letter? There was no need for you to come here—"

"I disagree. You wrote that you couldn't leave your father, remember?" he reminded her, impaling her with eyes of splintered black ice. "Although the man playing chess with the Honorable Delia Chillingsworth appears remarkably robust. And I came because, quite simply, I missed you, Victoria." He shook his head, his lips thinned, his expression bitter. "That's rich, isn't it, since you didn't plan on coming back, did you, my dear?"

"Don't be ridiculous. Of course I—"

"No. Not even to say goodbye," he continued as if she hadn't spoken, and she said nothing further, because he was right. "We—Mother, Mary

312

and I—were simply expected to send on your luggage, weren't we?"

She flinched, flayed by guilt and by shame. She really should have gone back, at least once, if only to tell Mary and Henrietta why she had left. . . .

"I don't know what you mean." She tossed her dark head so that the trio of pink baroque pearls that dangled from each earlobe swung madly. "Look, couldn't we discuss this later? I was just going to lie down. I have a dreadful headache—"

"To hell with your blasted headache," he snarled, striding across the room. Catching her by the wrist, he dragged her up, off the padded stool. "I deserve an explanation!"

"For my headache?"

"Don't play games with me! You know damned well what for! For leaving me."

He tugged her to him, so that their faces were only a hairsbreadth apart. Anger crackled all around him like jagged frost-fire.

"Ever since that damned fall, you flinch whenever I touch you. Jump like a frightened rabbit at the sound of my voice! Why won't you believe me? I had nothing to do with your accident."

"Why should I trust you? It was your pin, after all! You admitted it!"

"All right. The bloody pin was mine. I'll give you that. A gift from Aimee that disappeared years ago, in India. I always assumed one of the houseboys had stolen it, until I put two and two together. About Kalinda, that is. Don't you see, Victoria? It's been her all along."

313

"A scapegoat. How very convenient," she jeered. "But if you're really as innocent as you claim, why did you take the pin from my wardrobe?"

He didn't bother to deny it. "From what Tom Foulger told me, I knew you'd found something in Calypso's saddle pad. When you acted as if I'd suddenly sprouted horns, I guessed you thought I was responsible." He shrugged. "I was curious. I wanted to know why.

"It occurred to me you might have tucked whatever it was into your pocket that day, for safekeeping. Lo and behold, I found the pin in your riding habit. An item that threw suspicion squarely on me. Doesn't that tell you anything?"

"Should it?"

"Cut it out, Victoria! Damn it, I'm no fool! If I wanted to murder you, which I don't—not yet, anyway," he amended through clenched jaws, "I wouldn't leave any clues to my identity! Whoever did this *wanted* suspicion to fall on me. Why? Because they wanted to get rid of you, Victoria, one way or the other. I'd say they succeeded, wouldn't you?"

"Why couldn't it be you?" she whispered.

"Why would I want you dead?" he demanded, plainly furious. He looked quite capable of murder in that moment. His eyes were dark as a starless night, blacker than Hades beneath lowering brows. "What the devil did I have to gain from your death? Or Aimee's, come to that?"

"There's an inheritance from my mother—"

"Money?" He snorted in disgust. "It's common

knowledge that the Blackstone fortune could last a man ten lifetimes, however extravagantly he chose to live them. No, if you're looking for a motive, you'll have to do better than that," he added grimly.

"Then perhaps . . . you're simply a—a Bluebeard," she tossed back in desperation, well aware of how foolish it sounded.

What was she so afraid of? Why did her heart pound so? Why couldn't she bring herself to admit that she believed him? In her heart of hearts, she knew he was innocent. He had nothing to gain from her death, not unless he killed for killing's sake. What was she afraid would happen if she let him love her. . . . and allowed herself to love him?

Foolish as it seemed, afraid she was. The very thought of loving anyone as much as she had come to love him terrified her, for how would she ever recover if he abandoned her, physically or emotionally? If, some day, he just stopped loving her . . . stopped being there when she needed him, just as her father had done? Safer to end it here, now, on her own terms.

And so she brought her chin up and stubbornly insisted, "For all I know, you could be a deranged lunatic! A—a brute who murders his wives for the pleasure of it!"

He swore, softly yet foully. "Blast it, Victoria. You're an intelligent woman. Tempting as the idea of murdering you might be at this moment, surely you can do better than that?"

"Swear to me, then," she demanded quickly.

"Tell me you were not responsible for your first wife's death, and I'll believe you."

"Not responsible?" he echoed.

He seemed suddenly taken aback, all the anger sucked out of him by her question. His features were a blank, enigmatic mask as he murmured heavily, "That's a horse of a different color, Victoria. If not for me, I believe Aimee and her infant son would still be alive. The knowledge that I was responsible for their deaths has haunted me ever since."

Stunned that he had admitted causing their deaths, she turned away, hugging herself about the arms. So this was it. Tears obliterated her view of the darkening park through the uncurtained window. Instead, she saw her future stretching ahead of her. *Empty. Loveless. Alone.*

"I think you should go now. We have nothing further to discuss." It was better this way. Surely it would be less painful if he left now.

"If it were not for me . . ."

How fragile happiness was! How frail was trust, she told herself. In just a few little words, her dreams of a wonderful new life with Steede had toppled like castles built in air. While her father built himself a new life with Delia, she must be alone. Again.

"Leave, or I shall ring for a footman to throw you out," she said desperately, her voice cracking. If he didn't leave, and soon, she would never be able to let him go.

She loved him, needed him, no matter what he

316

was, or what he had done—or what he might yet do!

The thought terrified her as nothing else could.

Steede's jaw hardened. His eyes flashed, black lightning striking in a face as hard and chiseled as granite. Her cool dismissal, her lack of faith enraged him.

"What about us, Victoria? Does what we had mean so bloody little you can throw it all away, just like that?" he challenged, snapping his fingers.

Before she could step away, he grasped her upper arms and yanked her toward him. "Can you?" he breathed, his voice a silky purr.

Oh, that voice! Memories of black velvet nights . . . of scented satin sheets. . . . of searing kisses and a touch that stirred her senses flooded through her like heated wine.

"Let go of me!" she protested, struggling to escape his grip.

"The devil I will, Victoria. That's not what you want. Not really. This is what you want. *Admit it!*"

For one endless moment, he hesitated, their mouths so close she could almost taste him. She closed her eyes as his breath rose, warm and sweet, against her skin. Then he cupped her chin, tilted back her head and crushed his lips over hers.

He kissed her savagely, deeply. Kissed her until her eyes darkened to the color of a storm-tossed midnight sea, brimming over with desire. Her knees buckled as his tongue stroked inside her mouth, relentlessly teasing, tasting her as he dragged her up against his powerful frame.

The electric contact that leaped between them made her gasp, as if lightning bolts crackled and sizzled from one to the other. With a low, desperate moan, she leaned against him, needing his support, needing him to cool the desire that seethed in her belly like lava.

"I knew it!" he crowed, triumphant.

Plunging his hand inside her scalloped neckline, he cupped her breasts. Fondled the silky mounds that felt strangely unfettered beneath her chemise and the slippery rose-pink bodice of her gown.

She'd discarded her busk, the confining corset, the stays and hooped petticoat. Her lush curves were free of confinement, he realized with a heady jolt of pure lust as he ran his hand down over her belly and hips, then up between her stockinged legs, until it was lodged snugly between her thighs.

The divided, scalloped drawers were open between the legs. They offered no protection against a lover's determined invasion, he thought, as he eased a finger inside her.

She curled her arms around his neck and leaned more heavily against him, uttering a low, helpless moan as her fingers caught in his hair.

God, she was wet, and so blessed hot she sheathed him like a fiery glove. If she told him to stop, he didn't know if he could. Or worse, *would*.

He wanted to take the combs from her hair. To free her Gypsy mane so that it tumbled over the two of them in wild black torrents as they made love. To strip off the rose-pink satin gown, the chemise, the layered petticoats, and devour her, inch by luscious inch, until the raging beast within was tamed and stilled.

"Say it, Victoria!" he growled thickly in her ear. His hot, raspy breath raised goosebumps on the bare skin between her long white gloves and her wispy organdy sleeves. "Say I mean nothing to you. That this leaves you cold."

Splaying both hands over her derriere, he drew her against the hard bulge in his trousers. Sealing his lips to hers, he wielded teeth and tongue in a kiss calculated to make itself felt in every part of her, then drew back and whispered thickly again, *"Lie to me, darling. . . ."*

Shaking her head from side to side, she pressed her palms against his chest. Made a mute, half-hearted attempt to push him away, although she could feel his hardness throbbing against her belly.

Her treacherous body quivered in anticipation. It had learned to expect pleasure from his. Wanted it. *Needed* it. Now, every nerve and sinew, every inch of flesh and bone, yearned to surrender. To yield to his dangerous seduction . . .

Little fool! she scolded herself. This isn't real. None of it is—not to him. His lovemaking is only a prelude, a single step in his murderous dance. It *must* be! Hadn't he admitted he was responsible for Aimee's death? For the death of their little son?

She had her own unborn child to consider now, she told herself, cradling her hardening belly. And while she might risk her own life for a few hours of pleasure in Steede's bed, she would not risk her baby's. . . .

"*Go!*" she whispered in a strangled voice, turning her head away. "I—never want to see you again!"

He grew very, very still, his expression as dark and closed as a padlocked door. The pain in his eyes was that of a condemned man as he looked down at her.

"Is that what you want? You're sure?"

She could not look at him. *Had* to look away. After what seemed an eternity, she nodded and whispered, "*Yes.*"

The single word, no louder than a sigh—and just as insubstantial in the firelit room—was loud enough.

A muscle ticked at his temple. His Adam's apple bobbed in his throat. "Very well, then. Goodbye, Victoria."

Turning on his heel, he strode out the door.

As he left, he jerked it shut behind him so forcefully Victoria flinched as if she'd been shot. As, perhaps, she had, she thought miserably. *Straight through the heart!*

As tears fell like rain, she told herself he had left just in time.

Another second and she would have begged him to stay. . . .

*   *   *

"Off home so soon, Blackstone? I thought you'd be staying for the weekend, at least?"

"So did I, sir," Steede ground out. He halted, but didn't turn around to face Lord Hawthorne in the marble-tiled entryway. A nerve pulsed at his temple as he set down his bag. "There's—ah—there's been a change in plans."

"Ah. Gave you your marching orders, did she?" Hawthorne asked softly.

Steede turned to face him. "Something like that, yes."

"Care to discuss it over a drink?"

"I'm not sure there's anything left to discuss, sir. Or that it's any of your damned business."

"Why don't you let me be the judge of that, aye?" Hawthorne suggested mildly.

Steede hesitated, then shrugged. "All right. What have I got to lose?"

"Well, now? What seems to be the problem?" Roger asked as he poured them each a whisky from the Waterford decanter in his study. "Has my lass still got that wasp in her drawers about you murdering your first wife?"

His jaw hardened. "I didn't murder anyone, damn it!" he insisted, his eyes hot.

"Aye, I know that, lad. Do you think you'd be married to my daughter if you had?" the Yorkshireman countered in a voice like a whip. "By dusk of the day you offered for her hand, I knew every last thing there was to know about you, my lad, good and bad." He cocked an iron-gray eyebrow. "And I mean *everything*."

"If you're referring to my former mistress, I

dismissed her within hours of Victoria's accepting my proposal," Steede supplied in a go-to-hell tone.

Hawthorne grinned. "I knew that, too. Handsome woman, though." He winked and clicked his teeth. "Very handsome. You've excellent taste when it comes to the lasses."

The ghost of a smile curved Steede's mouth.

"My daughter loves thee, son. You do know that?"

"I doubt it, sir."

"Do you? Well, you'd be wrong. I haven't been the best of fathers, but I know my daughter, nonetheless. She loves you, but she's fighting it. She's afraid, aye?"

"Of me?"

Hawthorne shook his head. "Nay, lad. Of loving you, then losing you. This way—her telling you to go—it's safer, aye? Less hurtful, less damaging to her pride than having you abandon her, as I did—without ever going away." Eyes moist, he shook his head. "I've a lot to blame myself for, Blackstone. But I intend to make up for it. To do right by my lass in this matter, so help me God. You love her, too, I'm thinking?"

His jaw tightened. "Would I be here, if I didn't?"

"By gum, you're a prickly bastard, Blackstone! This is your father-in-law you're talking to! I'm asking, lad. Do you love her, or nay? It's a simple enough question—a bloody schoolboy could answer it."

Exasperated, Steede glowered at him. "You know I do, you old devil!"

Hawthorne gave a thin-lipped grin. "That's grand. I'm glad to hear it. Then you won't be leaving just yet. If she's worth having, she's worth a bit of a scrap for, aye? You'll take a room in Whitby for a night or two, I'm thinking. Give her a chance to cool down a bit. Happen she'll come around right smartly, once she's had time to think things through. And if she believes you and Harry Coombs have gone back to Devon for good, so much the better."

"You think it'll make a difference?"

"All the difference in the world, lad. Trust me. Who do you think the lass takes after—in temperament, I mean?" He chuckled. "Aye. She's her da's little girl, through and through." He winked. "Thank God, she took her looks from her mam! Now, then. Another whisky before you leave?"

"Make mine a double."

"Right you are. Here you go. Cheers! Oh, and before I forget, there's something I'd like to tell you before you leave. Something I'd intended to say at your wedding."

"Sir?"

"Hurt her, Blackstone, and you'll answer to me for it, so help me God!" Hawthorne cast Steede a fierce scowl, his blue eyes so steely and pale Steede didn't doubt for a second that he meant it. "Do you hear, lad?"

"Loud and clear, sir," Steede declared wryly, giving his father-in-law a cocky salute.

Chapter Twenty-four

"I say, Victoria. Let's go riding while Rog takes his nap, shall we?" Delia Chillingsworth suggested in her jolly, forthright fashion the following afternoon.

A handsome, strapping woman in her early thirties, Delia had abandoned any hope of marriage and children once she reached her twenty-fifth birthday. Instead, she resigned herself to being the dutiful spinster daughter, doing good works about the parish and taking care of her aging, gouty father.

Then Roger Hawthorne had come along, and turned her orderly, if somewhat boring, world upside down with his proposal of marriage, which Delia had eagerly accepted. That she had done so as a result of affection for her much older suitor, rather than from desperation, as the gossips would surely imply, was quite obvious when one saw the couple together, Victoria thought fondly. They were clearly devoted to each other.

Her father's betrothed had pretty golden-brown hair that she wore swept up into a simple knot with side-curls, regular features and a flawless pink-and-white complexion any debutante would envy, despite her love of outdoor pursuits such as badminton, croquet, horseback riding and gardening. More importantly, she had the sweetest, most agreeable disposition of any woman Victoria had ever met.

Delighted with her father's choice of a bride, Victoria had wholeheartedly welcomed Delia Chillingsworth into the family, and given them both her unqualified blessing on their marriage. In the days since Delia's arrival at Hawthorne Hall, they had become close friends, allies united by the solitary mission of returning His Lordship to perfect health.

"I'd love to go riding," Victoria agreed readily. Her pregnancy was not very advanced as yet. A ride in the crisp, cold air was exactly what she needed. The outing would blow away the cobwebs in her head, erase the guilty images of little Mary, once again abandoned by a woman she'd called Mother, and of Steede, looking as if she'd struck him a mortal blow.

"Does Father still keep old Muffin in his stables?"

"Is Muffin the ancient chestnut? Yes, as far as I know. But I would have thought—well, Roger's always praising your riding skills. Wouldn't you prefer a more spirited mount? His new bay mare's a pretty creature."

"No, not today. In fact, I probably won't be riding any spirited mounts for the next six months or so. . . ." She let the comment dangle.

"Why on earth not, old girl? I always say a spirited horse is—oh, good Lord! How stupid of me. You're in what is known as an 'interesting condition,' am I right?" When Victoria laughed at her prim reference, Delia blushed and added, "Oh, gosh. A baby. I'm going to be a step-grandmother! Congratulations, old girl! Does Rog know?"

"Thank you," Victoria said warmly, amused by the idea of Delia as a grandmother. "And the answer to your question is no, not yet. I thought I'd tell him this evening at supper. Please don't say anything until then, all right?"

"Don't worry. I won't. Oh, how exciting! I hope"—she blushed—"I hope I shan't be too long in following suit. Once we're married, of course," she added hastily, in case Victoria should misinterpret her eagerness as an unseemly haste to consummate the marriage.

"Oh, of course," Victoria agreed with a smile. "I'll just run upstairs and change. I'll meet you outside, shall I?"

"Splendid," Delia agreed. She arched tawny brows. "Would Lord Blackstone care to join us, do you think?"

"Didn't you know? His Lordship was called

back to Blackstone late last night," Victoria lied smoothly.

"Oh! What a pity. I do hope everything's all right?"

"Some problem with the Home Farm," she said vaguely. "Nothing too serious."

"I'm glad. We're both very lucky, you know, Victoria. To have them, I mean. He's such a striking fellow, your Lord Blackstone, and such a gentleman. And my Roger's quite dashing, too, in an older, distinguished sort of way," she added.

"Aren't we?" Victoria agreed with a painted-on smile. "Fifteen minutes?"

"Fifteen it is," Delia agreed, beaming.

The two women soon left the Hall behind them. Their mounts' hooves clattered loudly over the cobblestones as they rode through the fishing port of Whitby, passing the cluster of red-roofed houses that huddled along the banks of the beautiful River Esk, including that of legendary navigator and explorer Captain James Cook on old Grape Lane.

Little fishing boats were coming into the harbor where, just half a century before, whalers had dropped anchor, creating a leafless forest with their masts.

Seagulls screamed and dipped white wings over the vessels, swooping low in the hope of stealing a taste of the fishermen's fresh catch, still silvery-scaled as it flopped about on the slippery decks.

From the steep cliffs, where the ruins of Saxon

Whitby Abbey loomed over the old town like a protective hen over its chicks, the two women turned their horses onto a narrow cliff path that led down to the wide sands fringing the bay.

In the summer months, horse-drawn chara-bancs loaded to the gills with noisy day-trippers arrived each morning from the factory and mill towns of the north. They disgorged brightly feathered factory girls and working men in their Sunday best of shiny brown suits and flat caps, all eager to spend a day at the seaside.

But few people came to Whitby Bay at this time of year. The beach was empty, except for a man Victoria recognized by his handlebar moustaches as the town's fresh-air fanatic, Colonel Percy Ripperton, now retired, who took his daily constitutional along the sands, come rain or shine, dressed in white woolen combinations.

The only other beach-goer was a scrawny stray dog nosing some dried-out tangles of smelly brown seaweed, in the hope of finding a dead fish.

Within moments, Victoria's hair was whipped free of its intricate braid, Delia's from its elegant knot by the blustery autumn wind that blew inland off the bay. Bearing the frigid promise of winter on its damp, cold breath, it painted vivid roses in their cheeks.

As the women cantered their horses along the sands, little wavelets edged with yellow foam danced up the beach to tickle their horses' hooves. When the waves, receded, they left the wet sand as smooth and unmarred as a bolt of pale-gold silk in their wake, Victoria saw.

If only we could do the same! Eradicate our past, erase our mistakes, as easily, Victoria thought with a wistful sigh.

"Forgive me for saying so, but that sounded very melancholy," Delia observed with a sideward glance. "Are you all right?"

"Perfectly," she insisted. Patting Muffin's neck, she forced a smile to hide her heaviness of heart. What had she done, by telling Steede to go? Had she saved herself—or made a terrible mistake? One she would pay for for the rest of her life?

"We'll ride as far as those rocks, then turn back, shall we?" Delia sang out. "By the time we get home, Cook should have tea ready. I don't know about you, but I'm starved!"

"Me, too. It must be the sea air," Victoria agreed, her mind only half on what Delia was saying. Instead, she remembered riding with Steede at her side. Looking up at him from drifts of colored leaves, or from the tiger's pelt spread before a crackling fire in his bedchamber . . .

Delia hesitated. "I've been wanting to ask you, Victoria. How much longer do you expect to stay at the Hall?"

"Stay? But the Hall's my home!" Victoria protested sharply.

At once, Delia looked stricken and apologetic. "Oh, gosh, of course it is! I didn't mean that you should leave! It goes without saying that you are free to stay for as long and as often as you wish, even after Roger and I are married. We wouldn't have it any other way.

"It's just that . . . well, I lost my mother several years ago, and have no sisters or aunts to call upon for help or advice. While you—! Well, you're such a dear, generous soul. I was hoping I might prevail upon you to help me with the wedding arrangements. I know it's an imposition—especially for someone in your condition—but I don't know where else to turn, and I really—"

"Enough said. I'd love to!" Victoria said warmly, feeling contrite. "You and Papa shall have the very best wedding ever! Aunt Catherine—Papa's sister—is marvelous at organizing things—and people. She'll help, too, I just know she will." She smiled. "Before you know it, I'll be calling you . . . Mother!"

Delia pretended to look annoyed. "Try it, dear girl, and I shall not be held responsible for the consequences."

Victoria laughed as they rode on, her heartache forgotten for the moment.

Steede tossed his cigar stub into the brass spittoon in the corner and nodded to the bartender to bring him another drink as he fished in his waistcoat pocket for the price of the pint.

Though not the sort of establishment he usually frequented, the Whitby Arms nonetheless provided clean, comfortable rooms, tasty meals and fine ales and spirits. Last night, after Victoria had given him his marching orders, he recalled sourly, he had taken advantage of all three, with special attention given the latter.

He had told himself it would be a marriage of convenience, he'd thought morosely as he drank. Their marriage, his convenience. He'd believed he could marry Victoria, and enjoy her considerable charms in his bed, yet remain unmoved by her in any but the most casual fashion out of bed.

Had he truly imagined he could have a mother for Mary, an intelligent, desirable woman in his bed, a new mistress to run his household, and not become involved? Not care? What a fool he'd been—and how bloody arrogant, too!—to think he could pull it off.

In ways he did not fully comprehend, Victoria—with her delightful mixture of contrasts—had become an inescapable part of him. Of his life. *Of his heart*.

Perhaps it had started with his first glimpse of her dignity, her hard-headed obstinacy and pride, as she high-stepped through the mud the night of their "elopement" to Gretna, he thought fondly. She'd been too stubborn to knuckle under, yet too bloody proud to cry. Or perhaps it had been when he saw her with Mary in the rose garden, their two lovely heads bent together over the fragrant blossoms. He'd glimpsed something in Mary's face that day that gave him hope his daughter was responding to Victoria's warmth and affection. Or perhaps it was the joyous way his bride surrendered utterly in his arms; changed from a cool, elegant beauty to a deeply sensual woman whose body came alive under his touch, humming like a plucked mandolin.

Or perhaps it was simply all of the little things that made Victoria . . . Victoria. The woman, he realized, God help him, he had fallen deeply in love with.

"Bloody fool!" he muttered to no one in particular.

"M'lord?"

"Nothing, Mr. Turbot. Just thinking out loud."

Blowing the foam off his pint in the common fashion, which drew him nods of greeting and approval from the other drinkers, who were mostly fishermen and farmers, he made his way back between smoke-blackened settles, chairs and tables to his seat.

The small table by the lead-paned bay windows overlooked the high street. From there, he could watch who came and went in the fishing and jet-mining town on the bay, while he considered what to do about the wretched woman he'd married. The woman who had taken it into her foolish head that he wanted to murder her!

He spent a few moments watching the passersby going in and out of the red-roofed shops along the high street, which offered trinkets of carved jet, scrimshaw and shell-covered boxes and jewelry, before resuming his former pastime—staring into the depths of his glass tankard as if an answer might be found there.

He was still gazing morosely into his pint when a shadow fell across the table before him. He looked up to find a breathless Harry Coombs looking down at him, chest heaving as if he'd run a mile flat out.

"Afternoon, m'lord!" he stammered.

"Harry. What is it, man?"

"I just thought you might be interested to know, m'lord. Her Ladyship is out riding with the Honorable Delia Chillingsworth. The ladies will be passing the Arms in approximately two minutes, aye?"

"Two, you say?" He tried to sound nonchalant, but damn it, he couldn't help the way his head jerked around like a lovesick lad's. Nor the way his eyes immediately turned to the bay window and scanned the cobbled street, hungry for a glimpse of her. No, he couldn't help it—but he didn't have to like it, damn it.

"Pah. What do I care?" he growled. "The woman's irrational! She'd rather be miserable and alone than ever admit she's wrong!"

"Eeeh, you're right there, you are. Happen she'd do just that, m'lord. She's stubborn, that 'un, just like my Lily, sir. Between you and me, I reckon Lady Vicky takes after Old Thorny," Harry confided. "But never mind that for now, sir. I saw summat today. Summat—or someone, rather—thee should know about, m'lord. It could—aye, it could prove a matter of life, and death!"

"That important, is it?" Steede whistled under his breath, impressed by the seriousness of Harry's expression and his grim tone. "Bartender!"

"Sir?"

"Another pint for my friend here! Come on. Sit

down, man. Tell me what's bothering you."

Without further ado, Harry told him.

Having received Dr. Walters's permission to take the air for the first time since the beating had laid him low, Lord Hawthorne was champing at the bit to be up and about the following morning, a Sunday.

Since chapel was the only outing Delia would allow him, and because he would, furthermore, be in his betrothed's delightful company, he was uncharacteristically eager to attend morning services in Whitby that Sabbath, despite having turned his back on religion since his Isabelle's death.

"Why don't we all go!" Delia declared, smiling across the breakfast table at Victoria. "And after the service, we'll come back to Cook's lovely cold buffet and you can rest, my dear," she promised Roger fondly.

"Nooo, you two go without me," Victoria urged the lovebirds, resting a hand against her abdomen. "I'm feeling a little under the weather this morning."

She shot Delia a warning look, for despite her intention to tell her father about her condition, she had yet to do so.

"Aaah," Delia said, winking and giving Victoria's hand a conspiratorial pat. "It's probably just a touch of autumn grippe. Go on back to bed, old girl. I'll have Em bring you up some clear broth and dry toast."

"Don't bother—I'm almost certain it won't stay

down, but thank you anyway, Delia. Father's the luckiest man to have you," Victoria murmured, kissing Delia's cheek. "If you'll excuse me . . ." Tossing her crumpled serviette to the table, she left them alone.

In her brief absence, her bed had already been made, her room neatened and dusted, she discovered. Removing her morning gown and shoes, she pulled on a ruffled dressing gown, turned back the covers and lay down in her chemise and petticoats.

There was no need to loosen her stays. At Lily's urging, she'd dispensed with them over a week ago, and to her surprise, the morning sickness had eased, just as Lily promised.

Today, however, she felt sick to her stomach for some peculiar reason. Apprehensive. Edgy. Perhaps Delia was right, she thought. Perhaps the nausea, the overwhelming tiredness, were the result of an autumn grippe, and nothing to do with her condition at all.

She dozed off, waking to find that the drapes had been drawn while she slept. The room lay in heavy shadow now, except for the narrow band of harsh light where the draperies did not meet.

She listened intently, wondering what had awoken her, but heard only the measured ticktocking of the ormolu clock on the mantelpiece.

The great old house that surrounded her was hushed and silent, suspended in the drowsy spell cast by Sunday mornings.

Delia and Father must still be at church, she thought idly, stretching and yawning. And Carter, the butler, was probably down at the public house, enjoying an after-hours drink and luncheon with his old friend Mr. Turbot, the Arms' proprietor.

Lily had Sunday afternoon off, as usual, and had probably gone to visit her parents, since Harry had returned to Devonshire with Steede.

And Cook—Cook would have left for her sister's cottage in Whitby for the day, after preparing the delicious cold buffet in the pantry, which served for their luncheon and supper, as it did every Sunday.

In the kitchen, the scullery and chambermaids were probably enjoying a few unsupervised moments with their feet up, giggling and sampling forbidden treats before they served the family their Sunday high tea, promptly at three.

As for the grooms, they'd be indulging in a clandestine game of cards down at the gamekeeper's cottage, keeping a weather eye out for His Lordship's return, for the master did not approve of games of chance, especially on the Sabbath, religious or not.

To all intents and purpose, she was all alone here. And, although there was no reason why it should, the knowledge made her uneasy. She felt—foolish as it seemed—as if someone were watching her. Had, perhaps, been standing over her, looking down at her while she slept.

Steede. Had he come back?

Raising her head slightly, she could see the armoire opposite the foot of the bed, where her undergarments, stockings, garters and nightgowns were stored. Against the wall opposite the window, where the light was best, stood her dressing table and stool, and behind it, an oval looking glass.

Unlike Blackstone Manor and her papa's Belgravia townhouse, here at the Hall her gowns were stored in a small room next door. The door leading to the dressing room was hidden behind a folding red-lacquer screen, painted with Chinese scenes of herons and wispy bamboo stalks. That door was, she noticed suddenly, ajar, revealing a wedge of darkness beyond . . .

"Hello!" she called shakily. "Lily? Is that you?"

There was so answer. Still, she was almost certain she had heard a furtive scuffle.

"Hello, I said!" Her voice rang out, sounding overly loud in the fragrant hush of powders and perfumes. "Who's there? Steede? Is that you?"

Once again, there was no answer, yet the disturbing sensation that she was not alone refused to go away. Perhaps it was one of the maids, playing a spiteful joke . . . ?

But in her heart, she knew no one at Hawthorne Hall would do such a thing.

Gooseflesh prickled down her arms. The fine hairs on her nape stood up on end. Had the dressing-room door been ajar earlier, when she came upstairs? She suddenly wondered, feeling suddenly chilled.

She couldn't remember.

For some reason, it seemed vital that she should.

Gingerly sitting up, she carefully swung her

legs over the edge of the bed and stood, relieved to find the nausea had passed.

Creeping silently across the room in her stockinged feet, she tiptoed to the folding screen and peeked around a panel.

Too late, she sensed rather than saw the malevolent shadow that swooped down on her like a great black raven.

Her last coherent thought was that she'd been wrong, terribly wrong about everything.

"Steede!" she screamed.

Her terrified cry was cut off as a weighty hand clamped over her mouth. Coarse fingers pinched her nostrils together, cutting off the air.

She couldn't breathe—couldn't breathe— couldn't—breathe . . .

Blackness.

"Well, well. Good day, Blackstone! Still here, I see."

"Where's my wife? Is Victoria still inside the church?"

Hawthorne frowned. His son-in-law seemed curt to the point of insolence this morning. Not so much as a hail or a fare-thee-well.

"Why, no. She didn't choose to accompany us to chapel this morning. A touch of the grippe, Delia thought. She's resting at home. If you're intending to have it out with her, I recommend you wait a day or two—"

"Is she alone, man?" Steede demanded, cutting the older man off as he gripped Hawthorne's shoulder. His eyes were a glittering black, his jaw hard as he rasped, "Quickly! Answer me!"

Hawthorne looked shocked, taken aback. "Let me see. There are the—er—the maids, and then there's . . . no, no, they all have the afternoon off. I suppose . . . well, yes, I suppose she is alone, to all intents and purposes. But why do you—? Good God, man! You've gone white as chalk! What the devil is it?"

"Ned Thomas was spotted at his father's farm yesterday afternoon, sir." Steede almost spat the words out in his haste to be gone. "Harry immediately notified the authorities, but when they went out to the farm to arrest him, they learned from his mother that he'd slipped out when he saw them coming. Neither they, nor Harry or myself have been able to find him since! I came to warn you and Victoria that he was back and spoiling for trouble. When I saw your carriage in the churchyard, I thought—well, I naturally thought Victoria would be at church with you, sir—"

But even as he spoke, Steede was racing for the hired nag that Harry was holding.

"Go!" Hawthorne bellowed. "I'll be right behind you."

He and Harry needed no second urging. Wheeling their horses about, they gave the beasts their heads.

The house appeared deserted when they rode up. Nor did anyone answer their calls as they searched the sprawling mansion, floor by floor and room by room.

When Steede burst into his wife's apartments,

he saw at once that a lacquered Chinese screen had been overturned, as well as a milk-glass lamp and several other items.

A violent struggle had obviously taken place in the room.

Claws of foreboding sank deep into his gut as he raced back the way he'd come.

Harry caught him by the shoulder as he spilled out of the kitchen door, which opened onto the stableyard and the stables and carriage houses across the way.

Silently, Coombs pressed a finger to his lips and pointed to the stables.

"He's in there," he mouthed.

Steede gave a single, curt nod. "And my wife?" he mouthed in return.

"I saw him carry her inside."

Carry her? Oh, God! Then Victoria was either unconscious—or dead. His gut clenched in pure terror. He couldn't lose her. Not now. *Wouldn't lose her!* He loved her too much to let her go. . . .

Motioning Harry to wait, he sprinted across the stableyard, then ducked silently into the shadows of the stables.

She came around to find Ned Thomas crouched over her. He was breathing thickly as he yanked the fronts of her wrapper apart, ripping the sash in the process. With a quick, hard pull, he jerked down her under-chemise, baring her breasts. The ribbon that gathered the neckline tore as he did so.

He sucked in a breath, the air whistling through his teeth as he ogled her.

"Not a sound out o' you, bitch," he warned, his pewter eyes kindling with a cold, cruel gleam as he covered one breast with a callused hand, and squeezed. "One squeak, and I'll brain thee."

She lay unmoving in the straw, unresponsive as a log while he groped at her. How strange. It was as if what he was doing was happening to somebody else. As if she, in some peculiar way, was merely an onlooker, a casual observer, rather than a victim. Besides, on another level, she knew he would have derived enormous pleasure from her resistance. . . .

She had to buy some time. To think how she would get away.

He must have carried her downstairs, then outside, to the stables. To the place her father had surprised them together months ago, Victoria realized with a shiver, opening her eyes and looking up at him.

His clothes and body were dirty and unkempt, and there was a desperate air about him that boded ill for her. In fact, he bore little resemblance to the handsome Ned she remembered. But then, neither was she the naive, innocent girl she had been that long-ago day. There was little doubt in her mind what Ned intended to do to her, she thought with a shiver.

"Why did you bring me here?" she demanded, trying to reach the part of the man she'd once known and loved, if that part had ever truly existed except in her romantic imagination. "Why are you doing this to me? I loved you! Why would you want to hurt me, Ned?"

"You, love the likes o' me? Ha! Not bloody likely," he jeered, fondling her stockinged leg. His pewter eyes gleamed, feral in the shadows. "What thee wanted was the same thing I wanted at that mine, my lass. Revenge! To get back at your bloody father!"

"You almost killed him!"

"Aye. Aye, I did, didn't I?" he sneered. "I should have gone back and finished the job. Happen I'll finish it yet. And after our bit of fun, you'll be my ticket out of here, aye, lass? What do they call it? My hostage!"

"Take your hands off me," she insisted, her belly heaving in disgust as he squeezed her thigh, bruising it.

"Don't ye like a dirty miner touching your lily white teats, Your Ladyship?" he taunted. "Don't ye like these filthy working-class hands all over ye? Well, that's too bloody bad, because I'm going to do more than touch thee, ye snobby little teaser. I'm going to make ye squeal."

Stunned, she realized he was opening his breeches. She had to get away now or it would be too late!

"Please," she whispered, her voice breaking as she curled her fingers into tight, hard fists. She drew up her knee, outwardly submissive, inwardly coiled to fight or flee, or both. "Please, Ned. Don't do this . . ."

*　　*　　*

Steede stood in the shadows, temporarily blinded while he waited for his eyes to adjust to the gloom.

Yet even as he stood there, he heard the sound of flesh striking flesh, followed by a thick, pained male grunt.

"You bitch!" he heard Thomas rasp. Then there was the sound of a ringing slap, followed by his wife's whimper of hurt.

"Victoria!" he roared.

"Steede!"

Her cry acted like a red flag to a bull.

With a bellow of rage, Steede lunged frantically from stall to stall, searching for her as she exploded from the farthest stall.

Barefoot, she ran down the long aisle between the rows of partitions toward him. Her hair was a wild black torrent against her torn wrapper. Her eyes were huge in her pale face. Her clothing was disheveled.

"Oh, Steede! Oh, thank God!" she cried, throwing herself into his arms.

"Did he hurt you?" he demanded, tracing the red marks of a hand across her cheek.

"No," she assured him, but her torn clothing, the raised welts across her cheek, the tears brimming in her eyes told a different story.

"Go on outside," he ordered through gritted teeth. "Harry's waiting. Go to him."

"But what about y—?"

"Do it!" he cut her off. Chucking her beneath the chin, he added in a gentler voice, "I'll be fine. I promise."

"See that you are," she whispered fiercely. Giving his arm a quick, hard squeeze, she quickly brushed past him.

"Come on out, you bastard!" Steede roared. "Just you and me! Not the women and old men you usually prey on!"

Ned Thomas stepped into the aisle from one of the horse stalls. He wore a flat brown cap, a soiled collarless white shirt tucked into brown moleskin trousers, and leather braces. He was smiling wolfishly—and carrying a pitchfork.

"Put 'em up, Yer Lordship," he sneered.

Steede obliged, his fists raised before him, ready to jab, to block, to wrest the pitchfork from Thomas's hands. His weight was balanced on the balls of his feet, and an unholy grin added an evil cast to his features.

"Come on then, you bastard!" he taunted. "Come and get me!"

He danced left as Ned suddenly lunged forward, hefting the pitchfork at his face, yet he felt the rush of air as the wicked tines flashed past his cheek.

Hissing a foul oath, he jerked his head aside, reached for the pitchfork, grappled it out of Thomas's hands and hurled it into a heap of straw, out of reach.

Thomas howled with rage, drew back his knotted fist and swung a punch at Steede's head.

Momentum carried the miner straight into the piledriver Steede held ready to drive into his gut.

With a grunt, Ned reeled backward, the breath slammed from him.

"What's up, old son?" Steede jeered as he scrambled to his feet. "Not much fun with your bare fists—is that it? Or perhaps hitting a woman is more fun?"

"Shut thy bleeding mouth, else I'll shut it for thee, Blackstone!" Ned threatened, landing a lucky punch on Steede's chin.

He shook his ringing head as white lights danced in the red haze of his vision. "I'll see you in hell first!" Steede panted.

Blood and sweat sprayed like drops of paint as, suddenly darting forward, he caught Ned under the chin with a solid thwack. The uppercut sent the miner staggering backward several feet.

"I had her first, ye know. Yer wife, I mean. Lady Vic-tor-ia," Ned taunted, his expression sly as, bobbing and weaving, he fought to stay upright, wiping the blood from a split lip on the back of his hand.

"Couldn't wait, she couldn't, she were that eager for it. Crawled all over me like a she-cat in heat." He grinned and lewdly waggled his tongue at Steede. "Just beggin' me for it, she was! Well, what's a man t'do, aye?" He jerked his hips, lewdly pantomiming.

Steede knew, on one level, what Thomas hoped to do, yet the other levels didn't give a damn about reason. A crimson rage exploded through him, adding fury to his fists.

Slamming blow after blow into the miner's head and chest, immune to those that hammered his own body in return, he drove Ned out of the gloomy stables, into the harsh glare of the stableyard, where Harry and several others were waiting.

"Come 'ere, you!" Harry began, reaching for Ned, but Steede waved him back.

"Get away, Harry. He's mine. You can't have him. Not yet."

Hammering blow after blow at the laborer, Steede backed him up against the woodshed wall. He held him upright there, one forearm planted across Ned's windpipe as, his chest heaving, he paused to recover his breath.

Despite the bruises, the cuts, elation sang through him. Nothing had ever felt as good—or as right—as giving this bastard the thrashing he deserved.

"Enough, m'lord! Have done, sir, before ye kill him. I'll take him now, aye?" bellowed a loud voice.

Strong hands gripped his shoulders, pulling him off battered, bleeding Ned Thomas.

No longer supported by Steede's forearm, Thomas slid limply down the stone wall and sat there, like a marionette with its strings cut.

His fair head lolled to one side, the dirty hair streaked with blood from a hairline cut. His nose was shattered, both lips split and bleeding, both gray eyes so badly swollen it was impossible to tell if they were open or shut. Most of his face was mottled a dark bluish hue, evidence of the livid bruising that would appear in the next few hours.

But it was not enough for Steede. Not for what

Thomas had tried to do to the woman he loved. . . .

With a bellow of fury, he lunged at him again.

"Now then, sir. Enough's enough," Mr. Lovett insisted sternly, catching Steede's upper arms when he tried to drag the miner upright once more. The older man was surprisingly strong. "Come away wi' ye, lad!"

"Get your hands off me!" Steede growled, trying to shrug Lovett off.

"No, son. Lovett's right. Ye've taught Thomas a champion lesson, ye have, but enough's enough. Let the authorities have him now. We're proper proud of ye, we are, me and your lady here. Aren't we, my love? But let Harry take him for ye now, aye?" urged Lord Hawthorne, one arm around his daughter, the other around his betrothed.

Nodding slowly, Steede stepped back, his head bowed, wiping a trickle of blood from his mouth on the back of his fist as, on Lovett's orders, Harry and the other stable hands carried Ned Thomas away.

"Oh, Steede!" Victoria cried. She ran to him, half afraid he would want nothing to do with her. Nor could she blame him if he didn't. . . .

But to her delight, he opened his arms.

She flung herself into them. Joy filled her as his weary arms tightened around her in a fierce embrace. He lifted her, swung her high and around, so that her petticoats flew out.

"I didn't mean it, I swear I didn't," she sobbed when he put her down. Gently, she cupped his poor, battered face between her hands in a desperate bid to make him understand. "Please don't go. Don't leave me. *I love you, Steede!* I love you so much. I've loved you for weeks and weeks—almost from the very first. It's just that—I didn't know what to believe anymore! And I swear to you, I never did—what Ned said—I didn't, ever—I swear it! It was just kisses, nothing more."

"Hush." He pressed a finger to her lips. "I know."

She bit her lower lip, blinking back tears. "Oh, your poor, poor mouth."

"It's nothing."

"Oh, but it is! I've been wanting so much to—"

He kissed her then to shut her up, as much as anything; a long and infinitely sweet kiss that stole her breath away. She could taste his blood and her tears on his lips, their salty tang mingled with the sweetness.

"Steede, there's something I haven't told you. Something wonderful . . ."

"About the baby?" he asked, placing his palm against her belly.

"But how did you know?" she exclaimed. "Delia? Did you—?"

"Delia didn't have to tell me anything. I'm your husband, remember? I've noticed the changes in you. In the way your body feels," he murmured, his voice a seductive caress. "Lusher. Fuller. Ripe as an ear of wheat . . ."

"And?" She held her breath, her fingers crossed. Please, God, let him be as glad about the baby as she was.

"Nothing could make me happier—except for what you just told me."

"That I love you?"

He nodded. "That you love me. As I love you, with all my heart. It didn't start out that way for me, any more than it did for you. I didn't think it mattered whether we loved each other or not, but I was wrong. In the end, love matters. It matters more than any of it."

"Amen!" she whispered fervently.

He grinned down at her. And, although the puffy lips, the cuts on his swollen eyebrow, the livid bruising marred his striking features, he'd never looked more handsome.

"Call Alf and t' other lads t' cart him away, Harry," Lovett urged his future son-in-law.

He nodded at Thomas, still slumped against the wall, his jaw slack, his mouth gaping. Blood dribbled from his nose to stain his grimy shirt-front.

"T' Whitby constables are coming to fetch our Master Thomas. Aye, and they're bringing a warrant, too! Get a move on, lads. Unless I miss my mark, Lord and Lady Blackstone are wanting to be alone!" he added with a rare wink for Steede.

"Hmm, you taste different," Steede murmured later, running his tongue down the valley between her breasts, then gently biting each nipple in turn until it hardened. "Like a ripe, juicy peach."

"Liar," she accused, squirming with lazy contentment on the rumpled bed linens, enjoying his seductive kisses and caresses.

She ruffled his ebony hair, running her fingers through the inky waves at his nape. "But don't stop. *Oh, yes*. Right there! Hmm. That's *love-ly*," she murmured as his tongue danced over her belly, rimmed the well of her navel, then moved lower, to where a triangular sea of midnight curls lapped at the creamy flesh of her belly and thighs. "Sooo lovely . . ."

Speech was impossible after that. So was thought. She could only feel, one incredibly pleasurable sensation building on another, until her climax burst over her like champagne rain.

In its wake was blessed calm—and a deep contentment more precious than gold.

"My turn," Steede promised thickly.

He turned her over so that they lay curled on their sides, like spoons in a drawer. Bracing a hand on either side of her bottom, he drew her back, eased her onto him, burying himself to the hilt with a practiced dip of his flanks. Her startled gasp as he entered her made him chuckle, yet she eagerly pressed back, onto him.

"Surprised? Don't be. There are more ways for a man and a woman to make love than you could ever imagine, my sweet," he murmured, nuzzling her throat. Her scent intoxicated him, a heady yet elusive blend of hyacinths and talcum powder and the sweet fragrance of Victoria, the woman. "This one comes highly recommended for women in your condition."

She giggled. "I highly recommend it, too, my

condition be damned!" she declared naughtily. "How many ways are there in all, do you suppose?" she wondered aloud.

He grinned, his black eyes flashing in the murky light of her room, where the fire had died down to a heap of glowing embers.

"Be damned if I know. Let's count them, shall we?"

She drew his hands up, so that they cupped her breasts from behind. "I thought you'd never ask. . . ."

They dimly heard the dinner gong bonging soon after, but not even Cook's fabled cold buffet was enough to tempt them from the banquet of sensual delights on which they feasted.

"I want to tell you how Aimee died," he told her much, much later when she lay warm and loose in his arms, filled with the lazy afterglow of their lovemaking. "And why I consider myself responsible."

"It's time," she agreed softly as he sat up.

While she wound the sheet around herself, he pulled on his trousers, then rose to light a cheroot. The sharp odor of sulphur filled the room as he struck a Swan Vesta to do so.

"I should have asked you point blank weeks ago, instead of jumping to such silly conclusions."

"No, I'm to blame as much as you. I thought I could simply forget about it, but I was wrong. I wonder. Where should I begin?

"I suppose it really began after Mary was

born," he decided after several moments of smoking in silence. "The physician who had attended my daughter's birth asked to meet with me in private after he had examined Aimee. That day, he told me that very rarely, women go into a marked mental and emotional decline following the births of their children," he explained. "In his opinion, Aimee was one of those women.

"In the days, then weeks following Mary's birth, Aimee's moods were very odd, you see. She could be elated one moment, cast into the sloughs of despair the next. It quickly became apparent that she was quite incapable of caring for our little daughter. And so I engaged Kalinda as the baby's ayah and wet-nurse. The physician recommended that Aimee have no more children. Her labor had been a long, grueling one, and her mental state afterward had proven precarious, to say the least. The doctor told me that mothers in Aimee's condition sometimes tried to harm themselves or their infant children before they recovered. Others never got well, but ended up living out their days in asylums.

"I loved my wife, Victoria. I couldn't bear to think of her being shut away for the rest of her life. And so I explained what the doctor had said, and told her that, for her own good, because I loved her, we must discontinue marital relations."

"That poor, poor woman," Victoria murmured. "How rejected she must have felt." She bit her lower lip. "And how awful for you, too, my love."

He nodded. "I won't deny it. It was torture. Aimee was a beautiful woman. I desired her, and yet I was prepared to forgo all intimacy if it meant she would be well again. Aimee and the little daughter she'd given me were my entire life, until . . ."

He broke off, seeming unable to go on. She stroked his cheek, where bruises showed as livid shadows beneath the tanned skin.

"Until what? What happened to change everything? Don't stop now. Tell me!"

He sighed heavily and tossed his cheroot into the fire behind the bedroom grate. "Until I learned Aimee had a lover. The man served as adjutant to my regiment's commanding officer. Tristram Blake, his name was. She claimed she took tea with the colonel's wife, Miriam, several afternoons a week, and that Blake was merely her escort. But when it became obvious that she was with child—a child that could not have been mine—I knew my suspicions were correct. I confronted her, and she admitted it. She said that Blake had abandoned her when she told him about the baby.

"I offered to stand by her until after the baby was born, then I would resign my commission and return to England with little Mary, alone. My brother, John, had been killed in the first year of the Crimean, you see, and my father had quickly followed him to the grave. As the new Earl of Blackstone, I was needed to run things here in England.

"Well, in due course, Aimee gave birth to a healthy son—a child that, like our daughter, she took little interest in. She either lay abed in her darkened rooms, weeping, or rose to scream at our terrified servants and fill the bungalow with peals of hysterical laughter.

"When Baby Johnny was six weeks old, I told Aimee I had arranged passage for her and the infant on a ship bound for England. I suggested she return to her father's household while I filed for the divorce. She refused. She said she would never return to England. That the shame of a divorce would be too much to endure.

"I told her she was just being hysterical. To pull herself together. When I left her a little later that evening, she still seemed upset, but composed. Resigned—or so I thought. As I went out, I heard her telling Kalinda to bring the baby's bassinet into her room. I remember feeling encouraged that she was finally showing an interest in her baby." He shook his head. "Then I retired to my study to attend to some paperwork.

"Two hours later, I heard screaming. I ran toward the sound, and found Kalinda and Mary on the veranda outside Aimee's rooms. Smoke was billowing from the windows. Kalinda was screaming that a fallen lamp had ignited the hangings. The draperies had caught instantly. The bed linens, too. Within seconds, my wife's rooms were engulfed. I carried Mary outside into the garden, as far from the burning bungalow as I could get. After ordering Kalinda to stay with her, I went back inside for my wife."

"And Aimee?" Victoria whispered.

Steede closed his eyes, as if to shut out the awful images he saw even now.

"Aimee . . . Aimee was standing in her room, encircled by a wall of fire. She held the baby in her arms and . . ."

"Tell me, whatever it is. There will be no more secrets between us!" she urged, squeezing his hand.

"She was *laughing*." He shuddered. "Oh, God. Her nightgown was smoldering. Her beautiful gold hair was frizzling up, and yet—she was laughing. The baby—that poor little mite—was screaming and coughing. And then—and then he wasn't coughing anymore. He was still. Not making a sound.

"While all of this was happening, I was going half out of my mind trying to get to them. The buckets of water the servants threw on the fire were useless. Each time, the heat drove me back, hotter than a furnace! My eyebrows were singed, my hair burned. In desperation, I soaked a blanket in water, threw it over myself and forced my way through the flames to get to them. Even so, I was too late."

He stated it simply, but oh, the horror in his voice, in his expression, Victoria thought, deeply moved. And what self-condemnation, too.

"The smoke had overwhelmed them," he went on. "Aimee and the baby were both dead, and Mary"—he shuddered—"Mary wouldn't stop screaming. Some nights, I still hear her in my head."

But she had never spoken since that night, Victoria thought with a shudder.

"These past three years, you held yourself responsible. But why? It was not your fault—none of it was."

"That's not so. I *was* responsible—don't you see? If I hadn't threatened to divorce her—"

"Nonsense! Aimee was the one who chose to be unfaithful, not you. She gave you precious little choice in the matter, as I see it. And you were far kinder than she had any right to expect. You denied yourself a husband's rights solely because you loved her and wanted to protect her. And even after she had proven herself unfaithful, and borne another man's child, you allowed her to remain in your household until she had been safely delivered. The fire was a tragic accident. You have nothing whatsoever to reproach yourself for."

"Then you'll come home with me in the morning? Home to Mother, and Mary?"

She smiled, and it was a wonderful sight! As dazzling as the sun coming out, he thought, remembering a time when he had wondered how it would feel to have her smile at him that way.

Now he knew . . .

"Yes, my love. We'll both go home."

Chapter Twenty-five

Sam, the Blackstone under-groom, was waiting at the station for them with the carriage when the train pulled into Blackstone at dusk of the following day, carrying Victoria, Steede, Harry and Lily.

"How's everything, Sam?" Steede asked as Harry and Sam together wrestled their luggage up onto the carriage.

"Fair enough, sir," Sam responded with unusual curtness. He inspected the toes of his boots, refusing to meet Steede's eyes.

"Sam has a wasp up his breeches, wouldn't you say?" Steede murmured in Victoria's ear as he handed her up into the carriage.

"A wasp up his breeches? You really did spend a lot of time with my father, didn't you?" she said, laughing. "You're even starting to sound like him!"

"God forbid!" Steede shuddered, leaping in after her.

"Oh, I just can't wait to see Mary again," Victoria exclaimed as the horses pulled away from the station.

"Nor I. When shall we tell her about the baby?"

"Soon. We must give her time to become accustomed to the idea of a baby brother or sister."

"Do you know when . . . ?"

"I believe you will become a father again very close to our first wedding anniversary, m'lord." She saw his eyes darken with concern, and cupped his battered cheek. "You mustn't worry. I spoke with Dr. Walters when I went into Whitby yesterday. What happened to Aimee is quite rare. There is no reason to fear that I shall be similarly afflicted."

"Thank God," he muttered, giving her a quick, hard hug.

In minutes, they were being bowled down the shingle driveway toward the twelve chimneys of Blackstone Manor, which rose like pointing black fingers against the fiery orange of the autumn sunset.

Yet even from a distance, it was apparent that something was very wrong. There were men everywhere, some streaming back toward the house across the lawns, others leaving it: gamekeepers and their lads who carried shotguns underarm; farm workers and shepherds who

360

tramped the fields bearing stout sticks and storm lanterns aloft.

When Steede stuck his head out of the window, the men greeted His Lordship respectfully with a nod, a muttered word, a touch of the forelock. Yet like Sam, not one would meet his eyes.

"What the devil's going on here, Sam?" Steede demanded. "Stop this bloody carriage and let me out!"

"Lady Henrietta said not t' say nothin', sir," Sam mumbled. He squirmed on his high perch as he looked down at his furious master. "Wanted to tell you herself, Her Ladyship did."

"Tell me what, damn it?"

"About Lady Mary, sir. She be gone! She's took her pony and run off!"

"Good God, man! When?" Steede demanded, suddenly white about the mouth.

"Yesterday afternoon, sir. Around teatime, it were. We've all been helping with the search. I expect the telegram Lady Henrietta sent passed ye, sir."

Sweet Lord! Had he won back his wife and their unborn child, only to lose his little daughter?

To Victoria, it was déjà-vu. The scene from the Whitby jet mines, all over again! But this time, the drawn, anxious-eyed men who milled about Blackstone Manor carried storm lanterns and flaming torches aloft as they set out to comb the woods, the rocky tors and treacherous high moors for a missing little girl and her pony, rather than a maze of cold, damp tunnels that riddled the bowels of the earth.

Victoria burrowed deeper into the folds of her long riding cloak. Although it was trimmed with rabbit fur at both collar and arm-openings, she shivered from a deep chill that had nothing to do with the weather.

Perhaps Mary would have been better off lost in the mines, she wondered. Dartmoor, lorded over by High Willhayes tor to the south, and over two thousand feet at its highest point, was a place of wild beauty. But it was also a place of quagmires that swallowed up the unwary, man or beast, leaving nothing behind to mark their passing.

Almost 350 square miles of empty moorland, rocky tors, woods and clear streams burbling over stones, Dartmoor was a place where Mother Nature ruled, harsh and indiscriminate.

She played no favorites, made no allowances for human weakness—nor for the fragility of little children. Only the strongest and fittest survived here: the rugged moorland ponies, the hardy sheep. The weak fell by the wayside and were lost.

Those few hardened convicts, both American and British, who in 1815 had tried to escape desolate Dartmoor Prison's forbidding gray walls at Prince Town—a bloody incident later named the Dartmoor Massacre—had soon discovered there was but one way to leave the infamous prison: in a shroud.

Those pitiful few who, down the years, had

successfully evaded the prison guards by scaling the prison's forbidding walls were likewise swallowed up by the treacherous moors, and seen no more. They paid for their temporary freedom with their lives.

Henrietta had come rushing out of the house to meet them the very moment the carriage jounced to a halt.

"Oh, Steede, Mary's gone—vanished—and her pony, too! We cannot find her anywhere! Oh, the poor, poor child . . ." the older woman cried, wringing her hands. She looked gray with worry, heavy-eyed from lack of sleep.

"Calm down, Mother. You'll only make yourself ill. Trust me. We're going to find her. Where's her nursemaid?" Steede demanded as he stepped down from the carriage. Lifting Victoria down after him, he strode into the Manor.

"Upstairs in her room. To give the wretched woman her due, she seems almost as distraught as I am," Henrietta said charitably.

"I'm sure she is. As would anyone who feared that their livelihood had run off and left them. Jessup!"

"Sir?" the butler responded smartly with a half-bow.

"Have Kalinda sent to me in my study immediately."

"At once, sir."

"Come, Victoria, Mama. This way," Steede murmured. Tucking Victoria's hand through his own, he led the way into the study.

He had seated the two women in chairs before

the fire, and poured them medicinal glasses of blackberry wine, when Jessup returned.

The butler's angular face was even more gaunt than usual, his large eyes as mournful as a bloodhound's.

"I regret there has been a new development, m'lord," he informed them gravely. "It appears the Lady Mary's nursemaid has also left Blackstone Manor. Regrettably, none of the staff witnessed her departure, or knows what direction she might have taken."

"Surely she has gone to find Mary," Lady Henrietta suggested hopefully.

"I believe that is unlikely, madam, since Miss Kalinda took all of her possessions with her."

"That wretched woman!" Henrietta exclaimed in anguish, springing to her feet. "How on earth shall we find Mary without her to tell us where to look! If anyone knows where my granddaughter has vanished to, it is that dreadful woman, mark my words!"

The search party's wavering amber lights, eerily glimpsed through a veil of thick mist, reminded Victoria of the old Yorkshire belief in "corpse candles," the balls of glowing light seen hovering over the graves of the newly interred. According to superstition, these wavering lights were the restless souls of those buried beneath the mossy headstones.

The ghoulish comparison made Victoria shudder.

Closing her eyes and clasping her hands tightly

before her, she offered up yet another silent prayer that God would keep the little girl she had come to love safe from all harm. That they would find her before the poor darling was forced to endure another night of terror and exposure, far from those who loved her.

Blinking back a tear, she felt Steede's warm, strong hand on her own. He squeezed it comfortingly.

"Chin up, Lady Blackstone," he murmured, his dark eyes glinting in the glow of the storm lantern. "We're going to find our little girl. I *know* it."

Our little girl. She swallowed over the lump in her throat. He was right. She could not have been more concerned about nor loved Mary more, had she given birth to her herself.

"Yes," Victoria agreed firmly, meeting his eyes. Her fingers curled around his and tightly squeezed. "We are."

"*Mary!*" Steede shouted, cupping his mouth with his hands. His deep voice was immediately swallowed up by the mist.

"*Mary!*" came the faint, thin sound of another searcher's disembodied voice. It reached them through the dense fog like the reedy echo of her husband's voice.

The caller could have been within feet of them and they would not have seen him, the mist was so thick.

In another few moments, they would have to abandon the search until first light the following morning. The fog, coupled with the treacherous ground underfoot, and unseen quagmires, made further searching a perilous undertaking for all concerned.

If, God willing, Mary had survived thus far, Victoria prayed with all her heart that she would stay wherever she was until it was light. *Willed* her to stay there.

"Dear Lord, watch over our little lost lamb," she whispered fervently. "Keep her safe in Thy tender care, and guide her back to those who love her."

"Amen," came Steede's deep voice, equally fervent, at her side.

But for what few moments they had left, they continued to call:

"Ma—ry! Maaaa—rrr—yyy . . . !"

Chapter Twenty-six

When dawn broke the following morning, it found the search party huddled in oilskins in the lee of Tamar's tor. They were soaked and exhausted, and still had no word of either the little girl or her nursemaid.

"You men, go on back to the house," Steede ordered half of the search party as the first lemon-yellow fingers of light streaked the charcoal sky to the east. "I've left instructions with my housekeeper that you're to be given a good, hot meal on your return. When you've eaten, I want you to go home and rest until noon. Then, God willing, you'll take our places—unless my daughter has been found in the meantime." He looked around the circle of tired faces. "Our heartfelt thanks to all of you, for helping in the search."

As the men dispersed, Steede turned to Victoria.

"My instructions included you, my love," he murmured tenderly, his expression concerned as he looked down into her upturned face. "Look how pale you are! You've already done more than any woman in your condition should do. Go on back to the house with Harry, here."

"Aye, Your Ladyship. Come along wi' me," Harry urged. "My Lily will be beside herself, worrying about thee, she will."

"Hush," she soothed Steede, placing a finger gently against his lips. "There's no possible way I can just go home and twiddle my thumbs with Mary still missing. Don't ask it of me, either of you," she implored Steede and Harry in turn. "For if you insist, I shall undertake a search of my own. And that, my dear, could well prove a far more hazardous undertaking."

"Very well, then. But when the rested men resume the search at midday, promise me you will go home." Steede placed his hand gently over her belly. "For our unborn babe's sake."

"All right. For his sake, I promise."

They rode through the woods at the edge of the moors, thinking—hoping—that perhaps Mary had strayed toward the village. The horses' hooves rustled as they walked them through drifts of colored leaves—the same drifts of scarlet, gold and russet in which she and Steede had once made love.

But the trees were almost bare now, and they found no little girl asleep at the foot of their massive trunks, like the babes-in-the-woods of the fairy tale.

In the end, she and Steede rode out of the woods and back up onto the high moors alone, leaving the others to beat the fields and the hedgerows and—horror of horrors—to drag nearby ponds.

The too-bright autumn sunlight slanted across the turf beneath their horses' thudding hooves, turning sere grass to antique gold.

They had been walking their mounts for a little over an hour, eyes narrowed, scanning the moors in all directions to spot even the smallest movement, when Victoria saw a thin column of smoke rising into the air.

"Look! Over there. What is it?" she asked.

"A shepherd's campfire, probably."

"Shouldn't we investigate?"

He nodded. "It's probably nothing, but it won't hurt to look."

They rode closer, realizing while still some distance from the fire that the camp did not belong to a shepherd, as they'd thought, but to a band of Gypsies.

As their horses neared the circle of colorfully painted *vardos*, the camp dogs came out to bark and snap at their mounts' heels. Several dark-haired women and children stood and stared as they rode closer.

Motioning Victoria to stay back, Steede rode closer. "Good day to you!" he called. "May I speak with your head man?"

"You are speaking with him, *gorgio*. Carlos

Lee," a swarthy, stocky man declared. Thumbs tucked into a wide leather belt, he had swaggered out from behind one of the painted caravans. "What does a fine *gorgio rey* want with my Gypsies, eh?"

"My little daughter ran away from home two days ago. She is just eight years of age, and has spent the past two nights out in the open, alone. I hope and pray she has survived this long, but another night—?" His expression was grave. "Has any of your band seen a small girl riding a black pony?"

"We have seen nothing. There are only Gypsy girls and Gypsy ponies in this camp, *gorgio*. Ride on!"

"Very well. How about a woman?"

Carlos's bushy black brows lifted. "You seek a whore, then find yourself a *gorgio* whore! Insult our women again and my brothers and cousins, they will slit your throat, eh?" He spat in the dirt, turned on a booted heel and walked away

"Wait! I didn't mean that, Lee. The woman I'm looking for is my daughter's nursemaid. An Indian woman. She may know where Mary has gone."

"Gypsies do not kidnap little children, nor nursemaids," Lee sneered. "This is a dirty lie told by *gorgio* mothers to frighten their children. I told you. We have not seen the child or the woman."

Steede nodded. "If you should find her on your travels, I'm offering a handsome reward for her safe return."

Lee smiled. "I shall keep that in mind, *gorgio*. Now, be off with you!"

Steede rode back to where he'd left Victoria.

"Nothing?" she asked. He looked so gray with worry, so very drawn, she ached to take him in her arms and comfort him.

"He said they haven't seen Mary or Kalinda. I don't know whether to believe him or not," Steede said softly. "I'll have a constable question him later. Maybe he can persuade him to talk. Let's go!"

It was as they were riding away that Victoria thought she heard someone call her name. A low call, little more than a whisper.

The hackles rose on the back of her neck as she reined Calypso in, for the sudden sensation of being watched was very strong indeed.

Shading her eyes against the bright light as Steede rode on, Victoria slowly turned in the saddle, scanning the rolling moors that swept away in all directions.

Her view was unbroken except for Steede and his mount, who were now several hundred yards to the west, and the colorfully painted and gilded Gypsy wagons, which formed a circle among the outcropping of black rocks and trees at the foot of the tor.

She caught the smell of woodsmoke and roasted rabbit on the wind.

Cocking her head to one side, she sat very still, listening intently.

There! That faint cry again! It sounded like someone calling her name. More than likely, it was only wishful thinking, coupled with an over-active imagination. Or perhaps the low moan of the wind, or the shriek of a hunting hawk as it rode the air currents, high above the moors.

"Here!" came the low cry again. *" 'Toria!"*

Gooseflesh prickling down her neck, Victoria spun like a top in the direction of that low, feeble sound, her senses alert.

Over there! The call had come from the east, from a smart black *vardo* painted with scrolling leaves and vines. The wagon was set a little apart from the others, and was the only one with a horse still harnessed in the traces. The other animals had been turned loose to graze.

Near the *vardo* grew low, gnarled thorn bushes. Slabs of black rock were scattered about like fallen dominoes. Rocks that were too small, surely, to hide even a child from view?

Had the sound come from the wagon itself, then?

Turning Calypso's head, she rode the mare slowly back toward the Gypsy camp and the black wagon, afraid to hope in case disappointment proved too crushing to bear.

" 'Toria!" the voice croaked again.

The single word, forced from a voice grown rusty with disuse, had come from the door at the rear of the *vardo!*

Goosebumps prickled down her arms. The hair on the back of her neck stood on end. The heart leaped in Victoria's breast as tears of joy sprang into her eyes. A sob burst from her as, sliding down from Calypso's back, she hurried toward the wagon.

Her steps quickened, going from hesitant and stumbling to a giddy, frantic rush. "Mary? *Mary!*"

"Here, 'Toria! I'm here!"

"Oh, dear God! It *is* you, darling. *Steede, over here! I've found her!* Mary, darling, I'm coming!" Victoria screamed, wild with joy.

A half dozen steps, and she could see the little girl, crouched in the open doorway of the wagon. Her cloak was torn and dirty, her face deathly pale, but she was alive.

Gathering Mary into her arms, Victoria hugged her, rocking her back and forth and kissing the little girl as tears slipped down her cheeks.

"Oh, Mary! Oh, darling girl, we thought we'd lost you."

Mary's arms wrapped about her throat. Her icy little fingers clung to Victoria, gripped tightly, as if afraid they would lose her again. A chilly cheek pressed against Victoria's own.

"I love you, 'Toria. Truly I do. Please don't go away again. I'll be good. I promise. I'll be so, so very good! Cross my heart and hope to d-d-die!"

Victoria pulled back to look at her stepdaughter. Tendrils of hair were plastered to Mary's cheeks. Her heart-shaped face was bluish with cold and anxiety. Dirt and tears made furrows that dripped off her chin.

Love welled up and overflowed her heart.

"Oh, darling girl, don't! I didn't leave Blackstone because of anything you did, truly I didn't!"

Victoria murmured as she bundled the child into her own cloak. "My papa was lost, just like you were, and I wanted so badly to find him. Didn't Kalinda tell you I was coming back?"

"I tell her nothing, memsahib."

Victoria's head jerked up, to look at the speaker.

Kalinda stood in the doorway of the wagon. She had discarded her Eastern sari and wore the colorful garb of the Gypsy women. Her straight black hair fell almost to her hips.

"It is because I am afraid, yes? If my bright jewel has you, memsahib, she no longer needs Kalinda. This is what I am thinking."

"Steede was right. You made my horse throw me, didn't you?"

The black eyes grew sly. "I had no choice. I had to be rid of you!" She shook her head. "But when my jewel ran away to find you, I know it is over. Sahib Warring will send this useless ayah back to India. The Gypsies, they are outcasts, like me. I knew they would take me in and so I came to join them—and found the Lady Mary, also."

"What were they going to do with her?"

"Wait a day or so, then tell Lord Blackstone they had found her on their travels. By then, he would have been eager to pay much gold, yes?" Her dark eyes gleamed.

"They will be angry when they discover she's gone."

"Very angry," Kalinda agreed. "So, you must take her and go, before they see you. Aiee, already they are breaking camp! Hurry, before it is too late!"

Kalinda was telling the truth, Victoria realized. All around her, the Gypsies were breaking camp. Gypsy menfolk were coaxing their horses into the shafts of their wagons. Gypsy women were folding satin quilts and pillows and stowing them inside their *vardos*. The cooking fire had been hastily covered over with earth.

Already, the first of the heavy caravans was rumbling down the hill, toward the London turnpike.

A tangible sense of urgency, of haste, rode the chill wind.

"Thank you," Victoria murmured, lifting Mary into her arms.

Quickly, she hurried to her horse and lifted the child up onto Calypso's back. "Hold tight."

Hitching up her skirts, she scrambled up behind her. Clicking her teeth, she urged Calypso away from the camp at a brisk trot.

"Kalinda told me a fib." Mary broke off, her little face filled with uncertainty now. "She said you went away because of me. That you were never coming back because I was a naughty girl."

"Kalinda was wrong to tell you that," Victoria said firmly, "because it wasn't true. None of it. My going away had nothing to do with anything you did. Remember what I told you, darling?"

"That when you love someone, nothing they do will make you stop loving them?" Mary said.

"That's right." She caressed the little girl's damp head. "Well, I love you, Mary. And I'll never stop. So, if you'll let me, I'd like so much to be your friend." *And someday, God willing, your mama*, Victoria added silently.

Mary's radiant smile, her eager, vigorous nod were answer enough.

"I didn't burn the picture of your mama, 'Toria. Kalinda wanted me to, but I wouldn't do it. I've got it right here. Inside my bodice." She giggled, and some of the color returned to her face. "It tickles."

"You can give it back to me later, darling. Steede!" Victoria shouted when they were within hailing distance. "It's Mary! I've found her!"

"What?" Steede bellowed as he cantered Mercury toward them. The huge gray stallion's hooves gobbled up the hard ground as it closed the distance between them. "Dear God, *Mary!*"

Before the horse had fully halted, Steede sprang down from its back and quickly crossed the few steps to their side.

Hauling Mary into his arms, he glowered at her, tears standing in his eyes. A nerve ticked uncontrollably in his jaw, betraying his inner turmoil.

"Mary Henrietta Warring, run off again and I shall find you and strap your bottom until you can't sit down for a week! Do I make myself clear, young lady?" he growled, his fear becoming anger now that she was safe.

When Mary bit her lip and nodded, her gray eyes swimming with tears, his arms went around her.

"Oh, kitten! Oh, my poppet, thank God, you're

safe!" He held her so tightly Mary began squirming to get free. "Oh, thank God!"

"Papa, stop!" Mary gasped. "I cannot breathe!"

Steede drew back, his dark eyes widening in disbelief. He looked over at Victoria, who was laughing and nodding, then back at Mary before him. His expression was incredulous.

"She spoke! Mary's talking!" he whispered, unable to believe his own ears. "My little girl is speaking again!"

"I know. Isn't it wonderful?"

"I—I'm very sorry, Papa," Mary whispered tremulously, fat tears rolling down her cheeks onto her father's riding jacket. Her lower lip wobbled. "Please d-don't hate me! And please don't send me away to b-boarding school! I couldn't bear it! I never wanted baby Johnny to die, truly I didn't! I just wished and wished he'd be gone, so I didn't have to share you or Kalinda with him."

More huge tears rolled down her cheeks and dripped off her chin.

". . . I 'member, Mama was so cross that night. She threw the lamp, Papa. I saw her! She was screaming at Kalinda about . . . about you. Then the f-fire gobbled up the curtains, and I—and I—! *Oh, Papa, Papa*, I was so frightened, until you saved me!"

Tears streamed from Steede's eyes as, still bundled in Victoria's cloak, Mary wrapped her arms about his neck and clung to him. Sobs wracked her little body.

"Listen to me," he said sternly, holding her

away from him so that he could look her in her eye. "What happened to your mama and Johnny wasn't your fault. None of it! Wishing your baby brother would go away had nothing to do with any of it."

"Truly?" Mary whispered brokenly.

"Truly," her father told her in a firm voice that brooked no argument. "Wishing something doesn't make it so. And as for you leaving Blackstone, my girl—" He shook his head. "I could never let you leave me, not until you're a big, grown-up girl." He hugged her. "We love you, Mary. Victoria and I would miss you far too much if you went away. Wouldn't we, Victoria?"

"Terribly!" Victoria agreed.

"You see? Now let's go home and tell Grandmama that you're safe and sound, shall we, darling?" he said softly, cradling her against his chest as he carried her to where the two horses cropped the coarse turf. "We'll talk about it there, poppet. I promise."

"And Victoria, too? *Please*, Papa?" Mary implored him, noisily sniffing back her tears.

Steede's laughing sable eyes met Victoria's over Mary's red-gold head. They were filled with tenderness and love for the two females in his life.

"And Victoria, too," he promised softly. "Victoria, always and forever."

Over their daughter's head, their eyes met and held.

Chapter Twenty-seven

"I must admit, I find myself quite overset by the daunting prospect of the wedding," Delia confessed, admiring the magnificent train with something akin to awe.

Ivory Brussels lace flowed from a band of silk orange blossoms at her hairline, down her back, then swept another twenty feet across the Aubusson carpet, ending in a stunning scalloped curve.

"I can't imagine what I would have done without any of you. Dear Victoria, and you, Lady Henrietta, and you especially, of course, Your Grace. My own mama, God rest her soul, could not have done more for me." Happy tears glinted in Delia's eyes.

"Nonsense, dear gel," Catherine, the Duchess of Lincoln, declared, inspecting her future sister-in-law through the lenses of her lorgnette.

The seamstress was arranging the drape of the bridal train, and the duchess watched with eagle eyes to ensure it was done precisely to her liking. "After all, you're soon going to be a part of our family, and families stick together. Isn't that right, Rettie?"

"It certainly is, Birdie, dear," Henrietta declared, laughing. "Blood is thicker than water, or so they say. Though I do believe that friendship is as close as many blood ties."

Victoria smiled as the pair exchanged fond glances. Even now, she had little difficulty imagining the older women as debutantes in their white gowns, making their coming-out curtsies before Her Majesty. They had become as noisy and giggly as a pair of schoolgirls again, since their reunion at Blackstone Manor last Christmas.

Only the loss of Delia's invalid father on Christmas Eve had lent a sad note to the otherwise joyous season, she reflected.

In the days following the funeral, Delia and Roger had sensibly agreed to postpone the March wedding they'd planned until mid-June. A six-month period of deep mourning, rather than the customary twelve months, would be sufficient to demonstrate Delia's sorrow and loss to the world at large. The good Lord knew, she had never failed her ailing father in private.

In poor health for several years, Chillingsworth had suffered terribly the last few months. In many ways, his passing had come as a blessed release, both for himself and for Delia.

Always a dutiful, loving daughter, it was time now for her to embark on her own life, to marry the man she loved, and have children of her own.

And so, as she had promised the day she and Delia rode their horses on the beach that fringed Whitby Bay, Victoria had written to the duchess, enlisting her Aunt Catherine's help with the wedding arrangements.

When Catherine's letter had arrived at Blackstone Manor, expressing her delight at being asked to help, Lady Henrietta had sighed wistfully and observed how fortunate her old friend Birdie was, to have been blessed by "three daughters, a niece and a sister-in-law to fuss over."

It came as no surprise, therefore, when Henrietta had jumped at Victoria's invitation to be a part of it all, and fortunate for Victoria that she had.

To be honest, she was often tired of late, a condition she blamed on her increasing girth and weight as her pregnancy advanced. Her belly was quite enormous, as round and hard as a large cannonball beneath her pleated blouses—or so Steede had whispered fondly that morning, just before he and her father, Ian Walters, Harry and Uncle Lovey left with the dogs for a day's shooting.

Consequently, she gratefully accepted any and all assistance that was offered nowadays, for she quickly grew tired. Indeed, it seemed her days were taken up by numerous catnaps, eating, or making countless visits to the water closet. Her days of tramping about the countryside in the snow, or watching Mary and Steede as they sledded down a snowy tor, were long past.

As her pregnancy advanced, she was drawing into herself, becoming preoccupied, consumed by thoughts of the child that curled beneath her heart, waiting to be born.

She arched her back, kneading a small achy knot at the base of her spine. "Whooah," she sighed.

"Shall I fetch you another pillow, Mama?" Mary asked, eyeing her anxiously.

Victoria smiled, as she always did when Mary called her Mama. It warmed her heart so to hear it.

She had not dared to hope the little girl would ever think of her as her mother. In fact, she would have been content to be considered her friend. Yet the bond between them had grown effortlessly, until it was as close as that of true mother and daughter.

"No, thank you, darling. It's very thoughtful of you to ask, but I'm quite all right. Just a silly old twinge in my back that won't go away. Has Mrs. Marsden finished with your fitting?" Mary was going to be one of Delia's bridesmaids.

"Yes, Mama."

"Then come cuddle up next to me."

Flashing a smile, Mary scrambled up next to her stepmother, squeezing herself into the narrow space beside her on the chaise.

"There! As snug as two bugs in a rug," Victoria

declared, dropping a kiss on Mary's red-gold head.

Catherine's head suddenly turned toward her. She reminded Victoria of a stork as she used her lorgnette to peer at her.

"Did I hear you correctly, my dear? Did you say you have a backache, Victoria?"

"Yes, Aunt. I did. But it's nothing. Really."

"On the contrary. A backache was my first indication I was about to deliver your cousin Imogene."

"And mine that John was on his way into the world," Henrietta declared, her concerned expression mirroring Birdie's.

Both women now stared at Victoria who, snug beneath several carriage rugs, lounged with her feet up on a wicker chaise longue before the fire, where she could observe the fitting of Delia's wedding gown in comfort. The chaise and the rugs had been her aunt's choice, not her own, for the older women delighted in pampering her. But for once, Victoria was enjoying the lazy life.

The seamstress who was sewing Delia's trousseau was not, for understandable reasons, the Widow Johns, who had been commissioned to sew Victoria's wedding gown. Victoria's gown—and it was truly breathtaking, covered in tiny seed pearls and rich lace—still hung under a layer of protective dust sheets in her dressing room. It would be several months—if she was ever fortunate enough to recover her figure after her child's birth—before she could wriggle her way into its slim bodice, even had she wanted to.

She sighed. Sometimes she felt the tiniest twinge of regret that she had never worn it. That instead, she'd been married under duress in a plain muslin blouse and a muddy skirt in a horrid blacksmith's forge at Gretna, and by so doing, had missed the glorious wedding gown, the flowers and wedding breakfast Aunt Catherine had planned for her.

Ah, yes, it was a very small twinge, but a twinge nonetheless. What an ungrateful wretch she was! After all, she had so many other blessings to be thankful for. She and Steede had never been happier. She had a wonderful, loving husband, a little daughter who adored her and who was now quite the chatterbox, and a mother-in-law who was an angel. Even the pony Sooty had been recovered from the tinker the Gypsies had sold him to! What more could she ask for?

Happiness. That was truly all that mattered.

"Victoria? Victoria, dear?"

"Yes, Aunt?"

"I said, are you certain there's another month till your lying-in, dear?" Catherine inquired, obviously not for the first time.

"Is it possible you miscalculated?" Henrietta asked.

"No!" she shot back crossly, yet in all honesty, she probably had.

She'd forgotten all about her monthly courses following her marriage, and could not have said with any accuracy when her last monthly might have been if her life depended upon it!

"I'm sorry. I shouldn't have snapped at you,

Aunt. It's just—oh, I don't know! It's as if it will never end! I can't wait to see my baby, to hold him—or her—in my arms, and yet—! There's a part of me that's afraid. What if I'm not a good mother?"

"What you're feeling is what we all feel in those last weeks as we wait for our children to be born, dear gel," Catherine assured her. "Restlessness. Impatience. Self-doubt. Believe me, you'll be a wonderful mother."

"You're already a wonderful mama," Mary whispered, looking older and wiser than her years as she squeezed Victoria's hand.

"Thank you, darling. That's the nicest thing anyone's ever said to me."

"You're welcome. Are we really going home tomorrow?" the little girl asked.

"Oh, yes, indeed. We shall catch the train in the morning. Are you so anxious to go home, then? I thought you loved it here?"

"Oh, I do. Grandfather Hawthorne is such fun! I love to go riding with him. But . . . I do miss Sooty."

"You'll see him again very soon. I promise," Victoria murmured.

"Victoria, dear. I don't think it's a good idea for you to travel just yet. Particularly if you're having backaches," Catherine said. "Please, postpone your departure for a day or two. What can it hurt?"

"I agree with Birdie, Victoria. You shouldn't be traveling at all in your condition—and certainly not this close to your confinement. I don't know what Steede can have been thinking of, to allow it."

"But I've been having pangs off and on for several weeks now. And not once have they come to anything! Besides, both Dr. Riggsby at home and Dr. Walters here say it's perfectly normal. Besides, I *had* to be here. I wouldn't have missed Del's fittings for the world."

She smiled up at Delia, whose radiant smile had dimmed to a doubtful frown now. "Lady Blackstone is right. You shouldn't have come, not if it's dangerous."

"Mere pangs are not the same as backache, child," Catherine said sternly. "Backache is of far greater consequence."

Victoria sighed. "Oh, all right. If it will put your minds at ease, I'll wait two days for the pains to subside again. Mary, what do you say? Could you bear to stay here another two days?"

"Well . . . will you read to me?"

"We'll *all* read to you," Delia promised.

"Very well, then, I'll stay," Mary said eagerly.

"Are you sure you're all right, my dear?" Steede asked as the steam train rattled along the iron rails two mornings later, traveling south toward London through rolling green countryside.

Patchwork fields of brown and yellow and tender green swept away on either side of the embankment; farms and houses, small towns and country villages were dotted about like children's toys.

"Of course I am," Victoria insisted brightly.

It was a lie if ever she had told one, though earlier, when they had made their goodbyes to Father and Delia and Aunt Catherine, it had not been. She had felt brighter and more energetic than she had in days. It felt as if the baby had shifted somewhat, and was no longer pressing on her waterworks.

But her sense of well-being had lasted only for the first hour of their journey to London, where they would have to change trains for Devonshire.

She had accompanied Steede and the others to the dining room, but the motion of the carriage as it rode the rails had left her as queasy as she'd been in the early months. She'd managed to eat only a mouthful of dry toast and a sip of weak tea before she returned to their first-class compartment. Soon after, the backache had returned in force.

She tried to enjoy the view through the window, and when that didn't work, engaged Mary in a rousing game of I-Spy-With-My-Little-Eye or I-Packed-My-Trunk.

"My turn!" Mary crowed. "I packed my trunk, and in it I put an elephant, an egg and a—and a—"

"Envelope," Steede suggested, whispering in her ear.

"Don't, Papa. I can do it. An—eel!"

"Jolly good!" he praised her. "Your turn, darling."

Victoria gritted her teeth and nodded. "All right. I packed my trunk and in it I put an—an elephant, an egg, an eel and a—oh, *baby!*"

"Baby begins with 'B', Mama," Mary scolded. "Try another word."

Steede shot an intent look at Victoria. "I don't think your mama's playing the game, poppet." He took Victoria's hand in his. "Is the baby coming?"

"I—I think so. Yes!" Her face was white. She put her hands on her stomach, features scrunching up in discomfort as it gave a visible surge beneath the demure pleats of her blouse, rising to a point. Seconds later, it relaxed again. "Oh. It's stopped. There. That's better." She shot Mary a game smile. "My word was elbow. Your turn again."

"Can you hold on? We'll be pulling into King's Cross in a few minutes," Steede asked. If anything, he looked more frightened than she did. "I'll get a cab immediately. We can have you tucked in bed at the townhouse in a matter of minutes, while Harry fetches a doctor from Harley Street."

"I'll try to hold on. I promise."

"Come along, Mary. Let's go out into the corridor," Henrietta urged her granddaughter.

As Steede had promised, the train chuffed into King's Cross Station only moments later.

Travelers, guards and porters were milling about, blowing whistles or wheeling stacks of luggage as Harry leaped from the still-moving train and flagged down a pair of horse-drawn cabs, one for Her Ladyship, another to take himself to Harley Street.

"Can you walk?" Steede asked, cupping her under the elbows.

"Yes, I think so." She sounded surprised. "It—it hurts less standing up."

He went ahead of her down the single step to the platform. Lily hovered behind her. When she reached the doorway, he lifted her under the arms and gently set her down on the platform. But he did not release her immediately.

"I love you. You know that? More than anything."

"I know. I love you, too. I always will. And you don't have to worry about me." She cupped his cheek. "I'll be fine."

"Victoria, what I said, about offering for your hand because I needed a mother for Mary—"

"Let me guess. It was lust, too."

He grinned. "How did you know?"

She giggled. "Because it was lust for me, too, at first."

"It was?" His brows shot up. He looked interested. "Really?"

She looked down at her swollen belly and gave a wry little shrug. "That's why I'm here, looking like this, wouldn't you say?"

He shook his head and laughed. God, she was lovely. And his. All his. "Kiss me, Lady Blackstone."

"Here, m'lord? With half of London watching us?"

"Why the devil not? After all, we're no strangers to scandal are we, my love? Now come here, you."

As his mouth crushed down over hers, she closed her eyes and kissed him back, suddenly breaking the kiss with a startled, *"Oh!"*

"What is it?" he cried. "Did I hurt you?"

"No! The waters have broken." She managed to grind out the words between pains. "Steede, the baby's coming! Imagine—imagine those—those wagging t-tongues if our child is b-born here at the railway station!"

As another labor pain engulfed her, he swept her up into his arms and into the waiting cab.

As he lifted her inside, he growled, "Let 'em wag!"

"Roger, dear. A telegram has come for you from Lady Warring," Delia said anxiously, taking the small white envelope from the silver tray Carter was holding.

"Good Lord, what now!" Roger Hawthorne exclaimed, springing to his feet.

Taking the envelope from his betrothed, he slit it open with a letter opener and withdrew the single sheet of paper within.

His worried frown quickly became a broad smile. "Well, I'll be damned! That's right champion! Look here. It says I'm a grandfather, Del! Eeh, lass, this makes you a grandmother, come June!"

"Give it here, you horrid man. I don't believe you," Delia protested, snatching the paper out of his hands.

But, it was true:

"On May 15 at their London townhouse," she

read aloud, "Steede and Victoria were safely delivered of a precious son, Jonathan Michael, a brother for Mary. Stop. Mother radiant, son robust, new papa proud but exhausted! Stop. Congratulations, Grandfather! Stop."

Roger Hawthorne gave a whoop of delight. Giving Delia a roguish nudge with his elbow as he headed for the liquor cabinet, he asked cheekily, "Now then. Would ye care for summat to wet the babby's head, *Grandmama?*"

DON'T MISS THESE PASSIONATE MEDIEVAL ROMANCES BY LEISURE'S LEADING LADIES OF LOVE!

The Lion's Bride by Connie Mason. Saxon countess and Norman knight, Ariana and Lyon are born enemies. And in a land rent asunder by bloody wars and shifting loyalties, they are doomed to misery unless they can vanquish the hatred that divides them—and unite in glorious love.
_3884-6 $5.99 US/$7.99 CAN

For Love And Honor by Flora Speer. From the sceptered isle of England to the sun-drenched shores of Sicily, Sir Alain and Joanna will weather a winter of discontent. And before the virile knight and stunning lady can share a glorious summer of passion, they'll have to risk their reputations, their happiness, and their lives for love and honor.
_3816-1 $4.99 US/$5.99 CAN

Dorchester Publishing Co., Inc.
P.O. Box 6640
Wayne, PA 19087-8640

Please add $1.75 for shipping and handling for the first book and $.50 for each book thereafter. NY, NYC, and PA residents, please add appropriate sales tax. No cash, stamps, or C.O.D.s. All orders shipped within 6 weeks via postal service book rate. Canadian orders require $2.00 extra postage and must be paid in U.S. dollars through a U.S. banking facility.

Name_____
Address_____
City_____ State_____ Zip_____
I have enclosed $_____ in payment for the checked book(s).
Payment <u>must</u> accompany all orders. ❏ Please send a free catalog.

Captive Legacy

Theresa Scott

"Theresa Scott's captivating writing brings you to a wonderous time and shows you that love inself is timeless."
—*Affaire de Coeur*

Heading west to the Oregon Territory and an arranged marriage, Dorie Primfield never dreams that a virile stranger will kidnap her and claim her as his wife. Part Indian, part white, Dorie's abductor is everything she's ever desired in a man, yet she isn't about to submit to his white-hot passion without a fight. Then by a twist of fate, she has her captor naked and at gunpoint, and she finds herself torn between escaping into the wilderness—and turning a captive legacy into endless love.

_3880-3 $5.99 US/$7.99 CAN

CONNIE MASON

BOLD LAND, BOLD LOVE

New South Wales in 1807 is a vast land of wild beauty and wilder passions: a frontier as yet untamed by man; a place where women have few rights and fewer pleasures. For a female convict like flame-haired Casey O'Cain, it is a living nightmare. And from the first, arrogant, handsome Dare Penrod makes it clear what he wants of her. Casey knows she should fight him with every breath in her body, but her heart tells her he can make a paradise of this wilderness for her.

___52274-8 $5.99 US/$6.99 CAN

Dorchester Publishing Co., Inc.
P.O. Box 6640
Wayne, PA 19087-8640

Please add $1.75 for shipping and handling for the first book and $.50 for each book thereafter. NY, NYC, and PA residents, please add appropriate sales tax. No cash, stamps, or C.O.D.s. All orders shipped within 6 weeks via postal service book rate. Canadian orders require $2.00 extra postage and must be paid in U.S. dollars through a U.S. banking facility.

Name_____
Address_____
City_____ State_____ Zip_____
I have enclosed $_____ in payment for the checked book(s).
Payment <u>must</u> accompany all orders. ❑ Please send a free catalog.
CHECK OUT OUR WEBSITE! www.dorchesterpub.com

"Each new Connie Mason book is a prize!"
—Heather Graham

Spirits can be so bloody unpredictable, and the specter of Lady Amelia is the worst of all. Just when one of her ne'er-do-well descendents thought he could go astray in peace, the phantom lady always appears to change his wicked ways.

A rogue without peer, Jackson Graystoke wants to make gaming and carousing in London society his life's work. And the penniless baronet would gladly curse himself with wine and women—if Lady Amelia would give him a ghost of a chance.

Fresh off the boat from Ireland, Moira O'Toole isn't fool enough to believe in legends or naive enough to trust a rake. Yet after an accident lands her in Graystoke Manor, she finds herself haunted, harried, and hopelessly charmed by Black Jack Graystoke and his exquisite promise of pure temptation.

_4041-7 $5.99 US/$6.99 CAN

DEBRA DIER

SHADOW OF THE STORM

He is her dashing childhood hero, the man to whom she will willingly surrender her innocence in a night of blazing ecstasy. But when Ian Tremayne cruelly abandons her after a bitter misunderstanding, Sabrina O'Neill vows to have revenge on the handsome Yankee. But the virile Tremayne is more than ready for the challenge. Together, they will enter a high-stakes game of deadly illusion and sizzling desire that will shatter Sabrina's well-crafted facade.

___4397-1 $5.99 US/$6.99 CAN

Dorchester Publishing Co., Inc.
P.O. Box 6640
Wayne, PA 19087-8640

Please add $1.75 for shipping and handling for the first book and $.50 for each book thereafter. NY, NYC, and PA residents, please add appropriate sales tax. No cash, stamps, or C.O.D.s. All orders shipped within 6 weeks via postal service book rate. Canadian orders require $2.00 extra postage and must be paid in U.S. dollars through a U.S. banking facility.

Name_____
Address_____
City_____ State_____ Zip_____
I have enclosed $_____ in payment for the checked book(s).
Payment <u>must</u> accompany all orders. ❑ Please send a free catalog.
CHECK OUT OUR WEBSITE! www.dorchesterpub.com

DEBRA DIER
LORD SAVAGE
Author of *Scoundrel*

Lady Elizabeth Barrington is sent to Colorado to find the Marquess of Angelstone, the grandson of an English duke who disappeared during an attack by renegade Indians. But the only thing she discovers is Ash MacGregor, a bounty-hunting rogue who takes great pleasure residing in the back of a bawdy house. Convinced that his rugged good looks resemble those of the noble family, Elizabeth vows she will prove to him that aristocratic blood does pulse through his veins. And in six month's time, she will make him into a proper man. But the more she tries to show him which fork to use or how to help a lady into her carriage, the more she yearns to be caressed by this virile stranger, touched by this beautiful barbarian, embraced by Lord Savage.

_4119-7 $4.99 US/$5.99 CAN

Dorchester Publishing Co., Inc.
P.O. Box 6640
Wayne, PA 19087-8640

Please add $1.75 for shipping and handling for the first book and $.50 for each book thereafter. NY, NYC, and PA residents, please add appropriate sales tax. No cash, stamps, or C.O.D.s. All orders shipped within 6 weeks via postal service book rate. Canadian orders require $2.00 extra postage and must be paid in U.S. dollars through a U.S. banking facility.

Name_____
Address_____
City_____ State_____ Zip_____
I have enclosed $_____ in payment for the checked book(s).
Payment <u>must</u> accompany all orders. ☐ Please send a free catalog.

CATHERINE HART

Fire & Ice

Beautiful and spirited Kathleen Haley sets sail from England for the family estate in Savannah. On board ship, she meets the man who will forever haunt her heart, the dashing and domineering Captain Reed Taylor. On the long, perilous voyage, she resists his bold advances—until she wakes from unconsciousness after a storm and hears Reed's shocking confession. She then knows she must marry the rogue.

But their fiery conflict is far from over. Through society balls, raging duels and torrid nights, Kathleen seeks vengeance on Reed's brutal passions and his secret alliance with pirates. At last she is forced to attack the very man who has warmed her icy heart and burned his way into her very soul.

___4303-3 $5.99 US/$6.99 CAN

Dorchester Publishing Co., Inc.
P.O. Box 6640
Wayne, PA 19087-8640

Please add $1.75 for shipping and handling for the first book and $.50 for each book thereafter. NY, NYC, and PA residents please add appropriate sales tax. No cash, stamps, or C.O.D.s. All orders shipped within 6 weeks via postal service book rate.
Canadian orders require $2.00 extra postage and must be paid in U.S. dollars through a U.S. banking facility.

Name_____
Address_____
City_____·State_____Zip_____
I have enclosed $_____ in payment for the checked book(s).
Payment <u>must</u> accompany all orders. ☐ Please send a free catalog

Exquisitely beautiful, fiery Katherine McGregor has no qualms about posing as a doxy, if the charade will strike a blow against the hated English, until she is captured by the infuriating Major James Burke. Now her very life depends on her ability to convince the arrogant English officer that she is a common strumpet, not a Scottish spy. Skillfully, Burke uncovers her secrets, even as he arouses her senses, claiming there is just one way she can prove herself a tart . . . But how can she give him her yearning body, when she fears he will take her tender heart as well?

___4419-6 $5.99 US/$6.99 CAN

Dorchester Publishing Co., Inc.
P.O. Box 6640
Wayne, PA 19087-8640

Please add $1.75 for shipping and handling for the first book and $.50 for each book thereafter. NY, NYC, and PA residents, please add appropriate sales tax. No cash, stamps, or C.O.D.s. All orders shipped within 6 weeks via postal service book rate. Canadian orders require $2.00 extra postage and must be paid in U.S. dollars through a U.S. banking facility.

Name_____
Address_____
City_____State_____Zip_____
I have enclosed $_____ in payment for the checked book(s).
Payment <u>must</u> accompany all orders. ❏ Please send a free catalog.
CHECK OUT OUR WEBSITE! www.dorchesterpub.com